DESIRE AND DREAD

From the moment Hadley met Ernst Dietmueller, she knew she should avoid this lean, elegant, brutally handsome man. Not only was Dietmueller a leader of Hitler's evil S.S., but he made it clear he knew the passionate pull he exerted over Hadley.

Now what she swore would never happen had happened. She had come to his isolated forest chalet, betraying the husband she loved and the child she adored. She abandoned herself to this man and the fiery physical ecstasy he brought her to with such ruthless skill and strength.

"Today we have become acquainted," he told her as he watched her dressing. "Next time, I will introduce you to some of the pursuits that most amuse me."

"There won't be a next time," Hadley said. "I should never have come." Then his mocking eyes met and held hers—and she knew she was lost. . . .

FABLES

FABLES

by
Toinette Harrison

A SIGNET BOOK

NEW AMERICAN LIBRARY

PUBLISHED BY
THE NEW AMERICAN LIBRARY
OF CANADA LIMITED

PUBLISHER'S NOTE

This novel is a work of fiction. Names, characters, places, and incidents either are the product of the author's imagination or are used fictitiously, and any resemblance to actual persons, living or dead, events, or locales is entirely coincidental.

NAL BOOKS ARE AVAILABLE AT QUANTITY DISCOUNTS
WHEN USED TO PROMOTE PRODUCTS OR SERVICES.
FOR INFORMATION PLEASE WRITE TO PREMIUM MARKETING DIVISION,
NEW AMERICAN LIBRARY, 1633 BROADWAY,
NEW YORK, NEW YORK 10019.

Copyright © 1986 by Toinette Harrison

First Printing, June, 1986

2 3 4 5 6 7 8 9

SIGNET TRADEMARK REG U.S. PAT OFF AND FOREIGN COUNTRIES
REGISTERED TRADEMARK—MARCA REGISTRADA
HECHO EN WINNIPEG, CANADA

SIGNET, SIGNET CLASSIC, MENTOR, PLUME, MERIDIAN
AND NAL BOOKS are published in Canada by The New American
Library of Canada, Limited, 81 Mack Avenue, Scarborough,
Ontario, Canada M1L 1M8
PRINTED IN CANADA
COVER PRINTED IN U.S.A.

PROLOGUE
MID-ATLANTIC, DECEMBER 1929

HADLEY GAZED AT her reflection in the amber-lit mirror as she combed through the already gleaming crop of platinum hair. The effect of the emeralds at her ears—to match her eyes—and her suntanned skin against the black satin dress with its plunging back and daring front dazzled, and was sure to be the talk of the evening.

Running her fingers thoughtfully over her body, she paused to linger on the nipple that had slipped through the front opening of the dress. The nipple hardened under her touch and she wet her lips and closed her eyes as a wave of sensuous feeling swept through her like an incoming tide. Instinct told her that this night, the evening she and her sisters would celebrate Nell's twenty-first birthday on the most beautiful liner of the day, the *Bremen*, would be a night to remember.

It would also be an opportunity for the men who had pursued Hadley since the start of the voyage to come together in open competition. She had enjoyed the attention of her fellow passengers, especially Ernst Dietmueller, a German war hero who had been a flying ace. So far she had spurned his attentions. She was well-acquainted with the newspaper accounts linking him with the beautiful aristocrats of Europe. He was used to having his way with women, and though this knowledge tempted her to provoke him, she did not intend to satisfy his desires. Dietmueller was forbidden fruit and that was fun with a capital F. To Hadley, fun was what life was all about and she could barely wait for the evening's celebrations to begin. She clipped on the emerald earrings that matched the green of her eyes, and with one last glance at her reflection, left the cabin for the ship's dining room.

Annabelle, known to her sisters as Nell, twirled back and forth before the mirror, her long red hair fanning out around her face. Today, at last, she was twenty-one, a grown-up woman in almost every way. Pinning some scarlet poinsettias in her hair, she looked critically at the matching silk dress with its exotic pattern and kerchief skirt. As tall as Hadley, but voluptuous in build, Nell envied her older sister's slimness and the icy calm of her character. But she was finally coming into her own and had grown content with her own individual style. Horace Ellerman always told his girls that the worst thing in life was to be like everyone else—a sheep destined to follow the lead of others—and Nell had taken the advice seriously. And with wondrous results! After all, her own individual style had attracted the Prince of Wales, and he had pursued her since their first meeting a year previously. Of late he had hinted that an American wife could be an advantage to a British sovereign. Would he take the relationship a step further tonight? Was it possible for him to propose of his own initiative even before she had been officially deemed a suitable marriage prospect? Overcome by excitement at the thought, Nell gulped a glass of water and then hurried away to meet her youngest sister in the adjoining cabin.

* * *

Frances Clementine, known to her sisters as Bunny, struggled to fasten her ice-blue crepe. The *Bremen*'s rich desserts were very much in evidence tonight—Bunny's chic new dress was straining at the seams. Frowning at the heavy cleavage visible through the V neck of the dress, Bunny took a needle and thread and carefully sewed up part of the too-generous split. Then she tried on a platinum bracelet, uncertain if it looked right. Putting on the spectacles she wore for distant vision, she stood back and gazed at herself. Why didn't clothes look quite right on her? And why did she have sisters like Hadley and Nell, so at ease with their sophistication? Bunny knew that part of the problem was her weight and she was forever trying to control her desire for food, but the sensuousness of her nature invariably triumphed and she succumbed to all the sensations a fine meal provoked.

Scooping up a stray blond curl, Bunny pinned it awkwardly back in place. Then another tendril fell, followed by part of her chignon. After a moment of deliberation, she released the curls, brushed her fair hair vigorously, and pinned a white rose on either side of her center parting. How could she face the evening ahead? And the scrutiny of fellow passengers? Bunny slumped on the bed to wait for Nell's knock at the cabin door. Lucky Nell! Bunny wished she too could be twenty-one instead of seventeen and just out of school. By the time she was twenty-one she would be as worldly as her sisters, knowing all there was to know about life, love, passion, and men. Blushing at her audacious thoughts, she poured herself another glass of champagne and promptly fell asleep on top of the bed, creasing all her finery.

* * *

The guests had already sated themselves with caviar from the Baltic, roast peacock stuffed with wild dove and whole antelope grilled on cardamom-scented embers. There had been soufflés of rose petal and African violet and a tableau created to resemble the New York skyline entirely made in spun sugar by the finest chef money could buy. Now, an after-dinner buffet had been set along one side of the ballroom, its spectacular length dominated by a display of carved ice in the form of a chain of mountains, the valleys filled with foie gras, caviar, and scarlet crayfish. Stacks of crystal glasses had been piled by the side of jeroboams of vintage champagne and there was a birthday cake six feet high in the form of the Ellerman summer house at Newport, Rhode Island, complete with its fabulous covering of American Beauty roses.

When the dessert had been served and enjoyed, coffee and liqueurs savored, Hadley rose and proposed a toast to her sister.

"To you, Nell. We all wish you good health, happiness, and the fulfillment of all your dreams. And to each of our guests, a long life and a merry one."

The Prince of Wales rose to reply on behalf of the guests, his dignity compelling attention, despite his diminutive size.

"Ladies and gentlemen, it isn't often we enjoy a dinner as splendid as the one we were just served, and even more rare that we eat such a dinner in the company of three women as beautiful as the Ellermans. I'm sorry Mr. Ellerman was indisposed this evening and could not attend the party, but I toast our generous host—and you, Nell, Hadley, and Bunny. I raise my glass to the future of you all." Though the prince's warm words enchanted all of the sisters, his gaze rested solely upon Nell. With a slight bow in her direction, he reclaimed his seat.

After the enormous cake had been cut and the toasts completed, some of the guests disappeared to change for the fancy-dress ball. Others remained at their tables, gossiping furiously about Nell's chances of marrying the Prince of Wales, who was obviously dazzled by her. As waiters cleared the floor and the orchestra began to play, there was much speculation about the worth of the sisters, estimates ranging from a million dollars apiece to five million.

John Angus Cameron, Duke of Fife, had no interest in the gossip about the Ellermans' worth. A man known in Britain for his taciturn ways, his dislike of personal publicity, his piercing black eyes, he had once distinguished himself in battle by leading what was left of his beleaguered Guards Regiment against eight hundred Germans, capturing their position. Cameron was not a man for talk but for action. And right now he was intrigued by the action of Bunny Ellerman. Throughout dinner, he watched Bunny with increasing intensity, amused by her appetite and the lopsided roses in her hair. She was not as startling in her beauty as Nell or Hadley, but there was a wholesome, luminous quality about Bunny that touched his soul. She was a good girl, with a touch of stubbornness in her eyes. And judging by her dress, she was given to belittling herself when she should have been blowing her own trumpet. Cameron was delighted not to have missed this Ellerman party.

The fancy-dress ball began at ten. The guests were announced by a majordomo in scarlet livery. Loud applause greeted Hadley, reed-slim and menacing as Al Capone, complete with spats, white fedora, and a wooden machine gun. Gasps of envy rose from the women when Nell appeared at the top of the stairs in a white satin crinoline four feet wide, the skirt shimmering with opalescent paillettes in the form of swans and fleurs-de-lis. With the dress, she was wearing a curly silver wig and the Ellerman diamond choker. Her grace and beauty were well suited to the queenly character she had chosen and many of those present looked to the Prince of Wales to see if he had taken the hint that the lady had royal potential.

Bunny was costumed as her sister's maid, in black silk with a white mopcap, apron, and frilly drawers. Black stockings on garters completed the ensemble, with Cuban-heeled shoes that felt far too small. On hearing the roars of approval for Nell, Bunny hesitated to enter. She was negotiating the difficult curved staircase when, blinded by the spotlights, she missed her footing and tripped unevenly down the last few steps into the ballroom below. Mortified by the suppressed laughter of her fellow guests, she was grateful to see Cameron hurrying over to her, arms outstretched, his dark eyes gleaming with obvious admiration. Straightening her hair and brushing herself down, Bunny grasped his proffered hand, reassured by his towering presence and the abrupt way he inquired if she was all right.

"I'm fine, thanks, Jack."

"Shall we dance or drink champagne?"

"Let's dance. They're playing my favorite waltz."

"Waltzing it is, young lady."

Silencing the laughter with a glance of pure derision, Cameron led Bunny to the floor and whirled her around. Holding her as tight as he dared, he enjoyed the scent of baby powder, lavender water, and heliotrope that was, like everything else about her, a mixture of child and woman, of innocence and promised sexuality. Closing his eyes, Cameron savored the feel of her soft body against his own, the gentleness of her hand entwined in his. In his opinion, Bunny was the epitome of femininity. His vague perception of "the youngest Ellerman" had changed—she was as close to perfection as he had ever found. What her opinion of him was, he had yet to discover.

At three A.M. the party was still going strong. Some of the guests had ordered breakfast and more champagne. Others were dancing the pallyglide. The orchestra was about to start its early-morning repertoire of soft, romantic music, when an officer hurried into the ballroom, whispered to the captain, and withdrew.

The captain beckoned to his first officer, gave an order, and left the room. The first officer hurried to collect the Ellerman sisters and followed. No explanation was offered until everyone was settled in the captain's cabin. Then he began to pace back and forth, eyeing them with obvious apprehension. He was trying to work out how to break news of this sort to three women of tender years. Were the girls the fainting kind? He had correctly assessed Hadley's hardness, Nell's warmth, and Bunny's innocence. He decided to address himself to the eldest of the sisters.

"Miss Ellerman, I have the worst possible news for you."

Hadley's face turned tallow-pale as she nodded for the captain to explain himself. Her heart began to pound wildly from shock and panic when he spoke.

"I have been trying to think of a way to explain what's happened, but I fear there is no gentle way to say what has to be said. A little over an hour ago your father committed suicide on the promenade deck. He left a note for you, one for the purser, and one for his lawyer in New York. If there is *anything* I or the ship's crew can do to help you at this most tragic moment, you have only to ask. In the meantime, may I, on behalf of the company, express my very deepest condolences."

A cry escaped Nell's lips; then she was silent. Grim-faced, Hadley took the note, read it, and passed it to her sister. The captain observed that shock had made Hadley's movements stiff, and drained her face of expression. He turned from her to the youngest of the three sisters, pitying Bunny as she wept quietly, her face ashen, her body trembling uncontrollably. Nell's husky voice seemed to fill the quiet room as she read the note to her youngest sister.

Dearest Hadley, Nell, and Bunny,

I hope someday you'll find it in your hearts to forgive me for what I know I must do. The truth is, I've let you down. I lost everything in the crash; on Tuesday our own bank had to close its doors. If I were a younger man I'd think of starting over. But as it is, I can't face being poor— nor can I face you, my much-loved daughters.

I brought what cash I could on board to avoid its going to the creditors. The Ellerman earrings and emerald bracelet are for you, Hadley; the diamond choker is for Nell and the six-strand pearl-and-diamond necklace for Bunny. The cash is with the purser. There is only five thousand dollars for each of you and it'll have to last, so don't use it like your dress allowances.

I won't give you any advice; just do your best to make a new life and be proud of what you are. I love you all.

Somewhere in the distance, the ship's orchestra was playing "Ain't We Got Fun." Outside, in the blackness of night, waves were crashing against the sides of the ship. Hadley listened to the uncanny silence within the cabin, wondering if the others could hear her heart pounding. Glancing at Nell, she saw her sister's hand clenching and unclenching on the white satin fan, the knuckles livid like her face. Bunny's eyes were red and swollen, her limbs jerking involuntarily from shock. Knowing that her sisters would want to be alone with their grief, Hadley took her leave.

"I'll go to bed now, Captain. I take it you'll make all the necessary arrangements for Papa's funeral?"

"Of course I will—and please call the ship's doctor if you wish to take something to help you sleep. If you need someone to talk to, come and see me, day or night. We are *all* at your disposal to do what we can to be of service."

Panic-stricken for the first time in her life, Hadley walked from the cabin and stood at the ship's rail, staring out at the moonlit water. Oblivious of the cold sea breeze, she thought of the father she had adored. Seemingly without warning, he had lost everything it had taken him fifty years to acquire, including the legendary Ellerman fortune. And what had he left to his daughters? The stigma of suicide, and that, Hadley was certain, would follow them to the end of their days. From this day on she and her sisters would be alone in the world. And they would no longer be rich creatures to be feted for their marriage potential. Overnight, they had become both poor and undesirable. The world of those unfortunate others—a realm to which Hadley had given no thought in her blessed life—was now her world. Her head began to spin. The unthinkable had become reality.

Startled to feel a presence at her side, Hadley recoiled. Dietmueller! The last person she wanted to see at that moment.

"Now that your father is dead and your money gone," he said, "you are going to need someone to look after you, Hadley. Let me help." He spoke softly in the Prussian accent that had caused such a sensation among the women on board, his pale face looming at Hadley from the darkness.

How could he have learned of her father's death so quickly?

"I'll choose my own protector, thank you, Mr. Dietmueller," Hadley replied coldly.

Dietmueller looked into Hadley's face, his body burning with desire. In the days of his youth he had been one of the handsomest and most eligible bachelors in Europe. Now, at forty, he had already loved and lost the one woman on whom he had doted, his wife, Alicia. First he had had to suffer her departure into the arms of a man half his age and then her death in a car crash. At her funeral he had stood like a statue carved out of granite, ignoring the whispers that the accident had not been an accident at all. No proof to the contrary had been found, however, and Dietmueller's position remained unassailable, though his reputation had taken a mysterious and somewhat sinister turn. He was a valued military advisor to the newcomer, Adolf Hitler.

Throughout the journey, Hadley had obsessed Dietmueller and he had watched her, dreamed of her, lusted after her as he had never done before with any woman, except the faithless wife who had left him after fifteen years for another man. He knew he had fallen in love with Hadley but that she did not love him. He wondered if she was capable of love and the thought provoked him to bait her.

"Ah, you are cold now, and a cold woman is the most exciting challenge in the world. You are not always cold, of course. I recall the other night your telling me I made you burn like a furnace. Not many men will be able to do that to you Hadley, but you know I can, and it will draw you back to me again and again, whether you like it or not."

"You're no gentleman to talk of such matters at a time like this. The other night I'd had too much champagne!" Hadley replied, furious at his tone.

"Someday I will make you beg me to love you. Until then, I shall enjoy stalking you as a panther stalks its prey. Nothing you do will remain unknown to me for long. No one you love will be safe from my jealousy. I am a powerful man and have means at my disposal of which you know nothing."

"Dammit, Dietmueller! My father just shot himself and you stand there talking of love and passion and stalking me like an animal. There's only one thing you can ever be sure of and that's that I'll *never* love you. You do something to my body when you touch me. You pop into my mind when I don't want you to, but you'll never own me. I don't want to be a substitute for Alicia. I'm Hadley Ellerman and I'll do what I like in life."

Dietmueller looked at her with something close to adoration.

"What will be will be, but you and I are two of a kind and you know it, whatever you say. My day will come, and in your secret heart you are curious. You want to know if you are a *real* woman and you know enough to have learned that I am the man who can show you."

Hadley ran back to her cabin and locked the door behind her. Only then did she feel secure from Dietmueller's penetrating eyes and his even more penetrating words. She needed to calm herself, and was about to take a shower, when she noticed on the dressing table a bouquet of fifty pale blue carnations surrounded by fern and silver ribbon. Picking up the card, she read the message. "To the most beautiful gangster I have ever seen." Angry that Dietmueller should send her flowers after all that had been said, Hadley threw the card away. Then, as she looked again at the silver ribbons around the exotic blooms, she decided to reexamine it, smiling faintly at the expensive cream paper, the oxblood ink, the gilded seal of an aristocratic German family. She realised that Dietmueller would never have access to such a card, nor would he think to send such flowers. She wondered what manner of man had sent them. Whoever he was, he had style. Hadley put the card in her purse, still pondering the identity of the sender. Perhaps on this, the most agonizing night of her life, something special was about to begin. Ever the optimist, she went to bed and lay awake thinking about the mysterious admirer who had, for a few precious minutes, driven all thought of the tragedy out of her mind. She hoped he was very, very rich.

Nell was crying herself to sleep. First she cried for her father and for the life of luxury she and her sisters had taken for granted. Then she mourned her lost future. For months she had been a little bit in love with the Prince of Wales, and now the friendship would be over. The heir to the throne of Britain could not romance the daughter of a suicide. Nell winced as she considered her uncertain fate. On her twenty-first birthday she had, in the space of a single night, been hurled from the golden pavilions of wealth to the dark labyrinths of insecurity. She was homeless and totally unprepared for earning a living in the hard, competitive world. Memories of childhood flooded into her mind and she wondered sadly if she and her sisters would ever be really happy again.

Bunny had stepped out of the captain's cabin into the arms of Jack Cameron. He had offered his handkerchief and let her blow her nose hard. Now they were in the ship's library and Cameron sat thinking and trying to assess what the future would hold for the sisters, whose names were synonymous with wealth, style, and sybaritic pursuits. He turned to Bunny and looked hard into her eyes.

"Tell me what I can do to help you."

"Right now, I just want to give Papa a beautiful funeral with all his favorite hymns and flowers."

"And after the funeral?"

Bunny shook her head, wiping her eyes and doing her best to appear grown-up, despite the paralyzing feelings of fear that were enveloping her.

"We'll all have to find work, Jack."

"But what can you do? None of you knows anything useful."

Bunny's eyes lit with sudden exasperation.

"You know, Jack, ever since I was little, everyone called me 'Poor Bunny.' They told me I couldn't do this and I couldn't do that and gave me the distinct impression that the only folk in our family who could do *anything* were Hadley and Nell. Well, it's got to stop right now. I know I never learned a useful thing in my life, but I have to change. I'll go back to school and learn bookkeeping or stenography or cooking. And don't you tell me I can't do it, because I have to. I'm going to learn to be independent. I don't know how, but I don't ever want to be this scared again."

"Bunny, we've been together a lot during the voyage and I've enjoyed every second of your company. I never met a woman who put me so much at my ease. I never met a woman I could talk with as I can talk with you. I'm thirty-nine and I never thought it possible that I'd feel like this about anyone. I don't know all the fancy words men are supposed to say at times like these, but I'm in love with you, Bunny."

Bunny gazed at Cameron, shocked by the outpouring of his feelings. Normally he was so reserved, so secret and silent. She was used to men proclaiming their love for Hadley or Nell. Indeed, many rejected suitors had cried on her shoulder in the past. Now someone was saying that he loved her, and the thought was both incredible and intriguing. But to tell her about it on the night of her father's death was in the worst possible taste! She blew her nose one last time and fixed Cameron with a stern look.

"Papa killed himself a couple of hours ago and I'm extremely upset. Someday I'll recover, but right now let's not talk about love. Please, Jack."

Cameron took off his jacket and put it around her shoulders. Then he ordered coffee and brandy for them both and stood looking down at the shiny golden hair and the two wilting roses on either side of her parting. Bunny had met disaster with tears, but she had also revealed her courage and frustration at the role she had been allocated in life. Unlike the hard-faced females who had emerged since the war, she was a real woman with a lush body and a mind full of maddening contradictions. Turning to her, Cameron struggled to retrieve himself.

"You're right to reprimand me for mentioning my feelings at this time. We Camerons are a mite selfish when it comes to love and I apologize. I'll say no more till we reach France. There's one thing you should know, though. They don't call me the stubbornest man in the Kingdom of Fife for nothing and I'll be talking of love again before you're very much older."

It was snowing when the Ellermans arrived in Paris and stood together outside the station, looking uncertainly around at the stately gray streets of the capital. In a square nearby, a barrel organist began to play a love song. Chestnut vendors were huddled over charcoal braziers, calling their wares and blowing into frozen fingers. In the crowded street, men were hurrying to work at the Stock Exchange and a little girl was running home with a baguette from the bakery on the corner.

While porters stacked their trunks at the cab-stand, the sisters shivered in a skin-stripping wind. Nell counted thirty-six cases and trunks and sighed, wondering where on earth they were going to go with this mountain of possessions.

Hadley's voice cut into her deliberations.

"Well, we'd best go to the Ritz. That's the hotel where we always stay and the only one we really know."

Nell watched as Hadley tipped the porters and ordered them to load the small cases into the cab, the trunks onto a horse-drawn wagon. Another fierce gust of wind stifled the protests that came to mind at the thought of the expense of staying at the Ritz. Hadley's confidence was catching and Nell relaxed as her sister explained what they would do.

"We'll register at the hotel, then discuss our future. Do you agree, Nell?"

"Of course I do."

"Everything will seem much better when we're warm and snug and drinking something delicious."

Bunny gazed in surprise at her sisters.

"Can we afford to stay at the Ritz now that we're poor, Hadley?"

"Oh, *do* shut up, Bunny! Of course we can and anyway we're not poor. You are *not* to mention that word again. We're the Ellermans and we've got to remember what Papa taught us, that we're special people. Think poor and you'll soon be poor. You just get *that* into your head."

Claud Auzello, the manager of the Ritz, hurried to meet the sisters at the entrance, his professional smile masking the fact that he knew all about Horace Ellerman's suicide. He was relieved to see that the girls were traveling with their usual pile of luggage, that Hadley ordered a suite, and that jewels were deposited in the safe, just as they always had been. Obviously the Ellermans had not shared the fate of many of their fellow Americans in the aftermath of the Wall Street crash. He accompanied the sisters to their suite with a flourish, then withdrew, closing the door behind him. He was lingering outside in the corridor when he heard Hadley addressing her sisters.

"Well, this is it, the first day of our new start in life. Nell, order some champers, will you? Bunny, stop staring at me as if I've gone plum crazy."

"Sorry, Hadley. I was just wondering how we can afford to stay here when—"

"I don't want to hear another word. A year from now things are going to be very different for us all, and ten years from now, who knows where we'll be or what we'll be doing? We've got to view the road ahead as a kind of adventure, that's all I know."

Auzello moved away, shaking his head in puzzlement as waiters hurried into the suite with silver buckets of champagne.

For Nell, Hadley, and Bunny, who had never ironed a dress, carried money, worked, traveled on a trolleybus, or bought clothes off the rack, a new life was about to begin. Each had one precious piece of jewelry and five thousand dollars, a tenth of what had formerly been their yearly dress allowance. The new life had started in style. Only Bunny kept wondering if it was wise to follow the old ways, when there was no longer a rich and indulgent father to pay the tab. For Hadley, the present was all that mattered, the future something to be thought of tomorrow or next year or never. For Nell, the familiar room was comforting, though she was well aware that economies must be made, and soon.

Outside the Ritz Hotel it began to snow, muffling the sounds of traffic and piling in graceful white lines along the window frames. Inside the warm, womblike suite, the Ellermans were drinking champagne, having put off till another day the moment of truth, the moment when they would have to face life in the real world, where spoiled little rich girls were a most unwelcome breed.

I

THE
PASSIONATE YEARS,
1930 – 1931

— 1 —
PARIS, JANUARY 1930

AT MAXIM'S, A former grand duke of Russia was dining on oysters and caviar. Two other titled Russian émigrés were among the waiters scurrying to please him. In the French Parliament there were arguments so heated a fistfight broke out. Democracy, some said, had gone wild.

In the Ritz Hotel, Auzello was leafing through piles of cancellations from American clients struck down in the aftermath of the Wall Street crash. On this crisp winter morning, he had also learned that the fashion buyers who normally came in droves at this time of year had canceled. The sole occupants of the hotel were the Ellerman sisters, a German count who had just arrived, and two elderly sisters from Southern France. The Duke of Fife, known to the Ellermans as Black Jack Cameron, was due to arrive the next morning, followed by the Duc de Nonancourt and his brother. Apart from this handful of guests, the only further bookings were for a party of titled Englishmen who were coming for a brief reunion in three weeks' time. Auzello shook his head despairingly. That, as far as he could see, was that. The gilded corridors of the hotel would be empty except for a privileged few—and an idle staff—for the foreseeable future.

Bunny arrived back at the hotel, her face flushed with excitement. In the four weeks since her arrival, she had had a number of false starts. The week she spent attempting to learn stenography proved impossible because of her bad coordination, and a trial forty-eight hours at a beauty parlor was equally fruitless. It took Bunny less than twenty-four hours to decide that she hated the frivolity of the clients nearly as much as the rapaciousness of the owner. Now she had enrolled for a six-month cookery course at the Tante Marie School in St. Germain. By the time she was through, she would, with luck, have reached *cordon bleu* standard. Bunny smiled contentedly and ate the remains of the quiche she had been given at the end of the first day's tutorial. Cooking was fun, and how better to earn a living than by doing something you liked? She rushed along the corridor to the suite to tell her sisters the good news, that she was at last on her way to a career that would make her an independent woman.

Hadley was painting her toenails. Normally she had a top-to-toe beauty treatment once each week, but Nell and Bunny had protested loud and long at this extravagance, so she had decided to do it herself. She frowned at a red smudge of varnish on the sunburned skin of her big toe. Dammit! Any moment now she would have to rush out and buy a little something from Chanel or Patou to convince herself she was not as poor as Bunny kept saying. Hadley looked curiously at her younger sister, puzzled by the glow in her face. She spoke with a certain exasperation.

"You look like the cat that stole the cream."

"I just finished my first day at Tante Marie and it was wonderful."

"You're not going to get tempted to abandon it

like you did the typing class and the beauty parlor?"

"Oh no, I just love cooking, it's so creative. I feel like I'm making something beautiful. I always did love being in the kitchen, but Papa put it out of bounds because he was scared I'd get domesticated."

"He was quite right, too!"

"I'm going to work so hard now that I've found what I like doing, I might be first in my class."

"How can you say that, Bunny, you never even boiled water! Anyway, what's the point of learning to cook? Only servants *cook*."

Bunny sighed. There were times when Hadley seemed unable or unwilling to accept that they were all going to have to work, that for the Ellerman sisters servants were a thing of the past. She spoke gently.

"When I qualify in April, I'll be able to get a job as a pastry chef or a second in a restaurant. Tante Marie's is a prestigious school and their graduates always get high-paid positions. It's what I want, Hadley. I don't want to spend every cent Papa left me and be without cash afterward. We all have to think of the future. You too, you know."

Hadley concentrated on the blood-red toenails, unwilling to listen to reality and relieved when Nell appeared with the evening papers, the realty sections marked in her specially mixed violet ink. Nell looked tired and Hadley thought ruefully that even her voice seemed strained.

"I've searched every newspaper and damn near worn my shoes out visiting realtors, but I can't find anything to buy."

Hadley shrugged, bored with the problems of the moment.

"Aren't there any houses for sale? I don't believe it."

"There are thousands, Hadley, but not in my price range."

Bunny listened as her sisters talked, as always the silent observer. But Nell's complaint about the exorbitant prices of Parisian real estate made her think of something.

"Why don't you buy out of the city, Nell? Country places could be half the price, like they are back home."

Nell gazed at Bunny. There were times when Little Sister's list-making, worrying, and insistence on punctuality drove her and Hadley wild. But there were times, too, when Bunny's simple way of thinking cut to the heart of the matter. She patted Bunny's hand and conceded that she was right.

"I suppose I could look in the country."

Hadley shook her head and spoke emphatically.

"You *can't* live out of Paris. You're not the suburban type."

Nell glowered at Hadley, who was spraying herself from a newly purchased huge cut-glass container of Patou scent.

"I can't stay here at the Ritz forever! We've *got* to talk about that, Hadley, and you know it. We've been here over a month and we just can't afford it."

"I don't want to think about perfectly horrible things."

Nell and Hadley faced each other like fighting cocks, watched in silence by Bunny. Nell's voice would have cut a lemon in half.

"You didn't want to think about it yesterday and you won't want to think about it tomorrow, but we *have* to make a decision. Dammit, Hadley, must you act like a goddamned ostrich forever?"

Hadley rose and stood before the mirror, gazing at the white satin dressing gown she had secretly bought from Chanel. White satin was definitely on its way in. In a year or so it would be all the rage, maybe even for ball gowns and opera suits. She shrugged at Nell's furious face and moved to leave the room, calling over her shoulder, "We'll talk about it later."

Nell leapt to her feet. "I think we should talk about it right now."

Hadley's voice was placating. "You're tired, darling. Order some champers and have an early night. I *promise* we'll talk about things tomorrow or maybe at the weekend."

Nell leaned forward and started to hammer the logs on the fire with an iron poker. Hadley was the end, the bitter end, there was no doubt about it. She called out to her sister as she disappeared with a mischievous wave, "Just quit ordering champagne and smoked salmon from room service, will you? We're not in the market for those things anymore."

Hadley's eyes turned steely. "I'll *always* be in the market for champagne. I won't ever be poor, you'll see. I intend to be a Ritz type for the rest of my life."

With that, she was gone, the door of her bedroom slamming on the sisters. Minutes later, Nell and Bunny heard the outer door of the suite closing and Hadley's light, quick footsteps in the hall.

Bunny turned to her sister and spoke with a certain hesitation. "I've been thinking of looking for an apartment near the school. I just have to move out of here."

"You're too young to live alone."

"You could live with me."

"I want to buy a place, Bunny. Papa always said money was only safe in bricks and mortar, and after what's happened, I think he was right. I only wish he'd remembered his own advice."

There was a long silence. Then Bunny took an apple pie from a greaseproof paper bag she had carried back to the hotel from the school.

"I brought you this, Nell. You never could resist apple pie."

"I found a good restaurant in the street behind the hotel. You want to go there for dinner?"

"Hadley too?"

"God knows. She just can't make economies. She doesn't want to accept that we're not what we were anymore. She's scared but she won't admit it."

"I'm scared too, Nell."

Nell put her arm around Bunny's shoulders, enveloping her in a cloud of Patou's Joy.

"Never be scared, Bunny. We've got to be brave now and tomorrow and always, and we've got to be proud of ourselves like Papa said."

"I'll try."

"Now, tell me about Jack Cameron. When's he arriving?"

"On Friday around midday."

"How do you feel about him, Bunny? I hear he's pretty rich."

"I think he's comfortably off."

"Do you feel he's right for you?"

Bunny shook her head emphatically, as though determined to convince herself as well as her sister.

"Love itself isn't for me right now. Papa's death gave me the biggest shock of my whole life and it forced me to make a lot of decisions."

"What kind of decisions?"

"I want to know I can live like an independent person before I ever fall in love and get married. I don't want to live my life relying on someone else all the while. I'm scared of doing that again, more scared than anything else in the world. And I'm scared of being in love. When you fall in love you can get hurt. Remember Aunt Maggie after Uncle Hiram left her for a younger woman? She was never the same."

"But what do you really *feel* for Cameron? You

were with him almost every day during the crossing. You must have liked him."

Bunny looked from her sister into the glowing embers of the fire, her mind running back over some of the special moments spent with Cameron on board the ship. Despite his taciturn nature, instinct told her he was a passionate man. She recalled the night they had first dined together on the ship. Over coffee, Cameron had described Lochalsh, his Scottish home, making the castle sound like something out of a fairy tale. There were red deer on the hillsides near Lochalsh and foxglove that turned the fields pink in summer. In the fishing village nearby there was a morning market, where the catch was sold on the quayside to eager buyers from miles around. Bunny smiled at the memory of all Cameron had told her, remembering the joy in his voice as he had talked of the bleak old house that was cold even in summer, but that he loved with all his heart. She had said nothing of Lochalsh to her sisters, because Nell and Hadley were so enamored of the idea of living in a castle that they were inclined to like the men who owned them for all the wrong reasons. She tried to imagine what the castle would be like, but she had no idea of the architecture and atmosphere of the area. Scotland and its majestic glens and lakes would, for the moment, remain a mystery.

Realizing that Bunny was lost in romantic daydreams of the man she was obviously fighting hard not to love, Nell spoke gently. "Have you any idea what Cameron feels about you?"

Bunny shook her head, uncertain how to reply. "He's fond of me and maybe more than fond, but he's hard to assess and I don't know enough about men to be certain. Right now all I can think of is that I must learn how to earn my living. If Jack wants me, he's going to have to be patient."

Nell kissed Bunny's cheek and held her hands. "Papa's death shocked us all, and you more than most, because you've always taken things so hard, but you're not to allow it to spoil the future. You can't deliberately try to avoid love or marriage, just so you won't be hurt. Love comes to lucky people and they say it's the most beautiful feeling in the world. So ease up on Cameron. Let him take you out and have fun together. He's a good man, even if he's disinclined to talk. I guess he's one of those strong, silent types who feel things clean down to their boots."

Bunny wiped a tear from her eye.

"I wish I knew as much about people as you do, Nell."

"Enough serious talk. Come on, I'll buy you a fifty-cent feast around the corner."

Hadley was in the Ritz bar, sipping a crème-de-menthe frappé and trying to still the panic Nell's outburst had provoked. Unaccompanied women were frowned on in the Petit Bar, but no one had had the courage to tell the lady. Hadley sat gazing at her reflection in the apricot-pink mirrors. She had decided to let her hair grow, aware that the garçonne look of the previous decade was becoming passé. Patou had decreed that the thirties would be the decade of glamour and sex appeal and Hadley knew that fit her perfectly. The world would be her oyster, provided she could find the right setting and the right man. For a moment she thought of Ernst Dietmueller and wondered where he was and if his threats had been real or the products of a mind obsessed with desire for a woman. Pushing an errant lock of hair back from her forehead, Hadley decided not to think of Dietmueller or the hotel bill or anything unsettling like trying to work out her future. Again, panic rose in her as she cast her mind back to the past, when the iron-willed Horace Ellerman had made all the plans for his daughters. With something of a shock, Hadley realized that she had never really made a decision in her life. She knew only how to live in the manner taught her by her father, and was now keeping to the routine, long after the good life had ended. Terrified by the thought, Hadley ordered another crème-de-menthe frappé. She was sucking the emerald liquid through a straw, when she looked up and saw in the mirror the reflection of what had to be the handsomest man in Europe.

He was about thirty-four years old, tall, blond, and powerfully built, with a craggy face suntanned to deep cinnamon. His eyes were bright blue, his hair side-parted and curly. His cheekbones were high, his chin strong, and there was a reddish light in the hair of the mustache. Dressed in gray, the jacket piped with suede, he was a commanding figure, the type of man, Hadley decided, who would look at home on a mountainside or in a palace, riding like a Tatar on a distant steppe or lounging by the sea on a white-sand beach.

Hadley's heart began to beat with a thunderous roar when the man walked to her side and put a cream card down on the bar before her. She recognized at once the writing in oxblood ink on the gilded heavy paper with its manorial crest. This was the man who had sent her blue carnations on the crossing from New York. She smiled happily at the query on the card: "Would Monsieur Capone care to have dinner with Count Kohler?" She nodded and smiled into his eyes.

"Monsieur Capone would enjoy that very much."

The young man extended his hand and introduced himself. "I am Karl-Friedrich Kohler. I come from Munich in Bavaria."

"Hadley Ellerman, late of Chicago."

"Would you like to eat at any particular restaurant?"

"Anywhere so long as it's not here. I'm so bored with the hotel I could scream."

"People do not usually express boredom with the Ritz Hotel."

"I'm not people."

"May I ask the name of your perfume? It is adorable."

"It's Patou's Amour-Amour."

Their eyes met and held each other for a moment. Then Karl spoke with a certain teasing charm. "Is love one of your great interests in life, Miss Ellerman?"

Hadley stared at him, caught off balance by the question. One moment he was admiring her perfume, and the next, prompted by the name, he was asking intimate questions. Or had he asked it to watch her reaction, to shock her? Hadley thought wryly that if that had been his aim, he had succeeded. She did her best to answer as nonchalantly as possible. "Love interests most women of my age."

"That's true, but some are interested only in an abstract way. They like to listen to others talking of their experiences or to read about love in novels."

"I'm not like that."

"What are you like? What are your hobbies and special interests in life, apart from having your own way?"

Hadley felt again a frisson of uncertainty as she looked more closely at this challenging young man. He had the air of a gentleman, but a streak that was hard and unyielding. He would be difficult to know and to please. She saw that Karl's gaze had settled on her mouth and forgot what she had been going to say. Despite herself, she laughed merrily.

"Are you a hypnotist, Count Kohler? When

you look at me like that, I forget what I was going to tell you."

"Good, at least I shall not easily be overlooked. Do you like Indonesian food, Miss Ellerman?"

"I never tasted it."

"Tonight we must do everything you never did before. We'll go to exotic places and see strange and wonderful sights. I shall ask you a hundred questions and you will answer them all honestly."

Hadley felt her strength ebbing as the mocking blue eyes settled again on her lips. She tried hard to reply in her usual brittle style. "I shan't do anything of the kind. I *always* tell lies."

"I don't think so. You are much too brave to be a liar. Put on your wrap, it's cold outside. First we shall go to Fouquet's for a pastis. Then we'll see where the magic carpet takes us. Are you ready for a very special evening?"

"I'm ready. Hold my hand."

Hadley looked down as he linked his strong, suntanned hands in hers. She wanted, suddenly, to put her arms around his neck and beg him to take her upstairs to make her forget all her problems for an hour or two. Instead, she walked with Karl from the bar, shivering when his fingers lingered on her shoulders as he covered her with her wrap. For the moment her troubles were forgotten and she began to feel alive and vibrant again. It was going to be a perfectly wonderful evening with a man every woman in Europe wanted. Hadley felt happy for the first time since the night of her father's death.

The following morning Nell was on her way out of the hotel when she saw Auzello and went over to say good morning.

"How are you, Claude? You look a bit peaked. Have you had another mail bag full of cancellations?"

"They come on the hour, Miss Annabelle."

"Where's the Valley of Chevreuse? I found an ad describing the most marvelous little cottage for sale there, but I never heard of the place."

"It is near Paris and very beautiful. I will send a map up to your suite and mark it for you."

At that moment two men appeared at the reception desk followed by a chauffeur carrying a pile of luggage. One of them was tall and elegant, with an aquiline face and the languid air of an aristocrat. He was dressed in a dark blue city suit with a red carnation at the buttonhole. The other man was short, stocky, and tough. He had brown hair worn long on the neck, twinkling brown eyes, and a checked Prince of Wales country suit that on someone with less poise would have seemed out of place at the Ritz. His manner was easy, his smile dazzling, and as their eyes met Nell felt for the first time in her life a strange weakness that made her light-headed. Embarrassed lest Auzello notice her reaction, she spoke briskly. "Don't tell me we're to have some new guests at last. Who are they?"

"The handsome one is the Duc de Nonancourt and the other his brother. They live at the Château Bel-Ami near Cheverny in the Loire."

"What do they do for a living?"

"The duke does nothing, naturally. He is a renowned yachtsman and an international tennis player. The younger brother manages the family estates, which are extensive. In my opinion, Bel-Ami is one of the most beautiful of all the châteaux of the Loire."

Nell watched as the two men moved out of the reception area to the stairs. The handsome one was the Duke of Nonancourt. Obviously *this* was her lucky day! She thought dreamily of a château on the Loire. What a perfectly wonderful notion, to fall in love with a handsome man and never have to worry about anything for as long as she lived.

Watching her, Auzello's eyes shone with admiration for the auburn curls that reached almost to her waist, the outlandishly stylish clothes and astonishing eyes. Nell's perfect manners and contrasting ability to swear in four languages fascinated him, and whenever he saw her he found his body becoming disobedient. Struggling to remember his position, he excused himself and hurried away to his office with a brief backward glance at the object of his admiration.

Guy-Simon de Nonancourt, the younger brother, was thirty-four, a man who loved the outdoor life, the estate that was his responsibility, and the beautiful women who pursued him despite his lack of a title. Suntanned, in perfect health, he was possessed of an enviable vitality and a golden charm. He tipped the porter, who had carried the bags into the Nonancourt suite, handed a briefcase to his brother, who was en route to a rendezvous at the family lawyer's office, and then hurried back to the hall to find Auzello.

"Tell me, Claude, who was that exquisite creature I saw you with when I came into the hotel?"

"That was Miss Ellerman. The family call her Nell, but her real name is Annabelle."

"Horace Ellerman's daughter?"

"Yes indeed, sir."

Guy congratulated himself—this was his lucky day. His brother was always urging him to marry money, but he had found it impossible to contemplate making love with a woman to whom he was not deeply attracted. By the French patrimonial law, all possessions of deceased parents were bequeathed to the eldest son, Guy's brother. So Guy had not a sou to call his own, only a humble cottage in the grounds of the château and a job he adored that was his for as long as Bel-Ami remained. He was therefore overjoyed that at last a beautiful and fascinating creature had come along, who was one of the wealthiest young women in the world. Hurrying to the flower stall outside, he bought a dozen red roses and had them sent to Nell's suite with a note. He also arranged for Auzello to introduce them formally on the lady's return to the hotel, leaving the manager, in his wisdom, to find a way of doing it without giving offense.

After lunch, Guy was drinking coffee in the writing room and waiting for his brother's return when he saw Nell entering the hotel. He leaned forward, the better to admire the Amazonian figure in its striking dark dahlia suit. He saw that her eyes were a vivid green and was impressed by the way her presence caught the attention of every man in sight.

Nell did not notice Guy's intent look as she took a bulky letter from the porter at the desk. She looked instead at the envelope, and hurried to the writing room to read her letter. But one quick look at its contents and she knew a dread that was so deep, she felt on the verge of being ill. The results were in ... but could this be true? Her face turned chalk white and she dropped the sheets as if in a daze. Suddenly tears began to stream down her cheeks and she buried her face in her hands and sobbed.

In light of her acquaintance with the Prince of Wales, Nell had been advised to have a medical checkup just before leaving the States, with particular reference to her ability to bear children. All potential royal brides were obliged to do this, and an aide, knowing the Prince of Wales's feelings for Nell, suggested the check. Nell had accepted that it was part of British royal tradition. Now she reeled in horror. The letter informed her in no uncertain terms that she would never have a child. It mattered little now that she was not suitable to be the prince's wife, but the diagnosis of sterility shocked her. In her own eyes she was no longer a real woman. From her earliest days, she had longed and dreamed of having at least four children. The very thought that yet another of her dreams had been denied her cut her to the heart.

Witnessing Nell's distress, Guy rose from his seat and offered his handkerchief.

"Forgive me for intruding, mademoiselle, but I cannot bear to see a beautiful woman cry."

Nell was sobbing so hard her face turned blotchy and she forgot she was with a stranger and clung to his shoulder, so in need of the sympathy he was offering at the very moment when she needed it most.

When he had settled Nell in a chair, Guy hurried to the hall, returning with Auzello, who made the formal introductions.

"My dearest Miss Ellerman, I beg you not to cry. I have to go out to a meeting of the local chamber of commerce and cannot care for you as I would like, so may I introduce Guy de Nonancourt. Guy, Miss Annabelle Ellerman."

"Enchanté, mademoiselle."

Nell clutched the proffered hand, then turned to Auzello.

"Hurry back, Claude. I've a feeling I'm going to need all the help you can give."

"You have it, of course. In the meantime, Guy will look after you. He is a good friend of the Ritz Hotel and understands what is needed in times of trouble."

"I don't know what the bad news is, but nothing in the world is ever as terrible as it seems at first." Guy tried to sound reassuring, touched by the distress in the beautiful woman's face.

When Nell continued to sob, Guy decided to take action and, scooping up the letter, led her firmly outside into the winter streets of Paris. Already workmen were taking down the Christmas trees in the Place Vendôme. The shops remained full of temptation, their windows masterpieces of originality. Some were decorated in red and gold, others in white and silver, and Cartier had a giant Santa Claus bedecked in gems, beckoning to passersby to enter its legendary premises. Wishing he were rich like his brother, if only for the day, Guy bought Nell a bunch of violets, then a bag of hot chestnuts, and they sat eating them in silence on a bench in the children's park near the Place de la Concorde.

A group of toddlers was playing tag nearby. One was screeching because he had fallen. Another was shouting to his mother to come and see what he had found. The children's nannies sat on a green-painted bench, knitting and gossiping, keeping one eye on their precious charges and the other on the watches they all seemed to wear. A little girl ran by, rolling a hoop, her blond ringlets bouncing. She paused before them and offered Nell a sweet.

Unable to wake Nell from an obviously painful reverie, Guy decided to invite her to lunch.

"I would like to take you to a very interesting place. It is called Chartier, and though it's inexpensive, they sell the very nicest beef daube in Paris. Afterward I shall show you some of the areas I adore. Here, take my handkerchief, blow your nose, and wipe your eyes. I hardly know you, Miss Ellerman, but—"

"Call me Nell."

"Before we lunch together, I would like to offer a word of advice, if it would not offend you."

"Go ahead," Nell said. "I'll try anything so long as it makes me feel better."

"I had only two great disasters in my life, things that seemed at the time to shatter my world. The first was when my father was killed in a road accident when I was twelve. The second was when I failed my pilot training course because of inferior eyesight. My brother, Charles, had passed with flying colors, as he passes everything, so I felt a total failure. The thing I learned from both of these experiences was that each, in later years, could be seen to have taught me something valuable and to have strengthened my character. The first drew me and my brother nearer Mama and nearer our roots at Bel-Ami. The house became our refuge and our true home, where previously it had been only a valuable relic from the past. The second taught me that when you fail at one thing, you find other things you can do better than you ever imagined. End of speech. But remember what I have told you. When one part of our lives goes wrong, often another becomes more interesting, more important. We just have to make the adjustment."

"I appreciate your sympathy."

"We'll drink some good strong wine with lunch, a Gigondas perhaps, and we'll talk about our lives. I expected this to be such a dull day, but it is turning into a very special occasion."

"Tell me about your life as Duke of Nonancourt."

"*I* am not the Duc de Nonancourt—my brother is."

Nell threw back her head and laughed at her error. When Auzello had told her the handsome one was the duke, she had taken it to mean the one she found perfectly wonderful, with his bronzed skin and laughing eyes. She had been delighted at the thought of finding such an immensely rich man, and he had turned out to be amusing, impressive, and attractive. But Guy wasn't the duke. Instead, she had chosen the poor brother, who could not offer the security she craved. Still, Nell thought ruefully, whatever his financial situation, Guy de Nonancourt was the one she admired, the brother she wanted for a friend. Of course, she needed money and the feelings of safety it brought, but unlike Hadley, she was not a gold digger. Nell's heart still dictated her actions, just as it always had.

Relieved that she had shown no sign of disappointment in the discovery of his situation, Guy began to talk of the home he loved.

"My life *is* Bel-Ami, our château in the Loire region. I manage the estate for my brother and I adore every moment of my work. I live in a cottage in the grounds, a very pretty place covered in yellow roses. I eat in the main house, because I burn pans very efficiently, but have never learned to cook."

"My sister's teaching me to cook too, but I've not much of a flair for it. And I'm hoping to buy a little cottage in the Valley of Chevreuse."

"Have you dined there under the apple trees at the old inn?"

"Not yet."

"I will take you there tomorrow. I adore the casserole of chicken and we'll eat three helpings of the *tarte Tatin*. Is it a date?"

Nell smiled at his enthusiasm, the look of happiness in his eyes, and agreed. For several minutes she had forgotten all about the news in the letter that had changed her life, and she was grateful. For the moment, she knew she must guard her secret and try, as Guy had suggested, to find a new direction.

Conscious that Nell was falling again into a melancholy state, Guy rose and took her hand.

"I want to show you the sights of Montmartre and this evening to take you to the jazz cellar in the Place du Tertre. If you want, we can go to the late show of the Folies Bergère afterward. Try not to think of what's making you unhappy. We are going to have fun together today. I might even buy you a glass of Montmartre wine. It's so bitter they say it can raise the dead."

"Let's hope between the two of us we have enough to buy two glasses."

"I'm sure an Ellerman could obtain credit, even in Montmartre!"

"Not anymore. Papa lost every cent before he killed himself."

Guy sighed resignedly. Just when he thought he had found a rich woman to admire, she turned out to be penniless. He held Nell's hand tightly. Well, he wasn't the duke and she wasn't the heiress he had thought. But money or no, this beautiful woman was the one he had dreamed of meeting all his life.

Nell smiled, guessing the meaning of his sigh, and hurried out into the street on his arm. It was a chilly February morning but the sun was shining and there was still a ray of hope in her heart.

At the end of February, over a month after she had started the course, Bunny arrived home from the cookery school in a state of total exhaustion. She had been on her feet since eight that morning and the long hours of standing were something she still found trying. She called for a bowl of hot water to be brought, emptied the contents of a tin of mustard into it, and soaked her feet to relieve the pain. At least the lessons were interesting—and she *was* preparing for her future. Someday, what she was learning would make her independent, and that was what mattered.

She was dozing peacefully in the armchair, daydreaming about the money she would make, when there was a knock at the door and the sound of Jack Cameron's voice calling her. "I'm back. Are you in there, lassie?"

Bunny hurried to let him in.

"I'm so glad to see you, Jack. When did you arrive? I've been lonely without you these past few weeks."

"I got into the Gare du Nord an hour ago. Are your sisters away? Why have you been lonely?"

"They're still here, but Hadley's out most of the day with Count Kohler and Nell's been getting everything set for the purchase of her cottage."

"When are you planning to move out?"

"I don't know. Hadley doesn't want to leave the hotel and Nell can't leave fast enough. They've been quarreling like wildcats. I just keep quiet and do what I'm told."

"But what do *you* want, Bunny?"

"I'm trying to find a little apartment near the school. I already have a place in mind."

"You're not thinking of living *alone?*"

"I may have to. I asked Nell to move in with me, but she's set on buying the country place. She can't afford Paris prices."

"You're too young to live alone in a strange country."

"I can't stay tied to my sisters forever, Jack."

"Stay on here a wee while."

Bunny shook her head despairingly. "It's too expensive and Hadley just *won't* stop ordering champagne and snacks from room service. I don't know why we ever came here in the first place and I've no idea how we're going to pay the bill."

Cameron thought anxiously that he had best talk with Hadley and offer to cover the first month's bill on the condition that Bunny stay on. But he had to make sure she was not told of his offer—it was in Bunny's nature to feel such a suggestion immoral. He looked at her, sitting there with her feet soaking in a mustard bath.

"That's what I like, a natural woman. When I went home to Scotland I kept thinking of you with roses in your hair, and now I'm back I find you soaking your aching feet. Everything else around here is make-believe, Bunny. You're reality and that's what I love about you."

He kissed her hands gently and looked into the wide blue eyes.

"Tell me more about your plans for the future."

"I'll qualify at the end of April if I work hard. Then I'll take a job."

"Where will you work?"

"I don't know yet, it depends on what I want to do, general cooking or specialties. I could work as a commis chef at the U.S. embassy if I'm a top liner, and in five years I'd become a second and eventually in charge of the kitchens. Or I could go to a restaurant and specialize as a pastry cook or fish chef or in the really tricky subjects like ice carving and spun-sugar design."

"Will you not come to England and let me care for you?"

Bunny gazed into the dark, anxious eyes and patted Cameron's hand, touched by his concern.

"I just have to learn to live on my own first, so I know I can pay my way in life if ever disaster strikes. When I know I can get by like ordinary people do, I'll come to England with you, I promise. Meanwhile, what about dinner? I'm famished!"

They went to a bistro in the Rue Brey. The Etoile Vert served the best goulash in the city and a chocolate mousse that provoked Bunny to three helpings. They drank Beaumes de Venise, a dark red wine of the Rhone, and then tiny glasses of anisette liqueur that came with rich, fragrant coffee in an old-fashioned blue porcelain pot.

After dinner, Bunny proposed they walk back to the Ritz so they could be together longer. Touched by this small admission of her feelings for him, Cameron put his arm around her shoulder and kissed her ear and her cheek. Then, under a starry sky, they sauntered from the Arc de Triomphe down the glittering length of the Champs Élysées, pausing here and there to look in the windows of fashion shops, jewelers', and patisseries full of ornate icing-sugar wonders. Crowds of taut-faced Parisians were sitting outside pavement cafés drinking pastis and watching the scene. And from small bars in side streets came the sound of jazz musicians and blues singers crooning the night away.

Realizing that Cameron was uneasy at the idea of her living alone in Paris, Bunny got him to talk about his home in Scotland. When Jack talked of Lochalsh, he forgot all his worries and was happy deep in his soul.

"And how is your housekeeper, Mrs. MacKay?"

"She's sulking because I've come to Paris again. Agnes doesn't approve of foreign places and foreign folk. She's descended from Black Molly MacKay, who personally cut the heads off a dozen of her husband's enemies after his murder."

"She sounds a bit of a monster to me."

"Oh, she is. Mrs. MacKay never met her match in the Kingdom of Fife and I don't believe she ever will. There isn't a man or woman born with a temper like hers."

They reached the Rond Point of the Champs Elysées and paused to admire a flower stall hidden among the trees. While Cameron moved away to make his choice from the blooms on display, Bunny stood at the side of the road watching the evening promenade of fashionable people.

Suddenly a man stepped out of a white Mercedes, flashing a smile at her. Without warning, he leaned forward and kissed her hand.

"Would you care to take an aperitif with me, mademoiselle?" he asked, weighing the priceless pearls around her neck and the lush lines of her body.

Bunny blushed furiously and put on her spectacles, the better to see this arrogant young man. To her chagrin, they steamed up, despite the chill of the evening. She was wiping them when

Cameron returned, his arms full of roses and syringa. Bunny was shocked when the young man turned and told the Scotsman to go away. She was delighted when Cameron, by way of a reply, pushed the adventurer so hard he fell like a sack of potatoes onto the sidewalk, much to the amusement of passersby. Then Cameron handed her the roses and walked on, taking her arm and continuing his interrupted conversation as if nothing untoward had happened.

"You'd best show me this place you're fancying taking."

"You'll not be able to see it in the dark. Can't we go in the morning when you take me to the school?"

"We'll go right now or I'll not sleep for worrying."

A host of conflicting emotions filled Bunny's mind. Cameron was like a rock, hard and craggy and difficult, and she both admired and feared that. She wondered what he would be like when he made love. In a voice softened by her reverie, she spoke her thoughts. "I often wonder why you chose *me*. Why didn't you make a beeline for Hadley or Nell like every other man?"

Cameron chose his words carefully. "You and Hadley are the tortoise and the hare. Hadley lives her life as a woman in a hurry and I can see no good coming of that. You're the tortoise. You may have started slow, but you'll win in the end." Reading confusion in Bunny's eyes, Cameron explained further. "You see, Hadley's beauty reached its peak when she was still very young. When that happens to a woman, she may find it hard to accept the changes that are inevitable with the passing years. You're slow to find your style, but when you do, you'll outshine everyone. You've a beauty that'll mature like fine wine and improve with age. Wait and see if I'm not right."

Bunny stood very still, her hand entwined in

Cameron's. Was it possible he was right? She thought of the tortoise and the hare of the Aesop fable and Cameron's statement that Hadley's beauty had reached its peak at a very young age. In the days of childhood she had wanted more than anything in the world to look just like her sister. And often she had sobbed when folk called her homely. On those occasions Papa had reassured her that she was a very special person and different from her sisters in an important kind of way. Perhaps he had been right. Perhaps Cameron was right too and someday she would surprise everyone, even herself.

They walked together through the medieval streets of the Rue de la Harpe and the Rue Saint-Séverin, pausing to admire the flamboyant outlines of the nearby church. The location of Bunny's prospective apartment ran parallel to the Seine in a maze of tiny streets that comprised the Latin Quarter. In one tiny alleyway Bunny pointed out a favorite curiosity, some subterranean windows heavily barred in latticed iron.

"Do you know what those are, Jack?"

"I can't imagine, though they look a mite sinister to me."

"The French call them 'Oubliettes.' In olden times they were underground prisons where enemies of the king were put and then forgotten forever."

Satisfied that the area, though cheap, was not unsuitable for Bunny, Cameron called a cab and asked to be taken back to the Ritz. He was thinking of the young man who had leered at Bunny's body and who had undoubtedly computed the worth of her pearls. He wondered warily how he was going to survive the months of separation from the woman he now knew he truly loved. One thing was certain, he was going to have to wait. Bunny had had a fearsome fright at the death of her father and was determined to seek independence. He could not blame her for that. During the period of the cookery course he would continue to visit Paris every month, but Bunny would be on her own for the rest of the time. Unable to bear the thought, Cameron decided to speak to her sisters immediately, to insist that they order Bunny to remain at the Ritz. There, at least, she would have Auzello to keep an eye on her, since he was nothing short of a bloodhound. Cameron decided to leave it to the manager's discretion to explain to Bunny how the bill was being paid.

As they paused outside the hotel, he looked down at her with longing.

"Will you kiss me, Bunny?"

She put her arms around his neck, stood on tiptoes, and pursed her lips. When he kissed her, she was shocked to feel his tongue forcing its way into her mouth. He had not done that before and it made her moan with pleasure. There was something so insistent in the feeling and Bunny responded without realizing fully what was happening. Before she knew it, she was opening her mouth and her arms to him. Then, as the kiss increased in aggression, she drew back with a gasp.

"You never kissed me like that before, Jack."

"You never let me."

Bunny smiled a secret smile at the feelings the kiss had provoked, the tautness in her breasts, the ripple of strange, sensual feeling in her innermost parts. With a shy glance at Cameron, she took his hand and they went into the hotel together. It was the first time she had ever known what it felt like to be wanted and to want with all her soul in return.

In the Ellerman suite, Hadley was dancing with joy. She was off to Africa in the morning and was delighted to be getting out of the hotel and away from the responsibilities of thinking about the future. For two months she would do nothing but enjoy herself. It had been a tricky business, though. In the four weeks since their first meeting, Karl had returned to Bavaria to collect a party of friends and equipment for a forthcoming safari. Throughout the three weeks of his absence, Hadley had longed to hear from him, but he had not written, nor had he invited her to join him on the safari, despite strong hints on her part before his departure for Munich. But then, on the night of Karl's return, the week previously, he had taken her to dinner at the Tour d'Argent and asked casually if she thought she could be ready in time to join him on the trip. She savored his words and the memory of the look in his eyes: *Would you like to leave these cold, damp days of February for the sunshine of Cairo and the excitement of the Kenya bush? Are you ready for a very big adventure, Hadley?* After nights of passionate kissing, when his lips and his hands had inflamed her beyond all measure, Hadley felt sure he was not talking only of the safari. Under the scarlet sunset of a Cairo night, Karl would surely make her his own, possessing her as she had never been possessed before. A shiver of expectation ran through her body at the thought, and she closed her eyes, the better to savor it. When she opened them again, she saw that Nell was close to tears. Immediately she had a pang of conscience and hurried to kneel at her sister's side.

"What's wrong? You've been as quiet as a mouse all day!"

"Oh, Hadley. Here you are about to embark on this wonderful adventure and all I can think of is how my dreams all come to nothing. I can't tell you how the doctor's report has changed me— and my outlook. It's as if the news has diminished me and made me lose all my confidence."

Hadley saw tears running down Nell's cheeks. She wanted to say that children were pests who ruined your figure and made a mess of the house, but this was no time for flippancy. For as long as she could remember, children had figured into Nell's scenario for the future. The news must have been a savage shock. Suddenly contrite at her own happiness, Hadley hurried to the phone and ordered champagne cocktails to raise their spirits. Then she went and hugged Nell to her heart.

"Cheer up, doctors can be wrong."

"This one's a specialist, recommended by the prince's aide."

"Oh, poor Nell! Everyone'll give you different advice on how to handle this, Nell. The fact is, you just have to accept it and change your plans for the future. It takes guts to accept a situation you cannot change, but you've always had plenty of spunk."

"Well, I seem to have lost it since I got that letter. I live my life. I even have fun, but all the time my mind comes back to the news. It's like a nightmare I can't awaken from."

"You'll find a new dream, I assure you, but it'll take time, lots of time. Lean on me, Nell. I love you, always have, and always will. Let me help in any way I can."

When Bunny arrived, she found Nell crying on Hadley's lap. Two waiters were serving champagne cocktails, their eyes discreetly downcast. Hurrying to dismiss them, Bunny handed the drinks to her sisters and waited for them to tell her what was wrong. First she heard the news of Hadley's departure, then the details of Nell's troubles, from which, thus far, the youngest sister had been sheltered. Soon Bunny cried as well, and the noise was deafening. Then, drying her tears, she tried to be practical.

"What you need is a holiday, Nell. If you can't

take a holiday, find yourself a handsome man and have a whirlwind romance. *That* will take your mind off everything."

Nell stared in amazement at her little sister.

"Bunny! I never heard you talk like that before. Whatever has gotten into you?"

Bunny beamed, delighted to have shocked both her sisters.

"I'm growing up fast! I guess you'll just have to get used to it."

Hadley burst into peals of laughter and soon the sisters' tears had changed into tears of mirth.

At six the following morning, Hadley was due to leave with Karl for Marseilles. This was the first leg of an epic trip that would include Cairo and the safari to Kenya. She had always dreamed of seeing the Nile, and the thought of visiting Egypt with the most desirable man in Europe was a dream. She knew instinctively that this was going to be a special year in her life and longed to make the most of every opportunity that presented itself. As she kissed her sisters good-bye in the hall of the hotel, she was brimming with excitement and anticipation.

"I promise not to forget to write, the way I usually do. Nell, here's my address in Cairo and, Bunny, here's the one for Kenya, so you've no excuse not to stay in contact."

Karl stepped forward and kissed the sisters' hands. "Have no fear, I shall take care of Hadley. Between us, my party includes four of the finest shots in Europe, a doctor of medicine and one of zoology from the University of Munich, so we are not entirely without resources."

Nell looked quizzically into the clear blue eyes. "It's not lions and tigers *I'm* worried about where Hadley's concerned.

Karl's eyes twinkled as he replied, "The human animals will also be kept at bay, with Hadley's help of course. Now we really must go."

Bunny called from the steps of the hotel, "Bon voyage. And don't forget the zebra skins for Nell's cottage."

Guy appeared on the stairs as the sisters were about to return to their rooms.

"I'm ready when you are, Nell. I know it's a little earlier than we planned, but we should try to avoid the first rush-hour traffic."

"I'll get my purse. Do you need anything before I go, Bunny?"

"No, I'm just fine. I leave for the school at eight, so I shan't start missing anyone till this evening."

Claude Auzello was informed by a vigilant member of the hotel staff that Hadley Ellerman had left the Ritz with Count Kohler for a long journey to Africa. Miss Annabelle Ellerman also appeared to be on the point of departure with Guy de Nonancourt, leaving only Bunny in occupation of the suite. On hearing the news, Auzello ordered an account to be made up and presented immediately to whichever of the sisters appeared first.

At eight, Bunny went downstairs to the reception desk and was handed the first month's bill by the bookings manager. One glance confirmed all her worst fears—the items on Hadley's room-service account seemed endless. Bunny stood ashen pale, feeling more alone than she had ever felt in her life.

Cameron hurried down the stairs from his room, ready to take Bunny to school, as was his custom when in Paris. One look at her face provoked him to turn on the clerk behind the desk.

"What has upset Miss Ellerman? I demand to know what is happening."

"Mademoiselle was given the first month's bill, sir."

"Dammit, man, why did you give it to *her*? I

agreed to pay it. Could you not have had the decency to give it to me?"

Bunny felt weak, confused, and angry with her sisters, herself, and the world in general. She turned to Cameron, her face still pale but her determination evident.

"You know perfectly well I won't let you pay that bill, Jack. We've just got to learn how to be independent, and we'll never manage it if some man keeps paying the tab like Papa used to. You can't take his place, and I don't want you to try. Tell Monsieur Auzello I'll pay somehow."

"Can't I do anything to help you, Bunny?"

"When I get back from school you can help me pack and move my own and Nell's things out right away."

"Won't you talk it over with Nell first? And can't you miss school for the day? You're as pale as death."

"I'm going whatever color I am. Now, please call a cab. I want to get away from this place and I don't *ever* want to come back."

Bunny said nothing at all in the taxi. She was thinking of the bill and trying to work out what the total cost of their stay would be. Figures loomed in her mind and she was tempted to accept Cameron's offer to run off with him to Scotland, far away from all responsibility. Instead, she gritted her teeth and resolved to learn how to cope. It was all part of growing up, after all, and becoming an independent woman, which was what she longed to be.

When Cameron delivered her to the door of the school, Bunny was already regaining her color and some of her courage. She looked into his eyes and smiled bravely.

"You're not to worry about me, Jack. I'm feeling better already. I may be young and inexperienced in life, but I'm going to be the toughest

Ellerman there ever was. Now, off you go. Meet me here at six and we'll eat dinner at La Coupole."

Cameron was to remember it as the moment when he realized that he was irrevocably and desperately in love with Bunny Ellerman.

— 2 —
CAIRO–BAVARIA,
SPRING–SUMMER 1930

SUNSET CAME AT six and the sky turned orange. Black feluccas sailed slowly on the Nile, their crewmen chanting age-old songs of the sea, and in the distance, the muezzin called the faithful to prayer from the roof of an onion-domed minaret. The terrace of the rose marble villa Karl had rented for their stay in the city held impassive statues of Sekmet, goddess of war, and Anubis, the black jackal of death. The statues looked out over the city of a thousand sensations. At this hour of the day, all the sounds of Cairo were heightened and the scent of musk, papyrus, and cardamom was stronger, more insistent. At six-thirty, darkness would fall with sudden finality and the night people would emerge; the smugglers, belly dancers, assassins, and mysterious men of no true nationality, who were spies real or imagined. Beautiful pampered creatures entered Rolls-Royces en route to an exciting evening at the gambling tables, in the bed of a millionaire, or in one of the gilded garçonnières of the Villa Loma, the most expensive private club in the city and a hive of erotic activity from dusk to dawn.

Hadley was alone on the terrace, looking out at

the view. The exotic atmosphere made her body ache for love and she was resentful of the way Karl had avoided her since the start of the journey. During the voyage, he had remained the perfect gentleman, kissing her hand at the door of her cabin and then leaving her alone in the heat of the night. By the time the ship approached the African coast, she had brazenly invited him in, but he had refused, saying it was not the time or the place. Since their arrival in Cairo he had taken her to see the sights and had been elusive but charming. Then he had disappeared from the city for a week to make the final arrangements for the safari to Kenya. He had returned the previous night and thrown a large party attended by every socialite of the international set in the city. And all the while he had kept Hadley at arm's length, a stranger to be admired but never touched. Now he had gone out with some male friends to celebrate the stag night of his cousin, Graf von Arnow, who lived in Cairo.

Furious at having been left alone, Hadley paced back and forth on the terrace like a caged tiger, unsure if Karl was making himself unavailable because he wanted to heighten her desire or whether he was uncertain of his own feelings about her. But now, in his absence, she made a decision. She would not stay here mooning over his intentions. She would go to the Villa Loma and have a night of exotic fun. She would dance with every man who asked her, eat a sensational dinner, and then she would let someone make love to her. Yes. That was what she needed. Her body grew restless at the thought of giving herself to a man.

Unlike her sisters, Hadley was no neophyte in the area of physical love. She had first been seduced at the age of fourteen, when one of her father's lawyers had skillfully made love to her. Since then, she craved the feeling that came when a man was inside her, the ultimate power sex gave her, and the brief respite from desire and escape from reality each orgasm brought. Then, all too soon, the throbbing, beating longing drove her relentlessly on and she became the predator, searching for oblivion.

Tossing her head defiantly, Hadley went to her bedroom and stripped before the mirror. For a moment she whirled around, smiling at a dozen images of herself reflected in the walls and ceiling. After she had bathed, she chose a blue Patou dress, a necklace of platinum chain, and a fur cloak of pure white fox. The dress had no back and was split from calf to hip. Hadley thoughtfully inspected her long suntanned legs, watching how they were revealed when she moved. The night was young. Perhaps before dawn she would find the satisfaction she craved, the heights of excitement that would push the decisions she knew she was soon going to have to make to the very back of her mind.

Leaving the unwelcome emptiness of the house, Hadley banged the door behind her and ordered the chauffeur to take her to the Villa Loma, closing the window between them when he began to protest. As they moved out of the palm-lined drive and into the city of shadows, she relaxed, satisfied in having shut the frustrating Karl out of her thoughts. Hadley resolved to banish him from her memory for the rest of the night.

The Villa Loma was on the shore, two miles south of the city center, surrounded by lush fields tilled in the hours of daylight by bullock plows and natives with mattocks. The exterior was of yellow and white stucco, the entrance pillared in the Italian style. The manager, Mr. Hamid, was famous for his discretion, and when Hadley walked into the yellow marble hall, he greeted her with deference, though a foreign female visitor who arrived alone was unusual.

"Welcome to the Villa Loma, Miss Ellerman."

Hadley was surprised at this familiarity. "How do you know my name?"

"It is my business to know the name of every beautiful visitor to our city."

"I assume you've no objections to my being alone?"

"Of course not."

"I'd like to eat dinner and then watch the floorshow."

Hamid snapped his fingers and a native in flowing white robes motioned for Hadley to follow. The manager watched with interest, admiring her elegant clothes and the aura of illicit sex that she exuded from every pore. Picking up the telephone, he dialed one of the upstairs suites, smiling when he heard the eagerness in the voice at the other end. He was just replacing the receiver with a satisfied smile when another guest appeared. The man was tall, slim, and had startling cold blue eyes. As he approached the newcomer, Hamid felt a frisson of fear, an emotion normally alien to his nature.

"May I help you, sir?"

"I want to watch the floorshow," the man said in a cosmopolitan German accent. "I shall be joined later by Herr Hollmeyer and Count de Janzé."

"Very well, sir. Do you wish a table near the floor, or perhaps a private room?"

"Near the floor, if you please."

Hamid snapped his fingers and Ernst Dietmueller was taken through to the cabaret room with its scarlet mosaic walls, where the scent of attar of roses hung heavy in the air. There, under a whirring ceiling fan, he took his place and ordered champagne, disinterestedly eyeing a belly dancer undulating sensuously above him. She was too plump for Dietmueller. He liked his women lean, hard, and nervous as thoroughbred horses—like the willful Hadley Ellerman. Dietmueller tilted his head back and blew a solitary smoke ring into the air. She would undoubtedly be appalled to learn that he had followed the Kohler party to Egypt, and that he too would be on safari with his friends in the area. In fact Dietmueller's family had been acquainted with the Kohlers for twenty-five years, and Dietmueller knew Karl well. Karl was an athlete, a patriot, a fine musician, and a decent man. But whether he excelled in the pursuits beloved by Hadley was open to doubt. Dietmueller felt a sudden pulse racing in his forehead and desire coursing through his body. He had told Hadley that to him the hunt was everything, and it was, to a point. But this was one hunt he hoped would soon be over. Only then would he reach the zenith of every sexual encounter he had ever dreamed of having—for only then would he have conquered Hadley Ellerman.

Hadley consulted the menu and ordered her dinner. "I'll have makhallal and the pigeon stuffed with rice and lemon."

While waiters moved silently between the tables and the first course of spicy pickled vegetables was set before her, Hadley looked with interest at her fellow diners. She was the only woman eating alone. The rest were Egyptians with their mistresses, foreign diplomats with visitors from less exotic lands, and, in a far corner, a rich Italian accompanied by three expensive ladies. Unaware that she was being observed from a peephole in the wall of the manager's office, Hadley enjoyed her meal.

Hamid turned to his visitor. "What do you think of her, Excellency?"

"She is thin, but her fire burns brightly. Arrange it for me, my dear Hamid. I do not think the lady will protest. She came to the Villa Loma for adventure, after all."

The Egyptian swept from the room and hurried upstairs to the suite he occupied whenever he was in Cairo. He had never made love with a foreign woman before and was trembling with excitement at the possibility of the night's sport. How pale her skin was, how fragile the body. He closed his eyes, wondering how she would react to what he had in mind.

Hadley had been taken to a private room to watch the floorshow and was sitting behind a beaded curtain that glittered red and gold in the reflected spotlights from the stage. Her eyes were wide and she was hard pressed to conceal her excitement. On the table before her was a bottle of arak. On the stage below, two naked dancers with gilded bodies were performing a lascivious native rite. The woman was voluptuous and extraordinarily beautiful. The man was tall and elegant, his ebony skin oiled to catch the changing colors of the light. As the atmosphere became more heated, the audience called for the performance to reach its conclusion, and Hadley was entranced to see the dancers end the ritual on a bed of frangipani flowers in a simulated cavern. The woman's body arched as the man's long, thin penis pierced her. Then, moving with balletic grace, she continued to reveal all while remaining mysterious and infinitely titillating. The muscles on her thighs stood out as the man's body quickened inside her, until, with a wild cry, the couple reached a crescendo of emotion and lay panting and spent as a gauze curtain was lowered.

Hadley poured herself a glass of ice water. Then she looked down at the audience, shocked to see Ernst Dietmueller sitting near the cabaret floor with two friends. One she recognized as Count de Janzé, the handsome French colonial who was renowned for his decadence, and who lived in Kenya. She did not know the other man. For a few moments she studied Dietmueller. The performance seemed to have left him unaffected. He was a sensual man, of that there was no doubt, yet the ritual of high eroticism had not aroused the slightest flicker of interest. Hadley shivered. Dietmueller's tastes must be highly specialized. She closed her eyes tightly, trying to shut out the memory of the night on the ship when he had kissed her so passionately she had almost let him possess her. When she had run away, he had pursued her, tearing the gossamer silk dress as she eluded him. She had reached her cabin half-naked, panting, and filled with emotions she could neither understand nor forget. She had not slept that night, and sometimes, still, she woke longing to feel what she had felt that night—the frenzied, voracious desire to give in and to be punished for doing so, the bittersweet, contrary urge to abandon herself to the dark side of her nature, the part of Hadley Ellerman she tried to pretend did not exist. Did he feel the same, unbearable need? Was that why he pursued her? Obviously he had followed her all the way to Africa, for it was surely no coincidence that he was here in the Villa Loma at the very same time she was. An involuntary frisson of apprehension swept over her, but it was immediately tempered by the mysterious sense of excitement she always felt when confronted with the forbidden and the dangerous.

Hadley was powdering her nose and applying fresh lipstick when Mr. Hamid entered the room.

"A very distinguished client of the club would like to meet you, Miss Ellerman. Will you please follow me?"

"Oh, yes? Who is this man?"

"He is the governor of the province of Rayyoum,

a most charming and cultivated person. I have no doubt you will enjoy meeting him."

"Where is he?"

"He stays in the Royal Suite when he comes to the Villa Loma."

The Villa Loma was certainly living up to its reputation for delivering adventure. Hadley smiled ruefully, imagining the disapproval Bunny and Nell would show if they knew what kind of "big game" she was hunting tonight. Hadley nodded and followed Hamid, her heart still thundering from excitement at the performance she had watched.

Hamid opened the door to a luxury suite and announced her. "Miss Hadley Ellerman, sir."

A tall, dark man in flowing robes and a keffiyeh who was sitting on a silk couch bowed his head and motioned for Hadley to sit at his side. A young girl brought her rose water for the ritual washing of hands and a gold flagon of lime juice to drink.

"You have the reputation for being a fine shot, Miss Ellerman" the man said, "and I hear you go on safari after your visit to Cairo."

"I'm traveling with Count Kohler's party."

"Are you also adventurous in love?"

Hadley licked her lips and gazed into the watchful black eyes. "I'm more adventurous than most women."

"I'm sure you are. That is why you came to the Villa Loma, is it not? I would like to show you one of our more intimate rituals of friendship. If you agree, I can promise you a most *rewarding* evening."

Hadley gazed at the smooth face with its inscrutable expression. He was handsome and confident, but what did he really want of her? She was certain he had enough women in his household to satisfy any desire. Was he simply eager to love a foreigner? Was her silver hair the attraction in this city of brunette beauties?

Taking her silence for assent, the governor rang a bell and three young women appeared and led Hadley away to an anteroom. She watched, fascinated, as a bath was prepared and scented with rose petals. Her clothes were removed and taken away, her jewels locked in a cabinet. First she was washed in warm, fragrant water. Then she was moved to a new room and showered in a final cleansing process. Maids shaved off all her body hair, lifting her arms and parting her legs so she was totally exposed. Then oil was massaged into her skin in slow, rhythmic strokes by three pairs of hands. Desire throbbed at Hadley's temples as she speculated about what the next few hours would bring. She began to writhe as the oil seeped into her skin and one girl's fingers plucked at her nipples, making them rise like small red peaks on the golden tan of her skin. Finally, while one of the girls massaged a point on the soles of Hadley's feet and the other continued to caress her breasts, the third rotated her clitoris until a forceful orgasm made her shudder. When she opened her eyes moments later, Hadley was surprised to find the three maids gone. They had left at her side a chiffon robe covered in blue and violet beads. She put it on and hurried back to the room where she had met the governor on arrival. Finding it empty, she moved on, until she came to a bedroom tented in pure white silk. Inside, she found a scene of Eastern decadence that was hard to believe.

The governor was lying on the silken coverlet, eating a pomegranate and spitting the seeds into a solid gold tray held by a naked serving girl. Another young woman, dressed only in a white transparent robe, was cooling the bed area with an ostrich-feather fan suspended at the end of a jeweled pole. Two beautiful women were lounging at the man's side, touching his skin, kissing his shoulders. Excitement rose in Hadley and she sat on the gilded emperor chair at the end of the bed. She had never in her wildest dreams imagined being part of such a happening, though she had read about the sensual habits of the East in books. She watched in wonder as the governor clapped his hands and the room emptied, as if by magic.

He offered Hadley a drink from a golden vial by the bed. "Let this liquid have its effect on your body. It will make you relax and feel things you never thought possible before."

He shook some white powder from another container, put it on the back of his hand, and sniffed it, first with one nostril and then with the other. Then he lay back and pulled the waiting Hadley toward him.

In the distance, a child cried out in the night and in the desert behind the city limits a jackal called. Hadley heard the sounds as if in a dream. She was luxuriating in the feeling the drought had provoked, the vibrant awakening of every nerve in her body. Without further bidding she kissed the Egyptian, as he grasped her by the hair and closed his mouth on hers.

"First I will love you," he said, his voice trembling with emotion. "Then you will do my bidding."

His tongue was inquisitive and hard. Hadley shivered as it moved over her breasts, her stomach, and down to the newly smooth pubic mound, flickering over her excited clitoris. His hands were soft but strong, and as he parted her thighs he used both to expose her. Then, his head bent low, he tasted the honeyed secretions that were flowing and making her ready for his penetration.

Hadley gripped the pillars of the bed head, impatient to feel him relentless inside of her. But instead, she heard movement and saw the

Egyptian take a large dildo from a drawer by the bed. She recoiled at the sight of its huge carved ebony form.

"What are you doing? Why don't *you* want to make love to me?"

"I wish to make love to you how *I* wish to do it. Relax. This instrument has been giving pleasure to our women for a hundred years."

"I don't want it! It will kill me. And I've no intention of being touched by something that's been around for a hundred years."

With that Hadley got up from the bed and ran toward the door.

"Come," the Egyptian said, "you have not let me join our blood in the ritual cutting of hands."

Hadley stared stonily back. "Please get my clothes. I wish to leave."

The Egyptian got up out of bed with a sigh. He had made an error of enormous dimension in approaching the foreign woman. He motioned for a servant girl in the outer room to bring Hadley's things. Then he spoke in a soft voice to her. "I beg your forgiveness for startling you. You are obviously unaware of some of our most exciting tribal customs. Now, if you will excuse me, I must leave you."

With a nod, he was gone, leaving Hadley alone with the maid who had hurried to bring her clothes, and with them a gift in a carved sandalwood box.

"His excellency asked me to present this to you before your departure, miss."

Hadley took the box and opened it. Inside she found a magnificent pearl. She snapped the lid shut and began dressing. She should never have come to the Villa Loma. She shook her head sadly, conscious again of the depression that had afflicted her since the death of her father. The only things that seemed to lighten the sadness were buying clothes, making love, and planning trips to far-distant places. Loneliness was a spe-cial torment. Even when she was with a crowd, she felt alone and was obviously prepared to do almost anything to avoid it.

Hadley left the room, walked down the long curved staircase, and almost collided with Ernst Dietmueller.

"Hadley, you look terrible. What on earth . . . ?"

His voice sounded almost human.

Hadley looked at him and smiled. "It's five A.M., Ernst, and I'm tired. Would you drive me back to Karl's?"

"Certainly. But tell me, dearest Hadley, what will Karl say when he sees us arrive together?"

"Karl's not my lover. And he doesn't own me."

"Well . . . how very disappointing for you. But perhaps your visit to the notorious Villa Loma rooms made up for your lack of a partner."

Hadley shrugged, unwilling to tell him that she had simply taken a random lover.

"I wouldn't dream of telling you, Ernst."

"Of course you would, and I shall enjoy listen-ing. The more I know of you, Hadley, the more I realize that you are the only woman in the world for me. Someday I will force *you* to realize it. Now, open the box. I want to see how generous the gentleman was."

Hadley laughed despite herself, and showed Dietmueller the pearl. Then they left the villa together in Dietmueller's car.

Hadley watched the sun rising over the hori-zon as they raced along the edge of the Nile. Soon the chill of evening would turn into the ennervating heat of day. On either side of the road, orange vendors, melon men, and spice boys hurried toward the market square. The silence of dawn had already turned into the cacophony of day as water vendors' bells mixed with the cries of crows, cows, dogs, and men calling *"Ma'alish"*—Never mind—to others who had just collided with them. Hadley wryly observed that the bustle and confusion of the scene matched that in her mind. Suddenly she needed Karl, to hold his hand, to be reassured that the world was still her oyster and he her true and loyal friend.

Dietmueller looked down at the long-fingered hands clutching the evening purse and sandalwood box. At the sight of the pale blue shadows that had appeared under Hadley's eyes and the faint bruise on her arm, Dietmueller felt a strange tenderness toward his companion. Yet he was also consumed with desire, barely able to control his longing to love Hadley, to inflame her, to conquer her. For the moment, however, he decided it would be best to be patient, to play the friend.

"I suggest you tell Karl that you and I went out to see the city. He may not be jealous, but he will certainly disapprove of a woman who went alone to the Villa Loma."

"You obviously know Karl. How?"

"His family and mine have been neighbors for many years, though he is not an intimate friend. Are you planning to marry him, Hadley?"

She frowned, unwilling to admit that that was exactly what she wanted but could not engineer.

"I don't know what I'm going to do and I'm sick of being asked about the future. Will you *please* try not to start one of your interrogations."

"Don't tell me you're having an attack of conscience. And, by the way, I don't believe you when you say you and Karl are not lovers."

Suddenly Hadley's eyes were filling with tears. Even Dietmueller was obliged to believe her words.

"Karl barely seems to notice me. We haven't been alone together since we were on the ship from Marseilles."

Dietmueller pondered this surprising statement for a moment. "Then Karl is a clever man."

Hadley reeled in anger. "That's an odd statement to come from a man so obvious about his own intentions," she sniffed.

"I merely meant that Karl is wise enough to know that for a woman who can command *any* man to do her bidding, the most eager suitor is always the least attractive proposition."

Karl was completing his packing when Hadley arrived and greeted him with a strained smile.

"I brought a friend back with me."

Karl shook Dietmueller's hand, but his eyes were glacial.

"What are you doing in Cairo, Ernst?"

"The same as you. I am en route to Kenya with two friends, Count de Janzé, who lives near Nairobi, and Herr Hollmeyer, an associate from Berlin. I hope to bring back some heads for my collection."

Karl turned to Hadley, his eyes searching her face. He noted the tiredness, the unease.

"What happened to *you?* We were all so very worried when you didn't return to the house."

"I met Ernst on the ship coming from the States, and we bumped into each other yesterday. He's been showing me Cairo by night."

"I'm surprised it took so long! It must have been a very thorough tour."

Well aware of her awkward lying, but unwilling to show his disappointment in front of Deitmueller, Karl treated the matter lightly. But Karl could not contain his fury at Dietmueller's parting words to Hadley.

"I am staying at the Hotel Ramses II. Do call me if you need anything."

Karl stepped forward, his face taut with rage.

"If Hadley needs anything, she will ask *me*. And now good day to you, Ernst."

Dietmueller savored his triumph.

"My dear Karl, you are very tense. Perhaps the heat has affected you. Take my advice and sleep a little after lunch. Some men find the atmosphere of Cairo enervating, too much noise and excitement for pure European stock, I believe."

Hadley walked up the white marble staircase, delighted to have provoked Karl into jealousy. There was something about him that fascinated her, and though she hastened to tell herself it was not love, she had no idea what else it could be. Like Bunny, she feared that powerful emotion, certain that love only made women vulnerable. But Hadley knew only too well that what she needed most in life was security, and there was no doubt in her mind that Karl could provide it, if only she could find a way to his heart. She thought again of the moment when their eyes had met and suddenly realized that he had known she was lying. She knew she must tell him the truth or be diminished in his estimation. The truth would offend, but the lie had hurt him more.

Throwing herself down on the bed, Hadley let the mosquito netting float in the breeze. Outside the wall of the house, women swathed in black robes walked past with heavy baskets of washing on their heads, and somewhere close by she could hear the creaking of a water wheel. How alien this world was to her. She thought of her sisters in Paris and tried hard to control the longing she felt for them. Bunny knew how to soothe agitation by massaging Hadley's hands with scented cream in times of terrible stress. Nell was great at listening to stories, giving frequently obscene comments and then proposing a splendid dinner in some bistro she had found on her wanderings. Within minutes, Hadley knew all her depression would lift and she would be laughing again. Instead, she was far away in a foreign land gazing at an image of the crocodile god Sobek that had been placed in a niche in the wall. How horrible it was, how sinister and evil! She picked up the statue and put it outside the door of her room. Then she lay down again, thinking of Nell and Bunny, until their images soothed her to sleep.

At midday, Karl went to Hadley's room and woke her. It was a beautiful morning and he wanted to share it with her, because it was their last in Cairo. Looking down at the suntanned body through the mosquito netting, he thought how beautiful she was and how wanton. He was bitterly disappointed that she had lied about her activities of the previous night. She had such style, he had expected her to be honest and to have the courage of her convictions. Raising the netting, he sat at her side and took her hand.

"Time to get up."

Hadley's face was soft with sleep.

"I lied to you about what I did last night, Karl," she said contritely. "I'm sorry. It's just I *hate* being alone in the house. I always have hated it and since Papa's death I can't stand it for a single minute. I went to the Villa Loma and had dinner and watched the cabaret. I'm not an angel, Karl, and it's best that you know it. I do crazy things sometimes when I need to be loved. It's something I can't always control."

Karl was silent for a moment. Then he took her in his arms.

"I was distressed when you lied, Hadley. The chauffeur had already said that you went to the Villa Loma, and when I arrived home I telephoned the club and was told you were occupied. I imagined you were with a man, and though I don't like the idea, I am well aware that I do not have exclusive rights to your company."

He looked into her face and thought how exciting she was, an intoxicating mixture of tempt-

ress and angel, innocence and decadence. He bent
forward and kissed her cheek.

"Come, we shall have a fine lunch and then
we will finish packing. We leave at dawn for the
safari. It will take a long time to get to Kenya, so
we shall have many days to make a real acquaintance with each other. Thank you for telling me
the truth, Hadley. You have no idea how much it
means to me."

She gazed into his eyes, her face tender.

"Why have you ignored me since we arrived in
Cairo?"

"I have been busy, Hadley. But you have been
so preoccupied, I thought it best to leave you
alone."

Hadley sighed, knowing he was right. "I never
used to think about anything but the moment,
but since Papa's death I just can't stop worrying
about my future. It's Bunny's fault. She keeps
telling me we're poor and we have to economize.
I don't want to be poor and I'm scared of trying
to get work. Do you think *anyone* would give me a
job? I can't do a single thing that's useful."

"I doubt you would ever need to contemplate
such a thing."

"Kiss me, Karl. I need you so."

He took her in his arms and held her close to
his heart. Then he bent his head and kissed her
gently on the forehead, the cheeks, and finally
the mouth. His body and hers touched as their
arms entwined and their lips met, and he heard
the sharp intake of her breath and the low sound
that came as the kiss provoked her. He tried to
step back, but he could not resist kissing her
again and exploring more fully the warm, wet
depths of her mouth.

Hadley whispered, as if in a dream, "I love
your kisses."

"And I yours, but I must go before it is too late
to leave you at all."

"Kiss me just once more. Do you want me, Karl?"

"Of course I do. Is there a man alive who doesn't?"

Hadley smiled, happy as a child with a splendid new toy. Then, throwing her arms around his neck, she kissed him with an urgent, deep-down longing that was all too real. Her thin hands touched his cheeks, her boyish body moved slowly, sensuously against his as their tongues fought and then surrendered to ecstasy. Hadley felt her pulse quickening, her body rising toward the climax of feeling as Karl threw her back on the bed and kissed her breasts and her neck and her mouth.

"You are the most fascinating woman I ever met."

"Are we going to make love?"

"Someday, perhaps."

Hadley looked momentarily angry. " 'Perhaps' isn't a word I like very much!"

Karl rose and kissed the tips of her fingers. "One should never be too sure of anything in this life. Now, hurry and dress. We must not keep our friends waiting any longer."

In the six weeks of their journey from Cairo to Nairobi, on whose outskirts they were camped, the party visited many local settlements—Thika, where coffee was grown; Njoro, which produced wheat; Naivasha, a sheep-and-cattle-rearing station; and Londiani, where flax was produced. Foreign residents in the region fell into two main groups. There were the "remittance men," reprobates sent away by families in England and Ireland because they could no longer tolerate the shame of their presence; and there were the true settlers, who had come for no other reason than that they longed to own land. These people worked from dawn to dusk, lived hard, drank hard, and ate such huge meals their appetites were the cause of endless amusement to the natives.

Hadley was sitting by the campfire watching the sun rise. In Kenya dawn came at six A.M., when thick dew covered the grass and there was a haze in the distance that filled the undergrowth with magic. The early-morning chorus of birds was deafening and everywhere emerald and crimson butterflies fluttered on the perfumed thorn blossoms that filled the air with one of the most intoxicating scents of Africa. The thing Hadley adored most about the country was the sky, the ever-changing, rushing, fleeting patterns of blue, pink, and gold that seemed to resemble the thoughts that so often raced through her mind. In this magnificent landscape, she felt very small and very unimportant. It was one of the lessons Karl had taught her during the past six weeks—that the wilderness forces man to put all things in perspective. Hadley hoped fervently that she had learned the lesson. She knew now what she wanted. It was simply a matter of finding a way to achieve it.

The native cook made breakfast for Karl's party: buffalo steaks for everyone, with eggs for Cousin Heine and his wife, fried rice and sautéed roots for Helmut Kraus and his daughter, because the professor's family ate no meat. Karl had hunted from dawn to dusk the previous day and spent half the night labeling and boxing samples collected for various universities and medical establishments in Berlin and Munich. Hadley thought how, when she woke in the small hours, she had seen his figure bent over a makeshift desk in his tent, silhouetted in the light of the storm lantern. She had longed to go and make love to him as she had longed every night during the six weeks of the safari, but something held her back. She had realized at last that Karl was his own man, proud, cautious, and determined to run the relationship his way. Hadley had resigned herself to letting Karl control the relationship.

They breakfasted under an awning amid the sounds of Africa, the ground vibrating to the gallop of zebras, the air noisy with the scampering of baboons and the slithering of snakes in the tinder-dry grass. Hadley listened as the rest of the party talked of their return to Europe, and wondered what would happen now. Their last stop was Nairobi, and the moment of reckoning would take place there.

Nairobi was known as the meeting point for all foreigners visiting Kenya. Its gardens were full of jacaranda, bougainvillea, and hibiscus, and acacia grew wild along the highways. In the city center Englishmen in khaki shorts mixed with Germans in bush outfits, ocher-painted Masai warriors, and pretty blonds in the latest Paris fashions, all hurrying to pin messages on the thorn tree in Kimaku Street for lovers, husbands, or guests due to arrive from the wilds.

As custom decreed, this was the first place Karl went. Pinned to the tree he found a card from his old school friend Freddie de Witt. He read it with a smile: "Come for dinner at seven. Can't wait to see you again." Karl registered the party at the exclusive Muthaiga Country Club, with its croquet lawns, pink-walled ballroom, and elegant golf course. Its reputation was as a deluxe haven for inveterate drinkers. At the Muthaiga Club drinking started soon after midday with pink gins, followed by gin fizzes at teatime, cocktails at sundown, and champagne and whiskey till lights-out.

One of the Muthaiga bar's most reliable patrons noted the arrival of Karl's party with great interest. Irena Stevens, the notorious ex-wife of an English landowner, legendary partygoer, marriage breaker, and opium smoker, shot an indolent glance at the new arrivals. Turning to her female cocktail companion, she said, "I hope Count Kohler likes redheads with blue eyes who drink pink champagne."

"He's in sixteen, why don't you go ask him?"

"I will. No time like the present."

Irena grabbed the open champagne bottle, went upstairs, and knocked on Karl's door. When he opened it, she thrust the magnum toward him.

"Hello, I'm Irena Stevens. I brought you a little prezzy to say welcome to the club."

"How very kind."

Karl weighed the predatory eyes, the wild expression, and the exquisite legs sheathed by a diaphanous white dress. Amused by her overt curiosity and the desire she made no attempt to conceal, he gathered two glasses and poured.

"To your health, Miss Stevens."

She sipped the drink greedily, her eyes traveling from his blond hair to the muscles on his arms and the perfect jodhpurs that drew attention to the area of her interest.

"Call me Irena, please. Can we get better acquainted, say, over lunch?"

"I shall be lunching with my party. This is the last day of our trip, as most of them are leaving for Berlin and Munich in the morning."

"How about dinner then?"

"I'm sorry. My companion and I dine with Freddie de Witt tonight."

"Oh—how lovely! And convenient. I'll see you there, then. Freddie's an old friend of mine." Irena downed the last of her champagne and left. She'd hook this fish tonight.

The de Witt household overlooked a lake pink from hundreds of flamingos that crowded its pellucid waters. The gardens surrounding the house were a riot of Nandi flame and scarlet bougainvillea, the air scented with eucalyptus and jasmine. When Karl and Hadley arrived, a dozen native boys were watering and clipping the lawn with pangas. One ran inside to call de Witt. "Your friends are here, sir."

Freddie appeared and threw his arms around Karl.

"My dear fellow, how are you? You've met my wife, Greta. This is Irena Stevens, whom I understand you've met, and these are my friends Josslyn Hay and his wife, Molly."

Karl looked into the indolent eyes of Freddie de Witt. The Englishman's reputation was even more scandalous than Irena Stevens' and he felt annoyed when Freddie's eyes began to wander over Hadley's body. The manners and mores of the foreign colony of Nairobi were alien to Karl and he knew suddenly that he wanted to return to his home, far away from this fast set whose ideas were not his. He introduced Hadley with a cool formality.

"Freddie, may I present Miss Hadley Ellerman. Hadley, my friend since college days, Freddie de Witt and his wife, Greta."

Out of the corner of her eye Hadley saw Irena watching Karl. She knew at once that the Englishwoman wanted him and asked herself what was going to happen. If Karl amused himself with this notorious creature, she would know that he had been withholding himself from her purely for reasons of caprice. If he resisted Irena, perhaps he was serious in his intentions toward *her*. Hadley decided to keep a close eye on the lady. The rooms at the Muthaiga Club had no locks and Irena was reputed to walk in her sleep, sometimes right into the bedrooms of a half-dozen men in the same night.

"Are you daydreaming, Miss Ellerman?" Freddie interrupted Hadley's reverie.

"I'm sorry, the nightjars kept me awake and I'm a little tired."

"I asked you when you were planning to return to Munich, but you didn't hear."

"I hope we return very soon. I don't think Nairobi's going to be my kind of place."

Ignoring Hadley's pointed glance at Irena, Freddie continued cheerfully, "Wait until you see the hunting lodge. That will be a surprise for you. There isn't another building like it in Europe."

Irena interrupted with a sweet smile, "Where do you actually *live,* Miss Ellerman, or are you the wandering kind?"

"I'm based at the Ritz in Paris."

"Are you? How lucky to be able to afford it after what's happened to you. Just *unspeakable* circumstances."

"My sisters and I are independent. Papa saw to that."

"But I heard he lost every cent he had. It just shows how unreliable rumors can be."

"Yes, it does. Because I heard you were in a clinic in Vienna with a perfectly *unspeakable* disease, Irena. One should never listen to gossip, really."

Karl almost choked on his champagne at Hadley's barbed reply, but his admiration for her nerve increased as she continued to converse with their fellow guests, ignoring Irena completely from that moment on. As the evening wore on, he looked now and again to Hadley and smiled. He was aware that she was as bored as he was by Freddie's endless stories of legendary drinking bouts. This was not her kind of milieu and it was not his. Karl made a decision to leave Nairobi in the morning with the rest of the party. As soon as dinner was over he made his apologies.

"My dear Freddie, Hadley and I have decided that we shall leave with the rest of my party in the morning for Alexandria. I do hope you'll forgive us if we return early to the club. We have to pack and arrange matters rather quickly."

"But, my dear fellow, I thought you were staying for at least two weeks."

"So did I, but Nairobi is not my kind of place and I cannot wait a moment longer to bring Hadley home and show her the hunting lodge."

Hadley's face lit with pleasure and she held out her hand and clutched Karl's. She had won! Karl was bringing her home! At that moment, it was as if they were alone in the room, so charged with desire was the atmosphere between them. All the more reason to be sure Irena was kept at bay until Karl and she were safely on their way.

Later that night, Hadley, unable to sleep, heard the sound of slow, steady footsteps along the wood-floored corridors of the Muthaiga Club. She peered out the door. Irena! Dressed only in a filmy red-and-gold kekoi, she held herself with all the confidence of a woman to whom men never said no. She walked directly to Karl's room and stepped inside noiselessly. Hadley moved quickly out of her room and along the corridor. She opened the door of Karl's room a fraction, shattered to see Irena pulling back the linen sheets of Karl's bed and feasting on the sight of his naked body with its broad shoulders, long legs, and sleeping penis surrounded by curly gold hair. Kneeling by the side of the bed, she took Karl's penis in her hands and began to play with it like a child with a toy.

Hadley watched in fascination as Karl's eyes opened and he sat bolt upright. Fearful of being seen, Hadley closed the door but remained listening outside. What she heard changed her life, for although she still wouldn't admit it, it made her fall in love with Karl.

"May I ask what you think you are doing?" Karl asked, cool with suppressed fury.

"I'm bringing your prick to life."

Karl pushed Irena away and rose from the bed. "Look, Irena. At five A.M. I leave with Hadley for

Alexandria. If you do not agree to leave at once, I shall personally throw you out of this room."

Hadley almost cheered at the words. Then she waited to hear Irena's reply.

"You try that and I'll scream blue bloody murder that you tried to rape me."

"It would be embarrassing for me to have to break a few of your teeth to keep you quiet. I don't advise you to try it, Irena."

"You're a bastard, Kohler! Who'd have thought it?"

"If you knew as much about men as I had imagined, you would have realized that I am interested only in Miss Ellerman."

"Then save your heroics for her."

Hadley heard a brief scuffle. Then Irena was shoved unceremoniously out into the corridor by Karl. Concealed in the shadows of a linen closet nearby, Hadley watched as her rival disappeared, banging the door of her bedroom furiously behind her.

Hadley hurried back to her own room and lay thinking of what had happened. Karl had said that his only interest was Hadley. Her heart beat thunderously from sheer joy and she wanted to rush to his room and love him until her strength gave out. Instead, she began to make plans to be the woman of his dreams. Somehow she had to make herself indispensable to him, the perfect partner and potential wife, the most beautiful and seemingly unavailable woman he had ever met. Hadley closed her eyes and said a prayer that she would be guided. This was no time for her to make one of her silly mistakes. She would do her best to remain levelheaded.

And Hadley fell asleep daydreaming of a future in the most beautiful hunting lodge in Europe.

— 3 —

BAVARIA, SUMMER 1930

THE HUNTING LODGE was indeed like nothing Hadley had ever seen before. She had imagined Karl living the rural life in the mountains above Munich in a modest wooden structure of the kind one so often associated with Bavaria—with balconies filled with geraniums, windows carved with peasant designs of cockerels, doves, and daisies. She was caught off balance when he drove her up a winding mountain road, stopped on a hill, and pointed out his home in the pine forest.

"That is the hunting lodge."

Hadley saw a dark red roof and two slate-blue helmeted towers rising above a sea of pine trees. The place was a palace. For once Hadley Ellerman was at a loss for words.

Karl drove on, turning off the road onto a narrow track that led through the woods.

"This is one of the two entrances to the lodge. Why are you so silent, Hadley?"

"I expected a log cabin, not a palace."

"Well, this log cabin has forty rooms and was built by a cousin of King Ludwig I. All the Wittelsbachs loved to build, and George was anxious to uphold the stylish reputation of his family."

Hadley's eyes widened when she saw the lodge directly ahead. Built on two floors with attics on the third that had elaborate oeil-de-boeuf windows, it was a baroque structure in the most elegant style. Hadley loved the cream-painted exterior, the splendid iron-studded doors, the stable block that lay adjacent to the house.

Karl led her inside and acted as guide.

"The staircase is baroque, as you can see, and that painting of hunting hounds was executed in 1750. It measures fifty feet by twenty-five feet. It was the only painting I could find large enough to fill the entire stair wall."

Hadley followed him to the garden room, wallpapered with scenes of Greek mythology by the French artist Dufour, then on to a minstrel's gallery, trophy room, games room, crystal room, and small garçonnière known as the Cabinet d'Amour. She was fascinated by this secret room leading off the master bedroom, with its erotic paintings of goddesses and satyrs and its rose silk chaise longue placed next to a couch of Turkish design that could be made to revolve, rock, or remain tilted at an angle. She turned to Karl with a radiant smile.

"This is a *real* love nest."

"I thought it would intrigue you. It was designed a hundred years ago by the king's mistress. I will show you the rest of the house later. For the moment, you must supervise the unpacking of your trunks. Then we will eat lunch. Frau Hoffman, my housekeeper, is a wonderful cook and she is delighted that I have a guest."

Hadley's luggage had been put in the blue damask bedroom. When she was alone, she sat on the bed and gazed up at a painted ceiling depicting the goddess Diana flanked by hounds and a stag. The bed was draped with the same silk as the walls, ostrich plumes forming a crown at its apex that undulated in the gentle breeze from the window. After the fierce heat of Africa, Hadley felt as if she had been transported to paradise. As she lay back she felt, for the first time in too long a time, deeply content.

Before going down to join Karl for lunch, Hadley stood at the window and took in the magnificent view. Far below was Munich, the cosmopolitan capital of Bavaria. All around the lodge were pine-covered hillsides, and beyond them fruit farms, where apple blossoms turned the landscape pink and white. She watched a country-woman throwing grits to a flock of white geese and a man painting fruit-tree trunks against disease. Scents of resin and wildflowers filled the air, and outside the room, in the corridor, there were clocks chiming and miniature glockenspiels sounding.

Hadley sighed. Suddenly she had the possibility of gaining what was most important to her—a secure future with a very special man. To protect that precious possibility she had to control her longing for love and not even daydream of other men. Somehow, she would convince Karl that she had potential as a wife and not just a mistress or lover.

In the library, Karl was at his desk going through lists of samples that had arrived in the house from Africa. He looked up with a smile as Hadley entered the room.

"Well, what do you think of the hunting lodge?"

"It's just wonderful. Freddie de Witt was right. There probably isn't another place like it in Europe."

"I'm afraid I shall be a negligent host for a few days. I must unpack some of these precious specimens and get them sent over to the university. Will you forgive me if I work for a couple of hours after lunch?"

"I'll help you."

Karl took her hand and kissed each of the fingers.

"You are a guest and should not be put to work."

"I'm a friend who doesn't want to be treated like a stranger. You can show me the rest of the house and the land later."

"We'll start after lunch, then. By the way, my brother and sister are joining us for dinner. I think you'll like them. Ilsa is thirty and married with four children. Joseph is thirty-two, unmarried, and the merry bachelor of Munich."

"Like you?"

"I am not so merry. Usually I stay alone in this house, and of late I have found my days somewhat empty. I am thirty-four and it is time I settled down with a wife and children. Do you like children, Hadley?"

She took a deep breath, momentarily thrown by the direction the conversation had suddenly taken. Knowing her answer was important, she replied with caution, "I think I'd like my own, but I'm not always fond of other people's. My sisters and I were pretty easy to raise. Nell was the only rebellious one of the three. She took to swearing when she started school at five, so Papa taught her what he called a truly bad word and forbade her ever to say it. Nell shouted 'mollusk' at everyone whenever she was annoyed until she was seven or eight. She never did realize it was harmless."

Karl laughed, delighted by the story. "I was a curious little boy—even then an adventurer. My first expedition was to a lake not far from here. I took frog spawn from the water and packed it in a jar before returning home. But I was so engrossed in my task, I forgot the time, and on the way back to the lodge it became dark. I lost my way in the woods and was not found until the next morning."

"What happened?"

"My mother sent me to bed without breakfast or lunch. I was just five and she thought me far too young to become an explorer."

A servant appeared and threw logs on the fire. Hadley settled by the blaze, happy to listen to Karl as he reminisced about the past. His reputation as a world traveler fascinated her and she longed to know about the exotic places he had seen and the ones he planned to visit in the future. She encouraged him to tell her about his favorite trips in past years.

"I like India best, particularly traveling from there into the Hindu Kush and along the route of Marco Polo. It's always tremendously exciting to me. On each trip I take I bring back samples for museums and scientific establishments, so all my training has not been entirely wasted."

"What kind of training did you do?"

"I went to the University of Heidelberg and studied biology, botany, and zoology. I made a career out of my hobby, which is travel."

"And what of the hunting lodge? Is there much for you to do here?"

"My family owns all the forest and farmland around the lodge. We are trying to develop new trees that will grow despite the fohn, which is a vicious wind that has been known to drive some people to suicide. I keep myself very busy. Perhaps that is why I never have time to find the perfect wife."

When the lunch bell sounded, Karl led Hadley through the long, narrow corridor to a dining room decorated with animal heads from every corner of the globe. Leopard skins had been placed on inlaid ebony floors and antique hunting rifles hung on one of the walls.

"Where are you going to explore next, and when?" Hadley asked as they ate.

"Why, do you want to come with me again?"

"I don't want you to vanish before I have the chance to really get to know you," Hadley replied quietly.

"I shall not be traveling until the winter, when I go to Venice for a holiday. Venice is one of my *very* favorite cities. Perhaps we could go there together?"

Hadley concealed her pleasure and drank her coffee in one gulp. "We'd best get back to the library and start sorting through the samples," she said. "I'll make the lists for you. I'm very good at that."

Karl approved of her eagerness to be useful and they went hand in hand back to the spot where the open packing cases had been stacked. For three hours they worked, putting animal heads for eventual display in the lodge in one area of the library and research samples in boxes in another. He was pleased to see that Hadley's interest did not wane, that she saw the tedious task through to the end. When the last of the crates had been emptied, he kissed her tenderly on the cheek.

"You're a very fine assistant. I must try to tempt you to take a permanent post here."

Hadley touched his hand wistfully. "Tomorrow we'll start on the big crates."

"Oh no, tomorrow, I show you Munich. You have worked hard enough."

Their eyes met. Karl took her in his arms and kissed her at last as she had been longing to be kissed. Relaxing, she closed her eyes and smelled the masculine scent of his skin and felt the pounding of his heart against her own. Feeling him harden, she grasped him around the neck, unable to conceal her desire.

"Don't tease me, Karl. Please don't tease me."

He smiled enigmatically, not yet ready to tell her what was in his heart, but as he caressed her he tried to say something of his thoughts. "Making love is not a frivolous occupation for me, Hadley. What I have in mind for you is something very special and lasting, so you must let me decide when the moment is right for us."

She sighed, wondering if he would ever make that decision. She tried not to show her disappointment as Karl changed the subject.

"I shall order tea for us in the English style, and some of Frau Hoffman's liebkuchen. Do you know what they are?"

"I never heard of them."

"The translation is 'love cakes.' They are cut into the shape of hearts and gilded with a special mixture. Frau Hoffman made a batch the moment she met you. She is a romantic soul and most impressed, as I am, by your beauty."

Later, they walked until sunset through the woods near the hunting lodge. Karl showed Hadley his horses, and then, as they left the stables for the dark glades of the forest, he pointed out some of the animals he loved. There were marmot and blue hares that left hand-shaped tracks, alpine voles and ptarmigan, recognized by their low whirring flight. Once, as they reached a high place and stood still watching the sky, they saw an eagle with a two-meter wingspan. Pleased by this rare appearance, Karl led Hadley on through a summer wonderland bright with blue gentians and fields of pink daisies.

"We really must return to the house to change for dinner. Why don't you wear one of your beautiful Paris dresses for Ilsa. She loves to see the latest fashions, though she has become too stout to wear them since the birth of the last child."

Back at the lodge, Hadley bathed and dressed in a violet gown with the new rounded bust and longer skirt. Her hair was still too short to put in the soft lines of the most recent fashion, so she chose some of the wildflowers she and Karl had picked that afternoon and pinned them behind her ears. She left the Ellerman emeralds in her jewel case and wore instead the heart-shaped diamond pin Karl had bought her on their return from Africa. Looking at her reflection in the mirror, she realized that she had changed in the past few weeks. For the first time since her father's death, she was feeling more secure. Karl was a tower of strength. A man who loved the outdoors as well as the life of luxury she craved, he could provoke her to ecstasy easily, and his achievements filled her with admiration. What more could any woman want? With one last twirl in the mirror, Hadley walked to the staircase and descended regally into the hall.

Karl stepped forward to introduce her to his guests. "Ilsa, may I present Hadley Ellerman. Hadley, please meet my sister and brother-in-law, the Baron and Baroness von Allgau."

Hadley shook hands, liking Ilsa at once, Karl's sister was plump and plain, but her face had a gentle expression, her blue eyes twinkled with humor, and the halo of sun-blond hair gave her an angelic appearance that belied the toughness of her spirit. Hadley tried not to show her disapproval of the gathered skirt and bodice with frill that were both quite unsuitable for the lady's ample figure. Then, turning to the baron, she took in a cold, formal face with gray eyes and white-blond hair. The baron affected a military way of speaking, though poor health had caused him to be rejected by the army. Hadley disliked him as much as she liked Ilsa.

Ilsa leaned forward and touched Hadley's hand. "Your dress is truly wonderful, Miss Ellerman. I love so much this unusual blue."

"I bought it at Patou before I left Paris."

"And what are the new season's colors?"

"Violet, blue, and white. But tell me about your family. Karl said you have four children."

Ilsa smiled, motioning for her husband to bring

out the photographs. Her voice was full of pride as she spoke of the children she adored.

"All but one of my offspring are almost grown up. Otto is twelve, Gretel eleven, and the twins ten. The new baby is eighteen months old."

Hadley tried to think of something polite to say about infants. "My father used to say that children kept their parents young."

Ilsa laughed delightedly, shaking her head at the idea. "I am of the opinion that they make the parents very old, Miss Ellerman."

Conscious of the baron's disapproving glances, Hadley was about to turn to Karl for guidance, when they heard the sound of a powerful motorbike outside the lodge. Within minutes the tall, dark, and elegantly mustached Joseph Kohler appeared in evening dress topped by a metal helmet. He apologized for his late arrival, handed the helmet to the butler, and stepped forward to be introduced to Hadley, genuinely pleased to meet the woman Karl had mentioned so often in his letters.

"I am so very happy to meet you, Miss Ellerman. Do forgive my late arrival, but my car broke down and I was obliged to borrow a motorbike from a friend."

Karl smiled across at Hadley.

"I told you Joseph would arrive late and have some interesting excuse. We must borrow the motorbike, so you can learn to ride one, Hadley. There are so many things I wish to teach you, I think you will be obliged to stay here for months," Karl said as he lightly touched Hadley's shoulders.

A shiver of excitement ran through her body at his touch, taking her breath away and hardening her nipples. Images of Karl lying naked on the bed at the Muthaiga Club suddenly entered her mind, as they had done so often since that night in Nairobi. She had never wanted any man so much in her life, and, she thought to herself, she had never waited so long for one either.

The baron scrutinized Hadley with disapproval. She was too beautiful, too wild and sensual ever to be acceptable as part of the family. He wondered why Karl had invited her to the lodge. He had never had a female houseguest before and was usually disinclined toward women of the frivolous type. While Hadley moved across the room to enter the dining hall, the baron resolved to make a check on her past. He would call the center of intelligence gathering—Ernst Dietmueller's office—in the morning. Though Dietmueller was still in Africa, the baron was confident that his inquiry would be dealt with in the usual efficient manner. This was a matter of real importance. It was obvious that Karl wanted Hadley for a wife and not merely a lover.

At midnight, as they stood together under a full moon, waving to the last of the departing guests, Karl turned to Hadley, his hands outstretched.

"What do you like best in the whole world?"

She grasped his hands, thought awhile, and then replied, "Kittens, emeralds, and crème-de-menthe frappés."

"No, there is something you like more than all those."

"Surprises!"

Karl kissed her tenderly and led her into the house.

"I am the man who would like to arrange many wonderful surprises for you, and I have one now, which I hope you will enjoy. Come, Hadley, let me show you the last secret of the hunting lodge."

He led her from the salon down a flight of winding steps carved into the solid rock of the mountain. Then, opening an iron door, he turned on the light, flooding a grotto with amber illumination. There were stalactites hanging from the ceiling and a quaint cockle boat on the water.

"We call this the Venus Grotto. The water is warm and comes from an underground lake. The boat was built for King Ludwig I, as were the peacock chairs and the aeolodion."

"What is that, a musical instrument? It's wonderfully ornate."

"It combines a piano with a harmonium, and the sound is very special. Take a seat and I will show you how it works."

Hadley sat on one of the magnificent chairs depicting a peacock with its tail in full display. She watched entranced as Karl took his place at the aeolodion and played a selection of popular tunes, ending with a love song she had told him she adored. When he came back to her side, she clutched his hands and kissed them, leaning her head on his shoulders and closing her eyes. Her voice faltered with tension when she spoke. "I'm scared I'll wake up and all this will have been a dream and I'll be back in Paris wondering what to do with my life."

"Don't be afraid, Hadley. Everything in the hunting lodge is real. It has all been in existence for decades and will be here long after we are gone. I want to make love to you, Hadley. I want you. Come with me. I've been keeping this last surprise for someone very special, you see."

In an arched chamber off the lake there was a bed made by the same craftsman as the chairs. The bed head was of dazzling white and gold, depicting a swan. The foot of the bed showed the animal's head, gracefully curved as if in imminent flight. The sheets were of crisp white linen, the coverlet of Oriental silk that shimmered in the light of the solitary candelabrum. From the bedside they could hear the lapping of water and the ticking of a clock on the far wall. The rest was silence. The room had the secret, enclosed perfection of a seraglio.

Hadley looked down at the bed and began to feel nervous. She wanted their lovemaking to be perfect and knew just how much depended on Karl's reaction to her body and her sensuality. She looked at him with a wistful smile.

"I'm scared, Karl."

"I am too, but I like the feeling."

He untied the back of the dress, kissing her shoulders as he slipped off the bodice, revealing Hadley's small, firm breasts with their blunt-ended nipples. Karl put aside the bodice and unzipped her skirt, bending forward so Hadley could step out of it and kissing her hips as his cheek brushed her skin. He was thrilled when she shivered and stumbled in her uncertainty. Her fingers were still trembling as she began to undress him, unbuttoning the jacket and fumbling with the studs in his shirt. Karl bent forward and kissed her cheeks.

"Relax, don't be afraid. This is not a competition on which our lives depend."

"You have no idea what it means to me."

"You think too much. How can a woman as beautiful as you have so many doubts about herself?"

He pushed her gently back on the bed and kissed her on the mouth, running his hands lightly over her body. He enjoyed watching her reaction as he explored her nipples and the moist folds of her innermost parts. As he lingered over their kiss, fascinated by the writhing of Hadley's body, she began to run her fingers over him, encircling his nipples and then his stomach and pubic hair. When she took his penis in a tender grip, her fingers titillating, Karl could stand the provocation no longer, and, parting her thighs, he pushed slowly, sensuously, deep inside her, exultant at the heat and passion of her response. Moving gently at first, he quickened within her, holding her down until her cries of pleasure told him it was time to fill her with the outpouring of his love. Then closing his eyes, Karl allowed his body to dissolve into Hadley's. It was a moment of supreme ecstasy and he knew he would never feel such pleasure and force of emotion with another woman. Tenderly he took Hadley in his arms, trying to still the languorous movements of her body as the aftermath of orgasm took her strength away.

After a while, Hadley sat up and gazed into Karl's eyes.

"Do it all over again."

"I want to do it again and again for always. Oh, my love, please don't cry. This is a wonderful moment for us both."

Wiping away tears of relief and happiness, Hadley kissed his cheeks. Then she snuggled in his arms, longing for Karl to tell her he loved her. Instead, he lifted her from the bed to the water.

"Now you can pretend to be a mermaid!"

Hadley swam back and forth with all the eagerness of a child. Karl followed, diving under the water and lifting her into his arms. As their bodies met, he became hard again, his penis forceful in its thrust against the softness of her body. Hadley felt herself being pushed back against the side of the pool. Then, as his lips came down on hers, she wound her legs around him and let the undulations of the water push her slowly, sensuously onto him. Moaning with pleasure at the feeling of the warm water and the lusty man, she dived under the surface, teasing him by trying to elude him for a few seconds. Karl caught her and whispered in her ear, "You are like an eel. You escape too easily."

"Pin me down, Karl. Make me your prisoner. I want to belong to you."

Piercing her body, he brought them both to a

rapid climax, overcome by emotion when he felt
Hadley contract again and again as orgasms took
her breath away. Filled with pride at the success
of this first lovemaking, Karl picked her up and
carried her back to the bed. Then, entwined in
each other's arms, they slept until morning.

Upon his arrival in Munich, Dietmueller was
informed that Hadley was in residence at the
hunting lodge. Though that information chagrined
him, he received the news of Baron von Allgau's
requested dossier with delight.

It would be fascinating to see what turned up
in the Ellerman family history, what skeletons
rattled in the cupboard of the beautiful young
woman from Chicago. One thing was certain, the
baron had done him a favor in asking for the
report. Under a display of the game trophies
brought back with him from his safari, Dietmueller
considered the situation.

Though he had no intention of marrying Hadley himself, Dietmueller was incensed to hear
that she and Karl were rumored to be engaged.
He had dreamed for so long of possessing her
that he could not bear to think of her belonging
to another man. Hadley was not only just like
him—amoral, selfish, and ruthless—but also the
most beautiful woman he had ever seen: sensuous, yet unattainable, mulish yet vulnerable. The
thought of Hadley Ellerman filled Dietmueller
with a primitive longing. He would have her,
that was certain, just as soon as he could get the
vilifying facts that would make it impossible for
a man of Karl's position to marry the lady.

Later that day, in the Marienplatz, Dietmueller
saw an antique silk Bokhara shawl in a dealer's
window. It cost a fortune and he was not a rich
man, but Dietmueller bought it, knowing that
Hadley was a person who demanded perfection.
Nothing less than a masterpiece would impress

her. As he touched the ivory silk with its intricate detail and subtle nuances of shade, he imagined it draped over her naked body when they made love for the first time. The image of Hadley swathed in silk that matched her skin floated before his eyes, and Dietmueller clutched the shawl to his face, closing his eyes and wishing fervently that it had the scent he adored, the warm, enticing odor of Amour-Amour, the fragrance of Hadley Ellerman.

In the morning, Karl and Hadley breakfasted together. There was ham, salami, liver sausage, brown bread, black bread, and slices of venison marinated in claret. Having served themselves from the side table, they returned to the table to open their mail. Hadley smiled across the table at Karl, her eyes sparkling.

"I got a letter from my sister Bunny. Good Lord! Just listen to this."

She began to read, a thoughtful expression on her face.

Dearest Hadley,

Thanks for sending us your address. Though Nell and I wrote to you at the Muthaiga Club, you apparently never received our letter. Nell's cottage is looking so pretty I truly envy her. She has a whole acre of hollyhocks and delphiniums, but not much furniture. She says she's not buying anything else till she's sure she can afford it. Charles and Guy de Nonancourt are *both* in love with her. Charles buys her expensive clothes from Chanel and Guy grows her all her favorite flowers in the hothouse at Bel-Ami. I don't think she'll have much trouble in deciding which one she likes best, but in the meantime she's having fun.

I graduated from school last week and Jack Cameron threw a party to celebrate. He's proposed again but I haven't accepted. I'm determined to try my wings before allowing some man to clip them.

Nell and I moved out of the Ritz soon after you left for Kenya. (I'm mentioning this in case you didn't get any of our letters. Since we haven't heard from *you* beyond your change of address, Nell and I can't be sure.) I've taken an apartment near the school and I'm getting used to being alone. In the beginning I used to go sit in the café next door because I was scared. Then they gave me a bill for forty dollars' worth of coffee and snacks in the first month and that soon put a stop to the indulgence.

When are you coming home? Do write to me so I can tell Nell. And send me a check toward the Ritz bill. Nell's given me her share and I'll pay everything I can when I get a job. I didn't accept anything from Jack. It's a question of trying not to lean on every man in sight. I'm just *never* going to be that kind of woman.

Let us know what's happening in your life— in twenty-five pages or less!

Hugs and kisses,
Bunny.

Hadley reread the letter and then looked at Karl with a wry smile.

"And we used to call her 'Poor Bunny'! Now she's the only one of us who can get by entirely on her own. It's odd—Nell and I were always so worried about her, particularly after Papa's death. Bunny seemed so overwhelmed."

"Perhaps she just showed her feelings more than you and Nell, Hadley, but *you* are the one who remains upset. You spend nearly every waking moment asking yourself what is going to happen in the future. And for that no one can find a definite answer."

Hadley pushed her plate away, suddenly unable to eat. Karl's words provoked panic in her. Suddenly it all came clear. She had been the dependent one, always leaning either on her father or on the current man of the moment. Worst of all, Hadley realized that *she* was the woman Bunny had unwittingly described and refused ever to become. How would she ever find the money to pay the bills she had so blithely run up at her couturiers, beauty parlors, and expensive hotels? Hadley thought of Bunny struggling through the grueling cookery course—ten hours a day of standing in front of a hot stove and nothing to show for it in the end but a piece of paper. But that diploma would enable Bunny to earn a living to the end of her days.

Even Nell was faring well. She had two men fighting over her and would probably marry the Duc de Nonancourt in the end. Hadley licked her lips and tried to swallow, but her throat was as dry as tinder. She had forced herself to ignore her father's death as much as was humanly possible, but her own helplessness overwhelmed her and she was hard pressed not to beg Karl to take her into his home and let her stay.

Watching her reactions, Karl was aware that tears were close.

"Are you jealous of your sisters, Hadley?"

She shook her head, hurt by the suggestion.

"I don't envy Bunny, plump and plain and having to wear glasses to see across the room, but there are times when I know in my heart that she's more of a real person than I'll ever be."

"And Nell?"

"I've always loved Nell. She has such style and beauty and such a big heart. But I can't say that I wish I were she."

Karl rose and looked out the window. He was deeply in love with Hadley, particularly now that he had seen her soul. Karl was more anxious than ever to marry her as soon as possible. Though he feared she would accept a proposal to assuage her desire for security rather than out of love, there was only one way of putting her love to the test of time. Karl knelt before her and said the words she had longed to hear.

"Will you marry me, Hadley? I love you and have loved you ever since the moment of our first meeting. I know it's not wise to marry such a short time after becoming acquainted, but I'm willing to take the risk."

Hadley's eyes filled with tears and suddenly she was sobbing as she had not sobbed since the day of her mother's death, a long time ago.

"Oh, Karl, of course I'll marry you and I'll be the very best wife any man could have. I just want us to be together, for always, here at the hunting lodge. When I'm behind these big stone walls I feel as if nothing in the world could hurt me."

"I shall see that nothing ever does. If you agree," Karl continued, "we can marry on the first of December and go to Venice for our honeymoon. That will give you three and a half months to prepare, and will allow Frau Hoffman time to cook enough food for an army."

In a haze of excitement, Hadley thought of the celebrations, the photographs in the newspapers, the reaction of her sisters and friends, but most of all of the wedding she had dreamed of all her life.

"I'll have to go to Paris to order my wedding dress. You'll come with me, won't you, Karl?"

"Of course. We can stay at the Ritz and visit Nell in her cottage and see Bunny settled in the new job. First, though, you must arrange every-thing. Write to your sisters and tell them the news, and to Monsieur Patou, giving him in-structions about the dress. When everything has been organized, we shall leave the hunting lodge for Paris. On your return, you will move into a hotel for the sake of propriety. Then we shall marry."

They stayed at the hunting lodge for four more weeks, making love and getting to know each other. The idyll was uninterrupted by visitors, except for Ilsa, who came to tea at four each day and charmed Hadley by making her feel admired and wanted. Slowly, inexorably, the relationship with Karl became comfortable, happy, and open. They confessed to each other all the secrets they had never told anyone, and Hadley's pride in the match she had made grew to be as strong as Karl's heartfelt elation.

On their last morning in Munich, Hadley and Karl made one of Hadley's favorite outings. First they hurried to the early market and bought plenty of hot white regional sausages that Hadley had come to love. From the market, they wandered the streets around the Leopoldstrasse, buying pretzels from stalls under blue-and-white-striped umbrellas. Hadley was no longer surprised to find herself enjoying this new mode of living. It was very nice to be greeted as a friend by all the traders, and even nicer to feel at home in the city.

On their way back to the hunting lodge, Karl explained his plans. "I have booked us on the *Orient Express* to Paris. We shall travel by car to Zurich, leave the vehicle with friends there, and go by local train to Lausanne, where we can pick up the express. I think it is going to be a very interesting journey."

Hadley began to feel like her old self again, the phantom of insecurity disappearing to the back of her mind.

"I adore the idea of traveling on the *Orient Express*," she replied with enthusiasm. "Perhaps we'll find a fortune in diamonds hidden in our compartment. I've heard of people doing that."

"I adore *you,* Hadley."

"And I love you so much I can't even put it into words."

"Don't try, just show me."

The morning of their departure found Hadley flushed with excitement. She was carefully arranging herself in the passenger seat of Karl's white Mercedes when she heard the sound of a vehicle approaching. Was Ilsa here to see them off? Hadley reached for the door, then stopped herself. Dietmueller stepped out onto the forecourt. Hadley felt herself go pale.

"You are going away?" Dietmueller asked Karl.

"We're off to Paris. We have a wedding to prepare for, as you may have heard. But what can I do for you, Ernst?"

Dietmueller clicked his heels and inclined his head to Hadley, his face blotched with fury.

"My felicitations, Miss Ellerman, and to you, Karl. When will the wedding be?"

Hadley answered with a radiant smile, "We'll marry here on the first of December and then go to Venice for our honeymoon."

Dietmueller smiled coldly and moved with Karl away from the car. "May I have a word in private, Karl?" He handed over a large manila envelope, explaining what it was in a voice of deceptive calm. "During my absence in Africa, the Baron von Allgau requested that some information be gathered by my office. I have brought you a copy as a friend. The original will be delivered to the baron later today."

"What is it, Ernst?"

"Read it when you have a moment. Considering your plans, it is important material."

Karl tore the top off the envelope and scanned the first page, his face hardening as he read the heading: "REPORT ON THE GENETIC BACKGROUND OF HADLEY ELIZABETH ELLERMAN." Furious, he turned to face Dietmueller.

"How *dare* you do this? By what right do you investigate my fiancée?"

"As I told you, your brother-in-law initiated the preparation of this report. I brought you this copy as a courtesy." Dietmueller lowered his voice further, continuing with a sneer, "Many among the more patriotic of our countrymen have come to value the purity of our noble German bloodlines. The baron was obviously concerned lest the family become, shall we say, *infiltrated* by less desirable elements."

Karl tore the report in half and threw it to the ground.

"I cannot believe that you would do this, Ernst. However, as you have seen fit to investigate Hadley—"

"You see, Miss Ellerman is part Jewish, my dear Karl."

"I don't care if she is part Chinese and part frog. I love her and I am going to marry her. Now I must ask you to leave and please make sure you say nothing of this to Hadley."

"I will be happy to send you another copy to the Ritz Hotel in Paris. You may need time to consider your actions, Karl."

"Don't waste your time. And from today on, never come to this house again."

Dietmueller's eyes hardened and his face became a mask of malevolence.

"You may be titled, Karl, but you are in no position to give me orders. Remember this, Count Kohler—now and in the future, *I* decide what must be done in this city."

Karl's fists clenched and for a moment Dietmueller thought he was going to be attacked. Then Karl spoke, his voice trembling with rage. "This is my home, and until a man in Germany may no longer call his life his own and his home his own, I shall do as I wish, and what I wish is for you to leave at once and never return."

Dietmueller strode to his car, slammed the door, and drove off at a furious pace. Karl was outraged that his brother-in-law should have instigated such an inquiry and shocked by Dietmueller's acquiescence to the request. For years their families had been friendly acquaintances. Now they were declared enemies. Karl felt Hadley entwining her hand in his.

"What's happened, Karl?"

"My brother-in-law asked Dietmueller's office to draw up a report on your family background. He says it proves you are part Jewish."

Unperturbed by the news, Hadley laughed out loud.

"That's true. My great-great-grandfather, Isaiah Elderman, came from Krakow. He changed his name when he reached America and married my grandmother, who was an Irish Catholic. We have a bit of every religion in our family."

Realizing that she understood nothing of the implications of her statement in present-day Germany, Karl continued, his face imperturbable, despite the turmoil within. "I told Dietmueller never to come to the lodge again. I shall tell my brother-in-law the same."

"But he'll forbid Ilsa to visit us!"

"My sister has been doing as she pleases for the whole of her life. She will not alter her ways now, whatever the baron may think."

Hadley became silent. She suspected what Dietmueller had done for the baron had been to hurt her, to put her in his power. But she couldn't let anything interfere with their plans. Her dream was coming true at last, and she would allow nothing to stop it. Not even Ernst Dietmueller.

Hadley arrived at the Ritz in a new sable jacket bought for her by Karl from the finest furrier in Munich. Under it she was wearing a suit of cream silk tussore, purchased from Chanel, with a tiny pillbox hat tilted to the side of her head and covered in spotted veiling. As she walked into the reception area, looking expensive, Auzello hurried forward to welcome her.

"My dear Miss Ellerman, how nice to see you back. Count Kohler, it is a privilege to be of service. Now, Miss Ellerman, I have news for you. Mr. Patou telephoned and asked that the first fitting for the dress be at two today if convenient. Miss Annabelle called and said she will come to dinner at seven. And Miss Bunny says she cannot come to dinner but will join you later for coffee."

Hadley, who had remained unperturbed, suddenly looked concerned. "Is anything wrong with Bunny?"

"No, nothing at all. She works from eight in the morning until five at the American embassy, you know. She has also started a private catering service in the evenings and tells me she is trying hard to make it profitable. It takes most of her time, as you can imagine."

"When's that Jack Cameron due back? I must have a word with him and tell him it's time poor Bunny stopped slaving like a native. She'll get ill and have a breakdown if we don't take care of her."

"If it's any comfort to you, Miss Ellerman, your sister seems to be thriving."

At seven Nell arrived for dinner. She was wearing a red sequined jacket over a new pair of black satin trousers bought for her by Charles de Nonancourt from Chanel. In her hair she had a red rose grown for her by Guy, who, to everyone's surprise and delight, accompanied her to the sisters' reunion. Thrilled to see Hadley looking so relaxed and beautiful, Nell hugged her older sister to her heart. Obviously Hadley had been right after all. She had spent every cent of her five-thousand-dollar legacy in the first three months on clothes from Patou and had hooked herself one of the richest men in Europe. Nell gave Hadley the wryest of smiles.

"Well, you always swore you were a Ritz type, and now I believe you. Are we going to wait dinner for Bunny or is she coming by later?"

"She said she'd have coffee with us at ten. How is the poor little thing?"

"I haven't seen her for three weeks. I only know she's been working hard from morning till night. I telephone her every morning at seven, but she never has time to talk. Since she learned to do something useful, she's been rushing off in all directions."

Hadley smiled indulgently at the thought of Bunny.

"She loves *earning*, doesn't she? And you, Nell, what's been happening in *your* life?"

"I've furnished the cottage on a shoestring and got myself a job with René Davide, the interior designer. It doesn't pay much, because I'm a learner, but at least it covers the food bills and the taxes on the cottage."

"Does it buy the new season's Chanel trousers?"

Hadley's glance was mischievous and Nell smiled.

"Charles bought me these and Guy chose the rose specially for me from the hothouse at Bel-Ami. He's something of an expert at producing the finest fruit, flowers, and wine in the Loire."

Hadley's eyes were challenging as she turned to Guy.

"Aren't you ever jealous of your brother?"

Guy replied without hesitation. "If I were, I should never admit it. In any case, Charles is so confident and so competent, I swear he could walk on water and probably teach me to do the same. I think I am very lucky to have such a fine fellow for a brother."

They were still laughing when Bunny was unexpectedly announced. Hadley looked up expectantly, wondering if her young sister would have changed much since their last meeting. Though her face had retained its softness, Bunny had lost a lot of weight.

Hadley kissed her affectionately. "We're so glad to see you! We thought you couldn't make dinner."

"My meal for six canceled so I came right over."

Karl rose and kissed Bunny on both cheeks, making her blush with his compliments. "My congratulations on passing the course and obtaining your post at the American embassy. You must be a very superior chef."

"I am. It's the first thing I was ever good at and I'm so thrilled I can actually earn my own living. Now, tell me about the wedding. When's it going to be, and where? You'll have to give me plenty of warning so I can put a week aside to come to Germany."

Hadley spoke in her usual teasing manner. "Listen to the big businesswoman of the family!"

Bunny laughed good-naturedly. For as long as she could remember, all the Ellermans had teased her, and despite all the changes in the family's fortunes, nothing had altered in the sisters' attitudes toward her. Only within herself were things different. The new Bunny was confident, secure in the knowledge that she could do something useful, that she could earn substantial money and progress to bigger things. Smiling across the table at Guy, who was one of her greatest supporters, Bunny asked about a report she had read in the morning paper. "What's this I hear about your opening the gardens at Bel-Ami to the public?"

"Only the parterres and the Italian garden. They are among the finest in Europe, and Charles and I felt we should display them."

"I hope you make a fat profit from the entries."

"We shan't charge to enter, but we hope to make a profit from the seedlings, orange trees, and buckets of shrubs sold in the nursery shop. If we do become profitable, we hope to add a new gazebo in the summer garden. Nell is going to come down to lay the foundation stone for us, aren't you?"

Nell took his hand and gazed enigmatically at the strong, broad palm. She had been longing to visit Bel-Ami, but had been avoiding it, apprehensive of meeting Guy's mother. She was still profoundly affected by the realization of her sterility and inclined to imagine that people knew about it merely by looking at her. She was also fast becoming aware that Guy was in love with her and that despite his recent confession to her of being without a sou in the world, she felt the same way about him. She had said nothing of her feelings, however, afraid to break the spell during their meetings in Paris and the Valley of Chevreuse. The day she told Guy she loved him would be the day she had to tell him her secret, and Nell was certain she could never do that. Guy could, no doubt, marry a woman who could not give him money, but could he be happy with a wife who was unable to give him children?

Bunny's enthusiastic questioning of Karl broke Nell's reverie.

"Next time you take Hadley with you, you must *force* her to write home. We know nothing at all of what happened in Africa. What did you see? Were you ever attacked by wild animals?"

"We saw every animal imaginable and ten thousand flamingos on a beautiful lake in Kenya. And, though this may destroy your fantasies, we were not attacked by anything more serious than an occasional fly."

Hadley interrupted Karl's reply. "That's not true! Karl was attacked by Irena Stevens at the Muthaiga Club."

Bunny and Nell spoke together. "What happened?"

Hadley continued, delighted by the look of astonishment on Karl's face. "Well, Irena went to Karl's room at night for a little light relief and he forgot his good manners and threw her out into the corridor. I just *loved* every moment of it."

Karl gazed at Hadley, dumbfounded by what he had just heard. "If I had known you were there, Hadley, I might have let her stay just to make you jealous. Though, to tell the truth, women like Irena make me run so fast I could win an Olympic gold medal."

Everyone laughed as waiters brought more champagne. Hadley was overjoyed that Karl got on so well with her sisters and that he had seemed to find a friend in Guy.

Indeed, Karl and Guy both believed that friends were one of the most important things in life, more important than politics. It was a belief they would both need to hold onto. The years ahead would be years of uncertainty.

— 4 —

CHÂTEAU BEL-AMI, 1930

THE CHÂTEAU HAD been built in the sixteenth
century for the mistress of Henri II of France.
Designed by Philibert de l'Orme, one of the great
architects of the Renaissance, its magnificent lines
were framed by a spectacular avenue of chestnut
trees and a lake where black swans preened in
the golden light of early morning. Constructed of
pale cream stone, the château's ivy-covered towers and dark blue roof could be seen from a great
distance. Honeysuckle twined around the windows, scenting the rooms with the heady fragrance that guests would associate with Bel-Ami
forever. On the grounds, staff hurried about their
work, clearing fountains, mowing lawns, and putting fertilizer on the new vegetable garden. It
took all of their combined efforts to keep everything as beautiful, well-ordered, and peaceful as
it had been for centuries.

The entrance hall of the château had twin
staircases that fell in a graceful sweep like the
train of a spectacular robe down to the hallway
floored in black and white. Red poppies had been
arranged to contrast with the starkness of the
floor as well as the somber torchère of ebony and
satinwood. At the windows, on colored glass panes,

were the interwoven letters D and H, with bows and moons to signify the eternal linking of the original owner with her royal lover. Bel-Ami was a château synonymous with romance, and Charles de Nonancourt and his brother were both hoping that love would come their way on this hazy autumn morning.

Nell stepped down from the train and hurried at Charles's side to the new Bugatti. He had met her at the station, handing her a bouquet of roses before telling her that Guy was too busy to come himself. Nell was disappointed. It was true that ever since their first meeting at the Ritz, Charles had showered her with gifts, notes, invitations to the theater, poems that did not rhyme, and finally, a proposal. Nell had adored the attention, but her heart belonged to Guy, and she accepted it, though the thought of being in love filled her with apprehension. She wanted Guy to propose but what if he did? She would have to tell him the truth of her condition. And what of the matriarch of the family? Madame de Nonancourt was a celebrated dragon, given to taking instant likes and dislikes to the friends of both of her sons. Suddenly Nell's uncertainty was more than she could bear and she looked appealingly at Charles.

"Where *is* Guy? I need to see him at once."

"I have no idea. He works from five each morning till nightfall and we can never find him. Sometimes he comes to eat with the family, sometimes he does not. Perhaps he is in his cottage. Do you want me to send someone to find him?"

"I'll see him later, when I've unpacked."

"Nell, I told you a week ago that I want to marry you. Won't you reconsider your decision?"

"I'm sorry, Charles. You know that I don't love you. I can't fathom marriage without true love."

"But you would learn to love me, Nell. I truly

believe we are well-suited and I do so need a wife."

"Oh, Charles. The time has come for me to admit to you—and myself—where I stand. I'm in love with Guy." Crestfallen, Charles stared at his feet while Nell continued. "I only realized it recently but I truly believe I've loved him since the first day I saw him arriving at the Ritz and thought *he* was the Duc de Nonancourt. I'm so sorry, but you mustn't be under any illusions where I'm concerned."

Charles sighed wearily, wondering if there was any hope of changing Nell's mind. He knew in his heart there was not, and spoke resignedly. "If you are really in love with my brother, I think there's something you should know. Guy's former mistress, Arlette de Saumur, will be one of our guests this weekend. Since she and Guy went their separate ways, Arlette has married, but she is still very possessive about my brother and violently jealous of his friends. She will be one of the six people who will dine with us tonight."

"Was Guy in love with her?"

"Here in France, a man makes love with his mistress but is seldom in love with her in his heart."

"Why did they stop seeing each other?"

"As soon as Guy met you he wanted only to be with you. Arlette was so furious at his neglect that she married one of her rich friends and has been busy regretting her haste ever since."

Nell looked up at the turrets and spires of the château. She had come to this beautiful place hoping that Guy would propose to her. Instead, his brother had done so and now she had no idea how to tell Guy all that had to be told. Tonight there would be the dinner party for the Nonancourt society friends, which Guy would certainly attend, but there would be little time to be alone with him before she was obliged to return to

Paris. Panic rose in Nell's mind. Now that she was sure that she wanted and needed only to be with the man she loved, was she to be denied the opportunity?

A butler in funereal black led Nell to one of the guest bedrooms, situated up a winding stone staircase. The furniture was in the style known as troubadour, with heavy Gothic chairs and a four-poster bed curtained in pure white damask. From the window she looked out on a forest of poplar and willows. She could also see a cottage half-hidden by hedges, flowering creeper, and a venerable apple tree. She wondered if that cottage was the little house Guy often spoke of with longing, the place he called his refuge from the world. The longing for Guy that filled her heart made Nell impatient to begin her search for him. First, though, she had to meet her fellow guests. Nell chose her outfit carefully; neither the cream-colored serge trousers she put on nor the blouse of coffee and black spotted silk had been given to her by Charles. Nell knew that Guy was secretly jealous of his brother's gifts. She smiled to herself at the thought of his possessiveness and hurried downstairs, hoping he would stay like that forever.

Nell was surveying the gathering in the drawing room from a quiet entryway when a young woman stepped out of the shadows and confronted her. She had wide blue eyes, curly blond hair, a childlike pout, and, when she spoke, a pronounced lisp. "You must be Annabelle Ellerman. I'm Arlette de Saumur."

Nell weighed the doll-like face, the slim, elegant figure, and the practiced pout—this was a determined woman, an adversary capable of anything. Nell collected her wits and spoke casually, as if she knew nothing of her acquaintance's past relationship with Guy. "I'm pleased to meet you, Arlette."

"I think you should call me Madame de Saumur, as we are not likely to be friends." Arlette studied Nell unabashedly from head to toe. "I must say you are not at all as I imagined."

"I'm intrigued to know what you expected."

"The Guy *I* know likes his women to have a certain hardness. As he seems to have chosen you in place of me, your personality intrigues me."

Nell regarded the sharklike mouth, the nervous fingers holding the long amber cigarette holder.

"If you'll excuse me, Arlette, I'd like to join the others."

"He has no money, you know, not a sou."

"Neither have I."

"And your father committed suicide. That will not meet with Madame de Nonancourt's approval . . . should she come to know."

Nell moved to pass Arlette, but the young woman blocked her way.

"I haven't finished speaking with you yet."

"Oh yes you have, Arlette."

"You *will* listen to me."

Disliking intensely the obsessive, spoiled manner, Nell raised herself to her full, towering height and spoke softly. "You were Guy's mistress and he left you, so you ran off and married another man. Now you're stuck with your choice, no matter how miserable it may make you. The fact is, Guy's in love with me. So why don't you settle down and stop playing the little girl? You've had your fun, now it's my turn. End of conversation."

With that, she pushed Arlette out of her way and entered the drawing room. Despite her poise in the face of Arlette's hostility, the confrontation had completely undermined Nell's confidence. Arlette might be selfish, spoiled, even deceitful, but she could undoubtedly offer Guy a family. In the name of honesty, Nell would have to deliver the news in nearly the same breath in which she pledged her love. She wondered desperately if he would even wish to see her again. Angry at herself, Nell regretted that she had not informed Guy of her situation at the very start of their friendship.

A flurry of activity attracted Nell's attention to the center of the room. It was the dowager Duchess of Nonancourt, presiding over a group of friends. Nell admired how well Guy's mother had kept her legendary looks, noting the resemblance between mother and son. Guy's open, honest eyes were an exact reproduction of the dowager's, whose curious gaze Nell now evaded. With what look would the dowager greet Nell once Arlette had passed along her poisonous message? Furthermore, Guy's mother would obviously not be thrilled at the prospect of her son's marrying a woman who could never give him children, though at least Nell would have the chance to break the news herself. Arlette would be deprived of the opportunity to use that information against her. Still, despair buzzed through Nell's brain like a swarm of bees. Now she wanted reassurance. If only she could be certain that the man she loved loved her enough to accept even this horrible truth.

On seeing Nell's confusion, Charles hurried forward. "Let me take you to my mother, Nell. She's anxious to meet you." Taking her arm firmly, Charles guided his charge toward the thronelike chair at the end of the garden room.

At first glance the dowager duchess saw the suppressed emotion in Nell's eyes. Intrigued, she leaned forward and whispered a question. "Are you angry with someone, Miss Ellerman?"

Too overwrought to be cautious, Nell blurted the truth. "I was accosted by Guy's former mistress, who's very angry that she isn't the present one. I almost had to garrote her to get in here."

Madame laughed delightedly at Nell's turn of phrase. "You are very honest, I must say."

"It's one of my biggest faults."

"What did Arlette say to you?"

"She told me she was going to inform you that my father killed himself and that the Nonancourts were in danger of catching the malady if I were ever to enter their ranks."

"And what did you reply?"

"I told her to get out of my way. And I didn't tell her the whole truth, but I must tell *you*, madame."

Nell's eyes filled with tears as she struggled to find words to say what had to be said. Finally she took a deep breath and explained her situation. "I discovered some time ago that I can't ever have children. You see, there's no danger of anyone inheriting my father's problems." Nell's knuckles were white as she gripped the arm of a chair.

The dowager perched precariously on the edge of her seat, pressing her powdered face toward Nell.

"Young lady, this is hardly an issue you need to discuss with *me*."

"I realize that, madame. Still, I thought it best that you know. Guy and I have become very close very quickly, and—"

"Are you quite sure nothing can be done?" the dowager interrupted quietly.

"Absolutely. I shall never have a family and I have to learn to live with the knowledge. Now, my throat's gone dry from sheer nervousness. Where's Guy? Is he hiding from me?"

Madame was overjoyed by Nell's uncompromising manner. The young lady was quite different from anyone she had ever met before, so forceful and as transparent in her emotions as sheer chiffon. It must have hurt dreadfully to learn that she was barren, and it must have been an agonizing experience to lose the father she had adored. Madame rejoiced for her son. If the young woman had been the mercenary type, she would have chosen Charles and set her sights on marrying the title. As it was, Nell was sincerely interested in a man who had not two centimes to rub together. If she could not have children, it was not the end of the world. She was beautiful, spirited, and like a breath of fresh air in the staid atmosphere of Bel-Ami. Madame watched her unusual guest walk to the buffet. Nell bent forward so the butler could explain what everything was.

"That is a mousse of lark and woodcock, mademoiselle. Those are sandwiches of cucumber, and the others of peacock-tongue pâté. The pavlova is particularly fine and the strawberry tart quite perfect. Now, may I help you take something? Or perhaps you would like to wait for Monsieur Guy on the terrace? He asked me to let you know that he would be a little late for tea."

"What's your name?"

"Lemercier, mademoiselle. I was born here at the château sixty-three years ago."

"Thank you, Lemercier. I'm so glad to have met someone who knew Guy when he was little. You'll be able to tell me all his secrets."

Nell was on her third piece of cake, her second cup of tea, and Lemercier's fourth reminiscence when she saw Guy ride up to the house on a chestnut mare. Forgetting the guests sitting nearby and Guy's mother, who was still tracking her closely, the relieved Nell ran to the drive and called out, "Where've you been? I'm so pleased to see you, I could dance like a dervish! I met your mother a while ago, and Arlette de Saumur too. She was hardly the politest female I ever encountered."

"Charles was delighted to be able to come to the station to meet you. I swear he gets more possessive by the minute." Guy swung easily off his mount and took Nell's hand.

"He asked me to reconsider his proposal to me. Did you know he was planning to do that?"

"And did you accept?"

"Of course not. I told him I was in love with you."

Guy gazed at her for a long time, and then, handing the reins of his horse to the groom, held Nell in his arms and hugged her to his heart.

"Come with me and I'll show you my cottage. Then I must change before joining our guests for tea."

"Did you hear me when I said I'd met Arlette?"

"Of course, and I'm sorry she was rude. You understand that what Arlette and I had was nothing more than . . . an arrangement, don't you?" Nell nodded. "Well, one day she'll accept that too. Right now she does not want to admit it. She knows only that I love and need you—and that she has no place in the life I plan."

Nell held her breath, her heart beating so fast she was certain Guy could hear it. They had been out together frequently in Paris, mostly simple dates, walking by the Seine, eating roasted chestnuts in Monmartre, and visting the cool green glades of the Bois de Boulogne. He had kissed her passionately, and he was unsuccessful at hiding his tension whenever Charles appeared with a gift. But though Guy had told her frequently that he adored her, cherished her, enjoyed her, he had never spoken of love. Nell did her best to appear calm.

"My sister Hadley's going to marry Karl-Friedrich Kohler in Munich on the first of December. Will you come with me to the ceremony?"

"I'm afraid that would be impossible. In December we will have a conference at Nonancourt of estate-owners from all corners of Europe, and I must be here. But you and I can go on a trip together soon, perhaps to the South of France. I adore the Midi. You have never seen it, have you?"

So entranced was Nell at what met her eyes at the moment that she could not fathom a more seductive sight anywhere. Before her stood the cottage she'd glimpsed from the château window—Guy's cottage—and perhaps, her new home.

Nell stepped inside, enchanted by the scent of the full-blown roses trellised around the door and windows. The tables and chairs in the living room were littered with books, magazines, and newspapers. The walls were painted a pale biscuit shade, the curtains of heavy flowered chintz. Walking to the window, she looked out at the château.

"Are you ever envious of Charles for owning all this?"

"Never. He has the disadvantage of having to worry about keeping everything in good order. I have all the advantages, a free house, a beautiful outlook, and work on the land I love. I have enough food, a comfortable bed, and you. What more could any man want?"

"Do you really love me, Guy? You never talked of love until today."

"You needed time, Nell—time to decide what to do about my brother. After all, from a woman's point of view, Bel-Ami is preferable to my little house, and Charles has always been the good-looking member of the family."

"You're a fool!"

"That may be, but what I truly am is a second son, and second sons grow into realistic men, at least most of the time. It became obvious that Charles wanted you when you were staying at the Ritz Hotel with your sisters. I simply wanted to make sure you did not want him."

"I didn't and I don't."

"Then you're as big a fool as I am, and that revelation relieves me greatly."

Guy led Nell upstairs to the bedroom in the roof, where honeysuckle climbed through the window, invading the walls with long scented tendrils. Motioning for her to sit down, he kissed her cheeks and her hands.

"Wait till I've washed and changed my clothes. Then we can return to the house and have tea together."

"Why don't you kiss me? Don't you desire me, Guy?"

He walked over to where Nell was sitting on the edge of the bed and looked at her in puzzlement.

"When we first met, you were very upset and I knew what you needed was support and sympathy. Since then I have had to compete with my brother, who has bought you gifts and pursued you ardently. I was ferociously jealous, let me tell you, but I felt you needed time. So, of course, I desire you, Nell—and I am in love with you, very much in love—but to me your wishes are the most important thing in the world."

"Then I wish you'd kiss me and make me feel like a real woman."

Guy had taken off his shirt and was about to enter the bathroom when her words stopped him. With a determined glance in Nell's direction, he moved back and stood over her, a virile man full of pulsing desire. For a moment he hesitated. Then he kissed her on the mouth, running his fingers through her long hair.

"You're the most beautiful woman in the world to me," he whispered.

Pushing her back on the bed, he kissed her again, his tongue thrusting into her mouth, his hands on the silk blouse, unbuttoning and adventuring.

Nell closed her eyes as he caressed her, sud-

denly so leaden with longing she could not reply.
She felt his teeth on her nipples, his hands moving to unfasten her skirt. Then, suddenly, panic began to rise in her, and she sat bolt upright, terrified of his intentions.

"Don't, Guy."

"I want you. And I thought you wanted me."

"I can't let you make love to me, I just can't."

Guy rose, his face flushed, his eyes bright.

"Forgive me. It seems that I misunderstood your wishes after all—and when you said you loved me I went a little wild." Guy took both of her trembling hands in his. "Calm yourself, Nell, there is nothing to fear. I shall change my clothes and we shall go to tea, but remember: before you leave Bel-Ami I intend to love you as you never imagined being loved, even in your dreams."

"Please, Guy. Not yet. I just can't."

"Then just relax and smile for me. You look as if you were ravished by Attila the Hun, and I assure you I am a far more cultivated fellow than he."

Nell lay on the bed gazing at the ceiling and the bunches of dried flowers and herbs hung from the beams. Slowly she buttoned her blouse and tried to straighten her hair. At the moment when Guy had kissed her, she had felt as if her body was on fire. When he had caressed her breasts, she had wanted him with all her heart and soul. But when he had tried to move toward entering her body, she had panicked. She wondered why. She had been afraid whenever she thought of making love with Guy. Now that it happened, she understood. It was because her mind linked sterility with frigidity. She wasn't a whole woman. She loved Guy, but was she capable of reacting like a real woman? Would she remain frozen forever, no matter how ardent his advances? And what if he should propose marriage? Nell's heart began to thunder from terror. This was the moment to tell him the truth.

Guy came out of the bathroom in a clean white shirt and jacket of heather-gray tweed. Taking Nell in his arms, he held her to his heart.

"I adore you Nell, and I'm sorry I frightened you. I have the feeling something else is bothering you very much. Do you want to tell me about it?"

Nell gazed into his eyes, willing him to be patient. When she spoke, her voice was subdued, her face resigned. "I have something very serious to tell you, Guy, something I should have told you long ago. The news I had that made me cry when we first met in Paris . . . it was very terrible news to me. Guy, I can't have children *ever*. And I'm scared that I won't ever be able to be a real lover for you. I feel so incomplete, such a failure. My whole life fell down like a pack of cards when I had that letter, and I find myself unable to do even the simple things in life. I don't know how to ask you to forgive me for not talking about this before, for leading you on the way I did, but—"

Guy took her in his arms and kissed her cheeks and her ears and her fingertips.

"My dearest Nell. I love you with all my heart. I like children, but if you can't have any, well, so be it. It doesn't change my love or my desire for you, and it shouldn't alter your ability to enjoy our passion for each other. Listen, darling. If I have you and Bel-Ami and the prospect of growing old by your side, that will be more than enough to make me the happiest man in France. Now, dry your eyes and let's go down to tea."

Relief flooded through Nell like water on the parched sand of a desert. She wanted to sob from sheer happiness. Instead, she held Guy's hand and kissed it tenderly.

"You're the finest man I ever met. Thank you, Guy."

Madame eyed her son and then Nell's flushed face and agitated manner. Had they been making love? It seemed unlikely. Even Guy, with his passionate nature, would not do that on a day when there were important guests for tea, yet something had obviously disturbed the young lady. Madame motioned for Nell to join her.

"What are you going to wear for the ball tonight, Miss Ellerman? Tell me all about your dress."

Nell looked alarmed. This was the first time anyone had mentioned a ball.

"I thought we'd just be having dinner. Guy didn't tell me about a ball, so I brought nothing with me."

Madame thought for a while. Then she rose and excused herself to her guests.

"Come, Nell, I have something to show you."

Madame walked upstairs to a bedroom furnished in faded violet and pink. On the wall of the dressing room was the portrait of a beautiful woman, with vivid red hair and a choker of glittering diamonds. Her dress was low-cut in the empire style, with a long train of rich cream satin. Madame took a key and walked over to the trunk in the corner, amused to see Nell still gazing up at the portrait, taking in every detail of the majestic figure and sensational jewels.

"She's very grand, is she not?"

"Who is it?"

"That is a portrait of my mother at the age of thirty-five. She is something of a legend in our family. She was left a widow when very young and eventually became famous for her charitable works and also for her lovers. I want to show you one of her dresses."

Inside the trunk, wrapped in tissue paper, was

a dress of ivory satin, the same one worn in the portrait. Its condition was perfect and it was only very slightly yellowed with age. Madame smiled gently at Nell's expression.

"Try it on, my dear. If it is too small, we can certainly make some alterations. Felicienne, my maid, is an excellent seamstress."

Nell took off her clothes and crouched forward so Madame could throw the voluminous skirt over her head. It was a touch too short, but otherwise perfect.

Madame de Nonancourt stood back to admire the effect.

"It is marvelous, except for the length. I must ask Felicienne to add an underskirt of pink slipper satin. Wear it for dinner with the diamonds and earrings, as Louise did for her portrait."

"Thank you, madame. But may I ask why you are doing this for me?"

"Tonight we shall have six guests for dinner. Besides Guy's former mistress and her husband, I am expecting the Rothschilds, the Princesse de Polignac, and the writer Colette. I like you, Nell, and I want you to cause something of a sensation. To be truthful, I was always in dread that Guy might marry Arlette, who is such a shallow person. I wanted to adore my son's wife, you see, to feel about her as I would feel about the daughter I never had. And, Nell—I would want my daughter to *shine*."

"That's very kind, madame, but we're a bit premature. Guy hasn't asked me to marry him . . . yet!"

The two women laughed at this. Then Madame summoned her maid and put Felicienne to work on the dress before she and Nell returned to the sitting room, where Guy and Charles were deep in conversation. From the distant drive they could hear the sound of a car approaching. It was the Princesse de Polignac and her friend Colette.

The new arrivals were opposites, the princess tall, slim, and elegant, the writer short and thick-bodied. Colette spoke in a rolling Burgundy accent that made her hostess laugh.

"What are we going to eat tonight, madame? I like to look forward to my meals, you know. Food is one of the greatest pleasures in life."

The dowager smiled and caught the writer's arm. "Ah, yes, my friend. But first an aperitif—a small pleasure to whet your appetite for those yet to come."

Over drinks, Madame introduced the gregarious author to the greatly relieved Nell, who had been celebrating her newfound peace of mind, moving easily among the guests gathered in the great room.

Intrigued by Nell's looks, Colette leaned forward and asked a question. "What brings you to France, Miss Ellerman? There are so few Americans in Paris since the Wall Street crash."

"I work as an interior-design trainee for René Davide."

Colette turned to her friend. "Why don't you use her, Pol? She's far better looking than the Countess de Vries." The Princesse de Polignac looked the bewildered Nell up and down, then nodded. "Would you like to pose for *Vogue* magazine, Miss Ellerman?"

"I'm far too tall and hefty for that!"

The princess was amused by her candor.

"Oh no, Miss Ellerman, you are not. You are a beautiful Amazon and if you pose for us I shall put you on the cover. All the thin women in Paris are trying to change their shape since the new clothes came in. We are looking for *real* women, and that, my dear, is exactly what you are."

Arlette moved closer to the exchange, looking more uncomfortable by the minute at what she had managed to overhear.

"I'm surprised that you should need or wish to work, Miss Ellerman. Your father built up a great empire in his day. I was an admirer of the innovative way he did business."

"Papa lost everything in the crash. Even his bank had to close down, and all he'd worked for nearly fifty years to acquire just vanished overnight. He wasn't the only one, of course. A lot of his friends are still living from hand to mouth."

"And where do you reside?"

"I have a cottage in the Chevreuse Valley and I travel to Paris each morning from there."

"You don't wish to return to America?"

"I'm very happy right here for the moment."

Arlette, suddenly aware of her husband's maneuverings to edge closer to Nell, flushed red with anger.

Nell turned away from her, taking Guy's hand, conscious of the sigh that escaped his brother's lips. Charles, who had been so kind to her, seemed distracted since her refusal of his proposal. Though she wanted to comfort him, she remembered the simple wisdom Guy had passed on to her in the cottage—only time would soothe Charles, just as it would heal her.

The crystal ballroom of the château was walled in gold and gray. Chandeliers imported long ago from a palace in St. Petersburg gleamed like a thousand jewels, each one hung with billowing masses of lily of the valley, violet, heliotrope, and fuchsia. At the windows there were curtains of white silk damask, with designs of arabesques and guelder roses. Around the walls stood kingwood and lacquer *meuble d'appui* cabinets full of priceless porcelain objects. At the door, where the guests were announced, two massive Nubian statues in ebony and gilt kept impassive watch on the scene.

Guy and his brother were standing together receiving their guests. They had been a handful for dinner, but now neighbors and friends from Paris were joining the family for the ball, all impatient to meet the woman rumored to have enslaved both the Nonancourt men. This was no small feat, considering the contrast between the brothers—Charles was known to admire sophistication and a certain vulnerability in a woman, while Guy looked for beauty and the scent of danger. It seemed unfathomable that one woman could embody the combination of these opposing elements. Guy turned to his brother when the last guest had passed into the ballroom.

"Tonight I'm intending to propose to Nell. If she accepts me, I would like to announce the engagement during the ball. I've already discussed it with mother and she's given her blessing. Charles, I know how you must be dreading this, but I now must ask yours as head of the family."

Charles sighed, his shoulders sagging. For the first time in his life he had lost something that was precious to him. He did not relish the feeling.

"Are you absolutely sure about this, Guy?"

"I love Nell. I've loved her since the very first moment I saw her."

"Then we shall announce the engagement at midnight. I have a very strong feeling that this proposal is one our Nell will not refuse." Charles gripped his brother's shoulder. "My congratulations, Guy. I don't need to tell you that you are a very lucky man. And believe me, if I didn't love you as my brother, I'd be tempted to suggest pistols at dawn!"

As the orchestra began the lilting prelude to the first waltz, the guests looked increasingly puzzled by Nell's absence. They had expected her to lead off the dancing with Guy or Charles. Instead, she was nowhere to be found. Several of the more important guests were debating whether to proceed without her, when the major domo's voice echoed about the lofty room. "Miss Annabelle Ellerman."

Guy looked up, his heart missing a beat. Charles moved forward, the better to see this surprising echo of the past. And all around, a babble of excited comment from the guests almost drowned the lilting strains of the music, as Nell moved slowly, regally down the staircase. She wore the shimmering satin dress, the Nonancourt diamond choker around her throat, a bracelet of matching stones at her wrist, and she had arranged her hair in its usual style, but with a circlet of white camellias to hold it back from the face. She was alive, beautiful, and rosy-faced with excitement.

Guy took her in his arms.

"This is our waltz. The guests are waiting for us to lead off."

"I'm sorry I'm late. Felicienne hadn't finished the alteration."

"Mother told us she had a surprise for us and now I realize what it was. I'm so proud of you. Every man in the room must be sick with jealousy."

"Does that please you?"

"It makes me so vain I may be unable to get my head through the door of my room tonight."

"I'll help you force it in."

"Will you, Nell?"

Their eyes met and she shivered despite the warmth of the room. Then, as Guy whirled her around under the scented bouquets that hung in perfumed clouds from the chandeliers, Nell forgot everything but the romantic atmosphere of the moment. Outside, she could hear nightingales singing and the air seemed charged with anticipation. Enchanted by the reception she had received, she spoke with a certain wistfulness. "It's easy to forget the outside world here at Bel-Ami. It's a house that casts a magic spell."

"I adore it."

"But it isn't the real world, Guy. It's fairyland. You of all the Nonancourts should understand how different it is from Paris. There are strikes and people with no work and no money and everyone trying to make a fast fortune. Sometimes I get so tired of it all I wish I was a thousand miles away. Then I come here and everything seems so . . . unreal."

"I thought you were very happy in the city."

"My work's interesting, of course, one week helping to design a palace at Auteuil for the Maharajah of Baroda, another week planning the restoration of a Louis XIV house in Versailles. I love the variety and coming up with ideas, but making homes for the rich isn't reality."

"Your real life will begin once you're married. From that moment on you'll find your way and work for a purpose. Come, I have something special to share with you."

Nell followed him out of the ballroom and through the conservatory to the garden.

"Where are we going?"

Without replying, Guy hurried her through the Italian garden to a bower overhung with honeysuckle, climbing roses, and jasmine. The scent was intoxicating and as she followed him inside, Nell was enchanted by the beauty of the place.

"This is a truly wonderful bower. Was it built by the original owner of the house for her lover?"

"No, I built it for you. I wanted to propose to you here, so you would always remember the moment, even when you were old."

"I love you so much, Guy."

"I know I have no money and that my future will always be here on my brother's estate, but it's not such a bad thing. When we have enlarged the lodge, we shall have a comfortable place to spend the rest of our lives. It is not Bel-Ami, but it can be that 'real home' you crave. And most important of all, we shall be together."

Nell thought of Hadley, who was going to spend her future in a house built by one of the Bavarian royal family. Hadley always landed on her feet and always would, but whether she would ever be happy in her well-thought-out marriage was another question. Nell was a woman governed by her heart and not her head, and her heart clearly dictated that she spend her life with Guy in his cottage under the eaves. She closed her eyes, praying she could be a good wife, able to put the disappointment of her childlessness behind her. Impulsively she kissed Guy on the mouth, passion igniting. If only she could let him love her—now—it would take away all her fears forever.

"I accept your proposal."

"You've made me the happiest man in France."

"You'll have to be patient with me. You know how scared I am at the thought of making love."

Nell gasped as Guy grasped her around the shoulders and kissed her on the lips. When she leaned back against the flowers of the bower, her dress was pulled down and her breasts were exposed. She felt Guy's hands on her naked breasts, twirling the nipples. She writhed with longing, pleasure, and an odd feeling that had taken over her body, making her dizzy. To her surprise, Guy rose abruptly, straightened her clothing, and led her outside into the moonlight.

"We had best return to the ballroom and make our happy announcement. Oh, I almost forgot the most important thing. My dearest Nell, this is for you. Mother let me choose it from the family jewel box."

Nell gazed at a ring of rose diamonds and pearls in the form of a flower with leaves, stamens, and petals in different stones. Putting it on her finger, she waltzed instead of walked back toward the château.

"The ring looks very old."

"It belonged to Louise, my grandmother. Mother believes it will inspire you and bring you luck. That was a strange coincidence, wasn't it, that Mother chose Grandmother's dress for you and I chose her ring? We both see in you echoes of her personality, and perhaps we hope you will bring a new grace and honor to our family, as she did."

Nell held his hand and together they reentered the ballroom, where the orchestra was playing the tango.

On seeing his brother's radiant face, Charles stepped forward to make the announcement. "Ladies and gentlemen, I have something very special to tell you. Tonight Guy and Nell have become officially engaged. May I wish you both every happiness and may we at Bel-Ami be privileged to share a little of your joy."

Nell kissed Charles on the cheek, conscious of the pain in his eyes. When the applause had died down, Charles led her to the floor, while Guy went to join his mother on the terrace.

"You know, Maman, I am the very happiest man you have ever met."

"You're also the luckiest! Women like Nell are hard to find in these modern times. Ninety-nine out of every hundred would have chosen Charles because they love titles and handsome men."

"I'm lucky, but so is Nell. I shall love her for the rest of my days to the exclusion of everything else except breathing."

Guy and his mother were still chatting happily when Arlette appeared. She had had too much champagne and was looking very angry.

"You can sit there laughing while my heart breaks. How *can* you be so cruel?"

"Don't spoil a beautiful evening, Arlette."

"I'm so sorry, madame, but I loved Guy and gave myself to him. Now I find I am rejected, and it's hard."

"You're a married woman, you must forget the past."

"I can't and I won't."

Arlette burst into tears. Then she turned to Guy with a steely gaze.

"I was your friend for a long time, Guy, and our, shall we say, affection was deep. But now my love for you has been replaced by a hatred equally deep. Consider me your enemy, Guy. And the enemy of that woman you've chosen, too. I shall do everything I can to hurt her and to destroy once and for all her romantic notions of love and being mistress of Bel-Ami."

Guy looked with hard eyes at his former mistress.

"You're drunk, Arlette. You know perfectly well that my wife can never be mistress of Bel-Ami."

"She'll pretend she is. Why else would she put on such concern for Charles? She's the type to take over the world if she gets half a chance."

"Perhaps Bel-Ami was what *you* wanted so much. Perhaps that is why you're so angry at your loss. Well, I can assure you it is not what my fiancée wants. Nell is in love with me, not this house. Now, why don't you ask Henri to take you upstairs? You're obviously very tired."

Arlette ran and buried her face in her husband's chest. With a resigned shrug in Guy's direction, Henri took her upstairs, returning to the ballroom minutes later to ask his always-available mistress to dance.

Nell, a star among the luminaries in attendance, shared the glow of her happiness generously with all the gathered guests. Having worked her way through the crowd of well-wishers, she found herself in the company of Marc de Villalonga, the handsome and charismatic son of a Spanish nobleman and a French princess. After extending his congratulations, he explained his impromptu appearance at the château. He was visiting the area from his mansion in Paris and had been invited to the ball with the party of Henri de Saumur. Though Nell was taken aback to learn of his friendship with Arlette, Marc received her warmly. In light of his open, friendly manner, Nell could hardly turn down his invitation to dance. Taking her in his arms, Marc whirled Nell around the ballroom floor, talking of things he imagined would interest her, to bring the spark of animation he so admired to her eyes. He wondered if she had any idea of the effect she had on people when she spoke.

When the orchestra ended the waltz with a flourish, Marc found himself reluctant to give up his partner. Nell took a step back.

"I've so enjoyed dancing with you, Count Villalonga."

"Call me Marc. All my friends do and I hope to be a friend of yours and Guy's in the future."

Nell smiled, pleased by this tall, dignified young man with the glowing black eyes and the aura of proud Castile.

"Tell me about your house in Paris."

"It was originally owned by a countrywoman of mine, the Spanish dancer and courtesan Carolina Otero. Someday I will invite you there, but for now we must return to Guy before he takes an intense dislike to me."

At that moment Arlette charged into the ballroom and looked challengingly into Marc's eyes.

"You said you'd save this dance for me. *She's* already stolen *Guy*. Are *you* going to fall for her too?"

Nell swept Arlette aside with a dazzling smile. "Do go back to bed, Madame de Saumur. You're a married woman, and you must try to remember it. All the handsome men who once loved you have had to find new interests in life. It's the same way when every beautiful woman marries."

"Stay out of this, Miss Ellerman!"

Nell turned with a shy smile to Marc. "I promised to show you the water lillies. Let's go right now and see them by moonlight."

Arlette called her disapproval across the room. "Guy won't like it—he's very jealous, you know. At least he was very jealous of *me*."

Nell shrugged disinterestedly. "Then we'll take him with us, won't we, Marc? Good night, Arlette. Sleep well."

When they had seen the water lilies for which Bel-Ami was famous, Marc returned to his friends. He was remembering every nuance of expression on Nell's face, every moment when her eyes had lighted with pleasure or anger. Smiling wryly, he wondered if he would ever see her again. Or would her marriage to Guy make her simply a tantalizing dream that would haunt him for the rest of his days?

In the small hours, when the guests had gone and the château was deserted but for staff clearing the ballroom and dining hall, Nell lay in bed going over the events of that night. She could not sleep. Why had she accepted Guy's proposal without knowing whether or not she could ever be a real wife to him? The all-too-familiar fear of sex filled her with apprehension. Suddenly energized by her anxiety, she decided to grasp the nettle and find out once and for all if the fear was justified.

Slipping a wrap over the pale satin of her dressing gown, she hurried downstairs and across the courtyard. Her heart was thundering wildly as she ran in the direction of the cottage, through a field of scarlet poppies. On entering, she barred the door and wondered distractedly if she dared go ahead with her plan. Then, looking around the room and knowing without a doubt that this was where she wanted to spend the rest of her life, she told herself she had no alternative but to find out what Annabelle Ellerman was really like as a woman.

Nell made coffee, found some croissants, warmed them, and put strawberry preserve in a pot. Then she carried the tray upstairs and entered the bedroom under the eaves, surprised to see Guy sitting up in bed, wide-awake and obviously deep in thought.

"I brought breakfast for us both. I hope you don't mind, Guy."

He saw tension and desire passing through the expressive eyes and watched as Nell poured the coffee, noting the tremor in her hands.

"I'm delighted to see you, Nell, but why did you come?"

"I want to make love. I need to know if I can."

"You can't just set yourself a test like that. It could take weeks to adjust to the feelings love brings. Believe me, it's something that takes time for any woman."

Nell finished her coffee and rose from the bed. Slowly, deliberately, she unfastened the satin ribbons of her dressing gown, dropping it on the floor so she was naked before him. As he looked at her in admiration, she felt her cheeks turning scarlet and stammered her anxiety in a tiny, low voice. "Please make love to me, Guy. I want to begin to adjust to those feelings."

He put the tray on the floor and led her to the bed, gazing at her magnificent breasts, her tiny waist, her long muscular legs. Fire burned within him and he threw off his clothes and leapt under the sheets at her side.

"It will be best if we don't make love completely at first. Today we can just start to get to know each other's bodies by touch and taste and feel."

He ran his hands over her breasts, desire welling in him as he bent his head and smelled the feminine scent of her body. It was almost impossible to control his desire, and as he moved from her breasts to titillate her stomach, her thighs, and her inner folds, he was overtaken by emotion. Pushing her legs apart, he exposed her to the light, his hands moving expertly over the delta of Venus and then into the warm, wet core of feeling. As his fingers excited her, Nell tried to push him away, but he held her down and brought her to a climax of pleasure. Then, exhausted by the effort of controlling his longing to plunge inside her, he fell to her side, panting like an animal in heat.

Nell lay with her body touching his as if unconscious, her chest rising and falling, her eyes tightly closed. It was some time before she moved. Then she bent her head over his lips and kissed him. Slowly, as if in a dream, she tasted his chest, his stomach, and the rigid warmth of his penis. The hardness of it and the masculine scent of his body excited her and she rubbed her breasts against him, crying out when he pushed her away.

"Dear God, Nell, do you think I'm made of stone? What are you trying to do?"

"I'm trying to get you to love me as I want to be loved. I want to know if I can stand having a man inside me, because the thought of it scares me to death."

Abandoning all control, Guy pushed her back on the bed, excited by the intake of her breath and the sudden fear in her eyes. He began to kiss her with all the aggression and force that had attracted Nell to him in the first place. Then he mounted her, positioning himself ready to enter her, despite her sudden cries of fear.

"I changed my mind! I don't want to try to make love. Let me go, Guy, please let me go."

He closed his eyes, and whispered gently, "Too late, my love, too late."

Entering her body, he had to struggle to hold

Nell down as she fought to elude him. Her screams filled the room and he wondered anxiously if they could be heard at the house.

"No, please, I don't want to do this. I don't like it, I. . . ."

Suddenly her voice fell to a husky whisper and she began to move with his body.

"Oh, Guy, I feel so strange . . . Do that again, Guy. Do it again . . . oh, Guy, I feel as if I'm falling off a cliff."

In the pale light of dawn, Nell became the woman she had longed to be, her back arching in orgasm as Guy filled her with love. Then, with tears of relief in her eyes, she burrowed into his arms.

"I love you, Guy! I love you to death! I am a whole woman—I truly am!"

Wiping the sweat from his forehead, he smiled down at her.

"I'd best check your womanliness again in a little while. In the meantime, we'll sleep for an hour. I don't know about you, but all this excitement has tired me."

"Hold me tight."

He began to stroke her cheeks and to kiss the long curly hair.

"Now you can forget all your fears, Nell. Think only of the future and how you and I can live on my small salary. If you need to worry about something, worry about that. For me, you're the perfect woman and I told you a long time ago I am the best man for you. We shall be poor, but I promise you we shall be the happiest pair in France."

— 5 —

PARIS–BAVARIA, AUTUMN–
WINTER 1930–1931

BUNNY HAD GIVEN up her job at the American
embassy two and a half months after starting it.
The catering business she had begun on a shoestring was flourishing, despite the current eco-
nomic malaise. Bunny was now thinking like a
businesswoman. She knew she was lucky to be
living in France, a country much less affected by
the recession than England or America. The routine of most French society women precluded
even thinking about cooking, but since the war,
domestic labor had been impossible to find. Determined to cling to the old ways, the women
rose at eight, breakfasted, then saw masseurs,
midinettes, couturiers, and fitters. These were
followed by visits from bankers and brokers,
lunch, a rest, then lovers from four to five. Bunny
had wisely made her forte romantic and spectacular dinners for two, and this turned out to be an
astute move. From the start, she had made her
prices the highest in Paris, a seemingly insane
decision, but it was based on Horace Ellerman's
dictum that the rich liked to be seen to pay.
After the slow early days, the enterprise had
gathered momentum with alarming speed and

Bunny had been obliged to take on an assistant, known to everyone as the Orphan Severine.

Severine was two months younger than her employer, a small, dark, agile girl from the countryside of Calvados. She had applied for the post and won it in the face of stiff competition, by demonstrating with great skill how to grind huge blocks of chocolate by hand. From Severine's talented hands came the most perfect pastries Bunny's clients had ever tasted, though she had no idea how to cook meat, fish, or fowl. At first, she refused absolutely to learn, and Bunny, admiring the young woman's mulish streak, had let her be. Now, left to her own devices, Serverine was learning as fast as Bunny could teach her. She could barely read or write, but had a prodigious memory for recipes and everything else that interested her. Dishonest tradesmen who tried to deliver underweight were given a crack on the head with the soup ladle and her admiration for her employer bordered on idolatry.

Severine watched as Bunny opened the morning mail. This was always an uncertain time of day, because if there were too many bills, Bunny went into a decline. If there was a letter from Scotland or the confirmation of an important contract for dinner or lunch, Bunny would sing for the rest of the day. Severine made coffee and put a mug of it in front of her employer, topping it with cream and spooning in Demerara just as she liked it.

"Well, are we going to tremble all day or sing?"

"You know, Severine, you must be the rudest employee in Paris. I can't think why I like you so much."

Severine beamed at what she considered a great compliment.

"News must be good, then."

"Jack's coming to take me to Hadley's wedding. He arrives the day after tomorrow. We have a confirmation from the Duc de Chambord for lunch for twelve on Friday and the Montmorencys for dinner on Monday. You'll have to do that one on your own while I'm away."

"Don't worry. I can do everything that has to be done."

Bunny read the rest of the mail.

"What time's your new dress going to be ready, miss?

"This afternoon, though I still don't know if I was right spending all that money on frivolity. After all, I have trunkfuls of things still unpacked."

"Of course you were right. You can't wear something old for a wedding. Your sister'd call you 'Poor Bunny' again and you'd not like that one bit."

"That's why I went to Monsieur Patou. He's promised to transform me and I hope he knows what he's talking about."

"He's a live one, so they say. You just mind he doesn't try to get his maleness in you or you'll be transformed in a way you didn't bargain for."

"Severine!"

Severine threw back her head and laughed so raucously that soon Bunny was laughing with her. Then they sat in the kitchen working out the menu for lunch for six that day and the rose dinner to be served to two lovers in an apartment in the exclusive Avenue Foch in the evening. For the occasion Bunny had ordered the room to be decorated with pink roses and the table to be a vision of loveliness with an antique lace cloth, Moorish copper cutlery, and an exotic menu that included *truites en chemise, riz au safran,* chicken with truffles, and a soufflé of orchid petals with frangipane trimmings. The dinner would be a sensation, as all her specials were. Bunny smiled—her new life was under way.

* * *

Patou was suave, theatrical, and enigmatic. Over six feet tall, he had started his career as a Zouave in one of the celebrated French regiments in Africa. Now he presided over the salon in the Rue St. Florentin, a perfectly groomed figure with luminous gray eyes, dark hair, and the charisma of a dedicated ladies' man. Looking at his watch, he saw that it was close to two, when Miss Ellerman was coming. He would be seeing her personally. He was always a favorite of both her sisters, and being commissioned to design Hadley's wedding gown hadn't come as a surprise. Until three weeks previously, however, he had never met Bunny. Patou smiled at the memory of her nervousness. "I'm the plain one of the family," she had said, "but for my sister's wedding I want to look as good as I possibly can. Do you think you could work a miracle on me, Monsieur Patou, just for one day?" The designer had done better than that. Viewing the transformation of Bunny Ellerman as a personal challenge, he had used all his experience in deciding how best to change her, making a list of her good points—perfect legs, a beautiful skin, and a voluptuous figure that had once been plump, but had been pared down by overwork. Her eyes were lovely, but hidden behind glasses. Her hair needed styling. But, to the experienced couturier, these external flaws were easily remedied. The problem, for Patou, was redesigning the youngest Ellerman's self-concept. Bunny still thought of herself as fat and plain. She walked with her head down, as if ashamed of something, and was given to hiding in corners whenever she could to elude attention. A gambler of legendary dimension, Patou had decided to play his talent and knowledge of women against Bunny's inferiority complex. He knew he could transform the ugly duckling into a swan.

Bunny entered the showroom with its gray-and-beige staircase and amber mirrors. As Patou stepped toward her, she looked from him to the portrait of the designer painted in white tie and tails by his friend de Noyer de Segonzac. He had changed very little, only growing more distinguished and elegant with the passing years. She held out her hand to greet him.

"I hope I'm not late."

"You are never late, Miss Ellerman, and I am delighted to see you. We have much to do."

"I put aside two and a half hours for my fittings and that lesson you promised me."

Patou handed her a booklet with fabric swatches, drawings, and written instructions.

"I prepared this to help you choose colors for your clothes."

Bunny leafed through the manual, blushing with pleasure at the time he had spent thinking of her. Impulsively she bent forward to kiss Patou's cheeks. "Thank you for taking so much trouble over me."

Patou beamed. "For the wedding I am dressing you in cream silk and flannel, a suit and cloak with blouse to go under, and a matching hat. You are to wear very high heels with that outfit and at all times when you wish to be fashionably dressed. You must also try to keep to certain colors. The emeralds and fuchsias that Nell loves are not for you, nor are the hard blues and violets that Hadley adores. I have decided for the moment that you must dress in pink, cream, or gray. You can also wear black and white, but should avoid other colors until we have experimented with them."

Entranced by his authority, Bunny made notes in the booklet. She became alarmed only when Patou insisted she change her hairstyle.

"My friend Jack Cameron likes me the way I am."

"We shall not change you very much, but your hair needs shaping to make it look thicker. The coiffeur is waiting below with the makeup artist. When they have demonstrated their ideas, we shall go through your clothes."

Bunny watched as an expert coiffeur cut her hair and put it into a style very similar to the one she had always had, except that a side parting replaced the center one she had favored so long. Liking what she saw, she smiled with relief that she had not been made to look like someone else. But still, that small change made quite a difference. The makeup artist replaced her cherry lipstick with a dusky pink, used a swansdown puff to apply amber rouge to her cheeks, and worked closely on her eyes. Bunny was delighted to see that her eyes looked bigger and bluer, her whole face more alive. When the fitter brought the outfit and helped her into it, she stood in silence, wondering what Jack Cameron would think when she set eyes on the new Bunny Ellerman. She turned to Patou, shaking her head in wonderment.

"You really *did* work a miracle!"

"What I did was to show you just how beautiful you are. You simply didn't realize it before."

"Trouble is, I can't see without my glasses."

"You must ask your friend the Duke of Fife to hold you arm when you enter the church for the wedding. He will enjoy that." Bunny nodded absently, her eyes riveted on the sleek silhouette reflected in the gilt-edged, full-length mirror.

"In case you're still wondering how your friend the duke will react to the changes, rest assured that he expected them. And even *encouraged* them. You see, your friend asked me to make you a gift, and I have carried out his wishes. Mireille, help Miss Ellerman out of the suit and bring the Cameron order. And my own gift if it is ready."

Bunny cried out from sheer delight when Patou presented her with a silk georgette blouse in sugar pink, the jabot and cuffs frilled and flounced in the cavalier style.

"How beautiful! Can I put it on right now?"

"Of course you can. It is a small gift from me to celebrate your transformation."

"What did Jack order for me? He never said anything about it."

"He came here when he knew you had been invited to your sister's wedding and I had the impression he knew precisely what would suit you."

Cameron's order was brought, a white silk shantung outfit, the pleated skirt and fitted bodice lined with lavender blue. The other dress was a breathtaking evening gown of camellia-pink satin, its tiny bodice held by a single strap of diamante-trimmed rolled silk that resembled a snake as it trailed from shoulder to waist and then across the billowing skirt. It was the most beautiful dress Bunny had ever seen and she stood looking at it in awe, wondering if she would ever dare wear it.

"Did Jack really order that for me, or did you help him to choose it?"

"He said he wanted pink satin and very glamorous. I showed him two or three ideas and he chose this one."

"I just can't believe it. It doesn't seem like my kind of thing at all."

"He is in love with you, Miss Ellerman, and thinks you an exquisite woman. He is right. You really must try to learn that you can be anything you want to be in life, strong or weak, good or bad, plain or pretty. It is all in the mind, you see."

"Not all of it, though I have to admit I've never felt very pretty in the past."

"This afternoon, I wish you to practice a new walk. It is not elegant to hang the head and gaze at the floor all the time. Anya will show you how to do it and you must copy her. Then, each morning, practice for one-half hour when you rise until you don't need to practice anymore."

Bunny left the salon, her mind in a whirl. First she walked in the wrong direction. Then, remembering where she was going, she hurried to the cabstand near the Ritz and gave her address. Every few minutes, she looked at her watch. She had allocated two and a half hours to the meeting with Patou and had stayed well over that time. Now she had work to do and money to earn. Obviously, if the "new Bunny" needed time for frivolity, she'd have to schedule it more carefully. She leaned back with a sigh and closed her eyes, unable to resist thinking of the outfits Patou had shown her. She had been overcome by the glamour of Cameron's gifts and conscious for the first time that his image of her was very different from her own. Taking a mirror from her purse, Bunny stared at her reflection. Hadley and Nell had been beautiful all their lives and given to wild extravagance. She had been plain and given to economics. It was going to take some time to get used to being pretty. Bunny slipped the mirror into her bag. The question was, how would Cameron take to the transformation? Though she would rather have died than admit it, she was longing for him to be dazzled.

Nell arrived in Paris the following morning from her cottage in the country. Despite her plan to marry Guy in the summer, she had decided to retain the property. Once settled at Bel-Ami, she would give up her work, but the cottage would always be a useful base near Paris—and a much cheaper lodging than the Ritz Hotel. Guy's salary, while ample for two people dedicated to the idea of living as cheaply as one, would stretch only so far.

As soon as Nell's feet touched the pavement,

she hurried to Bunny's apartment to meet her sister and Cameron. Together the trio would continue on to Munich.

Expecting to be greeted at the door by an equally enthusiastic traveler, Nell was disappointed to discover that Severine would be her only welcoming committee. She put her suitcase in the corner and hung her outfits for the wedding in Bunny's closet and settled in to wait.

Severine entered with a pot of coffee and a couple of fresh-baked croissants. She poured for them both, then arranged herself regally in Bunny's chair, much to Nell's amusement. Then she began to talk about her employer.

"Mademoiselle's looking forward to the wedding. She's had her hair done and has even been practicing walking without hanging her head, just as Patou recommended. She has to have a rose-leaf infusion when she's finished wobbling on her high heels for an hour, but she'll manage it in the end. When Mademoiselle wants something bad enough, she gets it."

Nell wondered if they were talking about the same person. The Bunny she knew wouldn't dream of wearing shoes she couldn't *run* in, never mind high heels!

"Is Monsieur Cameron due to arrive today?"

"He is, and he won't know what is happening when he sees Mademoiselle in her new clothes. She's been painting her nails over and over for days. First she paints them, then she takes the polish off, and then she does them all over again because she gets so excited that she smudges them. What with that and falling off her shoes, it's been a most exciting few days."

"What's Bunny bought for Hadley?"

"We found a set of perfume bottles made for François Coty by Lalique. Mademoiselle told me that Miss Hadley collects perfume bottles, so she'll be happy."

"I got them a *oiseau de feu* lamp that cost far too much. I'll be living on lentils for the next three months if I don't take care!"

"Come and eat with us at lunchtime, there's always plenty of food."

Nell sipped her coffee and ate a delicious warm croissant, spooning onto it some homemade blueberry jam. She was thinking how they had always laughed at Bunny's priorities. Food came first, closely followed by warmth, flowers, comfort, and a happy atmosphere. Nell looked around the bedroom with its curved art-nouveau bed and Tiffany wisteria lamp bought by Bunny at the market of the Porte de Clignancourt and repaired by a student who lived upstairs, in return for lunches for a week. He had followed that first job by rewiring the apartment and mending every appliance he could find and was now unofficial second helper in the kitchen, in return for copious amounts of soup, tarts, and coffee. Nell shook her head in puzzlement at the changes in her sister's life. One minute she had been Poor Bunny, forever falling over her own feet and apologizing for her clumsiness. The next she had learned to cook and was moving toward financial success with a granite will worthy of their father in his heyday.

The trauma of Horace Ellerman's death had propelled Hadley into marriage, of this Nell was certain. In Nell's own case, it had caused fear to poison her life. Often she was afraid of simple things, like driving her car or meeting strangers. She remained less than her usual self, her confidence depressingly low, until Guy appeared like a luminous lantern at the end of the dark tunnel. This, she knew, was the route she had to travel back to normality.

But Bunny seemed to have gained rather than lost from the tragedy. In an age of uncertainty, she had had the courage to offer an expensive

service that combined good food with romance
and reliability. Nell shook her head, so full of
admiration for her little sister she could barely
believe it.

Cameron arrived at the Ritz and moved into
his usual room. Even before he had unpacked, he
dialed Bunny's number and was invited for
tea—by the now anxious Nell. Then he called
Auzello.

"I want to know about the Ellerman bill."

"Miss Bunny paid it off in full three weeks ago
and was given our receipt."

"And what was the total?"

"Though it's hardly customary to give out that
sort of information, I know you have Miss Ellerman's best interests at heart. The figure was
three thousand, two hundred and eighty dollars.
Miss Annabelle contributed seven hundred, Miss
Hadley's check was for one thousand, two hundred, and Miss Bunny paid the rest."

Cameron noted the amount. Bunny had remained adamant in her refusal to accept his
money, and damned if she didn't beat him to it.
Yet, he still felt responsible for the debt, having
announced his intention to pay. Cameron decided to invest an equivalent amount in shares
for her, shares he could hand over when she was
no longer in need of scruples about accepting
gifts from him.

Cameron arrived at Bunny's apartment at four
and found Severine in a foul humor and scowling
blackly. She had been reminded that in the morning she was due to have her annual bath and was
moaning that it would take a full day to recover
from the experience. In common with most of
the French, Severine normally washed herself in
sections, an "upper" or a "lower" as the need
arose. Only once a year was the cover removed
from the bath, the potted plants put on the floor,

and her skin totally immersed. To Cameron's amusement, the girl's teeth began to chatter at the very thought of the ordeal ahead, providing him with the perfect opportunity to tease her.

"Will I come and wash your back tomorrow?"

"Certainly not! Miss Annabelle has already threatened to do it. There won't be a gram of dirt left on me to keep the fleas away."

"Ah, so it's vulnerability you fear. No wonder Mademoiselle finds you such compatible company" Cameron began to pace the room.

"Is something wrong, Monsieur? You seem to be ill-at-ease."

"Where *is* Bunny?"

"She will return soon. She went to get milk and flowers. She said these were not fresh enough to put on the table for your visit."

"Did she like her new clothes?"

Nell brightened—another hint at the changed Bunny.

Severine rolled her eyes in mock exasperation. "Mademoiselle has tried them all on at least ten times, and every time she jumps up and down and screams from sheer delight. Monsieur le Boulou, who lives below, hammers on the ceiling with his walking stick for silence."

"She's a fine lassie when she's excited."

"It's hard to imagine her excited about clothes, though," Nell mused. "Perhaps she's finally found a substitute for chocolate mousse. Or perhaps she's finally grown to be more like her sisters."

"Just remember please to praise her hair. She has been worried in case Monsieur Cameron does not like the change."

"I'd like her if she had a feather in each ear and one up her arse, and she knows it."

"Pardon me?" gasped a startled Nell.

"I said I'd like Bunny whatever she wore."

Cameron was gazing out of the window when he heard Bunny's footsteps at the apartment door.

Turning, he looked in wonder at the new hairstyle, the high-heeled shoes, the shapely legs in their beige silk stockings, and the baby-pink outfit she had bought that afternoon. It was hard to assess exactly what had changed, but suddenly Bunny was not just pretty, but radiant, beautiful, perfect. The words to express his delight eluded him and he could only rush forward and hug her to his chest.

"I don't know who you are, mademoiselle, but you're gorgeous."

Bunny kissed him on the mouth, thrilled to feel his heart pounding against her own and relieved at his reaction. Cameron loved the changes, as she did, and though Nell had been shocked into silence, the Duke of Fife was all that mattered for the moment.

Two days later, Nell, Bunny, and Cameron stepped off the train at the station in Munich. It was a gray autumn day, with low clouds obscuring the jagged blue mountains all around the city. They were walking toward the barrier when they heard Hadley calling to them.

"Oh, Nell ... Bunny ... I'm *so* glad you're here. Give me a big hug and a kiss."

Radiant in a long cloak of blond lynx, with amber studs in gold settings at her ears, Hadley had enameled her nails blood red to match the trousers and cashmere pullover she had put on that morning.

Nell and Bunny exchanged glances. As always when they had not seen their sister for a few weeks, they were astounded by her impact, her energy, and the sheer beauty of her being.

Everyone started talking at once, and as Cameron listened he envied them their closeness. He had been an only son, always craving sisters and brothers, but having to make do with some distant cousins he had seen only twice a year. In the

summer he had gone alone to the Highland Games,
watching brawny Scots throwing cabers and enjoying the shrieking lament of the bagpipes that
were as dear to his heart as they were offensive
to the English. In time he had come to enjoy his
solitude, until the moment when he had met
Bunny. Since then he had longed for her company every minute of every day. He listened as
Hadley replied to Nell's probing.

"Children? I'm not intending to have any for
years."

"How are you planning to avoid them?"

"I've been to the doctor and if I can get the
knack of putting the device in, there'll be no
babies until I'm sure I want them."

Cameron glanced at Bunny and saw her em-
barrassment. She wanted a baker's dozen and
was old-fashioned enough to feel less than comfortable with Hadley's ultramodern ideas. He patted her hand and settled to watching the scenery,
while Hadley and Nell chattered on. Hadley was
telling them about her future brother-in-law.

"He's called the Baron von Allgau and he's
horrible. The first time we met he was very
disapproving of me, but Karl and I had no idea
he'd asked for a report on the Ellerman family
background."

Nell reacted with predictable annoyance. "How
did he get one?"

"He asked Ernst Dietmueller's office to investigate. You *do* remember the charming Mr. Dietmueller, don't you? Well, now he's head of a
kind of intelligence network that provides that
kind of a service in the interest of ethnic purity.
It's become very important to them to weed out
the 'undesirable elements,' which can mean any
kind of taint—from being Jewish to being crazy,
or even being a big reader of books."

Cameron listened hard. Adolf Hitler! The fa-
natic's obsession with genetic perfection had be-

come known in England and British Intelligence was already monitoring his rise to power. It was rumored that he would be the next chancellor of Germany. This, however, was the news made personal.

Hadley continued, unaware of his interest. "When the report was delivered, Karl tore it into shreds, but as soon as we got back from Paris the baron called and demanded that the marriage be canceled. Apparently the fact that I'm part Jewish on Papa's side is a matter of the greatest importance in Germany."

Nell laughed out loud.

"And did you tell them you're part Catholic and probably another couple of parts Buddhist and tap dancer too? Our family's got some very unusual ancestors, you know. Seriously, I hope Karl shoved the baron out of the door and told him never to come back."

Hadley shrugged in her usual flippant manner, determined not to let her sisters see how the incident had hurt.

"He did indeed, but Ilsa, Karl's sister, still calls. She's a pet. I just don't *think* anymore of what the baron did. Out of sight, out of mind."

"And what about Dietmueller?"

Hadley flushed. "Why do you ask about *him*?" she shot back. "I don't suppose he'll dare call again. It's as simple as that."

Hadley's face burned at the thought of the satisfaction, the curious thrill she felt when Dietmueller had tried to prevent her marriage to Karl. It was exciting to be so desired, even if the man involved brought danger and even a little fear into the peaceful luxury of her new life. Somehow that only added to the excitement.

The drive to the hotel took them along the misty green banks of the River Isar, allowing them to admire the elegant Renaissance facades of the buildings, the baroque churches with onion-shaped towers, the sound of glockenspiels ringing the hour. In the Marienplatz there were fountains and pavement cafés, tubs full of Michaelmas daisies, and men in lederhosen hurrying to work. To Hadley this was a familiar scene, but to her sisters it was a new world, far from the familiar chestnut-scented streets of Paris. Both looked warily about them, the echo of Hadley's chilling tale haunting their minds. Was their sister to be an outcast, even a target, in this picturesque near-fairyland?

At seven, when everyone had unpacked and rested briefly, Karl arrived to take them to dinner at the hunting lodge. He was obviously delighted to see them and shook hands cordially with Cameron, motioning for him to take the front passenger's seat.

"How good it is to see you again, sir. I am so glad you agreed to come."

"Call me Jack. We're about to become related, at least if I have as much luck when I propose to Bunny as you had with Hadley."

"I am indeed a lucky man."

Cameron wondered if marrying Hadley was such luck, so he spoke of general matters, unwilling to put a damper on Karl's enthusiasm.

"This is a very scenic road. Is this your land?"

"It is the public road that leads eventually to Berchtesgaden. In a few minutes we turn off to the private drive which leads to the house." Karl glanced back to make sure Nell and Bunny were engrossed in their conversation. "I hope you don't think my question too personal, but have you already made your proposition of marriage to Bunny?"

"Aye, lots of times, but she's always turned me down. I'm going to try again when I get her to Scotland."

"Did she give a good reason for her rejection?"

"She did, but not good enough to make me give up."

"I should not be so patient."

"Not many would, but my family all have the persistence of bloodhounds."

Cameron looked up to see the glorious facade of the hunting lodge, which had been floodlit for this special occasion. Entering the gilded hall, the duke frowned at the lavishness of the interior, which was not at all to his taste, though he appreciated that it had been decorated in the authentic style of the period. Turning to Bunny, he read wonder and a certain unease in her eyes.

"Well, lassie, how does this strike you?"

"It's very grand, Jack, but I wouldn't be at home here."

"Hadley's in her element."

"Nell's looking depressed."

"Well, Guy *is* penniless, after all. Nell's just been reminded, and none too subtly, that she'll have to scrimp and save for the rest of her life. She's mad about him, I know, but she isn't accustomed to the idea of of poverty. Seeing Hadley in all this splendor's probably a mite hard to bear."

When they had been shown around the property, cocktails were served. Ilsa was already there and Karl's younger brother, Joseph, arrived, late as usual, on a motorbike that had broken down twice en route from his apartment in the city center. Everyone settled happily to talking about subjects of interest, avoiding the traditional German prenuptial preoccupations of kinde, kuche, and kirche. It hadn't taken Ilsa long to realize that children, cooking, and church were as foreign to Hadley as couture originals were to her. Enchanted by the new woman in her brother's life and eager to help the couple settle, she contented herself by listening as Hadley chattered about the wedding.

"There'll be two hundred and fifty guests and

we're to marry here in the chapel, because that's the family tradition. We'll have the reception in the banqueting hall afterward, then dance till the small hours. The staff are going to roast whole oxen in a clearing in the woods and at five in the morning we'll serve breakfast and champagne. Karl and I'll be gone by then, of course."

Bunny studied the contrast between Hadley's radiant face and Nell's subdued manner.

"Where are you planning to honeymoon?"

"At the Romanelli Palace in Venice. We're going to pretend we're royalty."

Cameron watched Karl's brother intently. He had never taken his eyes off Hadley for a moment. When she talked of acting like royalty, Joseph smiled indulgently, obviously captivated by her. And captivating she was. Cameron turned his attention to the bride-to-be, assessing the changes in her since their first meeting on the ship. If anything, she was more beautiful now than she was on that voyage, but her beauty was of the dangerous variety. She was deadly beautiful, the kind of woman who would have been burned at the stake in centuries past because something in her emerald eyes tempted men to fall victim to her charm. Suddenly Bunny jumped to her feet and hurried from the room. Fearful that she was unwell, Cameron followed.

"Is anything wrong, Bunny?"

"No, I just can't stand hearing Hadley brag about her newfound wealth. It upsets Nell, and it upsets me."

"She'll change once she is settled to being married. Right now Hadley's drunk with her own success."

"She's in dreamland, Jack, and someday she's going to return to earth with a horrible bump."

Frau Hoffman had done her employer proud— the dinner was sensational. Goose-liver pâté was followed by eel soup, halibut stuffed with shrimp and asparagus, and a whole roast pig served with noodles and sour applesauce. They ate Bergkase, the mountain cheese of Bavaria. Then, with the coffee, they drank the powerful gold-flecked liqueur Karl had brought back with him from a visit to Amsterdam. Frau Hoffman served with it thin slices of baumtorte, a layered cake cooked with skill on a revolving spit. Even Bunny had to admit she was impressed by the culinary ability required to bring this tour de force off successfully.

While the guests talked and laughed, Ilsa made her good-byes.

"I must go now, Karl. I will see you in the morning. In the meantime, I pray that you and Hadley will have a fine day for your wedding."

Bunny rose when Karl's sister had gone.

"I think I too should be going, Hadley. I'm so tired I can't keep my eyes open."

Cameron shook Karl's hand and kissed Hadley's cheeks. "It was a fine dinner. You're a lucky pair to have such a cook."

"We're lucky her talents haven't settled on our waistlines," Hadley remarked tersely.

Only when their eyes met did Cameron realize for the first time, how tense Hadley was. She wanted this marriage more than anything in the world and she could not rest until it was guaranteed her. Cameron, ill-at-ease, took Bunny's arm and guided her out the door. As they stepped into the car, Nell came running after them.

"I think I'd best come with you or I'll have bags under my eyes in the morning."

On the way back to the hotel the trio sat in silence, Nell trying not to think how much she was missing Guy. In France she always felt at home. In Germany she felt inexplicably uncomfortable. She thought of the bedroom under the eaves of the cottage and the sweet love they had made there. Tempted though she was, Nell knew without any doubt that she would not trade Guy's little home for all the castles in Bavaria. Content with her life and her future, she fell asleep on Bunny's shoulder.

Cameron took Bunny's taut hand in his, conscious of the tension that gripped her. When she finally spoke, quietly so as not to disturb Nell, he understood what had been on her mind.

"I just *hate* the thought of that man asking for a report on our family background. It scared me and it scared Hadley too. That flippancy has always been her response to fear. I don't like the idea at all, Jack. I really believe my sister could be in danger. Men like that are fanatics in my opinion."

"That they surely are, Bunny."

"I'll stay for the wedding, but then I want to get right back to Paris."

"I'll change our tickets first thing and we'll go on the night train. I'll book a sleeper."

Bunny looked uncertain.

"You'll have to say we're married. They don't allow people to book sleepers who aren't."

"I'm forty years old and no railway clerk's going to stop me having my way."

Bunny smiled. That she surely knew.

In the morning, the mist cleared, and though it was cold, the sun shone over the mountains. By ten the sisters were in the hall, ready to leave for the lodge. Each waited impatiently, thinking the same thoughts: the first of them to walk, to talk, and to date, was now the first to marry. Hadley was still number one in the family, just as she had been from the beginning.

Cameron was in his room putting on a morning suit that smelled of mothballs. He shrugged: who gave a damn? He would be relieved when this extravaganza was over and he and Bunny could get back to Paris. In her apartment he would eat some wonderful lunches and take her out to dinner whenever she was free. He would kiss her as they lingered under the bridges of the Seine and do his best to resist carrying her off by force to his castle on the island.

Hadley was being fussed over by three maids and Ilsa, who was already weeping copiously from the sheer "loveliness of it all." Admiring the dress Patou had made, Hadley was enthralled. It was, as he had promised, a dream outfit, its billowing skirt appliquéd with ice-blue cabbage roses. The waist was tiny, the bustline high, the sleeves long and tight. Over each ear she was wearing circlets of lily of the valley, the veil attached to these and falling like a white cloud around her shoulders. She watched as Ilsa put the priceless Kohler diamond necklace around her throat, fingering the stones that fell from the triple choker in a waterfall of droplets that covered the cleavage of the dress.

Karl was standing with his brother in the family chapel, waiting for the bride to arrive. He was nervous and kept turning to his brother to check that Joseph had the ring. When he heard Hadley entering the chapel, he closed his eyes in a fervent prayer. Dear God, give us happiness and make her content with my love. Above all, I beg you never to let anything separate us.

From the vestibule Hadley inspected the chapel, now replete with decorations of yellow winter jasmine. As she walked up the aisle on Cameron's arm, she smiled at Nell and then stopped, mid-step, to stare in astonishment: was that really *Bunny?* She had never seen her sister looking so beautiful. Hadley took in every detail of the outfit, from the draped cloak lined with fox, to the silk blouse intricately tucked and pleated under the jacket. Bunny's makeup was divine, her hair a pale gold halo under the hat with its sweeping brim. Hadley's heart beat a little faster and she felt strangely disconcerted by the transformation. For as long as she could remember, Bunny had been plain, giving her and Nell a comforting feeling of superiority. Now, overnight, or so it seemed, she had changed. Hadley stepped toward the altar, angry with herself for her reaction but unable to control her feeling of jealousy. She had never in a thousand years thought that Bunny might become a rival.

When the responses had been given, the moment came for the rings to be exchanged and Hadley held out her hand, repeating the words after the priest: "With this ring I thee wed, with my body I thee worship, and with all my worldly goods I thee endow." A small voice within Hadley finished the vow of love for her: all her worldly goods amounted to very little. She could only hope to be a good wife and to give him her love and devotion, though even these gifts seemed unworthy of Karl. She looked gravely at the ring on her finger, then at the matching one on Karl's. Then, as the priest motioned for them to embrace, she raised her veil and kissed her new husband on the mouth.

Bells pealed a carillon as the couple walked together from the church. Photographers leapt to take pictures and retainers from the estate threw posies of scented woodruff and myrtle. A farmer walking by on the high road called a greeting and waved his hand. Finally the guests were grouped together for the official wedding photograph. Ilsa and her children stood at Karl's side with Joseph and the cousins from Schloss Durgan. Nell towered above Bunny, who stood with Cameron, her hand entwined in his. Bunny was smiling contentedly and Cameron was leaning down to whisper to her.

"I can't wait to see you in your pink satin."

"I still haven't figured out why you chose such an outfit for me. It didn't seem like my kind of thing at all."

Nell, who had overheard, turned to her sister and spoke with unusual sharpness. "Don't give us any of this humble act! After today, I don't ever want to hear you belittling yourself. That outfit of yours made me feel like your poor relation. As for Hadley, well, she nearly fell over her train when she saw you."

Bunny threw her arms around Nell's neck. "Say it again, say it again!"

"Like hell I will. You know what you did today—you nearly stole the show from Hadley, and she may never forgive you for it."

For the ball, the banqueting hall had been transformed with antique lanterns shaded in rose. The walls were hung with scented verbena and two orchestras were taking it in turn to provide continuous music. Outside in the grounds, servants were roasting oxen over fire pits and everywhere guests in impeccable evening dress were waltzing to the music of Strauss.

Hadley was in black velvet, sleek, tailored, and sensational. The high neck of the dress contrasted with her white-blond hair and the perfect suntan the dress exposed to the waist by its exotic styling. At her shoulder she wore a single red camellia that matched precisely the shade of her lipstick. At her side, Nell was in emerald silk, a billowing dress set off by a necklace of gold and crystal. Bunny had not yet appeared.

Hadley was about to take a glass of champagne to Karl, when she saw her sister entering on Cameron's arm. First Bunny had wowed them in Patou cream silk and fox, undoubtedly the most elegant creature at the ceremony. Now she had decked herself out in gleaming sugar-pink satin, the top hanging perilously over the edge of her breasts, a diamanté snake writhing sinuously from shoulder to hem. Hadley noticed that some of the men had stopped dancing and were staring in

admiration at the vision in pink. One hurried
forward and kissed Bunny's hand.

"That is the most beautiful dress I ever saw,
Miss Ellerman. May I compliment you on it."

"Thank you very much, sir."

Bunny glanced over to Hadley, secretly delighted that her sister was momentarily disconcerted. The tortoise had given the hare a preliminary warning that it was capable of a dangerous
turn of speed. For the first time in her life,
Bunny could not suppress a tiny smile of satisfaction.

From seven to midnight they danced and drank
champagne. Bunny kept all her dances for Cameron. Hadley danced with Karl and his uncle,
who had traveled from Vienna for the occasion.
Nell danced with everyone, her energy and vi-
vacity stealing the very breath away from the
staid citizens of Munich.

When midnight chimed, Karl and Hadley disappeared into his car. The guests saw them off
from the floodlit terrace, throwing rose petals on
the Mercedes and laughing delightedly as horse-
shoes clanked on the rear bumpers.

Cameron was smoking a cigar on the terrace
and waiting for Bunny to get her wrap, when he
saw a sudden movement in the rhododendron
bushes at the back of the lodge. Curious, he walked
over and stood looking up into the woods. Soldiers! There were soldiers watching the property down the entire length of the drive. What
did it mean? He moved inside and told Bunny to
go and find Nell.

"Get ready to leave, and fast. Something's happened that I have to tell the Hoffmans about. I'll
explain in the car."

Minutes later, Bunny, Nell, and Cameron were
racing back to Munich. Surprised to have been
virtually ordered to leave with them, Nell turned

to Cameron. "What's wrong, Jack? What happened to upset you?"

"There were soldiers watching the lodge from the woods. If I recognized the uniform correctly, they were personnel from a new unit called the S.S., a group that, I believe, answers directly to Ernst Dietmueller."

Nell's face paled and Bunny tightened her grip on Cameron's hand.

"What does it mean, Jack?"

"It means Dietmueller's making good on his promise. He's watching Hadley as he said he would, and stalking her as he promised on the ship. It's ironic that she's come to live here in the very seat of his power. I don't like it, Bunny, I can tell you."

In his office in the city center, Dietmueller was receiving the first reports on the Kohler wedding. As he looked at the photographs and read the guest list, he smiled. Hadley had married, but she had not escaped him. In fact, it was to the contrary. She was here to stay, and he would first show her his power and then play with her like a cat with a mouse. Dietmueller thought with relish that for him the game had only just begun.

II

THE YEARS OF DISCOVERY, 1932–1934

— 6 —
SCOTLAND, SPRING 1932

BUNNY AND CAMERON were resting comfortably in a first-class compartment of the *Royal Scot,* the fastest train from London to Edinburgh. She was in a pensive mood and thinking of Hadley, who was about to leave with Karl for yet another long journey of exploration. Hadley's days of loneliness were over and her letters were full of plans for the future.

But what would Bunny's own future hold? She had finally accepted Cameron's invitation to vist Scotland, because despite the success of her business she had come to realize that something was lacking in her life, something deep and satisfying. Somehow Jack's imtermittent presence was part of it, bringing on the lonely, isolated feelings that suddenly plagued Bunny despite her busyness. Never did Bunny wallow in the past as she did on the days of Jack's departure, often wasting most of the afternoon reminiscing about family outings now gone forever. The visit to Lochalsh would give her the chance to make some decisions, to see if she could accept the life Jack had offered so many times and the love he so obviously wanted to give. Sure that Cameron would propose again during her holiday, Bunny searched her mind for an answer that would not come. As she had been since the shipboard meeting, she was still torn between her need for him and the fear of dependency. Now that the inner conflict was beginning to exhaust her, she was determined that in Scotland she would stop procrastinating and make up her mind.

As they crossed the border, Bunny wondered if Cameron would be different once he reached his own home ground. She watched him gaze out at the countryside as they approached Edinburgh, as if he was drinking in every blade of grass and windswept hill. There was something very frightening about the prospect of accepting a proposal of marriage from the master of Lochalsh.

Cameron held out his hand and kissed Bunny's slim wrists as she linked her fingers in his.

"I'll wager you're regretting having left Paris."

"I am. I'm a person who needs a routine of living and who's scared of departing from it. But I want to see your home and I'm looking forward to having a holiday."

"Lochalsh isn't like the hunting lodge, you know. There's nothing frivolous about it, but I do love it. The love of home was inbred in all the Camerons. I just hope you won't freeze to death. The place is impossible to warm and sometimes we have to wear our overcoats inside as well as out."

"I'm sure it could be warmed. You just need expert advice."

"Aye, and a million pounds to do it!"

"What's Mrs. MacKay going to think of me? Particularly if my teeth are constantly chattering! You've told me so much about her, I'm kind of scared of the meeting."

Cameron shook his head. The thought of his housekeeper had sorely troubled him of late, though he had not communicated his fears to Bunny.

"She's a difficult woman. I suppose that in the end you'll either cry yourself to sleep or she will."

"Is there anything I have to remember not to say or do, any local superstitions, for example?"

"I don't think so. But the folk hereabouts *are* hard to know, so you'll have to be patient. It can take them years to give you a good-day in the street, because strangers are something they fear. They're like children, who need security and familiarity and cannot depart from it. That you can understand, at least."

"At the moment I understand that perfectly."

They stepped from the velvet-lined compartment of the *Royal Scot* into an old, rattling train with maple-walled interiors that had no cushioning at all. The train stopped at every station from Edinburgh, entering the Kingdom of Fife across the Forth Bridge and giving Bunny her first sight of Cameron's homeland.

Seagulls were swooping over ferries and fishing boats in the turbulent blue waters of the Firth of Forth. Quaint harbors dotted the coastline, and the names of the towns were like none she had heard before: Kirkcaldy, Lower Largo, Kilconquhar, and Pittenweem. Here and there she saw plantations of pine, larch, and spruce, destined for the paper mills of Edinburgh. And everywhere, in misty fields dotted with mayflowers and purple thistles, highland cattle with lyre-shaped horns stood watch over their newborn calves.

Bunny smiled into Cameron's anxious face, doing her best to hide her misgivings.

"I hope Mrs. MacKay's made a big lunch. I'm hungry."

"What do you think of Fife?"

"It's beautiful and mysterious and *real*. I've always been a country girl at heart, you know. I used to prefer Papa's house in the hills to the town house in Chicago. I could never stand cities for long, except for Paris."

"I'm beginning to feel the onset of galloping panic. I'm a man walking on the edge of an abyss. If you hate Lochalsh, Bunny, what am I going to do?"

As Bunny stepped from the train, she was rendered speechless by the welcoming blare of the local bagpipe band. Big men in tartan kilts walked slowly up and down the platform, playing a lively rendition of "Scotland the Brave." Then their leader stepped forward and shook hands with Cameron.

"Welcome home, sir. We had the word from Mrs. MacKay that you wanted the pipes for the young lady."

"This is Miss Clementine Ellerman. Bunny, meet Major Sullivan of the Camerons' Own Regiment."

Sullivan stood to attention, towering over Bunny with a twinkle in his eye. "Honored to meet you, Miss Ellerman."

"Thank you for the welcome, Major. I never heard the pipes before."

The soldiers looked into the eager, big blue eyes. How young the girl was! The poor wee thing would end by running home to her mother once she met Agnes MacKay. Cameron's housekeeper was known to have been in a rage ever since she had been told he was bringing Bunny back to Lochalsh. Convinced he had fallen for a fast woman, Mrs. Mac was ready to fight to the death to get rid of the newcomer. Sullivan led Cameron and his guest to the waiting gig and saluted them on their way. Then, turning to the musicians, he ordered them to play a favorite lament. It seemed a suitable tune for the occasion.

They drove through the narrow lanes, between dry stone walls, in the direction of the sea. Bunny saw fields of buttercups and wild cotton and

beaches full of violet sea poppies. The sheep
were black and gray, the rams long-haired and
fierce. She saw no people, except a shepherd in
the distance, hurrying over the brow of a hill
with his flock. Then Cameron pointed out an
ancient stone castle on the edge of the sea.

"That's Lochalsh, Bunny."

Following his gaze, she saw a craggy headland
that jutted out into the mist over the sea, linking
a small island off the sandy shoreline to the coast
by a causeway. On the island stood Lochalsh, the
castle beloved of every Cameron for centuries. It
was built of gray granite, its poniard turrets sup-
ported on rounded towers like giant tree trunks.
There were gun loops and spyholes in the walls
of the lower three floors, and windows only in
the upper stories, as befitted its fortified past.
On the walls of the courtyard Bunny saw heral-
dic designs carved out of stone, of warriors and
horses, gremlins and caryatids. The trees around
the castle were larches, the only vegetation that
could survive the cold, the gales, and the fury of
the sea. So she thought, Lochalsh is like its
owner—forbidding and awesome, but magnificent
all the same.

"It's truly impressive, Jack. I can't imagine
what it's like to live in, but it looks wonderful.
Now, hold my hand. I'm getting more nervous by
the minute."

"Before we go in, Bunny, I'd like you to know
that I've never brought a woman here to stay
before. I never wanted the place inspected or
interfered with. I like change even less than the
rest of the folk around here, though I'm the first
to admit that in the case of Lochalsh something
needs changing. I just don't know how to arrange
the place so it's more comfortable and fit for a
family. But now that you're here, I'd be happy if
you'd try to advise me."

Bunny entered the castle via the banqueting

hall, a huge bare stone chamber forty feet high at the apex of the roof. The only furniture was a refectory table that could seat a hundred, the claw-footed chairs that went with it, and some faded tapestries depicting Cameron ancestors in battle. At the center of the room was a raised hearth that would warm the place when lit, the smoke of the logs rising through a hole in the ceiling. The room smelled of damp, a familiar odor in all the great houses of the area.

Cameron hurried Bunny from the hall to his own sitting room, one of the smallest rooms in the house, and the only warm one. The walls were lined with books, the sofas were old and fat and upholstered in tawny velvet. A peat fire burned in the hearth and there was a faint scent of tweed, heather, and expensive tobacco. Outside, the wind began to howl and the trees to creak. Cameron rang the bell for Mrs. MacKay and settled Bunny in the chatelaine's chair.

"I fear there's a storm brewing. We often get them in the spring. Are you warm enough?"

"I'm just fine, Jack."

"You'll be in the tartan bedroom, where Queen Victoria once slept. She was powerful fond of the tartan and even had her knickers made of the stuff. Ah, there you are, Agnes. Come and meet Miss Ellerman and tell us what you've made for lunch. We're both as hungry as hunters."

Mrs. MacKay, who now loomed in the doorway, was six-feet-two and built like a battering ram. Her face was ruddy from long exposure to the elements and a lifelong devotion to home-brewed alcohol, which she made in a still concealed in the dungeons of the castle. Her gray hair was pulled back in a tight bun. Her eyes were dark and watchful, her lips pursed in a permanent moue of displeasure. She had, by sheer force of character, raised a family of six brothers and sisters after the untimely death of their parents, and had found them all respectable jobs, before becoming assistant cook at Lochalsh. She had married a tinker at twenty-five, but he had run off a year later, never to be seen again. Since then, Lochalsh had become Mrs. MacKay's life and nobody was going to take it from her.

Agnes MacKay inspected Bunny shamelessly, eyeing the smart tweed cloak with its fur lining, the sensible walking shoes and warm stockings. She was surprised that the girl was so young and seemingly innocent and told herself that the situation could have been worse. At least if Cameron insisted on marrying the lassie, she could be taught the ways of the house and relied on not to interfere. She shook Bunny's hand, determined to try to be friendly.

"I'm pleased to make your acquaintance, Miss Ellerman."

"It's good to meet you, Mrs. MacKay. I've heard so much about you."

"What did you hear?"

"They say no one ever won an argument with you and no one ever bested you in a fight. They also say no one ever will."

Mrs. MacKay opened her mouth and it was a full ten seconds before anything came out. At last she said, "I've put you in the tartan bedroom. That's the one reserved for royals. There's a blaze warming the room and wood aplenty in the baskets. Ring for Willie to come and bank up the fire when you need him. I'll be serving lunch at one sharp, so see that neither of you is late."

Cameron lit his pipe and smiled at the housekeeper. "What have you got for us, Mrs. MacKay?"

"There's smokies or hot cullen skink, then venison with bacon and plums. I made atholl brose too and the young lady'd best like it after all the trouble I took getting it right."

Bunny looked askance at all this, as Cameron patted the housekeeper's shoulder.

"Don't start your bullying yet, Agnes. Send Sarah up to show Miss Ellerman to her room."

"Sarah's busy—show her yourself!"

"I want Sarah. She'll be fending for my guest during her stay."

"Then I'll only have Willie to help me in the kitchen!"

"There's only two to cook for, not a regiment."

"Very well, but it'll be bashed neeps from now on, lunch and dinner, too."

When Mrs. MacKay had gone, Cameron poured himself a whiskey and sat back in his chair.

"In case you didn't understand, bashed neeps is mashed turnips. She'll be giving us those noon and night if I take Sarah away from her. She knows I hate them, so it's a serious threat."

Bunny laughed delightedly at the housekeeper's tactics.

"What were the other things she mentioned?"

"Hot cullen skink's a soup of haddock, potatoes, and onion with cream. Atholl brose's a sweet made of oatmeal, whiskey, and honey. You'll soon learn our language, Bunny. And perhaps Mrs. MacKay will learn yours, as well."

The room was large, the fire enormous, the curtains, which were drawn, of quilted triple-thickness velvet. Bunny threw them back to let in the sunlight, realizing at once why they had been shut, when an icy draft blew in through the windows. Closing them hastily, she turned to look around the room. The floor was stone-flagged and uncarpeted except for rugs on either side of the six-poster bed. The ceiling had been decorated with Tudor roses by an itinerant artisan in centuries past. The bedspread was of blue tartan, as were the window-seat covers. Bunny turned to Sarah, who was unpacking for her.

"Do all the windows in the castle let the draft in like this one?"

"Yes, ma'am. It's a cold house most of the year. We get icicles inside in the winter."

"Couldn't the windows be fixed?"

"I don't know. You'd best ask Mrs. MacKay. She knows about everything."

After a splendid lunch, Cameron took Bunny to see the estate. They rode out on stalwart horses, traveling from the shoreline to the forests inland and from the fishing stream back to the castle. The tour had to be cut short when rain came down in torrents, soaking them to the skin. Laughing and sliding on the muddy lawn, they ran back to the banqueting hall and then upstairs to their rooms to change.

Cameron called out to Bunny as he entered his bedroom, "I'll join you in five minutes, when I've washed the dirt off. Ring for tea, will you?"

She rushed to the bathroom, threw off her clothes, and stood under the hot tap, turning it full on and gazing up at the antiquated shower. But instead of the hot water she was expecting, Bunny was deluged with freezing-cold torrents. She leapt out of the shower, cursing the lack of facilities in the house. Then, having washed the mud from her feet, she put on a heavy wool dressing gown and rang for tea. Her teeth were chattering and she was furious. Was it too much to ask to have hot water in the taps in the middle of the day? She rang again, but no one answered. Minutes later Willie appeared and told her that Mrs. MacKay was resting after her efforts with the lunch and Sarah had been given the afternoon off.

Cameron appeared in a red striped dressing gown collared in raccoon that looked slightly the worse for wear. He shrugged apologetically at Bunny's raised eyebrows.

"My father wore this when he was in India in the army and I think half the rats in Kashmir ate some of the fur."

"I nearly froze to death in the shower! There's no hot water."

"Mrs. MacKay's having one of her spells of economy."

"Tell her to have her economy some other time. I don't like being dirty and I can't wash in cold water in this climate."

"You'll feel better when you've had your tea."

"I can't order tea. Sarah's been given the afternoon and off and Mrs. MacKay's resting."

Cameron sighed, unamused by his housekeeper's tactics.

"You realize, of course, that she's testing you."

"What do you mean?"

"Mrs. Mac's showing you who's boss, and me too for that matter. It's her way."

"The hell it is! Where's the kitchen?"

Cameron rose, visions of tiny Bunny and huge Mrs. MacKay battling for the keys to his kingdom filling him with alarm.

"Best not be hasty on your first day in the house."

Bunny drew herself up to her full five-feet-two.

"I need a hot drink, Jack, and I need it *now*. Or do you want me to spend my holiday in bed with the sniffles?"

Cameron followed her to the kitchen, situated in the windowless second floor of the house. In this bleak, dark room without light or modern facilities, Bunny made tea, found cake, and set out sandwiches on a tray. She ordered Willie to put the boiler on to heat the water. Then, satisfied that she had shown her independence, she followed Cameron back upstairs to her room. They were enjoying their second cup of tea when Mrs. MacKay stode into the room without knocking.

"I see you came into my kitchen and took what you wanted."

Bunny smiled pleasantly. "We were told you needed some rest."

"I don't like folk in my kitchen, miss."

"The kitchen belongs to the Camerons, not to you or me. Now, we mustn't quarrel. Jack and I are cold and wet and we needed something to warm us. That's the end of it."

"Not for me it isn't. I'll not have strangers giving orders in this house."

Cameron looked at Bunny's face, which was still and patient, while Mrs. Mac's was blood-red and sweating. Bunny spoke clearly and evenly, determined to show the housekeeper that she was not a child to be ordered about, but a guest, and one who might someday become mistress of Lochalsh.

"You're employed here, Mrs. MacKay, and I believe you're something of an expert on matters relating to Lochalsh. I see no reason for you to be difficult because I'm a guest in the house for two weeks. I need hot water for my baths and food and drink when I'm cold and hungry, and I don't think it's beyond your terms of employment to provide them. If you feel it is, well, you must say so. And, in the future, I'd like you to knock before you enter the room. If you weren't taught to do it, then I'd like you to learn how. House-guests don't like strangers in their bedrooms any more than you like strangers in your kitchen."

Cameron rose and walked to the window, turning his back on the two women as Mrs. MacKay replied, "I take orders from the master and not from his friends."

Cameron turned, his face like thunder. "Do you want me to repeat that rigmarole, Mrs. Mac? I will if you're in the mood to trifle."

She stood facing him square on like a fighting bull, furious that he was siding with Bunny against her.

"I want to know where I stand and I want to know right now."

"Then I'll tell you. I've already proposed to

Miss Ellerman nine times and each time I've been turned down. While she's staying here, I'll be proposing again, and if she accepts, she'll become mistress of Lochalsh. I love this house but I'm the first to admit that it needs the patience of a saint and the strength of an ox to survive the cold in these rooms. Frankly, Mrs. MacKay, twenty years of your being in charge haven't improved things, because you hate change even more than I do. If Bunny accepts my proposal, the pair of you'll just have to find a way to get on. I'm eager to keep you, Mrs. Mac, but if you force me to choose between you and Miss Ellerman, I'm afraid you'll be in need of a new position. Now, take yourself off and start making dinner. I'm in no mood for arguments and red faces."

The next morning, Bunny ventured out to the fishing village to see the crab and lobster market and to rummage in the shops near the quayside. Relieved to be out of the house, where Mrs. MacKay had been sulking since their conversation of the previous afternoon, Bunny was shocked to see the villagers turn their backs as she approached. Then she heard one of the fishermen's wives calling out.

No one seemed free to help her at the fish market, nor did the clark offer assistance in the cheese shop. Jack had warned that these isolated folk were not kindly disposed toward strangers, but to Bunny this response seemed downright icy—and personal.

Only after a fruitless stop at the post office did Bunny understand the snub, for in the doorway she overheard one fisherman's wife whisper audibly to another, "That's Cameron's woman from Paris. She's set on ousting poor Agnes MacKay, and her only in the house for a day."

Bunny walked on, her eyes smarting in the blustery wind. Obviously Mrs. MacKay had briefed her forces and the war had been declared. The slight forced Bunny's stubborn streak to the surface and she vowed not to let the locals upset her. Still, the comment had cut deep, and as she stood gazing out to sea at the herring fleet fighting their way to sea against the gale, tears began to course down her cheeks. Soon her eyes were red from crying. When she heard the soft voice behind her, she started violently.

"Who's upset you? Do you want to tell me about it?"

Turning, Bunny looked into the cloud-gray eyes of a man who matched her short stature inch for inch. He was pleasant-looking, with a reddish beard and a merry smile, but as he stepped toward her, Bunny noticed that his cuffs were threadbare, his body slimmer than it should be. His handshake was firm, however, as he introduced himself. "I'm Ewan Forbes, the village doctor."

"I'm Bunny Ellerman, I'm staying at Lochalsh."

"I know. Folk have been talking about you for weeks, and now you're here, they're talking louder than ever."

"So I heard."

"Is that what upset you? Did you hear something bad?"

"Yes, I'm afraid so."

"Why don't you come to my house? I'll make us some tea. I haven't had a patient for near a month, so you can pretend you're having a consultation and I'll pretend I'm needed." Forbes led her to a gray-walled cottage, it's roof covered in yellow moss.

"You are needed, I'm afraid. I'm grateful to you for speaking when you did. You're the first friendly person I've met since I arrived."

"Folk in these parts are honest and true, Miss Ellerman, but they have a powerful fear of strangers. It's taken me a year to get accepted, and even now there are some who won't come near the surgery. I believe the local attitude dates back to the days when this coast was forever being harassed by the Vikings."

"What am I to do about Mrs. MacKay? She'll set everyone in the area against me."

"Ignore her. If there's anything Agnes loves, it's a fight—I've learned that by checking her pounding pulse—so deny it to her. If she won't do your bidding, let her think you can do without her. I'm assuming you know how to cook."

"I'm a professional cook. I have my own catering company in Paris."

They chattered on for an hour and Bunny learned how Ewan had worked his way through the medical school in Edinburgh, only to find himself after the obligatory year's internship in the village of Crail, the replacement for a much-loved doctor who had tended the fishermen and their families for thirty-five years. At first he had been completely ignored. Then, after his efforts in saving the life of a crofter's child with pneumonia, he had emerged to a handshake from one of the local farmers. It had been the first friendly gesture from a citizen of Fife. Others had followed over the next few months and now he held a weekly surgery, scraping by on the meager fees he collected when things were going well with the fishermen. If the herring catch was poor, as it had been for a few weeks, no one came near the surgery. Instead, they walked into St. Andrews and pawned what little they had in order to buy food. As the doctor talked, Bunny learned about the people of the area and was grateful for his insight and willingness to share his own experiences. By the time the clocks struck midday Bunny was beginning to feel a great deal better. She rose with a smile.

"I've taken a lot of your time and I must pay for it, Doctor."

Forbes shook his head. "When you send for me

to tend you, I'll give you a bill, but this was a
social call and I enjoyed every second of it. Don't
spoil the occasion by offering me money. I'd rather
think it was my first friendly visit from a
neighbor."

"I'm not a neighbor yet."

"I'm sorry. I understood you were to marry
Jack Cameron."

Bunny hesitated, still unable to commit herself on the vital question. Needing to share her
thoughts, she explained her situation with Jack.
"Jack's proposed a number of times since we
first met and he'll propose again during this visit.
I just find it hard to make a decision."

"Do you love him?"

"I think I do, but since Papa died I've been
awfully scared of being dependent on a man."

Forbes patted her shoulder reassuringly.

"You just ask yourself if you'd rather live by
yourself for the rest of your life and grow old
alone or would you rather be with him, sharing
his house and raising his children and making a
family life for you all."

Bunny walked alone back to Lochalsh, pausing
on the causeway to watch women collecting drift-
wood on the beach, their backs bowed against the
wind, their black shawls stark against the silver
sand and dark blue sea. North of Lochalsh, men
were wildfowling, the sound of shots disturbing
the calm. Inland, an old man was digging peat
for the fire, his dog barking excitedly as each
new clod was thrown on a cart in preparation for
the journey home. Bunny walked on, thinking of
what Ewan had said to her. Did she really want
to leave Paris and the business she had built up
so painstakingly over the years? The thought of
leaving Severine behind was unacceptable and
Bunny decided with a flash of her old humor
that if she accepted Jack's proposal Severine

would have to come with her. That'd give Mrs.
Mac a handful. But could Bunny herself settle in
this hostile, clannish region? Would her feelings
for Cameron be enough to sustain her? Or would
she fade like a flower without water in the narrow confines of Lochalsh? She shook her head.
She knew she loved Cameron, but that's all she
knew. The rest, time would tell.

On entering the house, Bunny went upstairs
and knocked on Cameron's door, kissing him impulsively on the forehead and both cheeks when
he let her in.

"I went to the village and I loved the market,
but one of the women announced—out loud—that
I was trying to get rid of Mrs. MacKay."

"They'll say worse than that before they accept you. I knew they'd take her side, though
most of them have loathed her bones for as long
as they can remember."

Suddenly Bunny saw the funny side of her
situation. After years of hesitation, she had come
all the way from Paris to see Cameron on his
own ground and had been met with opposition
on all sides. She decided to take each day as it
came from that moment on and not to try to
solve all the problems at once. Decision made,
she felt happier than she had felt in days.

In the dining room, Bunny was surprised to
see great bunches of wildflowers in pots on every
sideboard and surface. There were flowers of the
hedgerow, wild roses, and pale green sea thistles
that she loved, but could never pick because the
spines hurt her fingers. She turned to Cameron
with a smile.

"I wonder if Sarah picked them or if Mrs.
MacKay's making a peace offering."

"I picked them for you on Lochalsh land."

Touched, Bunny looked up into his big dark
eyes. Then, standing on tiptoe, she kissed the
suntanned cheeks. When Cameron made no move

to take her in his arms, she kissed him again full on the mouth, startled by the weakness that came over her when he grasped her and held her so tight it took the breath from her lungs.

"I'm so glad I came to Lochalsh, Jack."

"You've hardly had a Scottish welcome."

"Being here's made me realize something all the same. If I can love you and want you and need you when I'm half-frozen by the weather and totally frozen out by your neighbors, I must love you. It just took the cold to bring me to my senses."

Cameron laughed and led her to the fire, rubbing her hands to warm them. Bunny studied the portrait of some stern-faced ancestors that hung over them.

"That's my grandfather, Fortescue Cameron," Jack said with a smile. "He married a Dutchwoman, had fifteen children, and expired trying to get a sixteenth on his sixty-eighth birthday. We Camerons don't show our feelings much, but we're a passionate breed and we choose women who can match us."

So Jack's grandmother, too, was a Lochalsh outsider. Yet she survived quite nicely. Bunny closed her eyes languorously and leaned against Jack. Was she strong enough to become a Cameron? Lunch arrived, in the form of one huge pile of the mashed turnips Mrs. Mac knew her employer loathed. Bunny sent them back to the kitchen with the message that they were not to be served in the house again. The rest of the meal was admirable, a hearty soup of sorrel and root vegetables, roast pork in cider, and a damson tart served with clotted cream. Bunny turned to Sarah as she was clearing the dishes.

"Thank Mrs. MacKay for a lovely meal. That damson pie was a miracle."

Sarah's eyes widened and she hurried from the room. Minutes later, they heard the sound of crashing and banging in the distant kitchens, then pans being thrown and dishes dropped.

Cameron turned to Bunny with a wry smile. "Mrs. Mac only knows how to fight. If you compliment her on something, she gets confused and starts throwing things. Come now, the sun's shining and the wind's died down at last. Let's get out for some peace and quiet. I want to show you the home farm and my croft cottage."

They rode through the meadow and up the hill where the purple heather was fragrant and the honeysuckle wild. Cameron stepped down before a gray stone cottage that nestled against the mountainside. Inside, a roaring fire scented the room with the indefinable smell of Scotland. The only furniture was a table, a yellow-painted chair, and a bed covered in a patchwork quilt. On the table were a bottle of whiskey and an unopened tin of shortbread biscuits.

Bunny thought the place like something out of a children's book.

"What is this cottage exactly, Jack?"

"It's my refuge from Lochalsh. When I feel the need for privacy, I come here. Let's walk up the hill, Bunny. I want to show you the whole of the Kingdom of Fife."

Under the warm sun of a May afternoon, Bunny stood with Cameron, looking at the panoramic view. To the east was the sea, its deep blue perfection bisected by thrashing white breakers that crashed in majestic dominance on the white sand beach. The quayside of the village and the pink-roofed cottages gave way to fields crisscrossed by dry stone walls and then to the dark green of the fir-tree forests. To Bunny's eyes it looked like a giant patchwork of natural beauty. She thought sadly that if it were not for the unfriendliness of the locals, she could think herself in paradise.

Cameron led her back to the cottage, touched

when she whispered against the howling lament of the wind, "I love you, Jack."

She buried her head in his shoulder, smelling the mixture of tweed and tobacco that she always associated with him. The doctor's words kept echoing in her head: *Ask yourself if you'd rather grow old alone or with him*. Then Cameron's pleas came into mind: *What I offer you is old-fashioned love and affection*. Bunny felt him kissing her hand and suddenly the floodgates of emotion opened and she raised her face to his.

"Let's go inside and lie on that patchwork bed together."

He kissed her lips and her throat, so intent on her every move and reaction he forgot all about his surroundings. Then, feeling her weaken under his touch, he picked Bunny up, carried her back to the croft, and lay down on the bed with her, astonished at the effect she had on him whenever they were close.

Bunny's limbs began to tremble as she untied her blouse, and she was relieved when Cameron took over and lifted it off, unhooking the skirt and garters that kept up her woolly stockings. She wound her arms around his neck as he lifted back the patchwork cover and put her gently between the sheets. Then she watched as he took off his clothes, startled by the sight of his naked body with its powerful shoulders, heavy muscled arms, and rigid penis. Her eyes widened and she struggled to find words to ease her fear. "Are you sure that'll fit inside me, Jack?"

"It was made for you, Bunny, I promise."

"I'm not so sure, now that I've seen it."

She felt Cameron bending over and kissing her breasts, his hands on the nipples that rose hard to his touch. In that moment she felt all the madness that passion brings, and realizing that he was already lost in a world of his own, she surrendered all control. Her body became languorous

and warm and she wanted Cameron so much she
forgot everything, watching as he moved astride
her and then pushed inside the warmth of her
body. As he moved relentlessly back and forth,
Bunny heard herself crying out from joy. There
was a moment of suspended animation before
the climax of love that made them both soar like
birds on the wing. Then, as he lay back and took
her in his arms, Bunny opened her eyes and
smiled up at him, her face the picture of joy.

"You were right—it fitted just fine, Jack. I
suppose I'll have to make an honest man of you
now. Will you marry me?"

He stared, nonplussed at the question.

"Are *you* proposing to *me*, Bunny? Am I hearing right?"

"I am, Jack."

"I accept, and I'll not change my mind, so
don't change yours."

Then Cameron lay back, a smile on his face
even an earthquake could not have erased. Gazing at Bunny's naked body, he was aroused by
her lack of inhibition, the lushness of her breasts,
the roundness of her bottom, and the fullness of
her thighs. He began to touch her with longing,
trailing a finger delicately from the silky outlines of her shoulders to her breasts.

"I adore every inch of you, lassie."

"Teach me how to love you. I want to do everything you ever dreamed of doing with a
woman."

"If you tried that, we'd be here for a week!"

Bunny laughed, hiding her blushes in his chest
as he guided her hands to his body.

"Touch me here and take hold of me and provoke me. Then put me where you want me to
be."

As if in a dream, her hand moved from his
chest to his stomach and then to his penis. Before Cameron could say more, she had moved to

sit astride him, gently lowering herself onto his hardness. Her body tightened over his, and closing her eyes, she bent forward so her breasts were touching his cheek. Then, her body moving in tiny, oscillating strokes, she brought them both to the peak of feeling. Sunbursts exploded like fireworks within her and she gripped Cameron's hands, luxuriating in the feeling of power her body had given her. Finally, chagrined at her own wantonness, Bunny burrowed like a mole into Cameron's arms.

"Let's get married tomorrow, Jack."

"I'll get a special license as soon as I can get up from this bed."

In the dusky golden light of a spring evening, they rode back to Lochalsh. Before dinner, Cameron went out to make the arrangements for the marriage. Then, on his way back home, he saw Janet Reekie standing at the doorway of her cottage.

"Congratulate me, Janet. I'm to be married on Saturday and you're the first to know."

Janet thought of the girl on the quayside and how she had envied her fine clothes. "What's going to happen to Agnes MacKay?"

"She's been with me for twenty years and I've no doubt she'll stay for another twenty."

"She'll not like having a new mistress."

"And I'll not be dictated to by anyone concerning Bunny. Now, see you come and throw rose petals at Craithie Church, where we're to have our blessing."

"You're marrying by special license, then?"

"We are. I don't intend to give her a chance to change her mind."

Janet ran inside her cottage and told her husband the news. That night in the pub he told all his friends, and soon the village was buzzing with excitement.

When Mrs. MacKay heard the news, she took

to her bed. Bunny promptly commandeered an unused storeroom near the upstairs dining room and had it turned into an auxiliary kitchen. Supplies were delivered with surprising speed from St. Andrews. Workmen ran in and out doing her bidding and gossiping furiously among themselves about the young lady and her newfangled ideas. Within forty-eight hours Bunny was contentedly turning out tasty dishes for everyone's enjoyment, and from her own kitchen, not Mrs. Mac's. When Mrs. MacKay heard the household's rave reviews on the young Miss Ellerman's cooking, she experienced a nearly miraculous recovery and was about to return to work when she received a summons to come at once to the library. Putting on her best apron, usually reserved for weddings and funerals, she hurried upstairs.

Bunny pushed an envelope across the desk with a sweet smile. "This is for you, Mrs. MacKay. It's a little present from Jack and me to celebrate our wedding."

"Thank you, ma'am, you're most kind, I'm sure."

"You'll be leaving in the morning for Paris. Please, Mrs. MacKay, don't worry about a thing. Arrangements have been made for you to stay at my apartment and everything's been taken care of." The matron of Lochalsh looked on in horror. "My sister Annabelle will be there at the same time, so you'll have someone who speaks English to look after you. Nell's got a big decorating job on at the moment and she'll be staying in the city until the end of July. The cookery course I've enrolled you for is in English, so you've no language gap to concern yourself with. You'll be there for eight weeks and then you'll come home to Lochalsh. While you're away, my assistant, Severine, is going to come here and be taught some of the Scottish dishes by Sarah and her mother. I want all the staff at Lochalsh to be experienced in French, English, and Scottish cooking, so when we entertain we'll be able to ring the changes and do Jack proud."

Mrs. MacKay stared at the tickets and at Bunny's address written on a crisp white sheet of paper. Then, her face ashen, her lips trembling, she moved like a sleepwalker from the room. It was, Cameron said later, the only time anyone had ever seen Agnes MacKay speechless.

On a sunny morning with a clear, crisp breeze from seaward, Bunny and her new husband emerged from the town hall with their witness, Ewan Forbes. At Craithie they had a ceremony of blessing, at which the doctor was also present. There were no villagers to throw rose petals and not a soul to wish them well. Determined to show their continuing disapproval of the new mistress of Lochalsh, the entire village remained barricaded behind locked doors and shuttered windows.

Cameron invited the doctor to return home with them. "Come, Ewan, you're our only guest, so you can't refuse."

Looking at Bunny, radiant in a pink lace suit and tilted beret of velvet rosebuds, Forbes smiled roguishly.

"I'd love to come to lunch, but are you not going away on your honeymoon?"

Bunny stepped into the car. "We're planning to spend our honeymoon in bed at Lochalsh."

Forbes almost laughed out loud at the scarlet blush that spread over Cameron's dignified face. Bunny, he knew, would blow the cobwebs out of the master of Lochalsh, then the house, and finally the villagers. He wondered wistfully if she would ever succeed in opening the locked boxes of the fisherfolk's minds.

They were motoring along the road that led to Lochalsh when they heard the siren the village used to signal disaster. Not realizing what it was, Bunny turned to her husband. "What's that horrible noise, Jack?"

The two men exchanged anxious glances. Then Cameron ordered Willie to turn the car and make for the harbor. On the way, he heard a local farmer calling the news: "The fishing fleet's gone down with all hands, sir. For God's sake, go and help the women and children."

Bunny's cheeks paled. Cameron, stunned, explained how once before, almost a hundred years previously, the disaster alarm had sounded after every fisherman in the village had been lost in a freak storm. Now something similar must have happened again.

On the quayside, weeping women, already dressed in black, their shawls damp from spray, were waiting for the news they knew would never come, that their husbands were safe and well.

Bunny stood by as Cameron and the doctor moved among the silent crowd. Not knowing anyone's name and conscious of their hostility, she could only remain apart. She took off her pretty wedding hat and put it on the back seat of the car. Then, wrapping a waterproof around her shoulders, she beckoned for some of the children to come into the back seat out of the rain. One entered and sat paralyzed with fright, staring up at her. Another followed, and soon a dozen stunned and silent youngsters were huddled together, their heads bowed, their faces mottled with tears. Realizing that she must do something, Bunny stepped out of the car and called to the women. "I'd like to take your children home with me until . . . until the news comes in. Have I your permission?"

They nodded, too shocked to disagree, and so Bunny ordered Willie to drive her back to Lochalsh. There, within two hours, she had organized a makeshift dormitory on the third floor and fed the children. When they had been put to bed, she told Sarah to watch over them. Then she returned to the harbor and sat alone in the car, watching and waiting until dawn came and with it the news that there were no survivors of the disaster. From this day on, Crail would be a village of widows and children, most of them destined for the poorhouse.

At sunrise, Janet Reekie came up to Bunny, gazing for a long time at her. "You brought us the bad luck and we'll never forgive you for it," she finally said.

Bunny closed her eyes, too tired to argue, too distracted to reply. Then she heard Janet weeping as she trudged home alone to her children. She wanted to go after the woman, to offer solace, but she knew that this was not the time or the place.

At eight A.M. Bunny and Cameron returned to Lochalsh and their first full day of married life. She was silent and subdued, aware that the ill luck that had come to the village on her wedding day would have to be reversed somehow or she would forever be known as a figure of doom, an albatross around the neck of this superstitious community. She bent over and kissed her husband, holding his hand tightly to give her courage.

"Don't worry, Jack. We'll help the women and see them through. First we'll have a sleep and then we'll make our plans."

"I love you, Bunny, I'm so sorry your wedding day was ruined."

"We're together and that's all that matters to me."

"Come to bed, Bunny. I want to show you you're the most loved woman in the world."

LOCHALSH, SUMMER–
AUTUMN 1932

BUNNY WAS IN her bedroom reading the morning papers. On page three there was a picture of the American socialite Mrs. Simpson, standing with her friend Lady Furness at the Prince of Wales's party at Osborne House. There was also a picture of Miss Unity Mitford at her coming-out ball, her pet snake draped around her neck. Bunny put the paper down and lay for a moment, unable to concentrate, thinking of the imminent visit of Ewan Forbes. She was almost certain she was pregnant, and the thought of becoming a mother filled her with such emotion she could barely contain herself.

But there was something else she wanted to discuss with Forbes—an idea she had had to give employment to the widows. She had worked out the plan in her usual meticulous way and had thought of little else for days. Bunny rose and put on a dressing gown, aware that this was going to be a very special day. If she was pregnant, Cameron would be overcome with joy, and if Forbes felt that her idea for the widows was feasible, she would put it to her husband over dinner so they could start to develop it together.

Bunny's mind turned to thoughts of Mrs. MacKay, who was due to return from Paris. From that moment on, the peace they had enjoyed during her eight-week absence would be over. They had received no letters from the housekeeper since her arrival in Paris, though Nell had sent regular reports on the lady's progress in learning a few words of French and accustoming herself to foreign places. Bunny took out the last letter and reread it, smiling at her sister's words.

Dearest Bunny,

Your battleax of a housekeeper just got her diploma and smiled for the first time since she arrived in Paris. She went right out and had it framed. Since then she's done nothing but check her tickets and her passport and her luggage. It's clear to me she wants to make dead sure she gets back to Lochalsh. She knows Severine's decided to stay on there and I suppose she's wondering if there'll still be a job for her. After the trouble she's had on the course and the effort she's made to accept the new ideas, she deserves a break, and if she gives you half a chance, make the gesture.

Guy and I get married at the embassy in Paris in August. We'll have a quick ceremony, no frills and no guests except for Charles and his mother. Thanks for the invitation to spend the honeymoon at Lochalsh. We accept, of course, and we'll notify you of our arrival date. I had a note from Hadley saying she and Karl are off to Iceland. After this, they won't be going away for ages, because he's got to get down to some work on the estate. It'll give Hadley a chance to play mistress of the house for the first time, though knowing her, who can tell what she might do? No more news at my end. How are things with the black-hearted Scots? Are the locals accepting you any better than before? Guy sends his love.

Yours,
Nell

Bunny was folding the letter when Severine carried in the breakfast. As she left, Ewan Forbes entered the room, shook hands with Bunny, and smiled.

"You look remarkably well and not at all in need of my services. What's wrong?"

"I'm wondering if I might be pregnant. How soon will you be able to tell?"

"It depends. Three months perhaps. We'll examine you and see how you are."

"Don't tell Jack until we're certain. He'll start telling me to lie down all day."

"Where is he?"

"He had a message from Janet Reekie and went to meet with the women. Since Katy Muir killed herself he's had to go down there every day and sometimes twice a day. So far, he's been paying their food bills, but he can't go on doing it. There are twenty-five widows and forty children and we just can't afford to keep them all forever."

"They'll have to go to the poorhouse and they know it."

"Not if I can help it, they won't. I've had an idea that could keep them all in work for years to come. You remember telling me about a man who'd worked all his life in the whiskey distillery at Glenlivet. Could you give me his name and address?"

"I can send Fergusson round to see you if you like. Are you fancying reviving the distillery?"

"I'm wondering if it would be possible. Those women need work, and more money than filleting herrings ever earned them. Because it's less risky, I'd prefer to capitalize on something that this area's been known for in the past. I chose whiskey because the distillery's for sale. I'm certain with the right advice we could make a profitable business out of it. Come and join me for breakfast, Ewan. I just hate eating alone."

Forbes ate with relish, mulling over Bunny's

plan. Ironically, her biggest problem would be those who stood to benefit most from the business—the women themselves. Because they were fisherfolk born and bred, that was the extent of their ambition. It was, in fact, all they knew to be. He wondered if Cameron knew of his wife's plans and if he approved of them. But one look into Bunny's eager face reassured the doctor. This was a woman who wanted to start a family more than anything else in the world. She wouldn't deal behind her husband's back. Forbes rose and motioned for her to prepare for the examination while he went to wash up. Then, when he had checked her thoroughly, he talked with Bunny while she dressed.

"It's a bit early for us to be sure you're pregnant, but I'd bet you are. I'll examine you again in three weeks' time."

"I hear you invited Severine to the cinema."

"I had to. I like the girl very much, and as for her cooking, well, it's the stuff dreams are made of."

When Bunny had dressed and returned to his side at the table, Forbes began to talk of the distillery. "Once it was a fine place. Then the plague came to this area and the work force was decimated. The distillery never recovered. It's been empty for years and it's in an awful state of disrepair."

"Send Mr. Fergusson round, will you, Ewan? And I'd like to talk with Janet Reekie too. Will you ask her to come to Lochalsh for lunch a copule of days from now?"

When Forbes had gone, Bunny went to her dressing room and put on the suit Cameron liked best. Then she stood looking out at the summer scene, the fields full of dog daisies and cornflowers, the kestrels wheeling above a turbulent blue sea. While she was standing at the window, a tortoiseshell butterfly with orange-and-black wings settled briefly beside her. Bunny was absorbed in her plan for the distillery. It would take a lot of money—everything she had, in fact—and would be the gamble of a lifetime. Ever since her father's death, she had saved the cash he had left her, depositing it with the bank at a substantial rate of interest and watching it grow, augmented by the profits from her catering business. The only substantial amount spent had been the settlement of the Ritz Hotel bill. She also had in her possession the Ellerman pearl-and-diamond necklace that was worth a great deal of money, and two thousand pounds' worth of shares her husband had given her as a birthday gift. To gamble everything was madness, but the widows were women without hope, substantially worse off than the Ellermans were even during their darkest days. Left to their own devices, the widows would soon make the dreaded trip to the workhouse with their children. There they would spend the rest of their days picking hemp and living in cells, regimented by wardens and humiliated by the fact that fate had decreed they end their days in an institution. Did she want to keep the pearls and diamonds under such circumstances?

During the day, Bunny visited the distillery again, this time with the local builder and architect, who would prepare final estimates of the work to be done. She was determined to approach the task with the utmost professionalism and to make certain that she could cover all preliminary costs alone.

That night, as she lay at her husband's side, Bunny told him of her plans. Cameron listened to what she had learned from Fergusson that day, how much the owners wanted for the building and how she hoped someday to sell the whiskey in London and New York, as well as in Edinburgh and Glasgow. It would be the most expensive whiskey on the market, a gamble of seemingly lunatic dimension in times of depression, but Bunny was convinced, by experience, that the rich always had the money to buy the status symbols they craved, just as they had with her catering service. And Lochalsh whiskey would be the ultimate. Impressed by her plans, Cameron could see only one flaw, the same one Forbes had mentioned.

"You could make the place pay and carry out any plan you choose, that I know. My only doubt is whether the women are your equal in ambition and confidence. They see themselves as herring filleters, and it'll take them twenty years to change their minds."

"I used to think of myself as Poor Bunny, fat, useless, and clumsy, and it didn't take me twenty years to change. Once disaster struck me down, I changed fast, thanks to you and my own efforts. If I can do it, so can they."

"They're ordinary women, Bunny, and you're not."

"I love you, Jack."

Bunny felt his lips on hers as they lay together in the four-poster bed, the fire glowing orange in the hearth in the moonless darkness of night. She returned the kiss, opening her mouth to admit his tongue as she would open her body within seconds to the thrusts of his manhood. Closing her eyes in ecstasy as Cameron bent to kiss her breasts and her stomach, she forgot all about the future and allowed herself the luxury of being loved. When she heard her husband's breath quickening with her own and as their bodies beat against each other with ever-increasing speed, she felt the cramplike ripple of orgasm running like an arpeggio through her core. Her knees lifted and her back arched as waves of passion died and she felt her body filled with the outpouring of her husband's love.

Afterward, as she lay in Cameron's arms, half-asleep, half-awake, and drowsy with exhaustion, she could not resist a smile when he spoke.

"When I'm making love to you, I feel ten feet tall, and it's something I cannot resist. I shall never tire of it and I pray you won't either."

"I don't know if I will or not. You'd best give me lots of practice so I can get used to it."

"Close your eyes and go to sleep before I feel provoked to give you another lesson."

The morning was sunny, with a playful breeze that made the sea choppy. Bunny and Cameron got into the car and drove to the station to meet Mrs. MacKay. Neither felt like talking, each one conscious that the housekeeper's return might be the start of a turbulent period in their lives. Primed on Mrs. MacKay's way of thinking by Ewan Forbes, Bunny had made her plans. The doctor had told her that to Agnes MacKay, Lochalsh, its owner, and dependents in the area were the most important things in life. She was rigid in her traditional manner of thinking and terrified of losing her job. Above all else, Forbes had said, she needed to feel needed. Bunny hoped she could hit the right note with the housekeeper on her return. If not, she was resigned to the fact that Mrs. MacKay's long service with the Camerons might have to end.

Mrs. MacKay was sitting bolt upright in her third-class compartment, peering out of the window whenever the train reached a station, in case she missed her destination. She looked with wistful eyes at the fishing boats of Lower Largo and thought how bright they were, how typical of the area, and how sadly they must be missed in Crail. She wondered what was happening to the widows, her friends, and more important, what was going to happen to her. During her stay in Paris there had not been a single day

when she had not sobbed for Lochalsh in the
privacy of her room. At first she had been horrified that not a single person spoke English. Then,
after Nell had given her a tour of the city and
dinner in a bistro, where the food was delicious,
she had accepted that Paris had a very special
atmosphere, though she remained terrified of
crossing the road, terrified of the men who kept
kissing her hand, and, most of all, terrified of
never seeing Scotland again. It had not taken her
long to realize that she knew very little about
cooking and that she was going to have to learn.
While practicing the basics, she had thought endlessly of Bunny, who had enrolled in an inten-
sive six-month course in French when she had
never even boiled a pot of water. The mistress
had courage, that was certain, and courage was
something Mrs. MacKay admired above all else.
Grudgingly, as Nell had talked about her sister,
she had come to know Bunny better. It was obvious that the young lady had always been the
underdog, overshadowed by her beautiful sisters.
Only now was she emerging as a person in her
own right. Mrs. MacKay had begun to wonder
how she was going to make her peace with Bunny
without losing her dignity. Now, as the train
drew into the station at Lochalsh, the problem
was still taxing her.

Cameron stepped forward and greeted Mrs.
MacKay. "There you are, Agnes, and in a new
Paris hat."

"Miss Annabelle gave it to me."

Cameron eyed the gray velour with its cock
feather at a rakish angle. Then, concealing his
amusement, he led Mrs. MacKay to the car, where
Bunny opened the conversation as if nothing un-
pleasant had ever passed between them.

"It's good to have you back, Mrs. MacKay. How
was Paris?"

"I liked it well enough after a wee while, ma'am,

and your sister was most kind, but I didn't take kindly to getting sent off like a convict and it'll take me some years to forget." Mrs. MacKay grimaced and remembered to try to hold herself in check.

"How were the lessons?" Bunny said, nonplussed.

"I thought I knew about cooking till I got to Paris, but I soon realized my error. It was a shock to my very bones, I can tell you."

"Severine had the same experience at this end. She did nothing but sob for the first three weeks, but now she's quite an expert at poachers' broth and Cumberland sausages, though she needs your advice on cooking venison. The last lot she made nearly broke our teeth."

"I'll show her, and she can put me through the tricks of French pastry. You need cool, light fingers for that, and mine are made of lead."

Cameron listened as Bunny told Mrs. MacKay her plans. "I want you and Severine to work out the cooking schedules between you. We've also decided to import some stoves from Scandinavia to heat the castle for the winter. You'll have to feed the men and generally make sure they behave themselves. I want the first-floor storeroom to be filled with logs during the summer, so we're ready for the storms and gales. We seem a bit short of linen too. If you make a list of what you need, I'll go to Edinburgh and buy it."

Suddenly Mrs. MacKay felt very tired. She had been so sure that on her return she would find herself usurped by Severine that her relief was immense and exhaustion claimed her. She glanced at Cameron out of the corner of her eye, but he was lighting his pipe, his expression impassive. She decided to venture a question about the widows. "What's happening in the town, sir?"

"I see the women every day and do what I can, but they need work and regular wages to give them some peace of mind. Bunny wants to talk to you about the widows, Mrs. MacKay. She's had an idea and will be putting it to Janet Reekie this afternoon. In my opinion, she'll need your support. Janet's more likely to heed you than she will my wife, though the idea's a grand one and the only thing that might keep that number of women out of the poorhouse."

"It'd take a miracle to keep them out, and even Madam can't make one of those! I don't believe there's any way to save them."

At a quarter to three, Janet Reekie gathered the widows for their walk to Lochalsh. Her face was pale, her eyes red-rimmed, because that morning she had visited the poorhouse at Anstruther on the instructions of the bailiff, who was due to evict her. The experience had been one of the most horrendous of her life and she had traveled back to Crail crying all the way at the very idea of taking herself and her six sons to that prisonlike establishment. So desperate had she been, she had even thought of suicide, as she had thought of it so many times since her husband's death. She knew that she could never kill her children, however, nor could she countenance leaving them alone and unprotected in the world. And so, despite her intense resentment of Bunny, she had come to see what the new mistress of Lochalsh had to offer. She was willing to work every hour of the day for a pittance, if necessary. Surely being summoned to Lochalsh must be the glimmer of hope in the black tunnel of despair.

Bunny was in the library when Janet appeared, followed by the group of suspicious widows. Momentarily taken by surprise, she motioned for them to sit on the sofas or on cushions on the floor. Then, pale with apprehension at the thought of the meeting, which she knew would make or break her own future in the area as well as theirs, Bunny explained what was on her mind.

"I asked you here, Janet, as spokeswoman for the widows, to put an idea to you. Your position right now is that you've no money, no jobs, and no prospects of any kind. You're all skilled herring workers, but since the disaster there've been no herrings to fillet. You can either move away and try to find work or you can go to the poorhouse at Anstruther, becaue there's nothing hereabouts for you. Is that an accurate summary of your situation?"

Janet nodded, biting her lips and pinching her wrists to keep from crying. "It is, ma'am."

Bunny chose her words carefully. "This area was once known for its whiskey, its glassblowing and etching. It was also famous for hand-woven tweed and knitted lace. Over the next five years I want to revive some of those local industries, starting with the whiskey distillery."

"But who'd work it, ma'am? The men are all dead, but for the ones who are too old to work."

"You would, Janet. You and the women will make the whiskey."

There was a long silence while the women gazed openmouthed at Bunny. Then they all began to talk at once.

"Whiskey distilling's skilled labor, ma'am, and we don't know about it. We're fisherwomen, nothing more and nothing less. We'd go bankrupt even if we could find someone to back us."

Bunny looked into Janet's hard blue eyes.

"What do you think, Mrs. Reekie?"

"Why ask me, ma'am? I know nothing at all about whiskey, and that's the truth."

"Could you learn?"

Janet recalled the terrifying events of that morning. "I'll do anything that keeps me and my lads out of the workhouse."

"Then you'd best be in charge of the operation.

Right, that's the first thing settled. Now all I have to do is raise the money to buy the place."

Janet looked at Bunny in mixed awe and alarm. Was the girl a fool or worse, an impetuous creature in love with the idea of charity? She wished Cameron was there to give his advice.

"Is your husband in agreement with you on this, ma'am?"

"Of course he is. Jack knows you can't let the tragedy take away your self-respect. If you were capable enough to become experts at herring filleting, then you're capable enough to be experts at whiskey distilling. And I'm going to sell the whiskey in London, then maybe in America."

Bunny rang for tea to be served, alarmed when most of the women burst into tears and started sobbing. She was wondering what to do when Sarah, Severine, and Mrs. MacKay appeared with silver trays full of scones, cakes, sandwiches, and patties. Willie followed with an urn of tea that looked sufficient for a regiment.

Bunny was astonished and relieved when Mrs. MacKay turned to the women and spoke in her parade-ground voice. "Sit up and get something to eat and stop that blubbering at once. Do you want Madam to think we Scots have no courage? And you, Janet, say something useful. You're to be given a chance to pull yourselves up by your bootstrings from the bog of despair. See you take the chance and be grateful, or I'll think every one of you deserves the workhouse!"

The women ate their sandwiches in silence and drank copious amounts of tea. Then, at a signal from Janet, they shook hands with Bunny and filed out of the room, leaving the two women alone. Uncertain what to say, Janet walked to the window and looked out at the sea as it pounded the rocks below the window. She was thinking how it had pounded her husband's boat into the deep, leaving her with no money, no home, and no future. When she had dried her eyes, she turned to Bunny and held out her hand.

"I've done nothing in the past to deserve your friendship, ma'am, but I'll promise you one thing: if you can raise the money to buy the distillery and keep us all out of the poorhouse, I'll work so hard I'll deserve your respect someday. I don't want my sons raised in that evil place, and if I have to learn new ways and new skills, I will. We all will, though the others don't know it yet. It'll be hard to change, but we'll do it."

Touched by Janet's words, Bunny led her from the house and outside to the forecourt.

"I'm meeting the owners of the distillery in the morning. I'll come and tell you afterward if we have the place or not. Then we'll go and sign the documents at Mr. O'Finoch's office in Edinburgh."

"What must we sign?"

"The deeds of ownership. I'm making the distillery a partnership between all the women as well as Jack and me."

"Dear God, ma'am, do you know what you're doing?"

"Not really. We'll just have to learn as we go along."

At noon the following day, Bunny agreed to buy the long-disused whiskey distillery for one thousand, five hundred pounds. She immediately took on Thomas Fergusson as adviser, equipment purchaser, and general tutor to the women. He was old, but one of the legendary whiskey makers of the area, who had worked forty years perfecting his art and drinking what he produced. When he commented that women would never be able to learn the business, Bunny responded by threatening to engage a younger expert to replace him. Fergusson agreed to meet the women and to do all he could for them.

As soon as the papers were signed, workmen

moved into the distillery. The widows were consulted, and those who wanted to live in the new accommodation Bunny had designed in one wing of the building were told to give notice to their landlords. Those who would not be moving into the distillery quarters would have their cottages repaired at Cameron's expense. Determined not to allow unsanitary conditions to bring illness to her workers, Bunny was convinced she had to get everything right from the bottom up. She allowed no protest, tolerated no tears, and ordered the women to report to Fergusson from the following Monday morning for lessons in the art of whiskey distilling. She was hoping they would feel more confident of their chances when they eventually entered the distillery, if they were already familiar with the processes involved. It would take two months for the work to be completed and a further week for all the equipment to be tested. By then the widows would at least have learned the the story behind whiskey making. Whether they would ever master the practical complications of the process was another matter. Cameron was unsure they could, but Bunny believed that what had to be learned in life could be, provided the desire was there.

On the day appointed for their first lesson, Bunny and the widows filed into the banqueting hall and sat on either side of the table, looking expectantly at Fergusson. He was wearing a kilt and a tam-o'-shanter with a red pompon, the true Scot to his fingertips. At his side there was a briar stick and his weather-beaten face and shock of white hair reassured even the most nervous of them.

Fergusson opened the proceedings with a challenge. "I've wagered the mistress you'll never be able to learn all that's needed, but she has faith in you and insists that you will. Today I'll start by telling you about the whiskey, which we call in Gaelic visage beatha, or water of life. You can take note and ask questions if you wish, and don't be frightened to interrupt. There's much you have to know and you'll learn from repetition in the beginning. Then, when we move to the distillery, you'll learn from experience and that's when we'll know which of you has the strength and the courage to make Lochalsh whiskey one of the great ones."

Fergusson cleared his throat and began the story.

"Here in Scotland, our whiskey is unique, because it's made from spring water that rises from the red granite and then passes through peatmoss country. In the early days, every highland laird had his own still, and fearsome stuff it produced, that could only be drunk by Caledonians and lunatics."

The women were delighted at this. Fergusson continued.

"There are seven stages in the making of whiskey and they'll be written on your hearts forever before we're through. The first is the cleaning of the barley. We do it by putting the grain in the steeps for two or three days. The second is the malting, when the barley's spread on the floor of the malthouse for eight to twelve days and sprinkled with water. When the sprouts are about three-quarters of an inch long, we turn off the water and have what's known as the green malt. The third stage is drying and grinding. The fourth is mashing, where the grist is mixed with hot water in a mash tub and allowed to soak. When the liquid has absorbed all the goodness from the grain, we call it the wort. The husks are drawn off and dried for cattle feed. The rest is cooled and pumped into vats for the fifth stage, which is fermentation. The vats for that will cost a pretty penny, I can tell you. Maturation is the sixth stage. At this time the whiskey has no color. It will need at least three years in oak casks to develop its flavor and its hue."

The women looked alarmed at this and Janet spoke the question on all their minds. "Does that mean we won't be able to earn anything for at least three years, Mr. Fergusson?"

"You'll not. Making whiskey's an expensive business for beginners. You'll probably need to be financed for up to five years before you can make a real profit. Now, I'll finish by telling you about the last stage, which is the blending. Blending's an art that needs experience. In the beginning I'll be chief blender, but I'm seventy-two, so you'll need to learn fast. Some of the great whiskeys blend up to forty malts with half a dozen grains. I'll need someone with a natural-born talent for the job and you'd best pray we can find at least one among you that has the gift."

When they had finished their discussion and asked their questions, everyone settled to eating lunch. There were soup plates of bacon stew with oatmeal bread and piles of fresh butter. As they ate, each of the women was mulling over what had been said during the morning. Janet likened the whiskey-making process to the preparation of a complicated wedding cake. She had often baked those for special occasions, spending weeks allowing the rich mixture to mature, having measured everything to the fraction of an ounce.

Milly Plat, once the fastest herring filleter in Fife, wondered out loud how Bunny could pay their wages for years on end if they were not earning a farthing.

"If we can't earn anything, how can you keep the distillery open, ma'am? We'd best teach the children the local crafts, so we can sell what they make in the big shops in Edinburgh and Glasgow. Do you agree?"

Bunny nodded her assent. "It's a good idea for

the children to learn the traditional crafts of Fife. They used to be famous in all of Britain and they only died out finally after the influenza epidemic in 1919 that decimated the population."

Loud Maggie Fine looked across the table at Bunny. "Can me and my son Rory try for the blender's job, ma'am? We've both got sensitive smell and taste and it'd give us security for life."

"Of course you can try. You must all try. The blender's the most important person of all, and Mr. Fergusson's not going to live forever. We must prepare ourselves now to replace him when he's too old to work anymore."

Maggie thought with longing of the coveted job, determined that either she or young Rory would win it against all competition.

All the women were smiling happily and chattering excitedly, when Cameron appeared and sat at the head of the table.

"I need the keys to the cottages of the women who aren't going to move into the distillery."

"What hours shall we work, sir?"

"You'll start at seven-thirty and have breakfast in the kitchen on arrival. Lunch'll be at midday, and at four there'll be tea, buns, and sandwiches. Then you'll go home, so you can meet the children from school. Now, Janet, tell me what you learned today."

Janet consulted the paper on which she had written in a clumsy hand the stages Fergusson had described.

"There are seven stages of the whiskey that must be written on our hearts forever, sir. Cleaning, malting, drying and grinding, mashing, fermenting, maturing, and blending. That's all we know so far."

"Well, it's a lot more than you knew this morning. My congratulations, Mr. Fergusson, and you too, ladies. Before you're through, I have a feeling you're going to make me and Bunny the proudest folk in Fife."

When the women left to walk home in the howling summer gale, Bunny and Cameron went to the new sitting room she had just designed adjacent to their bedroom. There, before a glowing fire, they sat hand in hand, not speaking but enjoying the scent of the peat and the feel of each other's presence. Finally Bunny broke the silence. "I went to see Ewan Forbes this morning."

"Are you ill?"

"I'm fine, Jack. I never felt better."

"Then why did you go to the doctor?"

"So that Dr. Forbes could give me the good news. We'll have our first child at the beginning of March."

Bunny was touched to see tears of joy running down her husband's cheeks, and thrilled when he took her in his arms and whispered his joy. "My dearest one, I've dreamed of having a son for so long. I cannot tell you what pleasure this gives me. Did Ewan tell you to rest and lie abed?"

"He told me to tell you not to fuss over me. I'm young and fit, and having children's something I'm built for. Though I'm not sure I'm built specifically for the production of *sons*."

Cameron leapt to his feet and rang for Mrs. MacKay, who appeared shortly with a black scowl on her face.

"I'm just through washing up after the feeding of the five thousand, and you ring for me."

"We're going to have a son, Mrs. MacKay. I wanted you to be the first to know."

She looked from Bunny to Cameron, unable to conceal her pleasure.

"May I offer my congratulations, madam, and to you, of course, sir."

Cameron poured himself and the housekeeper a glass of whiskey and Bunny a small measure of elderberry wine.

"To the boy and my lovely wife."

Mrs. MacKay refused to raise her glass to the toast, and, forgetting her newfound politeness, rounded on her employer.

"Just you watch that tongue, Jack Cameron. You don't know for certain it'll be a boy and I don't want Madam upset or disappointed if it's a girl, so I won't drink to a son. I'll give you a toast of my own instead. To the baby and its parents ... slenjtavor, mokarridge, great health, my friends."

Cameron raised his glass, his dark face radiant. "To the future and to Lochalsh."

Mrs. MacKay turned to Bunny. "Will you be able to carry out all your plans for the distillery in view of your condition, ma'am?"

"I don't intend to let having babies interfere with anything. We must try to get as much of the renovation of the castle done in the early months, so I can have a rest toward the end. Then, when the baby arrives, I'll need a girl to help me look after it, so I can continue my work. It's going to be hard for the first three years, when we're earning nothing at all. It'll make or break us all, though I haven't dared tell the widows that."

Mrs. MacKay returned to the kitchen and sat at the table, while Severine warmed up her stew.

"Madam's going to have a baby in March. I was the first to be told."

Severine poured them both a glass of wine, refraining from saying that Bunny had told *her* the minute she arrived back from the doctor's office.

"I am so happy, Mrs. MacKay."

"I wonder if she'll be able to manage her condition and keep on with all her plans."

"Of course she will. Madam can do *everything*."

"We'd best make sure we help all we can."

"We have agreed on the cooking. Next we shall move to the new kitchens and turn this horrible place into a wine store. We will do everything ourselves and surprise Madam with our great energy."

"The distillery isn't going to earn a farthing for three years."

Severine shook her head sadly. "I suppose Madam will have to sell the pearls her father left her. She told me once that the future of the widows and their children was more important than keeping her father's gift. Then she went to her room and locked the door so I would not see her crying. I hope so much she will not have to make such a sacrifice."

Mrs. MacKay sighed wearily, gazing at Severine, who had virtually taken over the kitchen and the stores and with a will of iron was making changes in the house. She could not help admiring the French girl, despite her fears, and tried to make her feelings known for the first time.

"When you first came here I thought you'd take over my work and I'd be given my notice."

Severine looked at Mrs. MacKay and found herself cutting her another huge slice of cake. Then she said, "Lochalsh could not continue without you, and now that there are going to be children, it cannot do without me, so we are both happy. You and I must do everything we can to provide support for Sir and Madam. It won't be easy, Mrs. MacKay, and we shall have a great battle to survive."

There was nothing in the world Mrs. MacKay liked better than a battle, and she patted Severine's hand contentedly.

"Aye, but we'll fight together and someday we'll win. Lochalsh'll be lovely and there'll be babies born and if we're lucky we'll keep the women out of the workhouse, though I still think we'll need a miracle for *that*!"

— 8 —
CHÂTEAU DE NONANCOURT, FEBRUARY–JUNE 1933

NELL WOKE AT seven and looked around the bedroom with its dark beams and big vase of winter jasmine. Though it was still dark, she sensed an unusual blanket of silence that puzzled her. She rose and went to the window, thrilled to see that it had snowed in the night. The garden was a gleaming fairyland, the fir trees edged with white, the lanterns frosted. In the deep blue light of early morning, she could see the fountain in front of the château, its cascade frozen in mid-fall, surreal shapes like phantom stalactites hanging from its copper bowl. Hurrying back to bed, she snuggled in Guy's arms.

"It snowed in the night and the garden's lovely."

"You sound so happy, Nell."

She sighed, closing her eyes as the scent of his body and the strength of his arms made her want him as she always wanted him when they were close.

"I'm happy with you and I love our cottage and our life together, you know that, Guy. But I'm not so happy with your brother's friends. I never realized what snobs the French were till we married! I'm often made to feel like a servant and I don't like it at all."

"I work for Charles, and to many of his friends in society I *am* a servant."

"I'm not used to being a second-leaguer."

"I never knew such things were important to you."

"Truthfully, neither did I. But after all, Guy, you virtually run this place, and I find it aggravating to be looked down on by our bone-idle neighbors!"

"To hell with neighbors. I care only what you think of me and what you feel about our life together."

Nell sighed, unable to put into words her annoyance at the petty slights, the patronizing attitudes, and the sly gibes of some of the family friends. The main problem at the beginning of the marriage had been her anguish at being childless. That had lessened, slowly but surely, by the sheer pleasure of being adored and constantly reassured by a loving husband. But another problem remained and Nell knew that there was little she could do to change it. She had never been able to accustom herself to poverty and doubted that she ever would. It was one thing to accept that there would be no new clothes, no exciting trips, and little else. She had accepted that willingly, because she loved Guy. But it was quite another thing to have someone like Arlette actually laugh out loud at her dated wardrobe. *My dear Annabelle, you really mustn't wear* that *again. The garçonne look went out years ago.*

At that moment Nell realized that she was, uncharacteristically, heeding other people's opinions of her, something she had never done in her life. The truth was, she hated being poor and having to save up for weeks for a new hat or pretty scarf.

Guy's salary was enough to provide the necessities for one man, but not for a wife. The cottage was free, the light and heat likewise, but still they were reduced to searching the shops for the most economical items. It was something she would never get used to, and Nell decided it was time to change her situation.

Guy was kissing her cheeks and stroking her hair. Then desire welled in him, and he began to make love to her. He saw Nell's hands reaching up to grip the carved pillars of the bed, her eyes closing as she entered the secret wonderland that was hers alone. But even as their bodies quickened and Nell opened her eyes to look up at him, he saw the tears in her eyes.

"I adore you, Nell. Don't let trivialities spoil things for us."

"I don't know what's gotten into me."

"Hadley was right, you are not the type to like being poor, but what can I do?"

"Make me feel all the things I want to feel, Guy. Make me forget everything."

He gripped her shoulders and pushed into her body with all his strength and force. Nell's thighs tightened on him like twin vises and suddenly he felt her contract from the force of her orgasm. Crying out, he released his love inside. Then he held her as he knew she loved to be held, close to the beating of his heart.

After a while they heard Marie-Brigitte, one of the maids from the château, arriving with her son, Luc. Marie-Brigitte knocked on the door, then entered carrying a breakfast tray loaded with everything Nell liked best and coffee that smelled delicious.

Nell sat up expectantly, surveying the heart-shaped rolls and selection of damson and rose-petal preserves.

"What's the big occasion?"

"It's Madame's birthday and she told me to bring your breakfast and ask you to join her for lunch. Luc helped me with the tray. He can never resist a visit to the cottage."

Nell turned to the little boy who had been such a joy to her since her arrival at Bel-Ami, organizing picnics, running errands, and playing the role of her very young but very devoted admirer. Taking·him in her arms, she kissed him resoundingly on both cheeks.

"How are you, Luc?"

"I didn't feel well yesterday, but I think I'm very well this morning."

"Isn't your birthday soon?"

"I'm going to be nine, Madame Annabelle!"

Luc beamed at Nell as she ruffled the corn-yellow hair, his eyes sparkling from sheer pleasure. When she handed him one of the brioches, his day was made. He had followed her around like a lapdog from the moment she moved into the cottage, a child who had fallen in love with the most beautiful lady he had ever met.

It snowed again in the afternoon, while the family was drinking coffee by the fire and Charles was telling everyone the news of the trip he was going to make.

"I'll travel by airship to England and then on the *Bremen* to New York. The races begin from Rhode Island on the first of March and I'm confident that we can beat any yacht the Americans produce."

"When will you come back?"

He turned to Nell and smiled affectionately. "I shall return on the first of May. Then I hope to take the airship from London to Paris. I find all the new machines quite irresistible."

Madame de Nonancourt shuddered. "I find machines of all kinds alarming. Do tell me, Millie, what news have you of Arlette?"

"There's a fearful scandal brewing, Aunt Lou! She's having an affair with a gigolo and goes dancing with him every afternoon at Ciro's. Henri's had a mistress for months, of course, but it's humiliating for him to be so openly cuckolded."

"Thank God, she never became part of our family!"

"Nothing Arlette does ever seems to go well. The other day she went to see the Princesse de Polignac to ask if she could be photographed for *Vogue* magazine. She was turned down, of course, because she isn't the type they need. I can't imagine why she wanted to do it in the first place."

Suddenly Nell realized there *was* something she could do to change her social and financial situation. She could model for *Vogue*. Hadn't Colette asked her, saying she'd be perfect? It was something she could accomplish without inconvenience to Guy or herself, and it would bring prestige as well as enable her to be dressed for free in return for promoting the couturiers' new lines. She resolved to go to Paris within the next few days to see Colette and the editors of *Vogue* magazine, provided, of course, that they even remembered her.

That night, Nell was lying at her husband's side when she heard a child crying. She sat up in bed, alarmed by the thought that it might be Luc. He had been pale for days and had said he hadn't been well the previous morning, yet he had seemed well enough when he helped his mother bring the breakfast. Nell waited for a while to see if the child was simply having a nightmare. She was just beginning to doze again when she heard the sound of sobbing and with it the clattering of locks being drawn, doors opened, and alarmed voices raised.

Nell got out of bed, put on her dressing gown, and wrapped herself in a thick Persian shawl. Then, stepping into her waterproof boots, she ran from the cottage in the direction of the staff wing, where Marie-Brigitte lived with her son. There she found a scene that took the breath from her lungs. Luc was lying in bed, his face ashen, his chest rising and falling with great rapidity. His hands were clutching the edge of the bedclothes, his face full of fear. Nell sat down and held his hand, looking to his mother for guidance.

"What's wrong with the child?"

"I don't know, ma'am. Luc's been feeling queasy and he's had a bad headache too. I thought he was exaggerating because he didn't want to go to school. Then, this afternoon, he went to bed without being told. He said he couldn't breathe and had a pain in his chest, so I made him an inhalation and it eased the breathing for a while. An hour ago it came back and the pain is much worse."

"We must call a doctor."

"Dr. Marquand's away skiing at the moment, ma'am. The only other doctor I know lives in Poitiers, and he won't come all this way in the snow and ice."

"Then we'll take Luc to the hospital. He needs immediate help."

"What hospital, ma'am?"

Nell looked askance at the resignation in the maid's face. "Where's the nearest one? Wake up, Marie-Brigitte. This is urgent!"

"There aren't many hospitals hereabouts, ma'am. There could be one in Blois or Tours."

"That's forty or fifty kilometers from the château! Are you saying there's nothing nearer?"

"Not as far as I know."

Panic rose in Nell's mind, but she fought to keep the fear from her face. There was no need to alarm the confused Marie-Brigitte any further. Instead, she rang for assistance and a footman appeared, rubbing the sleep from his eyes.

"Go and wake my husband and ask him to come at once. Tell him we have to drive Luc to the hospital."

The boy began to cough, clutching his chest to

ease the pain. Nell stroked his head, her terror increasing with each caress. The boy was as hot as an oven to the touch. Was it possible Luc had pneumonia of the kind that came on suddenly with fearsome force? Or was he simply in the grip of one of the illnesses of childhood? Taking her leave of Marie-Brigitte, Nell hurried from the room, promising to return as soon as she had dressed. She had never felt so helpless, so impotent to aid a loved one in need.

Guy drove wildly through snow and ice to the nearest hospital, forty miles away. Under normal conditions it would have taken an hour, but the roads had frozen and the car skidded constantly. It was five A.M. before they arrived, their faces drawn and tense. They had done everything they could to keep the child covered with blankets, but he was trembling violently with a high fever, his breath coming in rasping sounds that frightened them all.

Guy carried Luc into the hospital and came face to face with a stern-faced nurse who looked at him with some impatience. "We're not equipped for emergencies, sir. In any case, the doctor won't be here til nine."

"Call him and get him here immediately or I shall summon the gendarmerie."

Within minutes Luc was in an oxygen tent, watched over by the young doctor who had arrived in record time. Nell and her husband took their places in the waiting room, while Marie-Brigitte paced up and down the corridor, sobbing inconsolably.

It was seven A.M. before Dr. Guichet reappeared in the waiting room.

"You may come and see your son, madame."

"Is Luc better?"

"I'm afraid not. I'm sorry to say, his condition is worse. He has pneumonia, the kind that doesn't really manifest itself until cardiac complications begin. He asked to see you also, Madame de Nonancourt. Follow me, if you please."

Brushing the tears from her eyes, Nell followed the doctor to the room where Luc was lying alone, fighting for his life. She sat on the edge of the bed and held the child's hand.

"Can you hear me, Luc?"

The blue eyes flickered open and he tried in vain to smile.

"You'll look after Oki, won't you, madame? He's the best dog in the world—you said so lots of times."

"Of course I will. I'll give him some special things to eat so he won't miss you too much till you come home."

Luc closed his eyes and turned his head away. Listening in horror to the rattling of his breath in his lungs, Nell tried to shun the idea that he was dying, but instinct told her there was little hope. Bending forward, she kissed his forehead. Then she walked from the room, leaving the child alone with his mother.

At nine Dr. Guichet appeared with a nurse carrying a tray of coffee and a bottle of brandy. He sat opposite Nell and shrugged helplessly.

Madame, Luc died ten minutes ago. I'm so very sorry. Perhaps if he could have had medical attention sooner, perhaps if the hospital had been nearer, who knows, he might have lived. Perhaps nothing could have saved him. He was a very brave little fellow, but I could do nothing. The infection in his lungs was far too great."

Nell sat like a statue, tears streaming down her face. She was thinking of the day when Luc had given her his stone shaped like a cat's head and the morning he had brought her the first bluebells from the woods, with mushrooms gathered at dawn and put in a wicker basket. She had made an omelet with mushrooms and they had eaten it together in the garden. She drank the coffee Guy handed her, refusing the cognac and looking questioningly at the doctor.

"How many hospitals are there to serve the Loire region?"

"Two, madame, this one and the one at Poitiers. Neither is really prepared to deal with emergencies and we are unable to cope with surgical cases. Those we have to send to Paris, at least the complicated ones."

"Are there any hospitals for children?"

"For children only? None as far as I know."

Nell was silent. Guy's grandmother, whose precious ring Nell now wore, had made her life's work charity. During her life at Bel-Ami, this great lady had saved many widows and their children who had taken refuge in the château. Nell knew now that she must never be tempted to waste a second of her life. From this day on, she too must dedicate her time to something useful. Nell clenched her fists in resolve. She would fleece every patronizing aristocrat in the region for funds to build a children's hospital, and then another if she could raise more money. She would play the rich at their own game, giving them the adulation, publicity, and applause they craved until she had what she wanted. First, though, she must get her own status in order, or they would not give her a cent. Nell stopped crying, anger replacing anguish in her heart. She would not think of Luc bringing her posies in the early-morning light. She would think only of his ashen face and frightened eyes at the moment when they had both realized death had entered his small room. His pain would be her inspiration, his death the impetus she knew only too well she would need to sustain the efforts required.

Luc's death was the second great tragedy in Annabelle Ellerman's life. The first, her own sterility, had come close to breaking her spirit. She was unaware that the second would be the making of her.

On a crisp January morning, Nell arrived in Paris and went at once to Collete's Institut de Beauté in the Rue de Miromesnil. That such a distinguished writer should have opened a beauty salon had startled many of her friends and caused a sensation in the city. To Nell it seemed charming and original and she was delighted to see the lady again.

"We met once before when you came with the Princesse de Polignac to stay for the week with my brother-in-law."

"And now you are married and very happy, so they say?"

"I am and I want to stay that way. That's why I came to Paris. I need your help, madame. I want to earn some money and I've been wondering if your friend would still be interested in using me for the magazine."

Colette left the establishment in the charge of an assistant and led Nell to her private suite on the top floor of Claridge's Hotel. There, high above the Champs Elysées, she ordered lunch for them both, examining the beautiful creature before her with interest and a writer's eye. When Nell spoke of Luc, Colette recalled the day when she had met the child.

"He was a truly delightful little boy. He showed me where to pick wild mushrooms and talked all the time about you."

Nell spoke of her desire to build a clinic in Luc's name.

"I want to be someone those damned aristocrats who live near Bel-Ami will want to know, or I'll never be able to raise enough money."

"Will Charles not finance you? He's incredibly

rich and I wouldn't be surprised to hear he's still in love with you."

"He's promised me a donation, but I don't want him to do everything. This is something I want to do with my husband, not with his brother."

"So you wish to accept the Princesse de Polignac's offer to have your photograph in *Vogue* magazine? Hmmm. I think it's a sound idea. Once you are promoted as the new face of the decade, everyone will want to know you. I can help, of course. I shall write about you and then about Luc. I shall also give space to those who are very generous when you start the fund."

"Thank you. Your support could well tip the balance for me."

"Here's lunch, Nell. I'm so hungry I could eat a gorilla, provided it was covered in butter and garlic. By the way, I saw your friend Marc de Villalonga the other day. Perhaps you should approach *him* for money. He's so rich he could build an entire hospital if he had the inclination."

After lunch, Nell went to the offices of *Vogue* and was reintroduced to the princess and then to a diffident young Englishman named Cecil Beaton. The princess was overjoyed to see Nell again, and a sitting was arranged for the following week. Then the princess's assistants began to write notes and make calls to arrange with couturiers and set designers the lending of clothes and furniture for the session. Makeup artists were brought in to see Nell, and a hairdresser to discuss Beaton's requirements. He had decided to photograph her all in white, and when he had described what he wanted to do, he kissed Nell's hand and made his exit in the finest style.

"Have no fear, Madame de Nonancourt, I shall make you the sensation of the season. I shall surround you with lilac and jasmine and put you in the Hall of Mirrors at Versailles. You will be the person *everyone* wants to know, myself included!"

While arrangements were still being made with Chanel and Patou, Schiaparelli and Lanvin, another photographer was hastily summoned from his apartment nearby. George Hoyningen-Huene was intrigued when the princess explained that Beaton would be taking Nell's pictures and that she wanted a contrasting image. Charmed by Nell's larger-than-life style, he began to describe what he would like to do.

"I will use Madame as a creature from another world, an Amazon. I don't wish to use clothes from the designers. I shall photograph her in imperial sable and half-naked on a tigerskin. I shall put her in a medieval troubadour's outfit in the Château de Beau Rivage, which was built in the thirteenth century. Finally I will cover her with emeralds and diamonds and photograph her as an object of immense value in the window of Cartier. I adore the surreal style, and Madame's looks are well-suited to that. I'm sure Elsa Schiaparelli would dress her for nothing just to have such a splendid showcase for her creations."

It was six P.M. when Nell emerged from the offices and walked slowly toward the Champs Elysées. She was tired, hungry, and overwhelmed by all the attention she had received. She had gone only a few hundred yards when she heard someone calling her name.

"Nell, may I give you a lift home?"

Turning, she saw Marc de Villalonga getting out of a black Hispano Suiza car. She knew at once that Colette had telephoned him and told him where she would be. Nell thought of Colette's comment about Marc's wealth, and as she looked fondly at his handsome figure, she was wondering if she dared broach the subject of the Luc Dubois Fund.

"I'm so pleased to see you, Marc. Colette told you where I'd be, of course."

"She did. Now, may I drive you home to Bel-Ami, or are you planning to stay in Paris for the night?"

"I was thinking of staying at my cottage in the Valley of Chevreuse."

"Then I shall take you there, but later. First I invite you to dinner at my house."

"I'd like that. I'm hungry and in need of a bit of peace and quiet."

"How is Guy?"

"Busy, as usual. This time he's building a new addition to the main hothouse for an exhibition of rare orchids. I'm about to start work as a mannequin for *Vogue* magazine. It's another off-shoot of that memorable night at Bel-Ami."

"Colette told me your story—the *whole* story—and I should like to help. I like a challenge and so do you, if I correctly recall your conversation with Arlette on the night we first met."

Nell smiled wryly at the memory. "Getting money out of the rich will certainly be a challenge, but the cause is a good one, so I shall certainly do my best."

"I'll give you this now, so you don't have to ask me for money later. I'm sure you never asked a man for money in your life."

Nell looked at the check and swallowed hard.

"Are you sure you can afford such a large amount?"

"Of course I'm sure, and I shall give more from time to time. I should also like to volunteer to help you, if you'll allow me and if Guy has no objections. Sometimes it's easier for a man to ask other men for money. Guy can cover the Loire. I will cover Paris. I'll leave the ladies to you."

"I appreciate everything you're offering, and gratefully accept,"

"These are not easy times to raise cash, as you

know, Nell. Many rich people have property and land, but only a few have liquid assets of any substance since the crash of 1929."

Yet, at that moment, the Hispano Suiza glided toward a residence that had obviously suffered no such hardship. The house in the Rue Georges Bizet was built at the turn of the century in the Spanish style, with decorative iron grilles at the windows and an ancient studded front door that had been imported from a castle in Lérida. The interior was exotic, the floors of inlaid scented wood, the walls muralized with scenes of Castile and Aragon. There was a fire in the hall, another in the salon, and a massive open hearth in the dining room. The colors of the house were black, wine, violet, and scarlet.

Seeing Marc in this exotic setting, Nell appreciated his style even more than she had upon their first meeting. Her eyes twinkled as she gazed across the table at him, reveling in his open admiration and desire. How different life would have been if she had married a rich man like him! Then she thought of the check he had given her so casually. Hold on, Nell, she reminded herself. This is no time to allow your imagination to run riot.

They ate zarzuela and garlic chicken on a bed of yellow rice. The wine was intoxicating, the talk entertaining, her host attentive, and Nell relaxed for a few precious hours, listening to Marc's suggestions.

"You must launch the fund by throwing a Whitsuntide ball. Make the tickets very expensive and hard to obtain, so everyone will fight to be included. If you are wise, you will exclude a few of the people who have been difficult with you—for example, Arlette de Saumur and her friends. In that way you will begin to show your power. Let's make a list of guests who simply *must* come to the ball. You don't have to hurry away, do you?"

Nell sighed with pleasure. Hurrying away from this luxurious setting was the last thing on her mind.

Nell returned to Paris on Monday for her first session with Beaton. Never having posed for photographs before, she had no idea what to expect and was surprised to find the studio full of hairdressers, assistants, makeup artists, set dressers, Beaton's photographic assistants, stylists, and miscellaneous representatives of the magazine's editorial staff. The set had been draped with two hundred yards of white satin, the lush opalescent material tucked in folds to the walls and along the ground like a shimmering lake. When Nell appeared in a simple white Chanel dress, a wreath of camellias in her hair, there was a burst of spontaneous applause. Then, as she took her place before the photographer, the crowd drifted away and she was left to face his scrutiny.

It seemed like an age before the lights were to Beaton's liking. Then he began to speak. "I want to capture something in you that will be very hard to project. I want the aristocrat and the real woman, who is also a queen of society, the barbarian queen of Transylvania, and the American from Chicago who knows everything there is to know about life, love, and causing havoc."

"I'm no queen of society."

"You will be. Patience, my dear, patience. Now, head up, eyes to me, tuck your chin in, you're not a boxer. That is perfect, simply perfect."

For four hours Nell sat for Beaton in a selection of Vionnet clothes. The next morning, they were due to go to Versailles, where she would pose in the Hall of Mirrors in some of Chanel's more fanciful outfits. She kept thinking how much better at the job Hadley would have been. Her sister was in the habit of posing all the time, even when alone in a room. Nell smiled, knowing Hadley would be in her element to be the center of attention.

Nell was walking from the offices of *Vogue* when Guy caught up with her.

"Are you a very expensive woman or can a workingman afford you?"

"Guy! What are you doing here?" Nell paused to give him a warm embrace, then, suddenly energized, fell back into her brisk step.

He kept stride with her, looking anxiously into her face but saying nothing of the malicious call he had received from Arlette: "Your wife, it seems, has dined alone with Marc de Villalonga. After all, I'm still your friend, Guy, and I thought you'd want to know." He controlled his anxiety, however, and spoke as though nothing untoward had happened. "Marc de Villalonga called me to invite us to dine with him at Maxim's tonight. Apparently Arlette's been gossiping about you and him all over the city."

Nell blushed furiously, guilt at some of her thoughts of the previous evening making her ashamed.

"Arlette can go to hell. Why should we worry about what she says?"

"My darling, she has the vilest tongue in Paris, and you are about to launch your fund and cannot afford any problems. Once people know you, they will never believe anything Arlette says, but until you are a familiar face and we are a familiar couple, we must make sure we counter her statements."

"Do you dislike all this, Guy?"

"Not at all. I adore the idea of the fund and I love the idea of having a celebrated beauty for a wife. I can't say the same about Arlette's gossip."

That night, Nell and Guy arrived at Maxim's and entered the amber-lit interior crowded with the famous, the infamous, and the scions of aristocratic society. Marc was with a blond Milanese princess and in an expansive humor.

Nell bent to kiss his cheeks. "You look as happy as a three-year-old with a sand castle. What happened?"

"My dear Nell, the manager just told me that Arlette and her husband are due to dine here at nine, and I am delighted she will see us all together."

Nell chose pâté de foie gras with truffles, shrimp-en-croûte, and steak with Madeira-and-mushroom sauce. The Milanese beauty ordered the same with pasta to go with her steak. The four were talking about the Dubois Fund when Arlette walked in with her husband, made a beeline for Guy and kissed him resoundingly, holding him around the neck like a limpet.

"How lovely to see you, Guy, and Marc too. My, my, we are broad-minded! Nell, you look wonderful. And you have a new dress at long last! How exciting for you."

Before Henri de Saumur could interrupt his wife's cruel tirade, a tall slim young man with a matchstick mustache appeared at the entrance of the restaurant. He was wearing a dinner suit with satin lapels, his hair styled in long sideboards, his pale, cadaverous cheeks betraying the fact that he was one of the night creatures known to amuse Arlette. Evidently unaware of the presence of her husband, he stunned Arlette by kissing her dramatically before the shocked assembly of diners. Then he greeted her sotto voce. "My angel, I was *so* thrilled to have your call. I did not expect to see you till Thursday."

Henri, his body stiff with rage, stared at the simian-faced charmer who had made him the laughingstock of Paris. Guy gazed at his plate as if it had taken on a life of its own. Marc barely reacted at all, because he was the one who had arranged to telephone the gigolo, inviting him to dine with Arlette at Maxim's. Resentful of the rumors she was spreading about him and Nell, Marc had decided to teach the lady a lesson in her own inimitable style. He watched with interest as Arlette turned with a stricken face to her husband. "Darling, this is Alejandro. He—"

"I know who he is. He's your gigolo and the fellow everyone is talking about. I wouldn't have thought even *you* would invite him here to join us."

"I didn't, Henri. I swear I didn't."

"But now that he has so dramatically arrived, you must excuse me. I have work to do. I shall move my belongings to the club immediately and you will hear from my lawyers in the morning."

Arlette let out a wail of humiliation. "But, Henri, I'm your wife."

"Not for much longer, madame. I would rather live with a pack of hungry lions than remain one second longer with you. Guy, Nell, Marc, Marella, do forgive this most unfortunate scene."

Nell watched as Henri de Saumur marched from the restaurant, followed shortly after by his wife and her lover. Arlette's eyes were overflowing with tears. The gigolo was beaming like a general who has just had a great victory. Nell looked at Guy and thought how far removed he was from the trite world of high society that Marc, Arlette, and Henri inhabited. Impulsively she leaned over and kissed him, knowing without any doubt that he was the only man in the world for her.

They were drinking coffee and plum brandy when Marc handed her a list. "These are the contributions pledged so far by my friends in Paris."

"And these are the contributions from friends in the area of Bel-Ami," Guy added. "There aren't many big checks, but most of the families are

willing for you to use their houses and grounds
for fund-raising events in the summer. The
Lotbinières have also offered the free loan of the
Théâtre de Printemps here in Paris if you should
need it."

"Do thank everyone, Guy, and put their names
on the invitation list with details of their contributions."

Nell scrutinized the list Marc had given her,
smiling at Henri's name at the top, with a contribution only slightly smaller than his own. Nell's
list included Colette, the Princesse de Polignac,
the Duchesse de Ribes, and forty of the leading
fashion and social figures of the day. Some of the
contributions were small. Others were surpris-
ingly large. Whatever the total, a start had been
made. With luck, the fund would snowball as
socialites realized that the size of their contributions to the Luc Dubois Clinic Fund would dictate their entrée and status at the Whitsuntide
ball.

The next photo sessions lasted for over a week.
Gradually, as he realized her potential, Hoyningen-
Huene became intrigued by Nell. He took four
hundred pictures of her in the studio and more
on location. In addition, he borrowed a priceless
bejewled cape from the Musée Mayotte and put
it around her shoulders as she stood at the top of
a baroque black-and-gold staircase. The photograph of Nell, her foot outstretched as she prepared to descend, her heavy-lidded, sultry eyes
gazing down at the onlooker, the bejeweled cape
shimmering in the lights, made both of them
famous. She looked like a queen and a barbarian,
the astonishing personification of the new and
ravishing women, to be copied by anyone with
confidence enough to try. *Vogue* felt they had
found their face of the decade and Nell her place
in the sun.

On her return to Bel-Ami, Nell entered the

cottage and smelled lamb roasting over the fire. A leg stuffed with rosemary and garlic was hanging over the embers, a drip tray catching the juices. In the old black oven a braided bread was baking and on the table there was a bouquet of pink roses and a note from Guy. *Have gone to the Lancasters' to collect their contribution. I will bring back a gâteau for dessert. Can't wait to see you.*

Nell flopped down in the rocking chair, a look of contentment on her face. Though it had been fun to be feted and fussed over by the photographers in Paris, it was much nicer to be home, settled comfortably in her cherished cottage. She knelt and turned the lamb on its hook. Then, when she had checked the potatoes roasting among the embers, she sank again into the chair before the fire. She had made a good start with her fund and already had a third of the target money. Another third might be raised at the ball. Then she would spend the summer collecting the balance. It was conceivable that by the fall she would have enough to begin construction of the first clinic.

Outside the cottage the wind rose. It had been a long day. Lulled by the rustling of the foliage outside her cheerful refuge, Nell fell asleep and dreamed of the Whitsuntide ball.

Nell's issue of *Vogue* appeared on the stands the week before the ball and sold out within hours. Every socialite in Paris was eager to see whether the American had made a fool of herself or if she was as special as Colette's recent articles had implied. All were awed by the breathtaking beauty of the pictures. Nell's face and figure adorned not only the magazine's cover but also thirty pages of the interior, an unheard-of honor. The photographs were sensational, showing every facet of her strange, unworldly allure.

At Bel-Ami the telephone began to ring, until

finally Guy left it off the hook. Invitations arrived by the dozen and were replied to by the household clerical staff with the message that Annabelle de Nonancourt would be delighted to meet new friends at the Whitsuntide ball at the Ritz on the thirteenth of the month. Though all tickets had been allocated, donators, it said, could still obtain them in limited numbers.

Nell was in bed with Guy, opening her mail on the day before the ball, when she found a letter from Bunny. As always, she read it to her husband.

> Dearest Nell and Guy,
>
> We're in the distillery at last and have survived a few disasters like the machines going wrong and one of the women falling in the still. After a shaky start, the widows are getting more confident. We're also relieved that Mr. Fergusson's discovered someone with a talent for blending. It's Rory, Loud Maggie's twelve-year-old son. I've taken him on, despite his age, and he's even learned to spit out the whiskey, so he won't turn into a boozer. My stomach is so huge I can hardly get through the door and have to roll out of bed like a giant snail. I'll be glad to get back in shape again. Jack bought copies of your *Vogue* and gave them to all his friends. Mrs. Mac's put hers up on the wall. I truly believe you're the most beautiful thing our family ever produced. Hadley must be ill with jealousy.
>
> Hugs,
> Your sister Bunny

Nell laughed out loud at the thought of pregnant Bunny rolling out of bed like a snail. She was quite sure, however, that her sister would be the very best of mothers, just as she had already proved herself to be the perfect wife and budding whiskey tycoon. As Nell thought of the ball and the money she hoped to raise from it, she hoped fervently that she could have a fraction of the success her sister had had in life.

The ballroom of the Ritz Hotel had been decorated entirely in white. The guests had been ordered to appear in costumes of the Louis XIV period. When they arrived, their invitations were scrutinized by security guards, and gate-crashers were turned away. As they moved to the staircase leading to the ballroom, a majordomo announced the names.

Guy stood at Nell's side, looking proudly at the glittering scene. Though he would never admit it, he had been taken aback by his wife's success in attracting the leaders of Parisian high society to her ball. He spoke, however, with his usual laconic calm. "Well, you did what you said you would do, and they are all here. I wonder how they will take your little surprise.

Nell shook her head uncertainly. "They'll either reach for their checkbooks or be offended and go home. I wouldn't like to guess which."

Guy watched Marc de Villalonga entering, a beautiful titian-haired society woman on his arm.

"Marc certainly knows how to choose his women!"

Nell looked at her husband with anxious eyes.

"Do you ever envy your single friends, Guy?"

"Never. I am very happy with you and want no one else. I had enough years as a bachelor to last a lifetime."

Nell leaned over and kissed his cheeks.

"I wish we were rich enough to take Suite 105 and go up there togther. It would be like old times."

"I'm going nowhere until the announcements are made. I can't wait to see what happens."

After an elegant meal, the dancing began, only to be interrupted by the first unexpected announcement of the evening. At this, a dozen contributors to the fund were revealed, their donations recorded, and applause for their generosity encouraged. The names included Marc de Villalonga and Henri de Saumur, two of the most substantial backers. As everyone realized that all the contributions were going to be announced, there was a genteel stampede by some of the less-generous members of society to increase their contributions.

Nell watched as secretaries handed the latest figures to her husband, intrigued when Guy led her from the ballroom and upstairs.

"Time for champagne in Suite 105. I told Auzello you wanted it and he immediately thought it a good idea to offer you the use of it for the night. I believe he has been in love with you for years!"

"You're a schemer, Guy de Nonancourt."

"Would you change me?"

"Never in a million years."

Marc watched wistfully as Nell disappeared with her husband, kissing Guy at every step as they walked upstairs. He was about to reenter the ballroom when he saw Arlette standing behind a pillar watching him.

"You're in love with her, aren't you, Marc?"

"I admire Nell, Arlette. What are *you* doing here?"

"I tried to get in, but I didn't have a ticket."

Suddenly Marc felt sorry for the woman who was her own worst enemy.

"If you wish, Arlette, I can take you inside for an hour, but I think it best if you go home."

"Where's home? Henri threw me out and had all the locks changed. Can I come to your place, Marc?"

He looked into the brazen eyes, at the self-indulgent mouth and the hands that were never still. Then, with a shrug of regret, he moved away.

"I'm sorry, Arlette, it wouldn't work. As you have so often pointed out, my friends are not yours."

An hour later, Arlette threw herself from the third-floor platform of the Eiffel Tower, leaving a note on rose-pink paper tied to one of the stanchions.

> Annabelle de Nonancourt is to blame for this. First she stole my man, then she deliberately turned my husband against me. I have night-mares about her and I can't stand it any longer. Nothing is how I want it to be since I met her. I feel as if I've fallen into a deep hole and I won't ever be able to escape. Tell Guy I'll always love him.
>
> Arlette de Saumur

The following morning Auzello led Marc to Suite 105, waiting anxiously as he knocked on the door.

"May I come in, Guy?"

"Of course. What brings you here so early?" he asked.

"Don't look so miserable," Nell said. "I think we raised enough for two clinics last night, and I'm over the moon."

"Nell, Guy, there is an account in the papers about which you must know. Arlette killed her-self last night and left a note saying you, Nell, had ruined her life. I suggest you return to Bel-Ami and keep out of the way for a few days. After that, the journalists will have forgotten the incident and you'll be free to live in peace again."

Nell and Guy were speechless.

"I'm sorry to intrude at this time, but I wanted

you to know before the press invaded the hotel with their infernal questions."

An hour later, as Nell and Guy were about to leave the Ritz, Auzello hand-delivered a letter from Hadley.

Dearest Nell,

Please come at once. I've discovered I'm pregnant and I can't stop crying! Am so upset, I swear I could die. Karl keeps singing and I'm tempted to kill him. Hurry and call me.

Hadley

Nell turned to her husband. "Hadley's panicking, from the sound of it."

"She married Karl because she wanted money and security. She never wanted children. Children are reality. Karl adores her, of course, and needs her too, but there'll be problems for both of them once that child is born. I hope Hadley isn't tempted into doing something ridiculous to prove to herself that she isn't domesticated. She's one of those types who act first and regret later."

"Oh, Guy, I hope you're wrong."

"You know I'm right."

— 9 —

MUNICH, JANUARY–APRIL
1934

HADLEY WAS IN bed, surrounded by newspapers and fashion magazines. The front-page story in all the papers was the crash of an airship in the English Channel that had killed forty well-known men and women. One of the passengers had been Charles, Duc de Nonancourt. Nell and Guy were now the new Duke and Duchess of Nonancourt. Now Nell would be able to stop scrimping and saving and having economy drives, Hadley thought. From now on, it would be diamonds for her all the way. Hadley remembered the magnificent family jewels of the Nonancourts and thought with a certain irony that Nell, whose life had been blighted for so long by her childlessness and poverty, was suddenly one of the most famous faces in Europe and now a duchess to boot. Hadley asked herself with a certain unease of it was best to start at the bottom of the ladder of life and work your way up to the top. She had started at the top, a certain winner, or so it had seemed, and she constantly felt as if she was slipping, diminishing, deteriorating. It was a feeling that terrified her, because she never felt able to help herself, to stop the downward spiral.

Hadley quickly engrossed herself in reading

about Miss Barbara Hutton, whose husband had had her admitted to a hospital and force-fed because she was starving herself. She read furiously on. In Munich, Adolf Hitler could be seen eating sauerkraut at the Osteria Bavaria, his genial manner making it hard to believe the stories circulating about his intentions for the future. People were already talking about the possibility of war, and governments were sending diplomats to see the man of power in Germany.

Hadley threw down the papers and reached for her mirror, staring at her reflection in disgust. The feuille-morte taffeta housecoat would not fasten, the curly hair that had always been so lovely was suddenly out of condition, the face positively moon-shaped. Putting the mirror aside, she gazed into space, furious to have lost her looks to such a degree. She had hated every moment of her pregnancy. During it, she had suffered every malady in the medical journal, from headaches to fallen arches, nausea to flutterings of the heart. Angry with life, she glowered at the maid who appeared with the breakfast tray.

Gisela knew better than to look too cheerful in the early morning and greeted her employer with caution. "Good morning, madam. It is a fine day, but cold. Sir has gone skiing and asked that I tell you he will return at eleven to have coffee with you."

"He's nothing if not reliable! What's for breakfast?"

"Frau Hoffman has made the food in the style of New Orleans, as you asked. We have ham cooked in champagne, eggs in cream, pecan-and-cinnamon rolls with hot butter and brown sugar. I hope you will enjoy it."

Hadley thought of her husband skiing down the mountain and glowered at the breakfast she had ordered out of sheer self-indulgence. For months she had been confined to playing the drawing-room games that had always bored her instead of the tennis, golf, and skiing she adored. She was sick of Mah-Jongg, Parcheesi, and checkers, fed up to the eyeballs with whist, bridge, and cribbage. She turned on the BBC World Radio Service and heard a cheerful British voice singing "Ah, Sweet Mystery of Life!" Then, under the maid's watchful eyes, she began to eat.

Gisela spoke with exaggerated respect. "Frau Hoffman asks me to remind you that your sister is due to arrive on the train from Paris at two this afternoon. Also, Dr. Braun is expected at one."

"I want to meet my sister at the station."

"Herr Hoffman will drive you there."

Hadley stared at the girl, with her plaited blond hair and pale, insolent eyes.

"Did my husband say he'd be out?"

"No, but Sir is often out after lunch and does not come back until four. I assumed you would wish Herr Hoffman to drive you."

When the maid had gone, Hadley put the breakfast aside and returned to reading the papers. Inside her, the baby turned and kicked and did what Karl liked to call its morning exercises. Closing her eyes, Hadley tried to still the panic within her as she looked at the huge mound under the bedclothes. Dear God, would it never end? Was she going to spend her life as fat as a barrel? She was already two weeks overdue, inasmuch as she had been able to assess. Hadley did her best to concentrate on the newspaper. Lady Diana had thrown a fabulous party in Paris. Monkey fur was in for those with enough daring to wear it. Hadley scanned the other news. Hair was being worn up and in curls. The craze for Persian lamb continued, and wearing a pair of foxes with heads intact was de rigueur for luncheon appointments. The popular word of the season was "amusing." Hadley sighed, wonder-

ing if anything would ever be amusing to her
again.

Ignoring the meal Frau Hoffman had prepared
for her, Hadley got up and put on the jewels Karl
had bought her from the new Van Cleef and
Arpels African collection. She was trying to fasten the necklace, when she paused, the color
draining from her face as she felt an intense
pain. She ran to the telephone and called Frau
Hoffman.

The housekeeper entered the room, noting the
barely touched breakfast, the stricken look in the
mistress's eyes.

"What can I do for you, madam?"

"I think I have indigestion. I have a perfectly
horrible pain. You mustn't make any more of
those huge breakfasts!"

"Ah, the child is arriving at last."

Hadley's eyes widened in panic as another pain
hit her and sweat broke out on her brow.

"I wish I could go to sleep and not wake up till
all this is over."

"That you cannot do, madam. You must help
the child be born, as all mothers do. I will hurry
to help in every way I can. Don't worry, I will
not leave you alone for long."

Hadley sat on the edge of the bed, her hands
shaking, her face devoid of color. Nell would
already be on the train for Munich, so there was
no point in trying to telephone her. Hadley
thought of her younger sister and knew she must
speak with her at once. Bunny knew everything
about the problems of having children. She had
already had one son and was longing to be pregnant again. Hadley hurried to the phone and
asked the operator to connect her with her sister's number in Scotland.

Frau Hoffman returned to find Hadley pacing
back and forth like a caged tiger. Her face was
white, her fists clenched. When the phone fi-

nally rang, half an hour later, she called out in a loud voice, desperate to bridge the distance between herself and her sister, "Bunny, thank God they got you. It's Hadley, can you hear me all right?"

"We've got a gale and the lines are crackling, but I hear you just fine. What a lovely surprise."

"I'm in labor! Bunny, I'm so scared! It started about half an hour ago."

"Nell wrote me about her staying with you to help for a few weeks. Isn't she there yet?"

"She arrives at two on the train from Paris."

"Now, listen to me. No one ever took a month to get a baby out, so you just take your time. In a day or so everything'll be over. You'll have some pain and you'll be tired, but it's nothing you can't handle, and I'm telling you the truth. Have Frau Hoffman make you some raspberry-leaf tea and drink a pint now and a pint in two hours' time. Then do whatever you feel like doing."

"Do whatever I *feel* like doing?" Hadley shrieked. "I haven't been able to do *anything* in six months!" Hadley gasped through a contraction, then continued contritely, "What did you do?"

"I couldn't suffer lying in bed and started loading tinned foods onto the shelves of the new storeroom with Mrs. MacKay. I only went to bed at the end, but women are all different. A lot of them like to go to bed with hot-water bottles. Others need exercise. Janet Reekie told me she did a pile of washing before each of her six sons was born. Are you there, Hadley? You aren't crying, are you?"

"Oh, Bunny, I'm so scared!"

"Have a brandy and I'll call you at midday if I can get through."

"Thanks for everything, Bunny."

Hadley put down the phone, resolved to do everything her sister had advised. First she changed into a nightdress. Then, having asked Frau Hoffman to throw more logs on the fire, she sat in the armchair with her jewel box on her knees. She would sort through the pieces and clean them to make the time go quickly until Karl's return.

It was eleven A.M. when he finally hurried into the room. Hadley ran into his arms.

"Where have you been? I needed you."

"I am so happy to hear our child is coming."

"So am I. I want to be beautiful again. I'm so sick of all this."

Karl hid his disappointment in her response, as he had hidden it throughout the pregnancy. At first, Hadley had wanted to abort the child. Then, on learning that her condition was too advanced for that, she had become ill with tension. It had been like living with a time bomb, and it had been only recently that her temper had improved. Karl recognized Hadley's reactions for what they were—not filled with malice, but with fear. Now, as he watched her sorting through her jewels and making lists of the contents of the box, Karl loved her as he had never loved her before. Feeling her trembling as he held her in his arms, he looked into her eyes.

"Don't be afraid. Dr. Braun will soon be here and I will ask him to give you something to kill the pain."

"You won't leave me, will you?"

"Of course not. Now, here is the champagne. I have been told it is the best thing for ladies with labor pains."

When the doctor arrived, he was taken to Hadley's room, where she was lying in bed, her face covered in sweat.

"I shall not leave until the baby arrives, Countess, I promise."

He timed the pains and examined her carefully, shocked to find that in the days since his last examination, the child had shifted its position and was going to be born feetfirst. He turned to Karl with a helpless gesture.

"We must move your wife to the clinic. There is the possibility that this will be a complicated birth."

"Do what you must to keep her safe and well."

Hadley began to cry, aware that her husband had wanted the child to be born in the room where all the Kohler ancestors had entered the world. She felt like a fraud and a failure and was suddenly terrified of dying. Closing her eyes, she refused to watch as maids were called, a case packed, and the car brought around to the side door. Then she was wrapped in her favorite lynx cloak and carried downstairs by Karl. As she sat between him and the doctor, she watched the passing scene with weary eyes. The city was covered in snow, and here and there painted troikas passed by, their silver bells tinkling merrily. Memories filled Hadley's mind of the dreamlike days she and Karl had spent together, dining in the hunting lodge, skiing on the mountain, making love on a bearskin rug in the firelight glow. All that had ended with the advent of the pregnancy, Karl had suddenly seemed older and more responsible, less romantic and sexual. He had not made love to her after the fifth month and had slept in a separate bed in the same room for the last four weeks for fear of accidentally kicking her in the night. Hadley sighed, wondering if he would suggest love on the bearskin rug again after the child was born. Or did he enjoy his new role so much that his only interest from now on would be the baby?

At two P.M. Nell stepped from the train, surprised to see no sign of her sister or Karl. The journey had been long and she was tired and none too happy to be back in Germany. She scanned the faces of people waiting at the barrier and saw Herr Hoffman hurrying into the station concourse. Nell asked at once about her sister. "Where's Hadley? She said she'd meet me at the train."

"The countess had to go to the clinic. She was most upset and crying like a child. I am glad you are here to help her, madam. A woman needs her own family at a time like this."

"Then I'm about to become an aunt?"

Hoffman nodded, smiling.

"Let's go to the clinic right now."

"First we shall leave your baggage at the house, so my wife can unpack it for you. Then I will take you to the clinic."

Nell gazed out at the regimented flowers of the Hofgarten, with its formal beds and topiary hedges of yew and beech. Again she had the feeling of being ill-at-ease in the city, of wanting to go back to France on the next train. Instead, she tried to relax, telling herself that she must concentrate on helping her sister. Nell's face softened as she thought of the baby, and she closed her eyes, imagining kissing its cheeks and snuggling it in her arms. She was grateful to Hadley for allowing her to share these first precious weeks, weeks she herself would never experience.

Hadley lay staring up at the ceiling and listening to the glockenspiels sounding in the square below. She had heard them chime two, three, four, five, and six. Now it was almost seven and still there was no sign of the child. As a new wave of pain and nausea engulfed her, she held out her hand to Nell.

"You should go on your knees and thank God you won't ever have to suffer this."

Nell wiped the beads of sweat from her sister's face.

"Let Karl in. He's longing to share the experience."

"This is all his fault."

"He loves you, Hadley. It's only natural for husbands to want babies."

"Well, I never wanted any, and I'm never going to have another. Oh, dear God, the pains are coming back. Hold my hand, Nell. Can't you make them give me something to kill the pain?"

As Hadley's voice rose to a wail, Nell pressed a bell to summon the doctor. Then, despite her sister's instructions, she let Karl into the room.

Hadley began to moan, her hands clutching the sheets, her nails raking the embroidered coverlet. The two people at the bedside watched and waited, flinching when her cries grew louder, bringing the doctor hurrying to her side.

At nine the following morning, after a night none of them would ever forget, Hadley was taken into the surgical unit and delivered by cesarean section. Afterward she was wheeled, still unconscious, back to her room, where Karl was waiting hollow-eyed to watch over her.

Nell tiptoed after the doctor to the room where most of the new babies were sleeping in their cribs. Hadley's daughter was awake, her tiny fists clenched. She had long, dark eyelashes, high cheekbones, and golden hair with reddish lights. On the card at the side of the crib was her name, Venetia Yvette Kohler. Reaching out, Nell touched the child's cheeks.

"She's just lovely, Dr. Braun."

"I hope her mother agrees."

"How could she not," Nell murmured.

"The fact is, the countess specifically ordered that the child not be brought near her—not today, not tomorrow, and not within the foreseeable future."

A week after the birth of her baby, Hadley was recovering slowly from her ordeal. With the memories of the agony she had suffered still fresh in

her mind, she was resentful of the child she had
never desired. From the moment of its birth, she
had refused to see the baby and had demurred
when asked to see Ilsa. She did not *want* to be a
mother, a bovine domesticated creature like every
other woman in the world. Seething with
rage and terrified by the helpless fragility of
the baby, Hadley felt totally unequal to the
demands of motherhood. As always in moments
of trauma, she retreated into a world of frivolity
and fantasy.

First she read every fashion magazine in the
room. Then she had the clinic dietician prepare
a regime to enable her to get back her figure.
Then she became so bored she simply lay gazing
out of the window and seething with annoyance
at anyone who entered the room. She thought of
Karl, who was downcast by her refusal to see the
child and her determination not to breast-feed. If
he had wanted a domesticated wife, he should
not have married her. He should have wed some
fat hausfrau with plaits and impregnated her
regularly once a year. Hadley picked up her pen
and tried to finish a letter to Bunny, the only
member of the family who understood her feelings.
Bunny had told her that someday she would
want to see the baby and Hadley believed her
and had taken comfort from her words. Till then,
she would simply try to forget the hideous pain
she had suffered, the terror she had endured.
She would concentrate on getting her figure back
and on being ready to leave with Karl on his new
expedition to the desert. The alternative was to
stay at home with her husband and die of boredom
because all he wanted to do was be with
the baby. Hadley closed her eyes, trying not
to think of what was happening. When she opened
them, Ernst Dietmueller was standing by her
bed.

He looked very handsome, suntanned and lean. Dressed all in black, Hadley thought fleetingly that he resembled a character in a Wagner opera. Mesmerized by the look of desire in his eyes, she waited for him to speak, unable to resist a smile at his honesty.

"I won't bore you by asking how you like motherhood. I am quite certain you detest it. For the time being, you are free to act upon those feelings. No doubt your child is being well cared for and doted over by the rest of the family."

"But not by me."

"So I hear. I brought you some champagne and caviar. I recall you are very fond of both those things. I also brought this. It is a Bokhara silk shawl of great antiquity. I found it long ago in the establishment of a dealer in the city. Tell your husband you've had it for years or he will be angry."

"What are you doing here, Dietmueller?"

"You know what I'm doing here, and you know that I want. You must agree I have been very patient. Of course, I knew your marriage would eventually bore you to death. You're as addicted to excitement as some people are to drugs or drink. I have come to promise it to you."

Unfortunately, Dietmueller was right. Hadley *was* bored by everything settled and domesticated, and hungry for the burning emotional release she had not experienced for so long. Still, she would not admit her feelings to Dietmueller and answered defiantly. "I'm leaving for Ethiopia when I get out of this place, so don't build up your hopes."

"Your husband has canceled the expedition. He told Count Graf yesterday he could not bear to think of leaving the baby so soon after its birth."

Hadley glowered at Dietmueller, disappointed by what he had told her, and annoyed by the cynical amusement he took in it. She was shocked when he spoke again.

"I now have a chalet near the hunting lodge, on the opposite side of the hill, and I propose we meet there. Don't trouble to tell me you don't wish to. You were not made for housewifery. You were made for passion and the strange games people play when they are ruled by desire."

Hadley shut her eyes to control the images Dietmueller's words brought to mind, the sensations within her that she longed to control but could not. She took the glass he offered and sipped the champagne.

"Right now I don't know what I want. I feel as if nothing in the world could make me happy again."

"You are wrong. You simply need to escape a life that has grown old and tired. Come, I give you a toast: To old friends and new relationships. To excitement and all the forbidden pleasures of life."

Hadley raised her glass. "To the devil!" And she threw the contents of her glass into Dietmueller's face.

Two months after the birth of her daughter, Hadley had regained her figure and some of her good humor. She had not played with the child, but often went to the nursery in the still of night to stand over the cot looking down at the sleeping baby, full of nameless fears that it might have stopped breathing. The contradictions in her feelings for the child became stronger with every passing day, until finally something happened that made her confront her fears.

Nell had returned to the château after five weeks of lovingly caring for the child. An English nanny had replaced her. Miss Siddons was thirty-eight, bright, breezy, and affectionate, with a horsey face, a wry sense of humor, and the strength of a circus performer. Hadley was content to leave Tia with her without restriction. Then suddenly the new nanny was rushed to the hospital with appendicitis. Hadley panicked and threatened to run away if left with her child, but Karl was adamant.

"Tia is your daughter and you will look after her until Miss Siddons returns."

"I can't, I just can't!"

"Pull yourself together, Hadley."

"You don't understand, I just cannot look after her, I don't know how."

"Ask Ilsa."

"We can send to the agency in England and they'll dispatch someone right away."

Karl's face was hard. "You had a difficult time having Tia, and Dr. Braun told me to be patient, but now my patience is exhausted. You will look after your child, Hadley, and that is the end of the matter. I will not have a wife who shrieks every time she hears her baby cry, who refuses to hold her child, and who behaves as if the act of birth was the ruination of her life. Grow up! You are a mother now and must give up playing the spoiled child."

"Please don't leave me, Karl. I beg you not to leave me!"

He pulled away and was soon seen riding his white horse hard for the plum-tree meadow. Hadley watched as he cleared the fence and disappeared from view. Then she tiptoed into the kitchen, where she sat looking despairingly at the housekeeper.

"I want to call my sister Bunny, Frau Hoffman. Can you get the number for me?"

Frau Hoffman put on her spectacles and Hadley watched her clutching the receiver, speaking in her telephone voice. Then she turned to Hadley. "The operator says the delay is very short today, less than one-quarter of an hour. I will make you some coffee, madam. In the meantime, please try to relax. Tia is a baby, not a monster. She cries when she is hungry or wet and she loves to sleep so she can grow tall like her mother."

Hadley sighed. Deep down, she felt sorry that she had ignored the child for so long. It had not asked to be born, nor demanded care and attention. She knew she was in the wrong, as usual. She sighed again, suddenly uncertain of everything. Tia was a truly beautiful child. Hadley felt pride at least in that. Her deliberations were interrupted by the insistent ring of the kitchen phone.

"Hadley! How are you? We have a good line for a change."

"Oh, Bunny, the nanny's ill and Karl's insisting I look after Tia. I'm on my own and don't know what to do."

"Calm down, Hadley. If the baby cries, you change its nappy. If she still cries, you feed her. If you don't know how to mix the food, get Ilsa over to show you. When Tia's had her bottle, you burp her and then you put her in her cot, and that's the last you'll hear from her for ages. Now, why don't you ask Karl to bring you over here for a holiday. You sound as if you need it. Nell and Guy are coming in July and staying till the end of August. Guy'll be delighted if Karl can come. He's so scared on the sea, he turns green just walking on the beach."

Hadley laughed.

"Just remember, Hadley, she's a baby, not a machine, and all she needs is food and love and lots of sleep. There's not a thing in the world you can't do to make her very, very happy."

"I'll try, I really will, but I'm not *made* for this kind of life."

*   *   *

In the afternoon, the baby began to cry. Hadley changed the diaper and fed the child, burping her as Bunny had instructed and then placing her in her crib. In that quiet moment, Hadley noticed that Tia had the Ellerman green eyes. She folded her arms with pride. But within seconds, Tia's screams began to fill the house, terrifying the anxious mother. Hadley looked down at the baby, certain it was in pain. Gently she picked Tia up and snuggled her in her arms to try to pacify her distress, but she was alarmed to see the tiny face turning pale and the breath coming fast through the lungs. Panic-stricken, she ran to call the doctor.

After examining Tia, Braun realized that she had measles, a serious condition for a baby of only twelve weeks. A nurse was called and another engaged for the nights. Then Herr Hoffman was sent to the pharmacy for a prescription while his wife served tea to Hadley and the doctor.

Braun watched his patient with interest, his curiosity coming to the fore as he tried to assess her. She was shaking like a leaf and ashen pale from stress. Where was the hardness he had disliked in her on first meeting? Dr. Braun, as skilled at diagnosing emotional conditions as he was at pinpointing physical ones, smiled at his misgivings. Hadley's toughness was only a veneer—a cover to hide her childlike fears. He spoke gently, doing his best to reassure her. "Your husband meant well, but he should not have left you alone with the child. It has been obvious from the beginning that you were not taking to motherhood."

"I love Tia, Dr. Braun. I know it doesn't seem like it, but I do. It's just that I'm so scared of her. I'm even frightened to put her in the crib in case she suffocates."

"You are afraid, most of all, of yourself, aren't you? Sudden changes, like having a child, can make one stop and think, even reasses. Tell me, do you feel disappointed in your life?"

Hadley shook her head resignedly. "Since my father died, everything's changed. Till then I thought I was someone special and important."

"And now?"

"I've discovered I can't really do anything. All I'm good at is flirting and making love."

The doctor smiled despite himself at her honesty. "What would you like to do?"

"I don't know. I'm a person who needs other people to do things for her all the time. I can't earn a living and now I've discovered I can't even care for my own child. I don't understand how my sisters have changed so much and I've just stayed the same useless, decorative Hadley Ellerman."

"How did your sisters change? Tell me about them."

"The youngest, Bunny, was chubby and we all thought she was slow. Then, after Papa's death, she started working as if her life depended on it. First she learned to cook and ran a catering business in Paris. Then she married and went to live in a castle in Scotland. She has a son, a demanding husband, and a staff—plus she's running an entire industry to help a group of local women who were widowed by an accident at sea. She doesn't stop from morning to night and she's so *happy*."

"And the other sister?"

"Nell married a poor man for love and struggled to save up for every cheap pair of shoes she wanted to buy. Yet she's certainly made something of herself. Look, here's her photograph. Isn't she beautiful? She's the only person who's ever been given a cover *and* thirty pages of *Vogue* magazine all to herself. She's unable to have children, so she works at raising funds for hospitals for them. Now she's a duchess, but she and Guy still live in a little cottage. She doesn't even want to move to the main château. After all her good fortune, all she really needs is her husband's love."

"And you married Karl and came to live in a dream house in Bavaria. No doubt you thought you would live happily forever, but now you are bored?"

"With myself."

"And with your husband, I think?"

"There are times when I'm bored with Karl. He does everything at the same time and in the same way every day. He doesn't ever like anything to change. We eat at the same hour. He rides or skis at the same time each morning. We even make love precisely at ten each night."

"Have you told him how you feel?"

Hadley shook her head, tears beginning to fall. "I'm in the wrong, Dr. Braun. Since I was pregnant I've been angry with everything and everyone. I *love* Karl, but even so he annoys me."

The baby began to howl and suddenly Hadley could stand it no longer. With a quick good-bye to the doctor, she bolted outside and into the woods. Without realizing it, she made for the brow of the hill and looked down on the scene below. Then she knew why she had come this way. There was Dietmueller carrying logs into the mountain lodge he had recently acquired. Her eyed fixed on him, she walked slowly down the hill, pausing when he glanced up with an amused expression on his face.

"I knew you would come."

"How did you know?"

"Your husband left you alone with the child. Of course, you had to escape."

"Do you have a spy in my house, Dietmueller?"

"What I have is a perfect fire, some champagne on ice, and pâté brought back from Fauchon in Paris. Forget the hunting lodge and all its trivialities. You can enter the kingdom of fantasy, where all your dreams will come true, if you choose."

Hadley moved inside the house like a sleep-walker, conscious of his locking the door behind them. She was gazing at the blazing fire when she saw Dietmueller drawing the shutters and closing out the light. Then he poured the champagne and raised his glass to her.

"To you and me, Hadley."

"I hate you so much, Dietmueller."

"Ah, there is a very small line between love and hate, you know. Here, try some of this, and another glass of champagne."

Hadley was on her third glass of champagne when a sense of unreality filled her mind. She felt Dietmueller unbuttoning the back of her dress and knew she must leave now or be lost forever. She rose, afraid and unwilling to submit.

"I came here because I was scared of my baby. I have to go back now. I—"

Dietmueller tore off the dress with one sweeping motion of his arm. Then he grasped her by the shoulders and swung her toward him, bringing his mouth down on hers with a harshness that took her breath away. Hadley was mesmerized, her whole mind and body giving in to her desire to be dominated and held in the viselike grip of his obsession.

"You will stay and do everything I tell you to do. You want me and you always did. You just wish to imagine yourself the great lady like your sisters, when in reality you are a black-hearted whore. That is what you are and always will be. Accept it and enjoy it. Now, do you behave, or do I beat you into submission? The choice is yours."

He tore off her underclothes and threw Hadley down on the bed. He was panting like an animal and she could barely find the strength to ward him off as he bit her breasts and her stomach.

Then, as he was pushing her legs apart, Hadley made one last attempt to get away. Racing to the door, she began to unlatch it, but he dragged her back and hit her with such force she felt the blood running from her mouth to her chin. Shocked to feel desire running like a spring within her, Hadley watched in fascination and horror as he threw her clothes on the fire. It was all over. She was going to belong to Dietmueller forever. She felt a sudden lethargy come on her as he pushed inside her body, and then a desire more intense than she had ever known before. She knew she was doomed to damnation for this, but as Dietmueller's body enticed her to passion, she moaned in ecstasy. Dietmueller was a pleasure machine, devoid of love or pity; in short, he was just how she wanted him. In her moments of awareness, the instants when Hadley reminded herself that she must move away from him, that she must deny herself the feelings for which she longed, he hit her hard, until the pain and the shock brought her to orgasm and she lay, her body writhing from the onslaught of his desire. She barely noticed when he brought himself to a climax on the naked skin of her stomach. Then he stepped away and poured them both more champagne.

"You may go as soon as you have found something to wear. I have much work to do."

Hadley rose unsteadily, eyeing him with wonder. Automatically, she obeyed and began to search for something to wear.

Dietmueller came to her side and gripped her arm.

"Sit down on the bed. I said that only to see what you would do, to test your obedience. You cannot return home until your face is less red."

She sat on the edge of the bed, eyeing him warily.

"I wish to God I never met you. You've haunted me for so long."

"Nonsense! I intend to be the spice of your life from this moment on, the forbidden object you crave, the secret you cannot tell. That is what you need and what you will always seek in life. Here, you can put these on."

He handed her a pair of black trousers and a loose-fitting pullover. Then, with a wry smile, he threw his black uniform hat on the bed.

"Try it, it will suit you."

She put it on, her movements wooden, knowing—and wanting—what would inevitably happen. She kept her body stiff as Dietmueller lifted her toward him.

"Kiss me, Hadley, kiss me and be honest with yourself for once. Show me how much you want me and let me show you how much I want you."

Hadley let him push her back on the bed and undress her as if she were a child. She could summon no resistance and knew it would be hypocrisy to pretend that she did not want him. As he lifted her onto his penis, she felt herself filled by desire and knew that she was truly happy for the first time in months. Karl had been the symbol of youth and innocence, the good in her own nature, the right path she had tried so hard to find. Dietmueller was the jungle, where wild animals roam, the magician with death at his beck and call. Hadley felt her body dissolving as he uttered the words she longed to hear.

"I love you and I shall love you to the grave and beyond. Don't ever try to get away from me, because I will *never* let you go."

He did not cry out at the moment of orgasm, but simply pumped the love and the lust and the damning desire into her until he was spent. Then he rose, lit a cigarette, and kissed her hand.

"We shall have fun, you and I. Today we have become acquainted. Next time, I will introduce you to some of the pursuits that most amuse me."

"There won't be a next time. I should never have come."

His eyes bored into hers and Hadley looked away, unable to meet them. Then, without a word, she began to dress. Minutes later she was running to the top of the hill, where the wind was fresh and the air pure and clear. Her mind was in a turmoil and she could think of nothing but the sensations she had felt when Dietmueller was inside her, the feelings she knew she should deny. As soon as Tia was well again, she would go to Scotland. At Lochalsh, with Bunny and Cameron to protect her, she would be safe from Dietmueller's desire and from her own. Hadley wondered if she dared confide in Bunny. She could certainly not tell Nell, who would feel Hadley was unfit to raise Tia at all. Shame filled her, and with it a contradictory feeling of elation. Despite everything, Dietmueller's love and hate had made her feel like the women she had once been. For one brief time the old daring Hadley Ellerman had surfaced. The hausfrau had been submerged.

On reaching the hunting lodge, Hadley ran upstairs to strip off the clothes Dietmueller had given her. Then she tiptoed to the nursery and stood looking down at her sick baby. Within seconds she was sobbing her heart out from anguish. In one afternoon she had betrayed herself, her husband, and her child. In deceiving herself and denying her blacker nature, Hadley had deceived everyone who had ever cared for her. The future suddenly seemed devoid of hope. She was nothing without a man inside her. She was incapable of loyalty or of fidelity and had broken every vow made to Karl, who had married her and loved her faithfully to distraction.

Self-loathing filled her. She was now one of
the damned, like Dietmueller, and would have
to accept whatever retribution fate sent her
way.

—10—

LOCHALSH,
JULY–AUGUST 1934

THE COUNTRYSIDE AROUND the castle was a riot of color. Yellow gorse clad the hills, intermingled with deep purple heather. Wild fuchsia hedges skirted the lanes, and children could be seen wheeling Bunny's son, Charles, in his pram as they searched for blackberries to give to Severine so she could make pies for them to take home to their mothers.

Bunny and her husband were driving to the station to pick up Nell and Guy. Their hands linked, the couple glowed with happiness—Bunny had just learned that she was three months pregnant. Cameron had been in seventh heaven since the birth of Charles, and the prospect of a second child was the answer to all his prayers. He smiled proudly when Bunny spoke. "I'm so looking forward to having Nell and Guy see the changes we've made in the house."

"Just remember, you're not to work too hard while they're here. Visitors are tiring, and when Hadley appears, all hell will be let loose."

"She'll go riding and she'll make trips. Besides, what mischief can she get up to in these parts?"

"I don't know, but she'll find something."

251

They stood together on the platform, watching the train pull in, waving as Nell appeared with Hadley's daughter in her arms. Nell's voice was happy as she hurried toward them. "Guy's getting the luggage organized. He insisted on coming by train instead of in the yacht with Hadley and Karl because he's terrified of the sea. He made the baby his excuse, but it's really that he's the worst sailor since Kublai Khan!"

Bunny laughed delightedly. "But what are *you* doing with Tia?"

"Hadley left her with me a while back and I'm going to look after her during the holiday. I wish I could keep her forever, but as it is, I'm lucky that Hadley's busy or absent so often."

"Will you be traveling back on the train when you leave?"

"No, we'll be going by yacht with Hadley and Karl, whatever Guy says. I want to look after the baby till the last possible minute."

Bunny kissed the child's tiny hands, blushing with pleasure that Tia was already so like Hadley.

"She's adorable, Nell."

"She's the light of my life and Guy's too."

Guy hurried along the platform and kissed Bunny affectionately.

"How good it is to see you again, and congratulations on the news of yet another addition to the family."

They drove at a leisurely pace past whitewashed cottages with gardens full of red poppies. An old man picking apples from an ancient tree beyond his porch waved to Cameron, who stopped the car and shook his hand.

"Good morning to you, Robbie. What's happening in the world?"

"Things are better since my lassie came to work at the distillery. She thought of nothing but Fergus since he died. Now she talks of nothing but the whiskey. The old man leaned toward the car window. "I hear a new man's come to the village, a glassblower, so they say."

"Yes—my wife found him in Edinburgh and invited him to settle in Crail. We're trying to get together a group of craftsmen to teach the children their art. His name's Tom Cole and he hails from the Highlands originally."

"And did you hear that Easter MacGregor's back? He was once the finest stained-glass maker in Fife, though he's lived in foreign parts for years. I hear tell his travels may have softened his brain. He's staying at the Hark to Bounty and getting drunk each night from sheer boredom. Why don't you go and see him? He needs work, and those widows need some new men in the village, God knows."

Cameron smiled. "I'll do just that. Thanks, Robbie."

"Now I've a haunch of smoked venison in the storehouse. Would you like a piece, and some of the apples too?"

Nell looked up at the gaunt outlines of the castle and was glad it was summer. Bunny's letters always featured lists of work that had been done on the castle and Nell knew Cameron had spent a lot of money on the place since his marriage. In her opinion, however, Lochalsh would never be a real home. It was too cold, too damp, and too near the sea ever to be comfortable. She was shocked, therefore, on entering the banqueting hall, to find it transformed. There were enormous arrangements of yellow roses and wild buttercups on the refectory table. The windows had been replaced, the hole in the ceiling blocked, and a tanklike stove of embossed black iron installed at the center point of the far wall. From the hall, Nell followed her sister to the guest bedroom. There, the somber tartan had been banished in favor of chintz in ecru and pink, with cabbage roses and large green leaves. Here, too, the windows had been replaced and the fire lighted with fragrant logs. Delighted by the transformation, Nell turned and hugged Bunny.

"You've succeeded in making this monstrosity of a house comfortable!"

"It's better than it was, I must admit, and it didn't cost that much. We paid for the three biggest stoves, but Jack got the others free in return for letting Mr. Svenson use photographs of Lochalsh in his publicity. In Norway, the advertisement reads, 'If Svenson stoves can keep *this* place warm, think of what they can do for your house.' It's true, you know, the stoves are the best thing that ever happened to Lochalsh."

"How's the distillery?"

"Things aren't progressing there as quickly as they did in the house, I'm afraid. I'm running out of cash and Jack's put in all he can. I sold the shares he gave me a while ago and now all I have left is the money from the sale of my pearls. I thought I'd be able to keep the place going on the interest from that, but I'm not so sure. Jack isn't rich in cash, you know. He has land and the house and a military pension for his rank as colonel in the Queen's Own Scottish Highlanders. But he's having to consider accepting the job they've offered him, though I'm not so keen."

"What kind of job, Bunny?"

"Oh, something connected with the work he did in the last war for British Intelligence in France. Jack doesn't talk much about it."

Nell considered the reply.

"If he was in intelligence in the war, I suppose that's where he must have met Charles and Guy. But what are you going to do, Bunny? You can't go on throwing good money after bad."

"What *can* I do? I'll have to use the money from the sale of my pearls to keep the place going and pay the women's wages for another couple of years. After that, I'll have nothing left to sell."

Mrs. MacKay moved away from the guest-bedroom door, her face full of apprehension. She had been about to enter and wish Nell welcome when she had heard Bunny talking about her necklace. She hurried back to the kitchen and began to stir the soup furiously. Bunny's pearls had meant a great deal to her. They were all she had left of her father. Mrs. MacKay felt a solitary tear falling down her cheeks and was alarmed by her own reaction. Dear God, she was getting old, soft, and silly like the English. Pearls were only jewels, after all, and the widows of Lochalsh had put their very lives on the line by working all hours at the distillery. Still, it was a noble gesture on the part of the mistress and she was touched to the bone.

Hadley stepped from the yacht and into the waiting car, ignoring the shocked glances of the locals as they weighed the dress and jacket edged with shiny black monkey fur. Some of the children called out excitedly: "Are you headed for Lochalsh, ma'am?"

"We're going to stay with my sister, the Duchess of Fife."

One of the boys ran away, calling to his friends in the near-incomprehensible local dialect, "Charlie, did you see her, she's as scraggy as a wee ghostie. Mrs. Mac'll have to feed her six meals a day to keep her from falling down a rabbit hole."

Hadley sat at Karl's side, watching the road and gazing out at the waves pounding the whole length of the sandy shoreline.

"We got here just in time, Karl. There's a real Lochalsh tempest brewing."

"These can be treacherous waters."

"Have you ever been to Scotland before?"

"Once, when I was fourteen. I was working for the summer as a deckhand on a fishing trawler that plied between Bremen and St. Andrews. Many ships still come to this coast from Germany to fish for cod and herring."

Hadley wondered what kind of welcome she would receive at Lochalsh. Her guilt at what had happened with Dietmueller was so intense, she felt at times that folk knew what she had done just by looking at her. She shook her head, determined to try to banish all thought of Dietmueller for the duration of her stay. Nell would look after the baby with Bunny, and she would just let herself be spoiled. Hadley saw some of the village women dragging in the shrimp nets, their dresses soaked to the waist. She wondered why they did not use a horse to pull in the net, her mind as yet unable to grasp the extent of the poverty of the area, where a horse was worth its weight in gold. On the lane that led up to Lochalsh, Hadley inhaled the intoxicating scents of a Scottish summer, salt air, honeysuckle, heather, and pine. She took Karl's hand in hers and kissed it impulsively.

"I think I'll like it here."

"It is wild and beautiful like you."

"Do you still love me, Karl?"

"Of course, I shall always love you, and all the Valkyries in hell will not change my mind. But, Hadley, you're making it hard to put what I really feel into actions. For some time you've been drifting away from me, living in a secret world of your own, where I cannot touch you."

"You're imagining it, Karl."

"No, it's not imagination. When the child was born, you were full of panic, but you settled down again. Now you are totally changed. Is there another man, Hadley? Is that what our *real* problem is?"

Hadley tried to keep the panic from her voice. "I've been tired since I had the baby, so very, very tired. I'm sure I'll be my old self again now that I'm able to relax."

"Can you not relax at the hunting lodge?"

"Right now I need my sisters to help me get my confidence back. It's something that'll pass, believe me, if you just give me time."

Hadley entered Lochalsh and was greeted with a hug and a kiss by her sister. She stared into Bunny's big blue eyes, taken by surprise at the perfection of the white linen dress, the slim suntanned arms, the leather shoes of palest shell pink that showed off the perfect ankles. Yet again she found it hard to believe that this self-possessed young woman was someone she had once denigrated.

"I thought you said you were pregnant again. You don't look pregnant to me. You're thinner than I ever saw you."

"I'm only three months gone. It doesn't show yet."

"I looked like an elephant from day one!"

Bunny led her upstairs to the bedroom.

"You only felt like one. You could never be anything but gorgeous. Karl, come and look at the view from your window. On a clear day you can see for miles. Isn't it great?"

Hadley gazed at the room with its four-foot-thick walls and fashionable decor.

"Thanks for having us, Bunny. I didn't expect a room in the very latest style and colors."

"I did it specially for you, Hadley." Bunny looked at her watch. "Lunch is in ten minutes. Let's go have a drink before we eat. Willie's dying to show off how he's learned to make cocktails."

They ate a truly Scottish meal of soup made from shrimp and cockles, then rue that had been hung overnight, its throat stuffed with salt to make the small bones disappear. The fish was served with a sauce of shallots and rowanberries, followed by Mrs. MacKay's specialty, a casserole of lamb, potato, onion, and blood sausages with pickled red cabbage. The tart was one of Severine's latest inventions, combining almond, quince, and apple.

Karl raised his glass to Bunny and her husband. "Our thanks for inviting us, and my compliments on the meal."

Cameron raised his own glass. "To the Ellerman sisters, God bless them."

Utterly delighted to have the family together again, Bunny smiled across the table at Nell. Then, following her sister's gaze, she saw a look of such intense unhappiness in Hadley's eyes that she was taken aback. Obviously something was very wrong in her older sister's life and it was more than mere fear of looking after Tia. Bunny looked again at Nell, and together they watched as Hadley toyed with her food. She was eating nothing. She had already returned to her prepregnancy weight, but now it seemed she wanted to be even thinner. If she could be positively emaciated, Hadley had told them, she was certain she would feel beautiful again.

Nell went to her sister's room after lunch and found Hadley gazing out the window.

"Are you going to tell me what's wrong?"

Unable and unwilling to put her guilt into words, Hadley shook her head. "I have problems, but I can't talk about them."

"You've always told me your troubles before."

"Not this time. This time they're just too awful."

Hadley stood like a sphinx, her face pale and impassive, her voice contrite.

"In addition, Nell, all my troubles are of my own making. I just have to rest and get myself sorted out so I can find a solution."

For the first time in her life, Nell was afraid for her sister. What was it that was *so* awful Hadley could not even tell her? Had she fallen in love with another man? Was Dietmueller causing her trouble because of her racial origins? Had he made a threat to the family as a whole? Had he perhaps tempted Hadley into indiscretion? Nell walked to the door.

"I'm going to the distillery. Are you and Karl coming?"

"No, I want to sleep."

"I'll see you later, then. Hadley, I don't care what you've done. I just want to help. Don't lock me out of your life."

"There are some things you just couldn't understand, Nell. Nor would you want to."

Bunny drove through lanes lined with wild pink hollyhocks to the distillery on the hill. It was a big slate-roofed building, L-shaped and constructed of local granite. By the side of it, a stream trickled over the blue-gray pebbles of the area and yellow irises grew in the shade of an old oak tree. First she led her sister to the accommodation wing, where nine of the women and their children were comfortably housed. Each of the apartments had its own living room, bathroom, and two bedrooms. Bunny kissed some of the children who were working in the communal kitchen and then showed Nell to the interior of the main part of the distillery.

"It's too complicated to tell you all about the whiskey. You'll understand plenty by seeing the operation and meeting the women." Bunny's footsteps echoed in the long hallway that joined the two wings. "It's taken a long time for us to become a real team, but I think we've made it. At first, of course, they thought I was just playing the great lady. But now that they've seen their shares in the place and know they're part-owners, it's settled their minds."

The first thing Nell noticed as she stepped through the double door was the delicious scent of malting barley in the distillery. The trickle of running water, a hoe grating on the floor as one of the women raked the sprouting barley, and the lilting song of Millie Platt as she shoveled peat on the fire under the kiln were the sounds of the place, intermingled with the deep voice of Mr. Fergusson, who was discussing flavors with Rory as if the boy were a grown man and not a child at all.

Nell walked from one room to the next, daunted by the technical look of the place and the obvious complications of the process. She was about to return to Bunny when a red-haired man with heavy muscled arms appeared, stripped to the waist. Turning to her, he said with a dazzling smile, "Well, you're a pretty one. What's your name?"

Surprised by the familiarity of the greeting, Nell snapped a reply. "Put your shirt on and stop gazing at me as if I'm your lunch."

With that, she marched back to her sister.

"Who's that muscle-bound jerk in the distilling room?"

Bunny hurried to investigate and came face to face with a hulking stranger. Looking up at his great height, she spoke with sharp confidence. "Who are you and what are you doing in my distillery?"

"I'm Easter MacGregor, ma'am. You must be Jack Cameron's wife."

"I am, and this is my sister Annabelle, the Duchess of Nonacourt. Now, will you answer my question?"

"I'm making myself useful, ma'am."

"Well, I'd be obliged if you'd get up to the house and make yourself useful there. Mrs.

MacKay needs someone to load the wood store, and we don't have any vacancies here."

"Will I be able to sleep at Lochalsh, then? I'm a stained-glass craftsman by trade, and your husband said you'd find me work teaching the children a trade. That's why I came to the distillery."

Bunny eyed the solid torso and wondered what effect it had had on the widows. She spoke firmly. "We'll find you accommodation if you really can teach the children a trade. But first you'll go to Lochalsh and work for Mrs. Mac till the log stores are full. That's going to take about a fortnight."

Bunny turned to an impressed Nell, and they continued their tour. Easter laughed a hearty, happy laugh. With luck he would get a room at the distillery. After that, it would be simple to persuade Janet Reekie to let him into her bed. Irresistible to women from an early age, Easter was confident that he had it made. Even with Jack Cameron's wife as boss.

Hadley was in front of the mirror preparing for the picnic Bunny had organized, when everyone would swim in the nearby inlet. In the Schiaparelli two-piece bathing suit, with surreal fruits appliquéd to the bodice, Hadley was sure she'd shock the locals. The thought delighted her. At least none of them would ever forget her.

At that moment Mrs. MacKay appeared and gaped at her with ill-concealed horror.

"You'll need a dress over your nakedness and a pullover and stout shoes too. Where Madam's taking you's no place for those daft outfits."

"I'd rather you spoke only when spoken to, Mrs. MacKay. I'm not accustomed to being given instructions by servants."

"You're at Lochalsh and, with all respect, I'm here to look after you. So put your coat on or we'll be hearing the chattering of your teeth from the other side of the hill."

Bunny and her husband were loading blankets into the car in case the weather turned bad. Every few minutes Cameron stopped to kiss her, and twice took her in his arms.

"What have we to eat?"

"Cold lobster and grouse, pigeon pies, bottles of Montrachet '24 and Château d'Yquem '21, and plum and gooseberry tarts."

"It sounds delicious. I could eat it right now."

"You'll do no such thing!"

"How are Mrs. Mac and Hadley getting on? They're an unlikely pair."

"Mrs. MacKay's still treating her like a twelve-year-old."

"That's Hadley's fault for acting like one."

The group trekked off to the cove below the croft cottage, a long, hard walk after leaving the car. Above them, the sun was shining and Hadley could not resist rushing into the water. She screamed in alarm when she hit the ice-cold depths. Then, as she felt the ripples caressing her body, she called to her husband, "Come on in, Karl. It's cold but it's so clean I can see down to the pebbles."

While they swam from one side of the tiny bay to the other, Bunny set out the picnic and Nell and Guy held hands, watching as Hadley emerged, shaking her wet hair and laughing delightedly. As she looked at her dripping, happy sister, Nell realized that for the first time since her arrival, Hadley seemed relaxed. It was as if, once away from Germany, Hadley had rediscovered herself. The problem, therefore, must be nearer to home. With Karl ever the attentive husband and Tia such a bright, healthy baby, Nell knew that somehow Dietmueller was at the root of Hadley's troubles. Nell closed her eyes, praying fervently that nothing would ever harm the innocent child at her side, the only baby that would ever be given into her care.

Hours later, languid from their swimming, the picnickers were driving back to Lochalsh when they saw a yacht approaching the harbor. It was over two hundred feet long, with a beam of twenty-seven feet. The rigging was that of a screw schooner and it was obvious to all that it belonged to someone very rich indeed.

"Oh, stop, Jack!" wailed Hadley. "Stop so we can see the boat."

"It's not exactly a *boat*, now, is it, dear?" remarked Karl.

Cameron turned the car for the harbor and waited on the quayside for the yacht to berth. He was surprised to be hailed by an American voice. "Sir, could you direct me to the local boatyard?"

"There's no boatyard in Crail, but we can get help for you from St. Andrews if you're in trouble."

A figure, dazzling in sailing whites, emerged from a doorway near the bow. "Why, you're Jack Cameron, aren't you? I'm Neily Vanderbilt. We met a couple of years back when I went with a press delegation to Munich."

"Yes, I remember. It's good to see you again. Come and meet the family."

Neily bounded ashore, a solidly built man in his fifties with a twinkling smile and charming manners.

Cameron made the introductions. "This is my wife, Bunny, her sisters, Annabelle and Hadley, and their husbands, Guy de Nonancourt and Karl-Friedrich Kohler."

Neily gazed at the group, recognizing the Ellerman sisters at once. "Why don't you come aboard and have a drink?"

Cameron led his party to a salon lined with priceless inlaid walnut as Neily explained his problem.

"*Great Lady* was built by Fairchilds of Glasgow in 1905. I had a complete refit when I bought her four years ago, but now the engine's playing games."

"Where are you headed?"

"I'm going to drop off my guests, the Mahlers, in Hamburg. Then I plan to make for Le Havre or Calais. What do you make of the situation over in Germany, Jack? Everyone's convinced Hitler means to cause a war."

"I believe he will, too. In my opinion, war's inevitable, but my wife will tell you I'm the world's champion pessimist."

"Your government seems to think like you."

"They know it's impossible to deal with a madman. He's already given some VIP visitors the impression that he wants to rule the world."

"Franz Mahler thinks the same way. Come on, I'll introduce you to my guests, they're really a most charming couple and most concerned that *Great Lady* will balk at taking them home."

Mahler had iron-gray hair and a sweet smile. His wife was plump, with an Irish way with words that they all found fascinating. She greeted Cameron as an old friend. "Is it yourself, then, Jack? Dear God, I do believe you've forgotten me! I'm Mollie Brogan that was. My family came over from Ireland to live in Crail when I was fifteen, and I fell in love with you all the way down to my boots."

While everyone laughed at the expression of mystification on Cameron's face, the captain was instructed to show the ladies around the ship. This he did with style, explaining that the dining-salon table was always set for ten, in case friends should arrive. In the main lounge there were a grand piano and four large sofas covered in rose silk brocade. The master bedroom had been left in the Edwardian style, with carved walls and a bedhead covered with cupids and flowers. The bedspread was from Kashmir and on the floor there was a hand-knotted silk carpet from Isfahan.

On returning to the salon Bunny took a glass of champagne and enthused about what she had seen.

"The yacht's like something out of the Arabian Nights. I wanted to get into that fancy bed of the master suite and give orders for us to sail to the South China Seas."

"We'll be sailing nowhere till I get my engine fixed."

"Leave that to me."

Cameron rose and went ashore, his tall, lean figure striding across the quayside to the car. Bunny felt a sense of loss at his departure, but her attention was soon diverted to the German, who was gazing at Nell with something close to adoration. She listened with interest as he addressed her sister. "My wife and I saw your photographs in the *Vogue* magazine last year. Will you be doing more?"

"I've already done another cover for *Vogue* and more pages of photographs with a photographer called Man Ray. I'm also doing covers for *Harper's* and *Vanity Fair*."

"Here is my card. Do send Molly and me a copy of the *Vogue* when it comes out. We cannot always buy the magazine in Germany."

That night, Bunny lay in bed talking with her husband. "Nell's fascinating to men, isn't she, Jack? That German didn't know if he was in Aberdeen or Australia when she talked to him."

"If I were Guy I'd break his neck."

"He isn't jealous."

"Of course he is, he's just too stubborn to show it."

"Nell asked me about your work this afternoon. If there's a war, you won't have to leave Lochalsh, will you?"

"No, I'm too old for active service, and anyway, they have plans for this place if the worst happens. We're well-situated for secrecy and we'll probably be used as a training school for intelligence personnel.''

"They've already asked you, haven't they, Jack?"

Cameron hesitated, knowing he should not be discussing the matter with Bunny, but unable to keep anything from her.

"Aye, they asked me and I agreed I'd let them use Lochalsh and put myself at their disposal as head of operations. Don't be upset, Bunny. It may never happen.''

She put her arms around his neck and kissed him resoundingly.

"I'm not upset, I'm overjoyed. If war comes, I want us to be together with the children at Lochalsh. What you've just said's the best possible news. I don't care if they send a hundred trainees. We'll get by. At least we'll be *together*.''

"I love you dearly, Bunny. You're everything in the world to me.''

In the morning, Nell hurried into Molly Mahler's bedroom with a pot of beef bouillon and a plate of pills. Molly had felt ill during the visit yesterday, and Bunny had insisted she be brought to Lochalsh.

"I brought aspirin and the doctor's own tablets and a jug of beef stock, because Mrs. MacKay's convinced it cures everything. What did Forbes say?"

"He says I'm suffering from an infected ear and must stay in bed. I'm black with annoyance at the trouble I've caused.''

"Don't be, we're well-equipped to look after you.''

"Will you take Franz along to the distillery when Bunny shows Neily the operation? He was so moved to hear about the widows and children fighting to survive.''

"Where is he?"

"He'll either be outside looking through his binoculars at the birds or in the library buried in a book."

Nell found Franz Mahler in the library leafing through a volume on the history of the Camerons. She greeted him with a handshake and a smile, flattered by his obvious attraction to her. It was a boost to the confidence to be wanted, though Guy was the only man in the world for her.

Nell spoke of Molly in a reassuring manner. "Your wife's seen the doctor and he's coming again at five, so you're not to worry. I've taken her some pills and a jug of consommé, and she asked me to show you around the distillery."

"I should like that."

Their eyes met and he looked down, unable to conceal the desire that welled in him as Nell moved past and stood before the fire. She smelled of orchids and tiger lilies, jasmine and bergamot, and looked like something out of a fairy story. Mahler put the book down.

"At what time shall we leave?"

"Right now. Take a heavy coat with you. It's always windy on the hill near the distillery."

Nell walked with Mahler behind her sister and Neily as they went through each of the rooms of the distillery. She was impressed by the fact that Bunny told Vanderbilt at once that she wanted no money from him. To the man who received a thousand begging letters a day, this was something of a shock.

"Then am I to understand that I can tour your place without worrying about profit-and-loss ratios?" Vanderbilt smiled with relief.

"Frankly, Neily, our profit doesn't yet exist, except in our optimistic dreams."

Bunny, noting the financier's shocked expression, explained further. "You see, we've some time to go yet before we're ready to sell our whiskey. But you can help to get the business off the ground, if you're interested. I figure the only way we'll ever be successful with Lochalsh is if we attract enough publicity to make us a household name. If you would order some of the whiskey right now and give me permission to say you're a client, it would help to establish us with the right market. Guy's doing the same, and I intend to write to the Prince of Wales and ask for his help too. I want our whiskey to become the drink of choice for the names of note. That way everyone'll want some."

"How can I refuse such a flattering sales pitch? Permission granted, Bunny."

When the entourage reached the residential wing they found Loud Maggie crying her eyes out. Bunny hurried forward and inquired what was wrong.

"It's my youngest, ma'am, she's dead. She was killed in an accident in the early hours of this morning. She went looking for sea pinks, because she knew I love them, and she fell from the edge of the cliff. I've been trying to summon up the courage to come and tell you, but I've been too grieved to do anything."

Bunny sat at Maggie's side, her face very pale. "You'd best take the day off, Maggie, and I'll make the arrangements for the funeral. You have enough on your hands without that. I'm so very, very sorry about Katy. She was the dearest little soul and we all loved her."

"You once said you couldn't afford for us to be ill or absent, ma'am, so I'll stay at my post."

"This is different, Maggie."

"I'd prefer to go on working. The women'll help me like they did when Fergus died."

"We'll bury her in the bluebell field, where Jack and I are going to rest someday."

*   *   *

On a gray morning, the priest of Crail led a procession of women and children to the field that in spring would be azure with bluebells. Behind them were the sisters and their husbands and the guests who had come on the yacht. On Bunny's instructions, no one was wearing black. The children were in summer dresses, with wreaths of poppies and cornflowers in their hair. The women were in pink or gray. The coffin was white and covered with wildflowers from the hills, each bunch tied with satin ribbons. As it was lowered into the ground, Loud Maggie fell to her knees, her body racked by sobs.

The priest's voice intoned the final blessing. Then the grave was filled, the flowers placed over it, the last hymn sung. With many a backward glance, the procession walked slowly back down the hill to the road, where every man, woman, and child from the village was waiting to pay respects.

Cameron noted with a start that many of the locals had lined up to embrace Bunny and watched as the mourners shook her hand with fervent respect. He remembered the months of hostility when she had first arrived in the area, eavesdropping as Bunny talked to old Mattie about his lumbago and explained about heaven to one of the children. Bunny had turned the village folk around.

Moved by the funeral, Neily Vanderbilt was anguished when Mrs. MacKay berated him for his fears. "You can cry, but folk like you soon forget their sadness. Madam's had to sell her beautiful pearls and Sir's mortgaged himself to the eyeballs to keep those women and children in work. But you, you'll sail away in your fancy yacht and Lochalsh'll be forgotten!"

"I don't think so, ma'am. I've been mightily impressed by the women and children."

Mrs. MacKay glowered at Vanderbilt, whose

costly clothes and air of detachment offended her.

"That don't pay the bills, sir. But we'll see how impressed you've been *someday*."

Neily looked into the hostile face and vowed silently, with all the stubbornness for which his family was known, that time would tell.

Great Lady sailed for Hamburg on the thirty-first of August. Nell stood with her sisters calling good-bye from the battlemented terrace below the castle, smiling wistfully as Neily waved his panama hat and Mahler saluted in the time-honored way, his right hand across his chest. She was thinking of the conversations they had had concerning the war clouds that were gathering over Europe. Would they ever see Mahler and Neily again? Or would the conflict come suddenly, making enemies of friends? In the morning Hadley and Karl would leave for Munich. Nell shifted uneasily at the tension that again gripped Hadley, the haunted look that returned just as soon as her sister realized that her holiday was indeed over. As they walked back inside the castle, Nell made an attempt to cheer her despondent sister. "Let me help you, Hadley. Shall I keep Tia for a while longer?"

"I'd be glad if you'd take her till Christmas. Karl and I have decided to go to India as soon as we get back, and I don't want her dying of dysentery. When I saw that little girl's coffin being put in the ground, I just wanted to scream. I realized my baby could die too and I was scared deep down in my guts."

"But that's not all, is it, Hadley? Won't you tell me what's wrong? Don't you feel safe anymore in Munich?"

Hadley's eyes welled with tears. "I'm *damned* in Munich and I've only myself to blame. Dear God, what am I going to do?"

With that, Hadley ran from the room, colliding with Bunny, who looked askance at Nell.

"What is it, Nell? What's destroying our Hadley?"

"I tried to find out, but she won't say."

For a long time the sisters sat in silence near the fire. When Bunny finally spoke, her face was pale with anxiety. "We must revive our annual meetings at the Ritz on the first of May. We've missed a year or two because of our pregnancies, but we *must* keep in touch."

Nell sighed wearily. "You're right, of course. But, Bunny, I have a nagging fear that for Hadley our plans may be too little, too late."

III

THE YEARS OF LOVE AND LOYALTY, 1935–1939

—11—
PARIS, MAY 1935

PARIS WAS FULL of flower vendors selling posies of *muguet de bois*. It was the Day of Lovers and customary for men to give bunches of lily of the valley to the women they loved. By noon, every young man in the city had already rushed out to buy.

At the Ritz Hotel, a table had been set for three in the corner of the grill, a posy of stephanotis and lilac as the centerpiece, a tiny gift from the management for each of these most valued clients. The Ellerman sisters, who had stepped into their tempestuous adulthoods from this very hotel, were expected for their annual reunion luncheon.

Of the husbands, only Cameron had refused adamantly to allow Bunny to travel alone. Their second child had been born three months previously and she had been working furiously ever since. He had made her fatigue his excuse for making the trip, though in reality he was terrified that Bunny's blossoming beauty would provoke some man to follow her to the ends of the earth. She had suggested, in view of their current financial strain, that they stay in a small hotel on the Left Bank of the city, but Cameron had insisted they stay at the Ritz. Whatever the problems of the moment, he had no intention of seeing his wife humiliated before her sisters. He had been obliged to put his London apartment up for sale to raise money enough to help Bunny's program at the distillery. After that, there would be nothing left to sell but the land surrounding Lochalsh. Cameron looked at Bunny, resplendent in a shell-pink Hartnel suit he had impulsively ordered for her. She was humming a tune from Novello's *Glamorous Night,* a romantic musical they had seen together in London, and it made him smile despite his gloomy thoughts. There was no danger of the sisters thinking that "Poor Bunny" had returned.

Hadley was hurrying along the Rue de Rivoli and causing drivers to hoot their horns every inch of the way. Some of the men leaned out of their windows and blew kisses. One hit the car in front of him. Hadley waved and took a mock bow. Tripping lightly across the road, she stood for a moment looking up at the Ritz, memories flooding her mind. It was here that Karl had put the gilded card in front of her and invited her to dinner, and for an instant she fell in love with him all over again. But then she bit her lip, trying to shun the sad thoughts that came to mind. This had been a morning of bittersweet memories. Patou had greeted her at his salon with all the old elegance and wit, but she had known that he was a broken man, his reputation enjoying a brief Indian summer after the disastrous collection of thirty-two, when almost all his regular clients had deserted him. Well, Hadley thought, at least she was able to buy the zebra-printed dress she was now wearing. It was so chic, so different, so *her.* Bunny and Nell would be green with envy.

Nell stepped out of the taxi and gazed up at the facade of the Ritz. Its exterior was so com-

forting and solid, so reassuring in every way that
she could not resist a big smile and a tiny pirou-
ette of sheer joy. For the lunch date, she had
gone to Chanel and ordered a dress in her newly
favorite dove gray, the skirt very full, the waist
tiny, a prim white collar and large black taffeta
bow completing the pristine effect. Hatless, she
was wearing the Nonancourt emerald earrings
that picked up the color of her eyes. At her
shoulder there was a spray of lily of the valley
given her that morning by Guy. She was humming an old French tune she had been teaching
Tia during the child's most recent stay at Bel-
Ami—"Trois Jeunes Tambours." On seeing Auzello
waiting for her at the door, she kissed his cheeks
twice on each side for good measure.

"Hellow, Claude. Are they here yet?"

"They are in the bar. Miss Hadley is relaxing
over Manhattans and Miss Bunny is nursing a
Perrier water."

"That sounds about right."

"Come, I will take you through to them."

"Is everything ready for the ball on Saturday?"

"Of course, and I thank you for the invitation
to the grand opening of the children's hospital in
Paris. To be honest, I never thought you could
raise such an unprecedented amount of money.
It will be the talk of Paris for years."

"Well, it hasn't happened quite overnight, has
it, Claude? It took a year and a half, and most of
the team are near bankrupt from their efforts."

"Ah, but you succeeded. And here you are."

With a sweep of his arm Auzello presented
Nell to the table. The sisters hugged each other
and talked and argued and laughed, just as they
always had. Then, having hugged Tia, who was
going to the Children's Theater matinee with
her English nurse, they proceeded to the dining
room. The Ritz was just the way they had left it
as suddenly orphaned girls—the waiters fussed

over them endlessly and the maître d' did everything he could to attract Bunny's attention, just as he always had. They ordered scorpion-fish soup, followed by fillets of sole and pigeons with caramelized cucumbers and vermouth sauce. To keep them occupied while the meal was being prepared, they asked for a bottle of Krug. That would complete the picture. It was the same champagne they had fecklessly ordered on the day they had arrived, alone, uncertain, and knowing nothing of the future.

Hadley looked across the table at Nell. "Thanks for keeping Tia for so long. I'm truly grateful. Was she very homesick?"

"She was just fine. She's been coming to Bel-Ami for so long I think she regards it as her second home and she's secure because she knows that at the end of the holiday she always comes back to you and Karl."

"She may soon be coming home to only her mother, I'm afraid. Karl's been invited to join an elite corps of army officers called the S.S. Only one out of every three recruits at the training school gets through. They're the finest Aryans Hitler can find. God only knows what he's going to do with them—put them on display in the Marienplatz like toy soldiers, I shouldn't wonder."

Nell was wide-eyed at the thought of Karl taking up a military career.

"Why does he want to be a soldier?"

"Oh, you know Karl. He's patriotic and old-fashioned, and all his best friends are joining. In fact, he's in the training program right now. You can't imagine what they have to do. They're up at six each day and drilling till they're blue in the face. They do enough plank scouring and pipe claying and polishing to satisfy a field marshal and they have to be over six feet tall, blond, and of impeccable background. You know how Hitler worries about background. I sometimes wonder if *his* father was Jewish."

Bunny gazed at smiling Hadley, aware that she was not really as carefree about Hitler's obsession with Jews as she made out. As usual, her flippant attitude gave her away. Karl had told Bunny some time ago that Hadley was gravely worried about the situation of the Ellerman family background, since it might affect Tia's future safety. There had been intermittent surveillance of her movements, and worse, men who came to the hunting lodge on various pretexts when there were visitors from abroad. Of late, Hadley had even avoided inviting anyone of Jewish origin for fear that it might inflame the faceless officers who reported to Hitler on the activities of Germany's leading citizens. Bunny spoke gently, trying to find out as much as she could about Karl's new post.

"What is the function of the S.S., Hadley?"

"Oh, all kinds of specialized skills. The Waffen S.S. can dig themselves into the ground so fast the tanks never reach them."

"Do they use real tanks at the training school?"

"Oh yes. Those that don't dig fast enough get killed. It's a big incentive to learn fast."

Bunny made a mental note to tell her husband about Hadley. If she was in danger, she wanted Cameron to know everything. With all the simplicity of a child, Bunny believed that he would be able to help her sister if the worst occurred.

Nell began to tell her own news, watching her sisters closely for a reaction. "On Saturday I'll be giving the Imperial Ball at the Ritz to celebrate the opening of the first children's hospital in the city of Paris. It's taken ages to get the project off the ground, but we managed it in the end. The thing is, I need your help."

Hadley answered for Bunny and herself, as usual. "We'll do what we can, won't we?"

"Of course. What do you need, Nell?"

"I want us to pose for photographers after lunch. And I'd like you to come to the ball with me."

Bunny sighed audibly. Cash was tight. Would her offer to help cost her yet another new dress? She tried not to show her concern. "I don't have a ball gown with me, Nell."

"I'll borrow something for you from Chanel."

Hadley patted Nell's hand. "I have a dress and I don't leave Paris till Monday."

"Are you going right back to Munich?"

Hadley hesitated, her eyes flickering with what Nell took to be regret. "I'm going to Berlin first and then to Munich."

They were ordering their dessert when the photographers arrived. The professionals looked closely at the sisters, comparing their looks and personalities. The blond in the zebra print was gazing at her reflection in a hand mirror as she repowdered her nose and repainted her lipstick. She seemed unaware of her sisters and momentarily in a world of her own. Annabelle de Nonancourt was well known to the press and admired for her professionalism. They looked at the simple gray dress, the startling emerald earrings, the severe hairstyle parted in the center and pulled back hard, falling into a cascade of wild seemingly disordered curls down her back. The third sister intrigued some of them most of all, because she took no notice of their presence and simply continued to enjoy her cherry tart. When they were ready, they motioned discreetly to Nell and she nodded to her sisters.

"Let's raise our glasses and toast the future."

Flashbulbs popped. The sisters talked and laughed together. Then suddenly the men were gone and Auzello was motioning frenetically for staff to clear the floor of every trace of their presence.

Nell looked closely at Bunny, weighing the

calm face with its halo of pale blond hair dressed
in a circular roll with tiny kiss curls over each
ear. How content she looked, how regal and beautiful. She was shocked to think of that word in
connection with her younger sister. With a wry
smile, she inquired about Bunny's life. "What's
happening in Scotland?"

"Everything. It's been bedlam for months. Janet got married four weeks ago to Easter Mac-
Gregor. He's that brash young fellow who wished
you good morning, bare-chested, at the distillery.
He thought he could bed her and every other
widow in the area, but Janet soon instilled a new
set of rules in him. He proposed with the greatest obedience."

"How's the whiskey coming along?"

" As you know, I had to sell my pearls to keep
the thing going—don't glare at me so, Hadley,
you know it was necessary—and Jack's just sold
his London apartment. It was either that or close
the operation down, so we both did it willingly."

Nell and Hadley exchanged horrified glances.
"But you swore you'd never sell the Ellerman
pearls, Bunny. It's all you had—" Hadley was
cut off mid-wail.

"The whiskey's almost ready to market and
I'm going to New York next year to launch it."

Hadley stared at her sister as if Bunny had
sprouted two heads. "Why are *you* going over
there?"

"I can tell the story of the whiskey and how it
came about better than anyone else. After all, I
was involved from the ground up. And I'm hoping to organize an exhibition of all the Lochalsh
products while I'm there. I've asked Neily Vanderbilt to find someone to help me with the
presentation."

"What do you have apart from whiskey?" Nell
inquired.

"We've pottery, blue glass, etched crystal,

tweed, and a marvelous line of sheepskin carpets. I designed those myself and Jack and I have one in our bedroom. They'll cost a thousand dollars apiece and I figure I can sell a dozen, once folk see them."

"They're *very* expensive, Karl and I could buy them cheaper than that in Munich."

"If I've learned anything in business, Hadley, it's that rich folk like to pay for their luxuries. Besides, we need the money and there are lots of sheep in Scotland!"

In the afternoon, the sisters went shopping, just as they always had after lunch at the Ritz. Hadley bought a diamond clip from Cartier, Bunny some syrups from Fauchon. Money was short, but she could not resist buying a tiny quantity of *lait d'amande,* a treat Jack liked better than anything else in the world. Nell bought a pile of English novels from Smith's in the Rue de Rivoli. Then, their feet aching, the sisters adjourned to the tearoom above the bookshop and ordered muffins, buttered anchovy toast, and a pot of Earl Grey.

To Hadley it was like reliving the old and carefree days of her youth. But just as quickly as the refreshing feeling became conscious, she realized how far she had slipped into an abyss of degradation. Her shoulders sagged. The peak of her life had already passed. Now, under Dietmueller's influence, she would hit the nadir of her fortunes and there was nothing to be done. She had neither the strength nor the will to resist him.

Seeing Hadley's despair, Bunny whispered in her ear, "Is something wrong?"

"Nothing you can do anything about."

"Are you and Karl still happy?"

"He loves me and I love him. But life is more complicated than that, isn't it, Bunny? I can't work out the moves anymore."

On her return to the hotel, Hadley stood gazing at the telephone, fighting a losing battle, as always, in her resolve to end the relationship with Dietmueller. He had followed her to Paris and was staying at the German embassy. If only she had been able to stop herself from revealing the reunion plans to him . . . Finally she picked up the receiver and asked for the embassy, speaking softly when he replied.

"Ernst Dietmueller speaking."

"I'm back from my lunch date."

"How was your day with your sisters?"

"Fine. Bunny's a real-life tycoon and Nell's got plans to rebuild Paris."

"Come and see me at seven and I will introduce you to my old friend Elga, who is longing to meet you."

Hadley agreed, unable to find the will not to.

At ten-thirty, as Bunny and Cameron were drinking a nightcap in the bar, Hadley ran into the hotel, her face ashen pale. She and Dietmueller had spent the evening at the home of the notorious lesbian Baroness von Krietz. Shocked by what Dietmueller wanted Hadley to do and horrified by Dietmueller's evident enjoyment of her decline, Hadley told herself that she must break with him. But how to find the will to do the impossible?

Having followed her distraught sister upstairs, Bunny entered Hadley's room without knocking, to find her sobbing like a child.

"Whatever's wrong? You came into the hotel like a bat out of hell."

"Oh, Bunny, whatever am I going to do?"

"Tell me all about it."

Hadley felt a curious compulsion to relieve herself of the agony that had tormented her for so long, and averting her face, told Bunny all. When the ordeal was over, she felt a great relief, mixed with chagrin, shame, and a dozen conflicting emotions.

"What can I do, Bunny? For God's sake, help me, I'm completely lost."

"Well, you can't go on like this. Poor Hadley, I do love you so."

Unaware of the irony of the words, Bunny hugged her sister to her heart, drying her eyes as if she were a child.

"We'll think about all this again in the morning. In the meantime, you go and get into a nice hot bath and I'll put you to bed afterward."

Once Hadley was in the foam bath, Bunny rang the abruptly abandoned Cameron and told him where she was and that she would be late. Then she rang Nell and asked to see her before she went to bed. When Hadley emerged from the bathroom, Bunny bundled her into bed and handed her a book.

"I bought this at Smith's. You'll have fun reading it. It's a detective story about a young man called Maigret. I just *adore* him."

Bunny picked up the telephone and spoke to the receptionist. "If anyone telephones for the Countess Kohler, you are to say she's out. If anyone calls by to see her, you say the same."

Bunny kissed her sister good night and hurried downstairs to the lounge to wait for Nell. Her heart was thundering from worry and tension and she could barely keep from rushing to her room to ask Cameron what to do. If Karl found out about the affair, he would either divorce Hadley or shoot her through the head, and who could blame him? Bunny thought of Tia with her red-blond curls, joyful smile, and chortling child's voice. To Tia the world was a wonderful place, to be explored and enjoyed with enthusiasm. Was it possible Dietmueller might harm the child? He might even hold Hadley to their arrangement on the pretext of keeping Tia safe. Worse, he could get it into his head to do something to Karl. Bunny broke into a sweat just thinking of the dismal possibilities.

Nell was walking back to the Ritz, having slipped out to buy an early edition of the morning paper, when she saw a familiar figure ahead of her, striding toward the hotel. Her heart missed a beat the instant she registered—Ernst Dietmueller, the man who had pursued her sister so persistently on the ship. Could Hadley know he was in Paris? Then, with a certain grim resignation, Nell allowed it all to fall into place. Hadley and Dietmueller were lovers and *that* was what had been troubling her sister for so long. She fell into step behind the German, her heels clicking on the ground in the silence of night. Nell was about to follow him into the lavish lobby when he turned and addressed her. "I am Ernst Dietmueller. We met once before on the ship from New York."

"I remember."

"I wish to see your sister Hadley. When I telephoned the hotel, I was told she was out, and I am quite sure that if I ask at the desk I shall be informed that she is still absent. Will you be so kind as to tell her I will wait for her in the bar?"

"I'll do no such thing. Karl wouldn't let you visit Hadley at home and I'm damned sure he'd hate to see pictures of you in the newspapers drinking cocktails at midnight at the Ritz. Leave her alone, Dietmueller."

"You lack your sister's charm."

"I sure as hell do. What exactly is your business with Hadley?"

"Delicately put, madam. You must ask *her*, but I am sure you are old enough to know the answer."

"Why couldn't you have let her be? She might have settled down and been happy with Karl."

"She came to me, my dear woman, remember that."

Nell spat out her defiance. "Well, one thing's certain, she'd be better without you, and I'll do all I can to make her see sense."

"You wish to become my enemy—how very amusing."

"I'm not afraid of you, Dietmueller. Your power doesn't extend to Paris and the Loire."

"But someday you may return to Germany, and *then* you would be in my area of influence."

"Threats might work with Hadley, but they won't with me. Now, get the hell out of my way. I'm tired and I want to go to bed."

Dietmueller remained where he was, his arms crossed, his legs slightly apart.

Furious, Nell kicked him hard on the shins and as he cried in shock and pain, she pushed him aside and walked regally into the hotel, calling out to Auzello, who was watching in stunned admiration from the door. "If that man asks to see my sister Hadley, tell him to go to hell."

"He will have sore shins in the morning."

"He sure as hell will and he's lucky I didn't kick him in the balls as well!"

Bunny chortled joyfully when Nell told her what had happened. Then Bunny told her sister all that Hadley had confessed. Nell was responsible for Tia for nearly half of each year, and she was worried. The clocks were chiming two when the sisters finally walked upstairs to bed, each one gravely worried and uncertain how best to help Hadley. Nell was about to say good night when she remembered the photograph in the newspaper and handed it over with a smile.

"Show this to Jack and give him a big hug from me."

Cameron rose at five, as always, and turned on the light so he could look at the newspaper Bunny had given him. The photograph of the sisters was revealing and pleased him immensely. Had-

ley looked a little wild, her eyes staring at the
camera without seeming to see the man behind
it. Her thin body looked out of place in the vi-
brantly striped dress. Nell was poised as she
looked across the table to Bunny, who was in the
center of the group. Cameron examined the photograph of his wife, admiring the heart-shaped
face, the halo of fair hair, and the tiny kiss curls
at her temples. In the plain suit with its scal-
loped neckline, she looked like a queen, a slightly
amused expression in her eyes, a faint smile on
her lips as she raised her glass to her sisters.
Cameron considered what Bunny had told him
about Hadley and shuddered. He had once called
her beauty poisonous and now he had been proven
right. She was a disaster to any man who cared
for her, and most of all to herself. He walked to
the window and looked out as dawn lit the streets
with the pink light so typical of Paris. The sounds
of the city filtered through the window, the grind
of a flower seller's cart on the cobblestones, the
voice of a street singer, the gentle hum of cleaning appliances somewhere far below in the hotel.
Cameron went to the bathroom and shaved,
washed, and dressed. Then he wakened Bunny
with a kiss and ordered breakfast for them both,
with porridge, kippers, ham and eggs with sausage and fried potatoes.

While Bunny went to the bathroom to shower,
Cameron rushed down to the flower seller in the
square, bought some roses, a bunch of Bunny's
favorite marguerites, and a cluster of feathery
fern. He was about to return to his wife when
Dietmueller stepped out of a car parked near the
hotel.

"Mr. Cameron, as I recall. I am—"

"I know who you are."

"Of course you do. You are an English intelligence officer."

"I'm Scottish to the bone and I'll thank you not to call me an Englishman!"

Dietmueller looked uncertainly at Cameron's iron-willed face. "My apologies, sir. I wish to contact the Countess Kohler. Would you hand this to her?"

Cameron glowered at Dietmueller. "I'm no man's messenger boy. Hand it in at the desk, but I warn you, they won't deliver it."

When Dietmueller handed the letter in, the receptionist immediately passed it to a bellman who rushed the message to Cameron's room, as ordered. He was horrified to find the gentleman eating an enormous breakfast. With a shrug of Gallic disdain, he handed the letter over and hurried from the room, wrinkling his nose at the smell of Arbroath kippers and smoky bacon Cameron had insisted on bringing with him from home.

The theme of the ball was czarist Russia, the salon of the hotel tented in cloth of gold with Romanov violet trimmings. Some of the guests had hired costumes in the style of prerevolutionary St. Petersburg, and one of the leading hostesses of the city was in a sable cloak so voluminous the train had to be carried by two blackamoors in scarlet livery. Every woman present was wearing her best jewels and the room was full of the shimmer of satin, the glitter of diamonds, and the heady scent of ylang-ylang.

The Ellerman sisters appeared all in white, Nell in a shimmering beaded sheath by Lanvin, Hadley in a Patou extravaganza of ruched silk taffeta, Bunny in frothy organdy over sequins by Chanel. Each one had flowers in her hair, Nell the pink camellias that had become her trademark, Hadley white-and-emerald orchids, and Bunny a chignon of forget-me-nots that matched exactly the color of her eyes.

Photographers sprang forward, flashbulbs exploded, and when dinner was announced there was a burst of applause as Gypsy musicians appeared to lead the way into the dining room. The menus were printed on white slipper satin, the favors miniature copies of Fabergé eggs in gold and crystallite. Newsmen and photographers wandered among the tables snapping famous faces and trying to extricate themselves from the clutches of those who wanted to be more famous than they were. As at all Nell's charity functions, donators' names and the amounts they had given were read out at intervals throughout the evening and applause encouraged. On this most special night, as waiters hurried to serve champagne, some of the most generous of those present were called upon to take a bow, their faces pinpointed by spotlights, their pride in their own generosity evident.

The meal was presented with panache. There was caviar in silver bowls, then zakushki and a soup of wild funghi and egg yolk. Grilled imperial sturgeon with lemon was followed by the main course of flambéed beef served on sabers. While waiters ran back and forth, Gypsies flirted outrageously with staid matrons of French high society and everyone agreed that this was the very best ever of Nell's extravaganzas.

Guy arrived as the ball was beginning and sat with Cameron, who was watching the scene from a table near the dance floor. "Comfortable, brother-in-law?" Guy asked mysteriously.

"Well, yes—"

"But you're not *too* comfortable to consider taking a short trip, are you?" Guy's eyes were bright with mischief.

Cameron laughed. "Look, just what are you getting at?"

Guy explained to his brother-in-law the event

that was going to be the climax of the evening. "At midnight, after the last of the announcements has been made, we shall go by horse-drawn carriages to the hospital and the ribbon will be cut at the formal ceremony. Nell will do it herself. After all, this is *her* night. I just hope we shan't be arrested for stopping the traffic."

Cameron rapped a Gypsy violinist on the knuckles when his hands wandered momentarily to Bunny's bare shoulder. Guy continued imperturbably, resisting the urge to laugh out loud at his friend's peremptory manner.

"I still can't believe that Nell managed to raise the money for a Paris hospital. The other clinics she opened were child's play compared to this one, which cost many millions of francs."

"Your wife's certainly turned out to be an extraordinary woman, Guy."

"So has yours."

"Bunny's remarkable. I'm the luckiest fellow in the world, no doubt about it."

A folk-dancing ensemble from the Ukraine provided the opening of the cabaret. Then a choir of expatriate Russian officers sang "Kalinka," their voices bringing tears to the eyes of many of those present. The final act was the appearance of two Russian ballet stars who had come to Paris by special permission of the directors of the Bolshoi. As the lights were lowered and the spotlights turned to rose, the two danced the pas-de-deux from *Sleeping Beauty*. Enthralled by the artistry, many of the audience were heard to say that no one could organize a gala evening like the Duchesse de Nonancourt.

When the cabaret was over and the dancing began, Hadley wandered to the entrance of the hotel and took a breath of air. She was about to return to the ball when she saw Dietmueller drawing up in a black car. She wanted to run away, but when he stepped out and looked into her eyes, she remained rooted to the spot, his voice mesmerizing her.

"I want you ready to leave as soon as the ribbon has been cut. Do you understand me, Hadley?" She nodded uncertainly. "You have shown your independence, but it is time to stop playing games. We leave for Berlin on the one-fifteen train."

Hadley stood stock-still, taking in the black leather jacket, the familiar ebony cigarette holder in his hand. As his eyes searched hers, she thought of the moments when he had loved her, when her body had lived as it had never lived before. Then, unable to resist him, she walked back to the ballroom, her head in a whirl, her body trembling from emotions she could neither identify nor control. Within minutes she had given instructions for her bill to be prepared, her belongings packed. To her distracted and happy sisters, she said nothing—there seemed to be nothing to say. She would leave as Dietmueller had instructed, reassured that Nell would look after Tia until she was ready to take the child back again to the hunting lodge. Anxious to evade her sisters' sight, Hadley hurried out of the rear entrance of the hotel and into the arms of the man who had enslaved her.

At midnight, while the bells of Notre Dame boomed the hour, Nell stepped forward and cut the ribbon on the first Luc Dubois Hospital in Paris. The band struck up with a rousing version of the "Marseillaise," followed by the "Battle Hymn of the Republic." Then, amid riotous applase, a thousand white doves were released, their wings illuminated by the gold light of the curled iron lamps on the Pont Alexandre. It was at once a moment of satisfaction and spectacle for all of those present and a promise for the future. Here was Nell's gift to the children who were as much hers as they were her country's— in exchange she had earned the avid support of French society for years to come.

Returning to her room at the Ritz, Nell kicked off her shoes and threw herself on the bed. "God, I'm tired, Guy."

"It went well, though."

There was a knock at the door and Bunny and Cameron appeared and spoke quietly to Nell, who turned in alarm to her husband.

"Jack just saw Hadley leaving with Dietmueller. What shall we do?"

Guy shrugged resignedly, infuriating his wife. "We shall do nothing. Hadley's life is her own."

"But she has Tia with her! For Christ's sake, Guy, doesn't anything ever worry you?"

Cameron broke in on Nell's furious tirade. "I hope you'll forgive the presumption, but I asked for the little girl to be moved to your suite earlier in the evening, after my encounter with Diet-mueller outside the hotel. It became obvious to me then that he'd stop at nothing to have Hadley, and since I knew of her resistance—enforced resistance, though it may have been—I didn't want Tia to become a pawn. He's certainly unscrupulous enough to try to use her."

Nell looked helplessly at Cameron. "What are we to do, Jack?"

"For the moment there's nothing we can do. Tia's safe in your second bedroom. That's all that matters for now."

Cameron and Bunny returned to their rooms, their hearts heavy with foreboding. He voiced their thoughts as they sat by the fire looking into the flames. "That sister of yours is in deep trouble, I fear."

"Poor Hadley."

Despite his misgivings, Cameron smiled. "She used to call you Poor Bunny and now look what's happened. But as painful as it may be, you have to remember this: Hadley's every bit as obsessed by Dietmueller as he is by her. Unfortunately, if she isn't very clever, he'll destroy her. That's all someone like Dietmueller knows how to do."

—12—

NEW YORK, SPRING 1936

BUNNY LEANED AGAINST the ship's rail and scanned
the skyline of Manhattan. There was a sailing
schooner in the harbor and through the rigging she could see the skyscrapers and towers
of the city that had once been her second home.
Looking through the massive fore, main, and miz-
zenmasts, she remembered the little schooner her
father had bought when she and her sisters were
small, and the fascinating holidays they had had
aboard her. Bunny gazed at the jagged city skyline, pale gray in the watery April sun. Then,
closing her eyes, she said a prayer for guidance
and help.

She had told Hadley long ago that everyone, at
least once in a lifetime, must face a time of great
difficulty with even greater courage. This was
her time, her test. The whiskey was ready to
market and the Lochalsh Industries products too,
but in England buyers had been few and far
between. In the age of hunger marches and strikes,
not even the very rich wanted to admit hedo-
nism by drinking the most expensive whiskey to
come on the market in many a year. Had she
made a huge error of judgment?

Bunny returned to her cabin and sat on the

bed, deep in thought. She had planned the trip
to New York knowing it would be the deciding
factor in her life, not to mention that of the
widows. She had gone for broke, sinking every
penny she had left into the presentation that
would launch the Lochalsh products. She wondered if Neily Vanderbilt would keep his promise and come to meet her. Looking at the photograph of her husband and her sons she had put
on the night table at her bedside, Bunny struggled to hold back the tears. Jack had always accompanied her on her trips, but this time, at the
very last moment, he had been called to Berlin
by the Foreign Office, where he would act as
liaison between British and French intelligence
officers monitoring their prime ministers' meetings with Adolf Hitler. Bunny thought of their
final night in London, when Cameron had taken
her to see Astaire and Rogers in their latest movie
while the storm clouds of war gathered. Now,
alone, she felt bereft and fearful. Only the threat
of what would happen if she did not make a
success of the trip kept her from panic. There
was no alternative—she knew she must do what
had to be done. She'd sell the whiskey, market
the products, and return to Lochalsh with a full
order book.

On the quayside, a brass band was playing
"Bluebells of Scotland," and members of the press,
summoned by the British ambassador at Bunny's
request, were straining to see what the fuss was
all about. The source of the excitement, however, remained calmly at the ship's rail, waiting
for the rest of the passengers to disembark. Just
when she had satisfied herself that Vanderbilt
was not among the waiting crowd, she was handed
a telegram offering her his apologies for his absence. She had counted on Neily's support to
bolster her through the visit and now here she
was: no Jack, no Neily, and no confidence. Per-

haps Mrs. MacKay had been right after all—the Vanderbilts had *very* short memories.

When the last of the passengers was gone, Bunny signaled for Major Sullivan of the Camerons' Own Regiment to lead the way down the gangplank, watching proudly as he marched forward, playing the bagpipes as if his life depended on it. Bunny took a deep breath.

Unsure who this astonishing kilted character was, the photographers rushed forward to snap his picture. They had no sooner finished than they saw Bunny waving a greeting from the top of the gangplank. She was wearing a big pale pink hat with a sweeping brim. Her suit was fashionably broad-shouldered, tiny-waisted, her legs perfect in their beige silk stockings. It was her smile, however, that impressed, as well as the cheery greeting she called out. "Isn't someone going to say, 'Welcome home'?"

"Welcome home, Bunny!"

The photographers watched as she descended the gangplank, motioning from the quayside for a group of women and children to follow. They were all dressed in their Sunday best, with bonnets of white lace and hand-woven dresses. They formed a group as Bunny had taught them in the weeks prior to their departure, and as photographers, sensing news, bustled forward to capture the moment, Bunny made the introductions to the press.

"This is Easter MacGregor, our stained-glass expert, and this is his wife, Janet, head of the operation that produces the Widows Special Whiskey Blend. This is Rory, who's the trainee blender, and Mr. Fergusson, our business advisor and head blender."

Bunny distributed brochures describing the tragedy of the fishing fleet and the events that had followed. There were etchings of the castle of Lochalsh, photographs of the distillery and mountains, and a tempting description of the whiskey's distinctive flavor. Most important of all, there was a cunning piece about the prestige of the product and glowing endorsements from the precious few eminent people who had already been given the opportunity to taste this nearly miraculous potion.

When the photographs had been taken, the interviews given, Bunny herded her party into a hired bus that would take them to their hotel. Then, as they traveled from the Battery to midtown Manhattan, she drank in the passing scene. The kosher chicken market on Hester Street was a hive of activity, and nearby, the window of an Italian food store advertised famous cheeses with unpronounceable names that would surely have earned Mrs. MacKay's disapproval. A movie poster advertised Big Boy Williams in *The Law of the '45,* and a restaurant nearby was offering lamb stew at fifteen cents and pot roast at twenty. A line of indigents was forming outside and moving slowly forward. Uptown, near the more fashionable area of Central Park, Bunny was enthralled to see a carved wooden Indian in full Scottish regalia and tartan kilt outside a snuff shop. She cried out delightedly to the driver of the bus, "Please, stop! I've just got to buy that for my husband."

"They won't sell, ma'am, I can tell you."

"I bet they would for a good cause."

"You'd lose your bet."

It took the now consummately confident Bunny days to set up all the necessary equipment in the entrance of Blassingame's, the prestigious department store Neily had suggested for the exhibition. The press followed Bunny's every move as she supervised the details, and most of the widows were interviewed individually, their stories told in detail, stressing the human element of their struggle against their fates. The press worked

on the angle of twenty-five women and forty
children pitting their wits against destiny. Then,
when one of the little girls let slip the fact that
Bunny had had to sell her pearls and the shares
her husband had given her in order to keep the
distillery open, reporters besieged the hotel where
she was staying on Fifth Avenue.

"How come you were *that* short of cash, Bunny?"

"Despite what people may think, Papa left me
and my sisters a very small amount of money
and only one valuable piece of jewelry each. When
I had nothing left to sell and my husband had
already liquidated his real estate in London, the
Ellerman pearls put bread on the table—and malt
in the distillery." Bunny's fans chuckled with
delight. Developing a distillery is a very big long-
term gamble, gentlemen. It takes three years at
least for whiskey to mature, and you can't earn a
cent in that time. "Right now, everything we
have is tied up in the Lochalsh program. We're
lucky that people want to buy the whiskey."

"But why sell it here if you could have taken it
to England?"

"I'm American, remember? I thought I'd give
my countrymen a chance to be the first to try the
whiskey I believe to be the best in the world."

A week passed in the wink of an eye. As the
day of the launch drew near, Bunny grew increasingly tense. She was tired from the endless
preparations and exasperated by her futile efforts over the past few months to market the
whiskey in London. It had soon become obvious
that no one wanted the most expensive spirit on
the market and she had sent cases of the deluxe
product to members of the royal family as a last
resort. They had not even replied. She had hoped
for a royal warrant, but had received only silence. Now, despite her courage and resolve, she
was almost resigned to the fact that the enter-

prise was doomed to failure in New York also. Her daily attempts to reach Vanderbilt by phone had been fruitless. Neily had still not returned to New York and she had received no further messages from him. After all his promises of support, Bunny was bitterly disappointed.

She was pacing the room, trying not to think what would happen if things went wrong, when Janet appeared with a tray.

"I brought you some tea, ma'am. I thought you might need the comfort of it."

For a long time the two women sat together in silence. Then Bunny spoke her thoughts. "I'm scared, I wish Jack was here."

"We're scared too, even the little ones. It's a fearful gamble you've taken in bringing us all here to New York."

"I still stand by it, Janet."

Janet gazed in awe at Bunny, impressed as always by her mulish attitude.

"You know, ma'am, when I first saw you that day on the quayside, I thought you looked like a wild rose, all pink and scented. I was fearful jealous of your soft hands and your fancy clothes. Imagine me thinking you a jinx!"

Bunny smiled gently. "I'm glad you changed your mind. I rely on you, Janet, perhaps more than you realize. When you're near, I think everything'll go just fine."

"Oh, ma'am, if I could make it a success by wishing for one."

The papers blazed out the news that Wednesday would be the proving day for the widows of Lochalsh, their last hurdle in the struggle for survival. Within two weeks of their arrival in New York, there were few residents of the city who could not recognize the women when they walked in the streets. Thanks to the ever-attentive media, many of them were even greeted by name. The rich stayed aloof, however. They were the unknown quantity who would either ignore the venture completely or come like locusts to grab everything in sight.

On the morning of the launch, Bunny rose at six. She was so tense she could not eat, and ordered only coffee and toast for breakfast. Then she showered and put on her makeup. When she had sprayed herself with Floris *Bluebell,* she paused: for one mad moment Bunny swore that she could smell kippers and Lochalsh smoky bacon. Returning to the bedroom, she came face to face with her husband in full Highland dress tartan and Mrs. MacKay holding a breakfast tray loaded with Scottish specilties. Bunny threw her arms around the housekeeper's neck and then snuggled into Cameron's arms.

"Jack! Mrs. MacKay! This is the surprise of a lifetime!"

"Have you a kiss for me, lassie?"

"Oh, my lovely Jack, when did you get here?"

"I came on the plane and brought Mrs. MacKay with me. Agnes wants to put her shoulder to the effort, and you know what a shoulder she has! She's brought supplies of everything we all like best, so whatever happens, we'll eat well!"

Bunny turned again to Mrs. MacKay.

"Thank you for coming, Agnes. Your presence here will make all the difference to us."

"It was horrible on the plane, ma'am, but well worth it. Your husband's no fit company when you're away. But now that we're here we'll battle in the true Cameron style."

When the clocks struck ten, Blassingame's opened its art-nouveau doors. Pressmen, photographers, and public rushed in, only to be stunned by the astonishing sight spread before them—the entirety of the store's massive ground floor had been transformed into a Scottish village. Set designers had planted trees and flowers which bloomed beside a tiny waterfall and wandering stream. Some typical crofters' cottages had been faithfully reproduced and each was occupied by one of the Lochalsh women at work. Alice Smith was weaving her tweed at a loom, two children helping at her side. Tom Cole was blowing glass into elegant shapes, and another worker was stitching sheepskins with a curved steel needle. The potter was at his wheel, the glass etcher holding a thistle decanter against the light to check the perfection of the design. Easter was soldering a stained-glass window in shades of amber and rose. And everywhere children were working with their mothers, packing, boxing, and sticking labels on the luxurious whiskey of Lochalsh.

Waves of spontaneous applause filled the air. Flashbulbs popped and chaos broke out. Then a floor manager, in an attempt to keep order, called out that lines were forming. Sadly, they were not lines of rich people, for whom the whiskey and the products had been intended, but of the relatively poor who had clubbed together to buy a bottle to show their support for the women and children.

When the lines had been served, it became obvious that the publicity about the women had touched the hearts of many and they had put up the money to show support, a single bottle of whiskey being bought by two or three famillies. But none of the products had been sold and no big orders had been received for the whiskey. The widows' faces were grim, but they continued to enact scenes of everyday Scottish life. They were hoping for a miracle. And as the clocks chimed twelve they got one.

By noon, Bunny was wringing her hands, staring blankly through a display window. Her pessimistic reverie was broken by the sudden arrival of a fleet of chauffeured cars, led by none other than Neily Vanderbilt. Motioning the caravan toward the curb, he hurried in to shake hands with Jack and Bunny.

"Sorry I'm so late in arriving," Neily said calmly. "I had trouble with my boat and couldn't get back to New York in time for your arrival. I didn't expect you to be here, Jack."

"I'm here and I'm suffering. We all are."

"Suffer no more, the cavalry just arrived."

One of Neily's Rhode Island neighbors, on seeing the luxurious white fur carpets, bought forty of them, one for each of her bedrooms. Another purchased Tom Cole's entire violet-blue glass collection. A wholesaler from Boston placed the first major order for the whiskey. Another from New York followed. Then Neily's cousin, enchanted by the fur carpets, bought the rest of the rugs on display. New supplies were sent for to the hotel, but only six of the carpets remained and they were snapped up by two men who ran an interior-design business from a deluxe Park Avenue office.

By the end of the day, the exhibition had been both a wild success and a dismal failure. It was a success because the orders were better than anything Bunny had dreamed of achieving. It was a failure because they had virtually nothing left to sell, except the whiskey and a few leftover sets of crystal. As she and her husband sat together in the twilight of their hotel room, Bunny came up with an idea.

"We'll continue the exhibition for a while, but say all the whiskey's been sold and we have full order books for the other things and can't take any more."

Cameron looked out on the spires and towers of the city, marveling at her ingenuity, but unsure whether she was right.

"We need every order we can get, and you know it."

"Rich folk are contrary, Jack. If they think the

whiskey's available, they'll not want it. If they think they can't have any, they'll want it so badly they'll send all the way to Lachalsh for supplies. The biggest surprise of this whole affair's been the carpets. They've nearly saved the distillery on their own."

"There won't be a sheep in the Kingdom of Fife that can be certain of keeping his coat after this!"

Bunny sat on her husband's knee and kissed him on the mouth.

"You were so handsome this morning, I'm surprised no one put an offer in for you. Come to bed. I want to show you how a wanton woman makes love."

Cameron bent his head and kissed her on the mouth, wanting her with a great urgency.

"If you keep on like that, I'll be pregnant again," Bunny whispered.

"If you are, we'll call her Manhattan!"

"I love you ten million, Jack."

"I'm thinking we might cut short our visit and go home next week. By the time you've seen the wholesalers and thrown your party at the embassy, everyone that matters will have tasted the whiskey and made their decision."

"If you can get us all on the ship, book the passages."

The following morning, a cigar-store Indian was delivered to Bunny's hotel. She rushed to Cameron to ask how he had bought it.

"I didn't do a thing. Agnes heard you wanted it and she persuaded the owner to sell. She won't tell me what she said to the man, but he's coming to Scotland for a holiday in the spring and he thinks he's saved at least a dozen children from starvation."

On their return to Lochalsh, Bunny and her husband were met by Severine, who rushed out into the courtyard, her eyes alight.

"We had a most important letter this morning, madam. It's from the king! He's granted a royal warrant for the whiskey, and he invites you both to Balmoral for the weekend to tell him all about your trip to America."

Bunny threw her arms around Severine and then around her husband.

"Now we have the warrant, we'll be able to sell the whiskey all over England. We made it, Jack!"

"We did indeed, lassie."

Then, noticing that Severine was looking unusually coy, Bunny asked her what was wrong.

"Ewan and I are to be married at Christmas if you agree to let me take a holiday in the new year."

Bunny hugged Severine to her heart.

"Congratulations, I know you'll both be very happy."

Everyone filed into the banqueting hall, where lunch had been set out. There was venison broth with dumplings, whole roast lambs, and a series of gâteaux each one more astonishing than the last. Severine took a bow at the end of the meal to riotous applause from the assembled group, who were all ecstatic to be home.

Later, Bunny was in the sitting room when Mrs. MacKay appeared with the tea tray. Seeing that she was pale from fatigue, Bunny gave the housekeeper a hug.

"We're home, Mrs. MacKay, and we'll be staying here from now on, so you just cheer up. Have you any idea where Jack is?"

"He's on his way up here. He's been searching for something he hid long ago."

"Hid? What kind of thing?"

"I don't know, but he's been keeping secrets, that's for sure. I've been keeping one too, ma'am. Mr. Vanderbilt gave me a letter with instructions to open it only when I arrived back home. I opened it two hours ago and had such a shock I was obliged to lie down a wee while."

"What did the letter say?"

Mrs. MacKay handed it to Bunny, who looked disbelievingly at a check and brief note that had made the housekeeper cry for the first time in twenty years.

Dear Agnes,

Just to show you that we Vanderbilts don't *ever* forget, I'm enclosing a little gift for you to give to Bunny. Call it my contribution to the welfare of the widows of Lochalsh. It'll be enough to cover the cost of everyone's return passage to New York and the hotel bill.

My best,
Neily Vanderbilt

Bunny was shocked to the bone to see that the check was for twenty-five thousand dollars. She resolved to invest it for the future in the names of the widows and each of the children, grateful that with one magnificent gesture Neily had given them the priceless gift of security.

Minutes later, Cameron appeared with a dusty package, which he handed to Bunny with an embarrassed smile.

"You'd best put this on."

Opening the package, Bunny found the Ellerman pearl necklace in all its beauty. She looked uncomprehendingly at her husband.

"How did you get this back?"

"I sold the apartment in London, gave you half the cash to add to the sale of the shares to keep the distillery going, and I bought the pearls back with the rest. You didn't think I'd give them up without a fight, did you? They don't call me the stubbornest man in Fife for nothing."

Bunny sat very still as he clasped the pearls around her neck, tears of joy falling down her cheeks. Then she rose and wound her arms around him.

"Thank you, Jack, thank you for everything."

Cameron smiled. In a few minutes, he was thinking, he would take her upstairs for a rest that would exhaust him.

—13—

BAVARIA,
JANUARY—MARCH 1937

FOR CHRISTMAS, KARL had bought Hadley a Russian troika that had once belonged to Czar Nicholas II. They were planning to travel in it around the estate, with three white horses and dozens of silver bells to tinkle in the ice-cold air. Karl had also bought her a beautiful fox cloak and hat that were the most glamorous things Hadley ever owned. Wrapped in her luxurious gifts, Hadley admired her reflection in the mirror. How lucky she was to have such a generous, loving husband. Then she gazed at the child in the pink velvet dress, who was watching her in admiration.

"This coat is beautiful, isn't it, Tia?"

"Bootiful, Mama."

"What are you going to do while Daddy and I are out?"

"Hoffy's taking me to find treasure in the attic."

Hadley kissed the rosy cheeks, laughing as Tia held out her hand for some scent. She sprayed the tiny fingers with orange-blossom extract and then pinned a brooch of rubies to her daughter's dress.

"I'll be back at six and I'll come to your room and see what kind of treasure you found."

"Kiss again, Mama."

Tia stood with her nose pressed to the windowpane, watching as her mother stepped into the troika and drove away at Karl's side. The sleigh bells pleased the child and she waved merrily. Then she picked up the cat and carried him to the kitchen, where Frau Hoffman was making biscuits shaped like kisses.

"Patou could eat some cake."

"And you too, I suppose, young lady."

"I'd like some apple strudel."

Frau Hoffman put a plate of apple cake in front of the child and another in front of the cat, which it ignored completely. Tia ate her own and then the cat's portion, as usual.

"Patou's coming with us to look for treasure."

"He may find a mouse."

"Tante Nell once found a mouse and she jumped on the table and wouldn't get down. Uncle Guy said she was silly, but she wasn't."

"Do you like your uncle?"

"Oh yes. He has horses and sheeps and cows and unicorns and dragons at Bel-Ami, and none of them ever bites him."

"There are not any unicorns and dragons in the world nowadays."

"There are! Uncle Guy said they eat all his turnips, and he *knows*."

Hadley and Karl sat arm in arm in the troika, speeding through the woods to a spot where a fire had been lit. There they stepped down and warmed their hands. As instructed, the forester had left coffee near the fire and baked potatoes in the embers. Hadley smiled into her husband's eyes.

"We used to roast potatoes on the fire when we were kids back home."

"I love to see you happy."

Hadley thought ruefully that she had indeed been happy since Dietmueller left for Berlin two months previously. Her relationship with Karl was strengthening and they were daily growing closer and more loving. As Karl stoked the fire and pulled the steaming potatoes from the embers, Hadley reminded herself of this simple truth: if she could be happy for two months with her husband and child, she could be happy forever. She had to end the affair with Dietmueller and there must be no vacillation or hesitation about it. Relieved to have found the strength to make the decision, she resolved to concentrate her energies and love on Karl. She would do her best to make him forget that she had ever been anything but the perfect wife. They would be lovers again and the world would be golden.

A few days later, Hadley was in bed reading the morning papers when Gisela placed the breakfast tray before her. At the sight of it, Hadley's heart missed a beat: tucked into the clean linen napkin was a solitary ivy leaf, Dietmueller's signal to her that he was home. She had long suspected that the kitchen maid was her lover's spy in the house. Now, conscious of the girl's scrutiny, Hadley forced herself to eat and drink as if nothing had changed. Only she knew that everything had changed since Dietmueller's last visit to the chalet.

At ten A.M. Hadley arrived at Dietmueller's property and found him absent. Relieved, she decided to write him a note, telling him she could never see him again. She was signing it when she heard the sound of his car. Then he came through the door and took the letter from her. When he had read a few lines, he threw it on the fire.

"I have a surprise for you, Hadley. Take off your clothes—and hurry. I am going to give you the experience of a lifetime."

She stood quite still, gazing at him as if for the first time. Then slowly she backed to the door.

"I'm going home. I meant what I said in the letter. You just have to accept it."

Dietmueller reached her in a monent, his arms encircling her body so tightly that she flinched from the pain. Hadley felt him pulling off her jacket and unfastening the riding trousers. She began to struggle, but he was as strong as a titan and as she fell to the bed, horrified by what had happened, he secured her wrists and ankles so she was unable to move an inch. Hadley screamed in alarm when he took a slim brown snake from the box he had placed on the table.

"For God's sake, Ernst, that thing could kill me!"

"He is harmless, Hadley, only inquisitive. There, see how he moves with such speed and grace to the place where he can be happy."

Dietmueller watched as the snake writhed along the linen sheet, pausing when it reached the moist opening of the vagina, its tongue flickering like quicksilver. When Dietmueller opened the passage with his fingers, the snake insinuated itself inside Hadley, its body turning and coiling as it traveled deep within. She closed her eyes, holding herself so still she appeared dead. She was sweating from head to toe and trembling like a leaf. Then, after what seemed like an age, the snake began to emerge inch by inch from her body. Placing the snake on the bed, Dietmueller began to make love to her with manic, obsessive desire.

Unnerved, Hadley felt orgasm after orgasm racking her body, until suddenly her eyes closed and with a small cry she lost consciousness. She woke minutes later to find her wrists and ankles released. The snake was undulating over her stomach, seeking the place it had enjoyed, the place Dietmueller had opened for its brief adventure. Hadley hurled it aside and sat up, furious when

Dietmueller appeared with coffee and looked down at her with a cynical smile.

"You fainted from excitement."

"Let me go, Ernst."

"Never. I told you from the beginning I would never let you go. We were made for each other and we shall be together always."

Hadley tried not to think how the experience had thrilled her, how every nerve in her body had relished the sensation. It was always like that with Dietmueller, always the ecstasy his body provoked and the anguish of her betrayal of Karl. The snake had driven her to distraction with desire, but it had also disgusted her, with herself and with her lover. She closed her eyes, willing the strength to end the relationship. She was fearful of the reprisals to come, and doubted her own courage. Hadley sobbed with anguish. There was only one way to make sure she would never see Dietmueller again—she had to tell her husband everything, regardless of the consequences.

On returning to the hunting lodge, Hadley went to her room, showered, changed into a new dress, sprayed herself with her husband's favorite scent, and then went to join him in his study.

"I have something to tell you, something very upsetting Karl. You may not want to know me afterward, but I'm going to tell you all the same."

He looked closely at her, suddenly afraid. His wife's hands and body were trembling uncontrollably.

"I have known for some time that something is dreadfully wrong, Hadley, from your nightmares, from the haunted look in your eyes. Tell me everything now, my dear. *Please*."

She swallowed hard, and took a deep breath.

"Karl, this is very difficult for me." She turned to face the wall. "I've been ... seeing Ernst Dietmueller since four months after Tia was born.

I went to his chalet on the other side of the hill and that's when it all began. I don't know why I did it, why I'm like I am, why I destroy the things I love most. Perhaps it's because I'm scared of losing them, and I *am* petrified of losing *you*, Karl, but I felt I had to escape you to keep you. I know there's no way I can change what I've done, but try to understand—I was in a turmoil about my life. I didn't want to be domesticated, to be a mother, to settle down. I wanted to be the way I used to be in the old days." Hadley shook her head as if to erase the memory of her disillusionment. "I need your help, Karl. I've just told Dietmueller I can never see him again and I mean it, but I'm terrified of what he'll do to us."

"Why have you ended the affair after all this time?" Karl asked quietly.

"Karl, I'm truly happy with you, I realize that now. You may have separated me from my past, my days as a beauty, but you've shown me something else. I need to be a good wife, Karl, I just don't know how. I love Tia and want her to admire me. I'm disgusted with myself. I can't go on with the affair. I have to make a break and try to start all over again. The problem is that he's a man who likes his revenge."

Karl sat as still as a statue. Then he rose abruptly and led Hadley from the room.

"I want to be alone."

Returning to his desk, Karl sat thinking of the hypocrisy of life in Germany since the arrival of Adolf Hitler and those he favored, among them Ernst Dietmueller. Patriotism, they said, was everything. Was it? Or was it a rationalization for Hitler's demonic ambition? Love and respect for ones' fellow countrymen and for the fatherland was another ideal. Karl thought of Dietmueller's betrayal and wanted to kill him.

Hadley had shown great courage in telling him what she had done and she seemed to have meant what she said. At that moment, he loved her with deep devotion, despite the disillusionment that had hit him like a thunderbolt. But her revelation had changed life for them both, perhaps forever. Karl knew he could no longer remain at the hunting lodge. Heartbroken, his mind in a turmoil, he picked up the phone and asked for Cameron's number in Scotland. When the call came through, he spoke tersely, afraid that every word might be overheard.

"Something has happened and I need to see you at once. Can we meet in Paris?"

There was a long pause; then Cameron replied, "I'll be staying at the British embassy. I can get there by the day after tomorrow."

Hadley entered the room and stood looking uncertainly at her husband.

"Have you decided what to do about me, Karl?"

Karl responded wearily, "I love you and shall always love you. Whether we can ever be happy again will depend on the effort we are both prepared to make in the future. I am only human, Hadley—I have my pride and my dreams. I always wanted us to grow old together, and to grow in devotion. Now, perhaps, that dream has crumbled."

Hadley knew then that she loved her husband above all else and that she wanted to preserve the marriage if it was not too late. She spoke to Karl from the heart. "Nothing's ever going to separate us. I won't see Dietmueller again, I promise. I don't want to and I don't need to. Say it isn't too late."

"I hope it isn't, but I cannot tell you until I return from Paris what I have decided for our future. For the moment I must pack and leave. I have business there that cannot wait."

Karl arrived in Paris on the fastest train of the day and went straight to the Ritz.

Cameron arrived in Paris the following morning and went at once to the British embassy, where Karl was waiting for him. The two men shook hands. Then Karl explained all Hadley had told him and how he had reacted. He tried to put into words not only his disappointment in the marriage but also his disgust in the S.S. and its much-vaunted principles of loyalty and brotherhood.

"When I joined, I imagined I was going to be a member of a show regiment, something special to be displayed at rallies to the credit of my country. In the past few weeks it's become obvious to me that we are truly a fighting force and that it is Hitler's intention to invade and conquer all the countries that surround Germany. My friend Axel von Rootstein works at the Chancellery in Berlin and he has confirmed my suspicions. I think your government should be aware of Hitler's plans, so they will not be taken entirely by surprise."

"My government expects war."

"But I would like you to help me give what detailed information I can."

"Well, let's begin. There's no time like the present."

For forty-eight hours Karl remained at the embassy, detailing all he knew of German troop movements, placements, training programs, equipment, and numbers. He also made lists of every major military base about which he had been told. It soon became obvious that Hitler's energies were to be concentrated first on Austria and Poland and that he was well-equipped to invade whenever he wished. The possibility of invasion was not new to Cameron, but the military details were a revelation. At the end of the session he looked hard into Karl's eyes.

"From the moment you leave here, you'll be in danger. I'll keep your identity secret, but one thing I've learned in my business is that secrets are never secrets for long. German Intelligence will probably know you've been here and I'd advise you to leave Munich immediately."

"I intend to return and put my affairs in order and then travel with Hadley and Tia to Bel-Ami. I already rang Guy and asked if we could occupy one wing of the château until I can rearrange our lives."

Cameron stood at the window watching as Karl left the building and got into a taxi. As it moved away, a black Citroën pulled out and followed. Cameron sighed, foreboding filling his heart. Karl was a patriot and an idealist who had dreamed of the perfect marriage and seen it die before his eyes. He had wanted and longed to be part of a perfect Germany and had been brought down to earth with horrific suddenness. What would happen when he returned to Munich? Would the men in black be waiting for him at the station? Cameron picked up the telephone and called Guy's number.

"Cameron here. Karl's on his way to the station and being followed by two men in a black Citroën. I think you should telephone Hadley and invite her and the child to stay. Do it immediately, Guy."

"Of course. Is the situation that serious?"

"We'll need our wits about us if we're to avoid a disaster in the family. I'm returning home on the midnight boat train. If you need me, call me there."

Karl arrived in Munich soon after. The air was cool and clear, the sun shining. He was pleased to see Hadley and Tia waiting for him at the barrier. Suddenly he realized that he cared nothing for what she had done, for the unthinking, perverse desire that had made her let Dietmueller love her. He cared only for the future and keeping his family safe and happy. Quickening his pace, he ran to greet Hadley, kissing her resoundingly and then whirling Tia over his head.

Hadley looked anxiously at her husband.

"How was Paris?"

"It was beautiful, as always. I did what had to be done and tomorrow we shall be leaving to stay for a few weeks at Bel-Ami. Guy has agreed to let us use the guest wing of the house until further notice. You must pack and be ready to leave by morning. I already arranged for Nell to come and pick up Tia. She'll be arriving this evening at eight and they will go on the express at six A.M."

"*Why*? What's happened, Karl? Why can't Tia come with us?"

"You have to trust me, Hadley. Tia must leave as quickly as possible and I don't want her to travel with us, because we shall most certainly be in danger."

Hadley fell silent, thoughts zooming through her head like meteors in a night sky. It was obviously not the moment to ask what was wrong, so she got into the car, wrapped Tia's knees in a blanket, and sat in silence until they reached the hunting lodge. Then she turned to Karl.

"Is there anything you want to tell me?"

"I will explain everything when we leave the house. For the moment, take this and don't hesitate to use it if anyone tries to arrest you. Now, please go and pack your things."

Hadley looked at the pearl-handled revolver he had given her and began to tremble, but she asked no more questions, aware at last that their situation was desperate. Hurrying upstairs, she went to her dressing room, took out a pair of Vuitton cases, and began to pack her most precious things, the pure silk Patou blouses she loved, the handmade underwear, the jewels she had collected over the years, the butterfly in a glass case bought for her by her father. She took a minimum of everything, conscious that she must not arouse suspicion with a pile of luggage. She was about to rejoin Karl when she heard the doorbell ring. From the upstairs window she saw Dietmueller and two S.S. officers waiting to be admitted. Her heart almost stopped beating when Karl rushed into the room and kissed her gently on the lips.

"Ernst Dietmueller is here. Take Tia and hide in the room behind the grotto. Keep her quiet, whatever you do, and *go now.*"

"Come with me, you don't have to see them."

"If I don't, they will search the house and you may not have time to hide. Go, Hadley, please go."

"I love you."

"I know you do. Now, *please,* for Tia's sake, get out of here."

Hadley took her child down the servants' stairway into the kitchen and spoke with Frau Hoffman.

"Karl told me to hide with Tia in the room behind the grotto. Something's awfully wrong. You mustn't tell anyone where we are."

"Thank God Gisela has her day off, or we should have no secrets. I will listen at the door, madam, and tell you everything that happens with Sir."

Frau Hoffman hurried to the corridor outside the library, startled to hear Dietmueller's voice listing charges to be brought against Karl.

"You are suspected of having given German military information to your brother-in-law at the British embassy in Paris. You burned your S.S. uniform and visited Berlin three weeks ago to have lunch with your friend Axel von Rootstein, who is under arrest for theft of documents. Have you anything to say?"

Karl looked defiantly at Dietmueller.

"I have nothing to say to you, Ernst, now or

later. You betrayed our friendship just as you and those like you are betraying Germany."

"You are the traitor, Karl, and your wife is a spy. I have a warrant for her arrest. You will call her immediately. She is to be placed in my custody for interrogation."

"Hadley is not here."

"Search the house!"

Frau Hoffman stepped aside in time to avoid the two men who ran past in search of her mistress. She stood for a while in the hall, listening as doors banged and wardrobes were opened. It was almost half an hour before the men returned to the library and reported that they could find no trace of the Countess Kohler.

Dietmueller turned to Karl, his face livid with fury.

"I demand to know where you have hidden your wife!"

"Hadley left at eleven to go to lunch with friends. She took Tia with her."

"You are lying. My men have been watching this house ever since your return from Paris, and no one left."

Frau Hoffman crossed herself as Dietmueller continued.

"I will give you one minute precisely to tell me where your wife is hidden. If you do not reply, I shall shoot you as all traitors deserve to be shot."

Karl picked up a pen and wrote on the blotting paper before him: "Remember I love you and all the Valkyries in hell could not change my mind." Then he looked up at Dietmueller, his blue eyes mocking. He felt only a deep regret that he would not be able to dance the first waltz with Tia at her coming-out ball and that he would never again make love with the wife he worshiped.

Frau Hoffman heard two shots and the sound of a body falling. Ashen-faced, she ran to the kitchen and sat panting on the stool. Too afraid to cry, she listened to the clatter of the soldiers' boots as they ran down the hall. Then she moved slowly to the library and looked down on the body of the man she had served from the day of his birth. With a cry of anguish, she ran to find her husband.

Ilsa put down the phone, her hands trembling at the news Hoffman had given her. When she had recovered her composure, she ordered the estate manager to come to her, gave detailed instructions on what he was to do, and then dressed in a special version of the local costume, with long ribbons hanging from an ornate headdress and a dirndl bright with embroidered roses. Within the hour, she was ready to leave for the hunting lodge.

Hadley was sitting in the stone chamber behind the grotto with her daughter and Patou the cat. Tia was hungry and Hadley knew she would soon have to find food for the child. She kissed the rosy cheeks, enjoying the scent of her daughter and wondering despairingly how she could ever have rejected the child. To take Tia's mind off her hunger, Hadley talked of Nell's house in France.

"Tell me about Bel-Ami and what you do when you're there."

"I ride my pony and go hunting."

"What do you hunt?"

"Unicorns and dragons. Because they're very difficult to find, Uncle Guy and I pick mushrooms and take them back for breakfast. Unicorns and dragons sleep a lot, that's why we don't see them in the daytime."

Hadley held her daughter in her arms and kissed her tenderly.

"We'll be going to stay at Bel-Ami soon."

"I'll stay in the cottage, won't I? I have my

own personal bedroom there and no one else can
use."

Hadley smiled despite the tension of the moment.

"You can stay in the cottage and I'll make you
a second personal room in the house, with your
own crystal scent spray that no one else can
use."

"I love you, Mama."

They were entwined in each other's arms when
Frau Hoffman appeared with Ilsa.

"Time for Tia to leave, madam."

Hadley looked askance at the housekeeper's
chalk-white face and the tear marks on Ilsa's
cheeks.

"What happened?"

Frau Hoffman took Hadley aside and told her
of Karl's death. Hadley said nothing, but turned
with a smile to her daughter.

"Nell's decided to come from Paris to collect
you, but right now you're going to the fair. You'll
be the prettiest little girl there and I'll be proud
of you."

Hadley watched as Ilsa dressed her daughter
in an outfit that was a miniature version of her
own. Then, for a precious moment, Hadley held
Tia in her arms, terrified that she might never
see her child again. Suddenly she thought of all
the things she should have done to be the perfect
mother, the things it was too late to do now, and
her voice broke as she bade her child good-bye.

"Be good and don't forget to give Nell a big
kiss for me."

"And one for Uncle Guy too?"

"Yes, a big one for Uncle Guy."

Tia paused at the door of the hiding place,
something making her reluctant to leave her
mother behind.

"Can't you come to the parade, Mama?"

"I have to pack for us. Now, hurry and get in the flower wagon."

"We'll have tea and cakes on the terrace at Bel-Ami when you arrive, Mama. You don't have to worry. There aren't any dragons *there*."

Hadley watched as her child skipped away at Ilsa's side. A farm cart decorated with red and white flowers and ribbons was parked to the side of the hunting lodge, so near the wall no one would see one extra child joining the others as they drove away. There were two dozen laughing children of all ages on the cart, each one dressed in lederhosen and dirndls, their hair full of flowers.

Unaware of the tension in Ilsa, Tia joined in the singing and threw dried lavender at the officers guarding the gates. She was holding the cat, hoping Patou would not be tempted to eat the goldfish in the lily pond at Bel-Ami.

Frau Hoffman took dinner to Hadley in her hideaway, aghast at the blank ashen face, the red-rimmed eyes.

"Please try to eat, milady. You are going to need all your strength."

"I can't believe he's dead. I just can't believe it."

"Try not to think of Sir. You must think only of Tia."

Hadley took some soup, then sat again looking into Frau Hoffman's eyes. She was clutching the note Karl had left her, which Frau Hoffman had found.

"He looked so calm, didn't he, Hoffy?"

"He was not afraid of Dietmueller or of anything else in this world, milady. He had only one fear, and that was that you and the child would be harmed."

Hadley rose and paced the room, the anguish she had suffered making her strong for the first time in months. Somehow, she knew she had to get out of the house and out of Germany and that she must not go on the same train as Tia and Nell. On the contrary, she must try to lead the pursuit in the opposite direction from that her sister would be taking. In this moment of tragedy, Hadley thought of Bunny and longed for the safety of Lochalsh.

Dietmueller would expect her to travel by train. The desperate Hadley searched her mind for a reliable diversion. Then, remembering the yacht Karl had bought the previous summer, she thought of sailing it up the Isar and then driving the rest of the way to Bremen, where she would be able to get a passage to the Scottish coast on one of the many fishing boats that left the port each day. Hadley resolved to make as much of the journey as she could by water. But how to get from the hunting lodge to Ismaning, where the yacht was moored? Would there be roadblocks at every turn? She decided to walk there and asked Frau Hoffman to bring her things from her room.

"I want my walking boots, my brown antelope jacket, and my leather trousers. Pack a rucksack with some changes of underwear, a spare shirt, my crystal scent spray, the Ellerman emeralds, and all my best jewlery."

"You need food, not jewels, for your trip."

"I want to take them for Tia. I'll go through the underground tunnel to the gate and wait till the small hours to cross from there to the woods."

"There are men watching the house. They will surely see you if you try to cross the road."

"Karl always told me that at four A.M. even the best sentries sometimes lose their alertness and fall asleep."

"Shall we come with you, madam?"

"No, no, you stay. Someone must tell my sister what's happening and what I'm doing. She'll be arriving around eight-thirty tonight and she'll know nothing of what happened here. On second thought, get one of Ilsa's sons to go meet Nell at the station. I don't want her at the hunting lodge. I couldn't bear for Dietmueller to arrest her."

While she waited for Frau Hoffman to collect her things, Hadley thought of her husband's face in death. It had been a risk to go to the study to see Karl that last time, but one she had taken willingly. Tears fell again as she recalled touching the suntanned hands and kissing the fine-boned cheeks with their reddish-blond beard. The note was all she had left of their love and Hadley read it again to give her strength. *Remember I love you and all the Valkyries in hell could not change my mind.* He had forgiven her; it had been his last act.

In the black darkness of night, Hadley walked through the underground passage that led from her hiding place to the rear gate of the hunting lodge. She was without shoes, her feet kept warm by socks of thick oiled wool. When she reached the door that led to the gate, she stood for a long time listening, her heart beating from fear that one of Dietmueller's men might be waiting on the other side. At last she found the courage to open the door, and having waited for a few seconds, ran to the woods and into the darkness. As she put on her hiking boots, she hoped fervently that Dietmueller had not ringed the entire area with soldiers.

Nell arrived at the station and looked for her sister's face among the waiting crowd. She realized at once that something must be wrong, for neither Hadley nor the Hoffmans were present to meet her. She was moving uncertainly along the platform when a young man fell in step and offered to carry her bag.

"I am Ilsa's son. You are to come with me."

"Where's my sister?"

"Mama will explain everything. Please hurry, we must get out of the station as quickly as possible. The car is outside."

Nell was driven to an old farmhouse twenty kilometers south of the city, in the village of Sauerlach. It was surrounded by orchards dense with plum blossom and meadows where cows munched white daisies. Following the young man into the house, she came face to face with Ilsa.

"Sit down, Nell. I am afraid I have some very bad news for you. My brother was shot dead by Dietmueller at the hunting lodge at five-thirty this afternoon. Your sister and I managed to get Tia out of the house and she is waiting for you in the garden."

"Where's Hadley?"

"She plans to leave the hunting lodge and make her way to Bremen and then to take a fishing boat to her sister's house in Scotland."

"Bremen's five hundred miles away!"

"She told me to tell you to take Tia through the frontier at Innsbruck and then on the train from Switzerland. You cannot go on the train from Munich. Dietmueller will be watching the station and he will surely arrest you if he finds you."

"Is there no way I can contact my sister?"

"Best not to try, Nell. Your responsibility now is to Tia. You must get her out of Germany as soon as possible. I have here food, maps, and a car. If there are roadblocks, I must leave to you the decision on what to do. In the meantime, please eat something. I cannot let you stay here longer than one night, because Dietmueller often comes to the house with my husband. The baron has never had any liking for you or your family and since my brother married Hadley he has hated Karl. He could have telephoned Karl a warning, but he did nothing and I shall never forgive him for that."

In the morning Nell drove along the road in the direction of Bad Tolz. At her side, Tia was chattering happily. She had been told that she was going to play a game, that if asked she must say she was Nell's daughter and called Venetia de Nonancourt. Like all children, Tia loved games and was looking forward with great eagerness to pretending to be someone other than her true self.

They had traveled only twenty kilometers, when Nell saw a massive roadblock ahead. She turned immediately off the highway and pulled into a picturesque village where she sat for a while considering her position. One thing was certain; without papers for the car or the child, she would be unable to pass the block. She needed help, but knew no one in Germany. It was then that she remembered Mahler, whose admiration during his visit to Lochalsh had been very obvious. She wondered if he would remember her and, more important, if he would be willing to take a risk to help her. Would he be home or on military service? Nell hurried to the phone, closing her eyes in a brief prayer as she requested Mahler's number. She was conscious only that she must do everything possible to get her niece safely out of the country. The cost to her or to Mahler was unimportant. When she received the number and dialed, he answered the phone on the second ring. He was home! Nell did her best to sound calm.

"This is Annabelle de Nonancourt, we met at Lochalsh."

"I have thought of you so much since that meeting in Scotland! But where are you?"

"I'm in a village twenty kilometers south of Sauerlach on the road to Bad Tolz. There's a big green sign off the highway leading to it. I have my sister's child with me and there's a roadblock ahead. I'm not sure I can pass it." Nell hoped he would understand only that she was in danger and not question why.

There was a pause while Mahler digested the information. Then his voice came over the line, reassuring in its calmness. "Is there an inn nearby with a golden pig sign hanging outside the door."

"Yes, there is."

"Go there and wait for me. I will come at once."

When Mahler arrived, he kissed Nell's hand and looked searchingly into her pale, strained face.

"I will take you through the roadblock and then to lunch at Lenggries, which is on your way to the border with Innsbruck. After that we will have to see."

They passed through the block without question, Mahler's authority in the area being sufficient to satisfy the guard. As Nell sighed with relief and began to explain what had happened, Mahler shook his head despairingly. The situation was more serious than he had realized. He was uncertain how best to advise her.

"What you say is very grave. The frontiers will be heavily guarded and I cannot take you over; my authority does not extend to the south. What I am doing now could already cost me my liberty, but we will not think of that."

They stopped for lunch at Lenggries, startled when a radio announcement toward the end of the meal informed everyone that the frontiers to the south and west of the country had been closed to all but military transport.

Mahler made a plan. Nell thought of the risk he was taking, of the consequences to him of his actions, and felt guilty that she had involved him, but the child she loved was in terrible danger. She listened hard as Mahler described what she must do.

"My driver, Fritz, is a dull-witted fellow, but

he is devoted to me. Go outside and tell him I ordered him to drive you to Innsbruck. He will certainly believe you, and if he does not, I can confirm the order. When you arrive there, send him back to me. If you have difficulty at the border, show them this."

Mahler handed her his priority travel authorization.

"Better still, get Fritz to hand it to them. They will then believe, perhaps, that you are being transported on military orders. It is the best I can do."

"Thank you for everything, Franz. I hope I can repay your kindness someday."

"My dear Nell, I shall hope to meet you again under happier circumstances. At this moment my country is in turmoil and nothing is as it was."

Nell went outside, gave the order to the driver, who leapt up and opened the door for her. Inside the car, she held Tia in her arms, praying they could pass the frontier before any new orders were given by security headquarters in Berlin.

Hadley reached the boathouse at dawn, having slept for an hour after her arrival in the woods nearby. Now, cold, hungry, and tired, she swung open the oak gates, staring in alarm. The yacht was not in its place. She was trying to work out where it could be when she heard the click of a revolver, and turning, saw Dietmueller watching her. His voice was mocking, his face pale from tiredness and tension.

"You did well to elude my men, Hadley, but certainly you did not expect to lose me as well? Where is your daughter?"

Hadley remained silent as he approached and looked smugly into her eyes.

"You are under arrest. I shall personally conduct you to headquarters, where I will make sure you are thoroughly questioned by my men. Afterward I will have you released into my own custody."

As Hadley backed away from him, Dietmueller's face hardened imperceptibly.

"Come, now, Hadley. You must remember previously being held by me with *some* fondness, no? Now, please come. My car is over there by the trees."

"Where's Karl's yacht?"

"I had it removed."

When he turned and strode toward the car, Hadley remained rooted to the spot, conscious that if she went with him it would all be over, and she would never see her child again. She flinched as Dietmueller turned and shouted at her, "Come, this is your last chance!"

When she still refused to move, Dietmueller strode back toward her. He was a dozen paces from Hadley when she shot him through the chest with the pearl-handled revolver Karl had given her.

Dietmueller looked incredously at the blood trickling through his fingers. Then, stumbling, he fell to one knee, his face contorted with pain. With all the willpower he could summon, he found the strength to pull his revolver from its holster, and as Hadley looked down at him with a strange, distant expression, he shot her twice. Before he fell to the ground, he saw her blouse turning red and smiled. Then he stretched out his hand to try to reach her. He had always told Hadley he would never let her go. His dying thought was that he could take her with him.

—14—
GERMANY–SCOTLAND, APRIL 1937

HADLEY TOUCHED THE wounds in her upper chest, a few inches below the shoulder. She had felt little pain, only hearing the sounds of the shots. Looking down at Dietmueller, she thought of the long years when he had pursued her, the heights of passion to which he had provoked her, the madness that had made him kill Karl and try to kill her. Bunny's words kept echoing in her head. *There are times when we all have to show our courage.* This, Hadley knew, would be the greatest test of her life. Somehow, she must find the strength to go on. She thought of Tia and how the child had run back to make the invitation. *We'll have tea on the terrace at Bel-Ami, Mama. There aren't any dragons there.*

Hadley staggered uncertainly to her feet and started to walk to the entrance of a house hidden in the trees a few meters from the lake. The sound of the doorbell brought footsteps scurrying to the entrance and a woman with frightened eyes asked what she wanted. Hadley struggled to stay on her feet and to speak calmly.

"I've been shot and I need your help. Can you dress the wound for me? I just have to get to Bremen and out of Germany."

As tears filled Hadley's eyes, the woman opened the door, helped her inside, and called her husband.

"Bring hot water and the medical box, Joseph."

There were trunks and cases everywhere in the hall and Hadley realized that the couple were in the process of moving out. She sat quite still while the woman dressed her wound and bandaged it.

"Can you lend me some clothes? I can't walk around covered in blood."

"Of course I can, madam. They will be too large, but they are clean."

"And perhaps a bicycle?"

"We can do better than that. You can take our second car. Don't worry about returning it, we are leaving Germany ourselves. If we do not, we shall certainly be arrested. If you can get to Bremen it will be easy to get a passage to the English coast. Fishing boats leave for the North Sea very frequently both by day and by night."

An hour later, Hadley left the house, following the mountain road suggested by the couple. She was relieved that the wound felt numb, that there was no pain at all, only a faint throbbing deep within the wall of her chest. With each beat of her heart Hadley reminded herself of the dictum she had always lived by—all her life Hadley Ellerman had succeeded in getting just what she wanted. Nothing had changed. All she had to do was to keep the panic from her mind.

Hadley arrived in Kassell without incident and was soon hopelessly lost in the maze of tiny streets. Eventually she found a sign that led north, and as dusk fell, put into an inn at the roadside. She was exhausted and suffering agonies from a blinding headache. On reaching her room, she counted the money she had brought from Karl's safe and put a little in her purse. Then she called a doctor. While she waited for him to arrive, she tried to make plans, thankful that she had her jewels and enough cash to pay whatever the cost might be of the passage to England. She wondered if the docks would be patrolled by soldiers or if she would be able to enter the harbor without problem. Then, despite her unease, she smiled wanly. In her present condition she would be lucky ever to reach Bremen. She must think of that first and get her priorities right, as Nell was always advising.

The doctor examined the wound and shook his head.

"You must come with me to the hospital. I have no anaesthetic with me, and under these conditions there would be a very real risk of infection."

"Do whatever you have to do here and now. I accept the responsibility for the risk."

For what seemed like an age, he probed the wound, causing excruciating pain. Tears streamed down Hadley's cheeks and she bit her lips to keep from screaming in agony. She was about to tell the doctor to leave the bullet where it was, when he held it before her eyes.

"I am so sorry you have had to suffer, but the bullet was very deep. You have courage, madam, remarkable courage. I do not know who shot you, and I do not care. You are an unusual woman, and I wish you luck. The police are searching all cars on the main routes out of this town. Take care if you are the one they seek."

Hadley left the following morning at daybreak. Within half an hour she was driving in the direction of Bremen on a circuitous back road, telling herself all the while that she could make it, that she must let nothing prevent her from seeing her child again. She tried not to think of the pain in her chest and the leaden feeling in her arms and legs that seemed to be spreading. With a grim determination never previously tapped, she thought only of reaching Lochalsh and of getting well. Once she had her health back, she would keep her rendezvous with Tia at Bel-Ami.

Nell and Tia were two miles from the frontier when a car came up fast behind them. It was Guy in a Mercedes sports coupé waving her down. Nell called for the driver to pull to the side of the road. Then she ran to greet her husband.

"Whatever are you doing here? I only spoke to you on the phone last evening. How did you get here so fast?"

"I asked Marc to fly me in his private plane. He's a regular wizard at the controls, as you know."

"But why did you come?"

"You needed me and I knew you were in danger."

Nell began to cry, hugging Guy to her heart because his words had touched her deeply.

"How did you find me?"

"I went to the hunting lodge and then to Ilsa's place and lost you about twenty kilometers south of Sauerlach."

"I turned off the main road."

"I knew you'd probably gone onto a minor road, but there were two, so I took the gamble and here I am. Oh, Nell, I'm so glad I came. We have to get back to Bel-Ami as soon as we can. They brought in new regulations within the last hour and you have to have a special pass to cross through any German frontier until further notice. Mahler's chauffer won't be able to get you through."

"What shall we do?"

"You'll see. Dismiss the fellow and send him back to his base. This is one of those occasions in life when we must act first and ask questions later." He strode purposefully to get Tia. "Come,

Tia, we're going to play a game. You lie down with Patou on the floor at the back of my car and pretend you're hiding from dragons."

"Are they dragons from Bel-Ami?"

"No, they're from Berlin and they have *very* sharp teeth."

The frontier post had two points of entry, one for commercial and army traffic, the other for private vehicles. As all borders had been closed to nonmilitary personnel, there was an air of boredom and lethargy about the place. A solitary troop transport was passing through the main channel; the other was empty. Two sentries, their faces relaxed, were smoking by the side of the red-and-white painted pole that formed the only barrier.

Guy drove slowly toward the frontier, accelerating only when he was almost at the sentry box. Then, putting his foot down, he forced the car forward with a sudden surge of power. The barrier cracked, the soldiers leapt out of the way, then shouted for him to stop, but Guy drove on, his face determined, his eyes anxiously scrutinizing the road ahead.

Nell looked back and was horrified to see the sentries raising their rifles. Then bullets whistled through the car, shattering the windshield and sirens wailed as the soldiers began their pursuit. She turned to Guy, her eyes wide with fear.

"They're coming after us."

"They are wasting their time. This car can overtake everything on the road. It belongs to Marc's cousin, who lives near Munich. He guaranteed it."

Nell's heart beat so fast she thought she would faint. For comfort, she held out her hand and touched Tia's, amused when the child spoke in a tiny frightened voice. "Patou doesn't like this game. He's *cold*."

Guy spoke reassuringly. "We shall soon be home again at Bel-Ami, don't you worry. Are you all right, Nell? Put my scarf around your neck."

"I can't get over your coming all the way to Germany to help me. Why did you really do it?"

"It's not often that you need your husband, but today you did, so here I am. It's nice to be indispensable once in a lifetime."

Hadley drove into Verden, a town south of Bremen, seconds ahead of a German patrol that had pursued her for miles. Having put the car outside the crowded market hall, she hurried down a narrow street and took refuge in a watchmaker's shop. Her strength was ebbing fast and she knew that she would be unable to continue the journey without help. Bremen was not far away, but she could no longer drive, and walking was becoming difficult. She could barely feel her legs. She turned to the old man, who was peering at her over a pair of gold-rimmed spectacles.

"I have to get to Bremen without going through the roadblocks."

"Your shoulder is bleeding, Fräulein."

Hadley slumped down on the chair.

"I was injured a few days ago. Can you help?"

"It would be costly."

"I have money."

"I will call my son and ask him to come for you. Excuse me, please."

Hadley watched as the man locked the door of the office behind him. Then, distrusting his manner, she made her way from the shop and hid in the doorway of a kindergarten farther down the street. Within seconds, a police car screeched to a halt before the watchmaker's shop. Hadley slid to the ground inside a schoolyard, unable to stand for a moment longer. Somewhere, seemingly in the distance, she heard children's voices calling for the teacher to hurry over. Then a woman came to her side and tried to rouse her.

"Please tell me what is wrong, madam."

"I have to get to Bremen."

The young woman looked closely at Hadley, taking in the bloodstained shoulder, the pale blue marks of pain under her eyes, the flinching of her entire body as the police sirens sounded.

"Our school bus will be going along the Bremen road. You can come with us."

"What about the road-blocks?"

"The soldiers are not interested in children."

"How close to Bremen will you go?"

"About halfway. Let me help you. You cannot stay here, it is certainly too dangerous. If you are in trouble with the military . . ."

"I'm in bad trouble."

"Come, I will help you."

Hadley stumbled toward the bus, listening as the children were told that as she was unwell she would travel on the floor at the rear of the vehicle. As the bus filled with passengers, she felt someone covering her with a blanket. She closed her eyes against the noise and did not open them again until she heard a sentry calling for the driver to halt. Tears of fear and anguish began to fall down her cheeks as she looked up into the curious eyes of one of the young girls. Then she felt a weight on her legs and her back and her shoulders and realized that as the soldiers entered the bus the children at the rear had pulled the blanket over her head and sat down on her body to cover her from the scrutiny of the military. Hadley forced her fist into her mouth to stifle the pain. Then she heard the voices of the soldiers retreating and felt the weight vanishing from her body and the bus beginning to move forward. The schoolgirl who had covered her pulled back the blanket and wiped the sweat from her face.

"The soldiers have gone, madam. Please drink some of the water from my flask. It will help your fever."

When all the children had been put down near their homes, the teacher took it upon herself to deliver Hadley to the center of Bremen, using the schoolbus. Then, having settled Hadley in a corner of a harborside café, she whispered reassuringly, "I will go and find the captain of one of the ships sailing to the Scottish coast, but it will take time to find out who sails soonest."

Hadley pushed a roll of banknotes into the woman's hand.

"Take it, please take it, you might need to get out of Germany yourself someday."

The woman gazed at the money, then hurried from the bar. An hour later, she was back with a tall, handsome man in yellow oilskins. She motioned him to the corner where Hadley was sitting, her face bathed in sweat, her body slumped against the wall. The teacher looked anxiously into Hadley's eyes and then at the darkening stain on the blue blouse. Even in this extreme condition and in her borrowed clothes, she thought her beautiful. She did her best to sound confident as she addressed Hadley.

"This is Captain Westen of the fishing trawler *Die Meistersinger*, which will sail in forty minutes if you can be ready."

"I'll be ready."

The captain looked doubtfully at Hadley's tallow-pale face. Her condition was worsening fast.

"Are you quite sure you are fit to travel, madam?"

"Of course."

"Very well, we will go aboard at once. There are guards patrolling some parts of the dockside. If they approach us, I shall pretend you are a prostitute. Please forgive me if I am obliged to be familiar."

"How far must I walk?"

"Two hundred meters."

"I don't know if I can make it. I'm sorry."

While the teacher shook hands with Hadley and made a brief good-bye, the captain called to a burly sailor who was drinking rum at the counter, "Hans, this lady has had a little accident and needs to be helped. I will take her luggage if you will carry her."

Hadley lay in a bunk, dressed in an oversized nightshirt of soft cotton lent her by the huge man who had carried her aboard. She had slept for hours on first arrival, waking only when the ship began to roll alarmingly. She kept telling herself she was on her way to Scotland and safety, that she must will the wound to heal. Once she reached the coast of Scotland, Bunny and Jack would take over and everything would be all right again.

By afternoon of the second day, Hadley's condition had deteriorated as her fever increased. Her chest felt stiff and she could barely stay awake. She was conscious only of men who came and sat at her side, wiping her forehead and holding her hand as they whispered words of encouragement. Relieved that the pain had gone from her shoulder, she was puzzled by the fact that she could feel nothing at all from neck to waist on her left side. Reaching for a glass of water, she drank, but vomited before she could swallow. She felt her face being wiped with a warm cloth and saw that Hans was at her side, a gentle giant with eyes full of pity.

"Try to sleep, Countess. The captain is sending a message to your sister, but the storm is bad and we are unable to get into the harbor of Crail.

Don't worry, though, the *Meistersinger* is a very special ship and we will get there in the end."

In fact, the ship was in grave difficulties and they had had to radio for the St. Andrews lifeboat. He wondered how Hadley would fare when they had to transfer her from one ship to the other. The wound was festering, the smell from it permeating the cabin with the odor of rotting flesh. The sailor shook his head and took Hadley's hand in his own. Once, it was obvious, the woman had been very beautiful. He wondered sadly if she would live long enough to be beautiful again.

Bunny and her husband were finishing their dinner when Mrs. MacKay rushed into the room.

"You're to go at once to the harbor. The St. Andrews lifeboat's going out to rescue a German fishing trawler off the point. Your sister Hadley's on board and she's ill. I've called Ewan and told him to get over here immediately."

Bunny leapt up, her face paling at the news.

"Did they say what was wrong with Hadley?"

"No, but they were told a stretcher would be needed, ma'am."

When the lifeboat came in, Bunny was helped aboard and told to go below at once. Her husband looked warily into the captain's ruddy face.

"What's happening, Jock?"

"German trawler in difficulties, sir. They've engine trouble and are shipping water. The woman was shot a week ago and has been traveling ever since. She's seriously ill."

Cameron stood on deck like a statue hewn out of rock. He had to get Hadley back to Lochalsh immediately and have her examined by Forbes without causing Bunny too much upset. Then, if her condition was as serious as it sounded, he would notify Professor MacNaughton in Glasgow and arrange the very best possible care for her.

Bunny was pregnant and Cameron was terrified the violent rocking of the boat might make her ill. He hurried below to see if there was anything he could do for her, and found her sitting on a bunk knitting baby socks.

"Are you feeling sick yet?"

"I'm fine. Don't worry, Jack."

"Would you care for some tea? They just brewed up."

"I'd love a cup."

Cameron hurried away, returning minutes later with two steaming mugs of liquid. Bunny warmed her frozen hands, closing her eyes as her husband kissed her.

"You're not to start worrying about me, Jack. I've had two sons without a second of difficulty, and this time we'll be having a girl. Neither of us minds rough seas. Worry about Hadley. Right now she sounds as if she needs it."

In a storm that rivaled anything seen in the area for years, the fishing-boat crew and solitary passenger were winched aboard the lifeboat. Exhausted and close to collapse, Hadley felt men lifting her. Then, as she fought to retain some semblance of consciousness, she saw the blurred outline of Bunny's face coming into focus before her eyes and began to sob uncontrollably.

"Am I home at Lochalsh?"

A tear fell down Bunny's cheek at the mention of the word "home," and she reached out and took her sister's hand.

"You soon will be."

"My jewel case is strapped to my calf under the trousers."

"Don't start worrying about jewels at a time like this, Hadley."

"I brought them for Tia, like I promised."

Bunny looked at her husband, her face suddenly full of fear.

"Try to sleep, Hadley. We'll soon be home."

"I drove so far."

"Who shot you?"

"Dietmueller. He killed Karl and then tried to kill me, too, but I shot him."

They carried Hadley into the bedroom Bunny had prepared specially for her first visit to Lochalsh. She was unconscious, though from time to time she woke and was almost lucid. Bunny watched her till the storm abated and morning came with the sweet sound of birdsong. Then, as she gazed at the face that had once been one of the most beautiful in Europe, she saw that it was streaked with gray, the eyes sunken and hollow. Ewan had been and gone, shaking his head in despair. He could do nothing for Hadley but give her painkillers to dull the throbbing of the wound and sedatives to calm her fear. Bunny saw the red poison lines spreading from her sister's shoulder to her wrist and down her chest. Determined not to cry, she held Hadley's hand and wished her good morning as the green eyes flickered open.

"It's a lovely spring day and you're not to worry about a thing."

Hadley looked up at Bunny's pink-and-white cheeks, at the dress that matched her eyes, and at the Ellerman pearls around her neck. Her sister's back was unusually stiff, the smile a little forced. Something was terribly wrong. Struggling to remember everything she wanted to say, Hadley fought to voice her thoughts.

"Am I dying, Bunny?"

There was a long silence while the sisters looked at each other. Then Hadley turned and gazed at the sea crashing on the rocks below.

"Don't ever tell Tia about Dietmueller. Just

tell her I was beautiful and that I loved her so much."

"You mustn't say things like that, Hadley."

"Will you write her a note for me?"

Bunny wrote, tears falling as Hadley stumbled to dictate her last wishes.

Dearest Tia,

I am so sorry I won't be coming to Bel-Ami. Be good and remember always that you're a very special person. Bunny will bring the Ellerman emeralds to you and with them my very best jewels. I love you best in all the world.

Your loving mother

Hadley felt a wave of nausea and closed her eyes. Perhaps there was still a chance for her, if only she could find the strength to do what had to be done. She tightened her grip on Bunny's hand, smiling as she fell asleep and began to dream of Karl. He was riding toward her on a fine white stallion. When he neared her side, he paused to lift her up beside him and she reached out and kissed him, just as she had kissed him in the early days of their love. She felt a cool breeze in her hair and smelled the scent of alpine flowers as they galloped through the meadow together. Then, holding Karl tight around the waist, she leaned her head on his shoulder and let him take her with him over the sunlit crest of the mountain.

They buried Hadley on the bluebell hill overlooking the sea. Out of respect for Bunny, the villagers came with wreaths and garlands of spring flowers till the blue of the hillside was interspersed with the red of roses and the white of marguerites brought by the children.

When the service was over and the villagers had gone home, Bunny stood with Cameron, looking down at Lochalsh in all its glory, the granite walls sunlit, the monolithic structure surrounded by deep blue sea. She turned to her husband and kissed him gently.

"Poor Hadley, who'd ever have thought it would turn out like this?"

Cameron strode on down the hill, his face furrowed.

"Your sister lived a dazzling life and died before she got old, which is how she would have liked it best."

"But what of Tia?"

"She'll want for nothing. Nell loves her as if she were her own and so does Guy."

They walked past the distillery and called a greeting to Easter MacGregor, who was loading crates of whiskey into one of the new green delivery vans. Then they saw Severine, hurrying back to Lochalsh after a date with her fiancé, Ewan Forbes.

Bunny took her husband's hand and kissed it contentedly. It had been a long, hard struggle, but the Camerons of Lochalsh had made it together slowly but surely.

— EPILOGUE —
PARIS, MAY 1, 1939

THERE HAD BEEN no reunion in the spring, out of deference to Hadley. In May 1938 Bunny was still recovering from the birth of her daughter and had been too busy to travel. Now, while air-raid shelters were being dug in the London parks and all Europe was asking when, not if, there would be a war, the Ellerman sisters arrived at the Ritz. Both knew it would be the last reunion for some time, though neither realized it would be seven years before they would meet again in the old familiar room, with its elegant decor and ever-attentive waiters.

Auzello watched as Nell stepped out of the taxi with her husband, looking sensational in a dress of viridian silk. At her side, the little girl with red-blond curls and slanting green eyes was the image of her dead mother. She was dressed in dark blue velvet with a collar of white Malines lace. Behind them, Jack and Bunny Cameron were walking up the steps, holding hands like lovers. Auzello weighed Bunny's new short hairstyle and expensive dress of spotted silk. How beautiful she had become in maturity. It was impossible to believe that anyone had ever thought her plain. He kissed both the women like the old friends they had become over the years.

While the sisters went to the dining room, Cameron and Guy went to the bar and talked of Marc de Villalonga, who, distressed by the death of Nell's beloved sister, had returned to the hunting lodge two weeks after Hadley's funeral and arranged for the removal of certain small but valuable items. These he had transported back to Bel-Ami as Tia's only "inheritance."

Cameron was curious to know how Marc had got the trunkful of antiquities out of Germany. "How did he pass the frontier? There must have been guards."

"Oh, Marc, didn't drive, he put the trunk on the train, booked a first-class sleeper to Paris, and was out of Germany a few hours after he'd repossessed the stuff. If it hadn't been for him Tia would have nothing but the jewels."

"And where is he now?"

"Marc remained in Madrid after the war began there. He'll be back, though. He's more than a little in love with Nell and won't be able to resist seeing her."

Cameron frowned blackly. "I'd break the fellow's neck!"

"So would I, if I didn't know that he is one of the few remaining real gentlemen in Europe."

Flashbulbs popped as Bunny, Nell, and Tia ate their lunch. The little girl, conscious of the importance of the occasion, sat up straight, ordered her food with perfect poise, and constantly touched the Ellerman emerald brooch left her by her mother. She was about to order dessert when one of the photographers whispered a compliment. "You are as beautiful as your mother. That is the greatest compliment I can pay you. The countess let me photograph her on the night of the opening of the first Luc Dubois Clinic in Paris. I will send you a copy for your album."

FABLES 345

Tia turned to Bunny, her eyes wide. "Was Mama really the most beautiful lady in Paris?"

"She most certainly was."

Tia looked around the room as waiters hovered and the photographers made their way back to their offices. Then, turning to her aunts, she voiced her thoughts. "I like being at the Ritz Hotel, but only for the day. Tomorrow I have to go home, or the animals will start to miss me."

The sisters exchanged amused glances. Tia had inherited the very best of both her parents' natures, Hadley's looks and Karl's love of home. Someday, Nell said with confidence, she will run Bel-Ami with ease. In the meantime, the sisters would guide and mold her until she was ready to emerge to astound the waiting public with her beauty.

Bunny sighed as tears came to her eyes. The three Ellerman sisters had started life with such high hopes. And the wheel of fate had turned a full circle for them. Nell, both rich and famous, now was able to have what she had not wanted, a child. Bunny thought back to something Cameron had once said. Hadley had been the hare of the children's fable, the certain winner in the race of life. Yet she had known only failure before her tragic death. And Bunny, the tortoise, was beautiful and more content than she could have dreamed. The fable was complete. For those who remained, the future was golden.

ABOUT THE AUTHOR

Toinette Harrison is the author of THE
MISTRESS FROM MARTINIQUE and
CATHAY as well as several other popular
titles for Signet. She was an actress in
England before becoming a full time writer.
She lives in France.